Of Earth and Gold
© 2026 Shona Barton
All rights reserved.

No part of this publication may be reproduced, distributed, or transmitted in any form or by any means, electronic or mechanical, including photocopying, recording, or other information storage and retrieval systems, without the prior written permission of the author, except in the case of brief quotations embodied in critical reviews and certain other noncommercial uses permitted by copyright law.

This is a work of fiction. Names, characters, places, and events are either the product of the author's imagination or are used fictitiously. Any resemblance to actual persons, living or dead, or actual events is purely coincidental.

Cover design by S. Barton.
Map and Artworks by S.Barton

A catalogue record for this book is available from the National Library of Australia.

ISBN (Hardback): 9781764518123
ISBN (Paperback): 9781764518116
First edition 2026.
Printed in Australia.

To all my lovelies searching for their chance at love — a love where they are cherished, worshipped, and revered as the goddess they were always meant to be.
This is for you my Queens.

TRIGGER WARNING

This book contains material that may be sensitive for some readers. Please read with care.

Adult romantic and erotic sexual content
Explicit intimacy
Grief and loss
References to past trauma
Violence and threats of violence
Emotional distress and panic responses
Magical combat and peril
Power imbalances within fantasy political structures
Protective and possessive romantic dynamics
Reader discretion is advised.

CONTENTS

Prologue	1
Chapter 1	7
Chapter 2	15
Chapter 3	23
Chapter 4	31
Chapter 5	37
Chapter 6	47
Chapter 7	59
Chapter 8	67
Chapter 9	82
Chapter 10	97
Chapter 11	108
Chapter 12	119
Chapter 13	135
Chapter 14	145
Chapter 15	157
Chapter 16	167
Chapter 17	172
Chapter 18	181
Chapter 19	191
Chapter 20	201
Chapter 21	209
Chapter 22	221

Chapter 23	227
Chapter 24	234
Chapter 25	240
Chapter 26	248
Chapter 27	257
Chapter 28	268
Chapter 29	272
Chapter 30	278
Chapter 31	289
Chapter 32	297
Chapter 33	305
Chapter 34	320
Chapter 35	326
Chapter 36	331
Chapter 37	341
Chapter 38	345
Chapter 39	351
Chapter 40	357
Chapter 41	368
Chapter 42	374
Chapter 43	379
Chapter 44	384
Bonus Chapter	389

FAE REALM

- Air Court
- Sun Palace
- Wyvern Territory
- Sylvari Outpost
- Sisters of the Verdant Veil
- Earth Court
- Fire Court
- Water Court
- Dragon Bay

HUMAN REALM

LOOKOUT
CARVISH PROPERTY
FLORAL BEANZ
QUARRY
MISTY RIDGE
CRYSTAL HOLLOW
RIVERTIDE

Names and Titles Reference

Aodhan (Ay-den) (Also known as Aodh – Ayd)
Maricus (Mare-ih-kuss)
Kaelen (Kay-len)
Luc (Loo-k)
Harrid (Hah-rid)
Yasar (Yah-sahr)
Ellisar (El-ih-sahr)
Varyn (Vah-rin)
Nivara (neh-vah-rah)
Erif (Eh-riff)
Mo draganín (muh drah-gah-neen)
Ríganne (Ree-gahn) – A high fae title meaning Queen or High Sovereign
Rívaran— (Ree-vah-ran) A high fae title meaning King or High Sovereign
Fíralen (Fee-arh-len) - Elite assassins, outside normal hierarchy; answer only to the crown
Rívalis — (Ree-vah- less) - Goddess
Kárith — (Kah-rith) - Warriors / soldiers

PROLOGUE

Flour drifts through the air like pale dust caught in the morning sun, turning the kitchen into a snow globe of our own making. Caleb stands behind me at the old, chipped laminate counter, taller by a head, shoulders brushing the window frame. That easy grin lighting his face as though he were someone with zero cares in the world and not a shred of stress. The very same smile I recall in every memory I've stitched to home.

A smear of batter streaks his forearm from "helping," though he's done more taste-testing than mixing. Chaos rolls around us like a cyclone. Daisy — six years old, pigtails askew, face sticky with syrup — has declared herself "Queen Pixie Carvish of the Pancake Palace", barking orders with all the authority of a ruler in gumboots.

Oliver, four and solemn, is determined to eat two plates at once, his little hands working with the precision of someone convinced all his breakfast will vanish if he doesn't consume it right this second.

Nyxie, our black German Shepherd cross — all legs and oversized paws, still more gangly pup than guard dog, bounds through the fray, barking at every burst of laughter, tail lashing.

Then, all of a sudden, she clips the milk jug with her hip. It topples, crashes to the floor, sending milk everywhere. She dives in to lap it straight from the floor boards, smearing it further instead of cleaning it up. This sets off another wave of mayhem — Daisy shrieking, Oliver scolding, Caleb bending double with laughter that booms through the kitchen until even I can't hold back my own. I swat at his arm with the tea towel, pretending annoyance, but my cheeks ache from smiling.

"See?" he says between chuckles, still pointing at the small disaster spilling across the floor. "We need more room, Lil. Imagine this in a bigger place — a proper kitchen, your own café. Just think about it."

I shake my head, trying to keep my voice firm, but it wavers, because his dream is infectious. "You and your ideas. You're impossible. You've been trying to talk me into this for months."

He winks, cheeky as ever. "And you love me for it."

And God help me, I do. I wipe my hands on the tea towel, still kneeling, when Caleb rounds the doorway. The sun has a way of chasing him — catching in the light brown of his hair until it glints amber, pooling in the green of his eyes. Those warm, laughing eyes that always find me first — eyes that crinkle at the edges when his grin breaks loose.

He's carved from the soft poetry of soft flaws and easy charm: a worn plaid shirt with the sleeves shoved up to his elbows, forearms sun-browned and strong from years of work he never complains about. His jeans are scuffed at the knees, boots well past their prime — squeaking on the floor despite his insistence that they're "the most comfortable pair he's ever owned." There's the stubble, always a day too long, always making him look rakish — and the dimple that only appears when he's hatching something cheeky.

"Come on, hun," he says, tilting his chin toward the lounge where the noise has hit its peak. His voice is rich with mischief and certainty. The kind of tone that makes me want to argue and agree with him all at once. "Look at the kids. You know as well as I do, they need more space." I glance over at them — Daisy and Oliver locked in a heated debate over who stole the last scoop of ice cream, spoons clattering against the table like a war could break out. Nyxie paces between them, playing referee with solemn little huffs and a flick of the tail.

It's a mess. Loud, sticky, ridiculous...and yet it's ours. My chest tightens as I turn back to Caleb, his green eyes catching mine like they always do — steadying and knowing all at once.

"I hear you, but..." I push up from the floor, flicking residual batter and flour caked under my nails — the excuse flimsy even to my own ears. "What if this doesn't work? It's such a big commitment. Are you really ready to give up a stable job to help me run the café?"

Caleb's grin tilts wicked — half smirk, half trouble — dimples threatening. "Well, it'd be worth it just to have you serving me coffee every morning... maybe in a cute little maid outfit."

"Caleb!" I swat at him, trying and failing to hide the laugh tugging at my mouth.

"You know, you could always make me one in your very own maid outfit, the customers would love your plaid shirt and frills," I shoot back, and his answering bark of laughter is so infectious my own resistance breaks.

"Ugh, gross. Mum and Dad are kissy," Oliver groans from the hall, his little voice thick with the weight of disgust. Daisy follows with a dramatic sigh worthy of an actress twice her age.

Caleb chuckles, low and warm, and the sound wraps around me like a favourite blanket, comforting even in its mischief. Then his smile gentles, the humour falling away. "In all seriousness," he says, tone soft but steady, "we've gone over the plans, checked the numbers, walked the block a dozen times. It's perfect, Lil — it's like fate or something pulling us towards Misty Ridge. And if it doesn't work, it doesn't work. But at least we'll know we tried. Gave it our all. Stop over thinking. Trust me on this. We could use the room, and the kids definitely need more."

I look around the room, our first home, our little oasis. It was never meant for a family of four. A sigh slips from my lips. He's right. We do need something bigger. The kids need space to grow, to run. I look at Cal and instantly he smiles, a grin so wide it tells me he already knows.

"Finally," he breathes against my ear, relief rolling through his chest like sunlight after rain. He leans back and bellows down the hall, "Hey, Dais! Ol! You'll never believe it — she's finally decided!"

"About time, Mum!" Daisy yells back, bickering forgotten as footsteps thunder our way. Oliver skids into the doorway right after her, hair sticking up like a startled hedgehog.

"Yay, Mum..." he says with all the dry seriousness of a four-year-old, sounding so much like his dad that I worry soon I'll have two of them to contend with.

"We can still help with the design, right?" Daisy asks, eyes sparkling with excitement, already sketching colour schemes and curtain choices in her mind.

"Of course. Just make sure there's space for Nyxie in every room," I reply. Right on cue, the queen of the house swans into the kitchen, tail thumping, head held high as if she's understood every word. Daisy crouches to scratch her chest. "We should build her a throne room."

"Out the back, next to your dad's man cave," I add, followed by Daisy's innocent remark, "So he can hide when he's broken another pot." I look at Caleb, mock-shocked. "What do you mean another pot?" The whole kitchen erupts in laughter — big and ridiculous, but real. It feels good to dream. To plan ahead, to think of the future and all it could possibly be.

Dinner that night is loud and sloppy — exactly as proper dinners ought to be. Spaghetti eaten too fast, sauce streaking chins and shirts, Daisy pitching a tree house with her own water slide while Oliver campaigns fiercely for a soccer goal the size of the garage.

The house hums with our ordinary joy. Walls soaking in every laugh, every wild idea, every clatter of fork against plate. Later, I gather dishes, tucking away the nerves that try to edge in at the thought of change, because tonight should be easy. Tonight should be joy. Tonight is about embracing change.

By the time I wrangle everyone through bedtime — stolen

hugs, whispered secrets, last-minute demands for water, another hug and kiss goodnight. The house finally exhales, sinking into its serenity. Nyxie hops up beside me, a solid weight against my thigh, her sigh long and horse-like. I scratch behind her ear, and something calming washes over me.

Caleb slides in on the other side, the mattress dipping with his weight, his arm finding its place across my waist without hesitation.

"Night, gal," he murmurs to Nyxie, rubbing her chin before turning that smile on me. "What, no scratch behind the ear for me?" I roll toward him, tucking my nose beneath his jaw, breathing him in. "Only if you sit and shake."

I feel the rumble in his chest as he laughs. "I can if you want — I'll do anything you ask," he teases, voice playful and soft. I smirk into his chest and curl in closer. "Night, Cal. Love you."

"Night, hun," he whispers back, lips brushing my temple. "Love you too."

The house is quiet then, folded into the rhythm of our breathing. Just walls and a roof — but within them, laughter, love, and the memory of this moment. One to hold and treasure not knowing what the future holds.

Grief.

It's the hollow ache that gnaws at the edges of your soul, a constant ebbing, sinking deeper with every breath.
In a single moment, life fractures and the world tilts off its axis.
So the mind retreats, folding in on itself, whispering quiet prayers into the dark that one day, the memories might soften, and the heart might remember how to beat without breaking.

CHAPTER 1

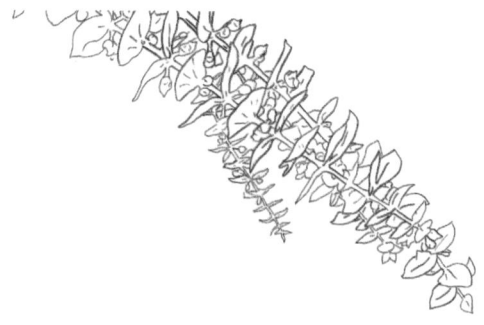

My reflection in the glass looks like me, and not me. A tired, worn woman gazes back — a face lined by too many dawns that came around too soon. Curls the colour of sun-faded wheat refuse to fall the way I want, dry and needing a cut. Freckles dust my nose, which still burns if I forget sunscreen for even an hour. My green eyes betray me, as they always do — holding too much if I'm not careful. I look away quickly, hating the person I see, needing to collect myself and put on my mask for the day.

I wash up for the morning and look at my hands. They are barista's hands — nicked by knives, scarred with hot water spilt, calloused by mugs, forever polished with the faint sheen of coffee oil that no soap scrubs away.

At my throat hangs a thin silver band, threaded on its chain. Without thinking, I spin it once between my fingers. The ritual steadies me. A reminder. A wound. A shattered heart.

I take a deep breath and start my braid — neat, practical, and out of the way. Clothes are my armour. I slip into my white boho dress, the fabric soft from a hundred washes. My favourite tan cardigan follows — its elbows stretched, sleeves frayed — and then the leather boots that have outlasted years of summer storms and the mat at the café door.

Familiar layers. Easy to wear. Easy to disappear inside. No thought required. A safe option.

I head downstairs, kids late and laughing. Daisy, eighteen,

pins her graduation form to the corkboard with a reminder that nothing is to be booked that month. Oliver, sixteen, trails behind — tousled and slow — already embroiled in an argument about whether his toast is too buttered or not buttered enough.

I let them spar — these small moments make my day. Their voices fill the house, patching the silence Caleb left behind in whatever rough way they can. It's noise that feels like life, even if it aches.

I study them both as if the morning light itself might burn their edges into my memory. Daisy's chin is decisive, all mine — stubborn and unflinching — but her crooked grin is pure Caleb. Oliver's gaze, steady and thoughtful, belongs to his father, though the hard set of his mouth is all me. They are stitched from both of us — fragments of two stories sewn into their own.

And gods, they are beautiful. But they'll drive me mad if they don't get a move on and end up late to school again.

Misty Ridge has changed us in ways I never expected, yet the walk to Floral Beanz remains a quiet constant I return to without thinking. The path to Floral Beanz runs alongside a clipped hedge of orange jasmine, its honeyed sweetness drifting across the frontage — a calming embrace for anyone who pauses near it.

From the road, the cafe looks like nothing more than a modest weatherboard shop pressed right up against the verge, softened by creeping vines. Timber tables dot the patio, and the small white picket fence forever begs for another coat of paint. It's a secret tucked into the garden. Exactly what we dreamed it would be: a quiet retreat for those seeking stillness, warmth, and a moment's peace. But there's more to it than what the road allows you to see.

The cottage was already here when we bought the property, waiting behind the hedge. Weathered timber walls and ivy-framed windows made it feel as though it had always belonged here. A perfect home for a café built on comfort rather than perfection. Window boxes spill with nasturtiums, while lavender and rosemary bracket the stone path in unruly but fragrant arcs.

Behind the café, a low stone wall runs the length of the block, crowned by that same towering hedge of orange jasmine. From this side, it's clipped neat and dense — glossy green and star-bright with blossoms in season. From the street, the tables, and every public angle, the living wall seals away the world beyond completely.

Opposite, the mountain rises — its green shoulder steady against the sky, ancient and unbothered by mortal troubles. It felt as though it had always been waiting for us, ready to welcome travellers and locals alike to our little nook beneath the peaks.

Just after eight, a wind chases itself down from higher on the mountain — not from the road, not from the valley, but from the quiet rise beyond the café fence. It carries the unlikely mix of spring grass and dry eucalyptus ash, cool and warm all at once, sliding through the open door and setting the hanging lights to a faint, uneasy flicker.

The bell over the door gives a startled chime.

And he steps inside.

For a heartbeat, I forget how to breathe. The air changes. As if the world itself has shifted around him.

He's tall enough to make the doorway look narrow, broad-shouldered in a way that speaks of strength not just worn but honed. His hair is golden, streaked with white and silver where the sun strikes, pulled back in a loose tie at the nape of his neck. A few strands fall across his brow with effortless disobedience.

The white linen shirt he wears — sleeves rolled to the elbow — clings just enough to suggest the defined muscle beneath. And there, faint beneath his skin, are lines of gold and silver — ink or scars, I can't tell — delicate skeins that shimmer and vanish with every shift of light, as if the patterns themselves are alive.

It's mesmerising.

He walks through like some kind of royalty — the sort that

carries the weight of knowing everyone else is beneath him, not worth his time or effort. My pulse stumbles, then surges. I can't look away. My cheeks flush with embarrassment, heat crawling across my skin, and I hope no one else notices my where my gaze lingers. I glance away, trying to snap myself out of whatever pull this is — but it's his eyes that pin me.

A blue so startling, so crystalline, it looks rimmed with molten gold — as though flame has left its mark inside him, silver rippling through the iris like lightning striking down within. They cut across the café like a soldier's blade — corners first, exits next — and when they finally sweep over me, something lances through my chest, quick and electric, stealing the air from my lungs.

I grip the counter harder than I should, trying to ignore the heat flooding my skin.

There's something magical about him — not that anyone else has noticed.

He's handsome, yes — I see the mums with prams eyeing him off like he's the only bottle of water on a desert island, want and need flickering behind their eyes. The tradies at the back table watch him too — not with interest, but with the quiet calculation deciding whether he's a friend or foe.

But to me, there's something else. His aura hums. The air around him seems to shimmer and glow — more than confidence, more than presence. It's as if he's a storm contained in human form. A presence too sharp, too heavy, like standing too close to the sun and daring to stare into the light — the glare blinding.

He doesn't smile. Doesn't even acknowledge the way people turn to look at him. He simply chooses the table furthest from the door — the one with the cleanest sight line of the room — and stalks toward it, hands in his pockets. He sits, posture straight, hands loose but controlled as he leans back against the chair — which has never looked so small beneath anyone else. He looks calculated, like a man trained his entire life not to show his hand.

I walk over to take his order, composing myself, mask firmly in place. "What can I get you?"

"Double espresso." His voice is low — velvet wrapped around stone — the vowels shaped by an accent that feels foreign with a dialect older than the café walls themselves. Then, with the barest pause, he adds: "for Aodhan."

He gives his name like a command. The moment it leaves his lips, the air seems to catch — snagging on the sound. His voice is deep, slow, deliberate — like he has all the time in the world and yet the world owes him every second.

I write it down, though my hand trembles faintly. I avoid his gaze and glance at his hands — veins tracing the backs, the tendons standing out against sun-bronzed skin, disappearing beneath rolled sleeves. I take another steadying breath, turn away, and make the coffee. When I bring it over, I tell myself to keep my hands steady — to keep my eyes on the cup, not on him...

I place it down and thank him quietly. He flicks his hand in dismissal, as if waving me away. All thoughts of him being attractive vanish in that instant. Arrogance replaces every single one. Nyxie lifts her head from where she lies by the counter. Her ears prick, and a low, warning rumble builds in her chest. She only does that with strangers who don't belong. I turn, murmuring under my breath, "Thinks he runs the place. Like some spoilt king."

He glances up at me then, and the weight of his gaze nearly buckles my knees. A nod — the smallest dip of his chin, so subtle it might be imagined.

"Then you understand the order of things," he says, a smirk playing on his lips.

And god help me, the way those words settle between us feels like a thread pulling tight. Thin. Invisible. Binding. I step back, pulse unsteady, and force myself to return to the counter — wondering how on earth he heard me.

Vivienne arrives ten minutes later in a blazer that could cut glass, heels clicking against the timber like a metronome. Phone tucked to her shoulder, she's already mid-conversation voice brisk, efficient. The kind that makes people scramble to keep up. Her eyes, sharp and assessing, sweep the café in one glance, noting and filing every detail before she's even hung up. Every bit the older sister, one always on edge and in control.

She leans down to kiss my cheek, the faint scent of citrus perfume and Rivertide air clinging to her. Then she sees him. One arched brow perfectly sculpted — says it all. Trouble. Capital T. She doesn't need words to brand him. Still, she offers a clipped, "Morning," that's both polite and edged.

He lifts his gaze, acknowledges her with the barest nod — and nothing more. Indifferent. Uncaring. Viv looks at me, the question written plainly on her face. I shake my head — no idea, not now. I already have enough to juggle without adding a hot, brooding man to the mix. She glances over to Sal, who is muttering darkly behind the counter about banks being crooks as she aggressively wrestles with the EFTPOS roll. I sigh, shaking my head at my technologically cursed manager. Viv lets out a sharp huff before marching over to save the machine and Sal from complete destruction.

The café settles into its familiar rhythm — the heartbeat I've built my days around, the business Cal and I poured everything into.

Mr Fisher claims his corner seat with the morning paper, though he reads it less than he broods over it. He calls out for another brownie, giving me a wink before glancing at the corner where Mr Handsome and Broody sits. There's something in Mr Fisher's posture — shoulders bent, body rigid, like someone's asked him to explain how the wifi works again. He gives me a nod and his big, heartfelt smile — the kind that says you're doing great; keep it up.

Then I hear the whispers.

"She's the one."

"Yeah — nearly six years ago now, couple of months off."

"Friend of a friend was first on the scene. Said it looked less like an accident and more like a maiming. Horrendous. Can you imagine?"

"Widowed young. Business to run. Kids. What a waste. He was a good-looking man too. Always smiling and happy to help."

I serve, smile, wipe, fold.

The repetition is a shield. The motions keeping me stitched together when I'd otherwise come undone. The pity, the comments, the sideways glances... the exhaustion of pretending I don't hear any of it. Sometimes I wonder if grief seeps out of a person in ways you can't scrub clean — like stains in timber, only visible in a certain light.

A noise similar to a bird screech peaks my attention and Mr Fisher chuckling in his corner, then I hear table six, not at all subtly "Well what was it we were talking about? I think something shocked me, because I can't remember?"

When I clear the stranger's table, he's gone. No chair scrape, no door chime, no farewell. Just absence — as if he was never here at all. Except he was. Beneath the saucer, a coin waits. Too heavy for its size, cool against my palm, stamped with a compass — the arrows a feather. I turn it over once, twice, and something strange pulses beneath my skin — a hum, soft but insistent, like gravity bending around it. It's nothing. Just metal. That's what I tell myself. And yet, my hand lingers, unwilling to set it down.

For the ward.

The words hum against my skin — not so much heard as felt, like someone pressed them into the marrow of my bones. I look around. It can't be — no one actually spoke.

Viv glances over, eyes narrowing as she knots her apron tighter. "Weird," she mutters, voice flat but edged, as if she felt it too. I pocket the coin, its weight dragging at me, and force myself to move on. Some mysteries can wait. The day still needs my hands steady and my heart stitched tight enough to last until tonight — until I reach my bedroom, hidden away and safe where his presence still lingers.

But memories start brewing too close to the surface today. I can smell butter spitting in the pan, hear the sizzle of batter too thin — remember the way the first pancake always burned because he was laughing instead of paying attention. Oliver riding high on Caleb's shoulders, king of the kitchen.

By the time I blink back into the now, my hand is moving in small circles, polishing the counter for no reason. Caleb on my mind again. Caleb, always. Everywhere.

I shut the window against a sudden gust, telling myself I have enough to worry about — the café, the kids — pushing back the ache that grief never quite lets go of.

And still, my fingers find the coin in my pocket. And I think of my father. Magic, he always said, was as real as rain. He treated it like a lifeline — warding the doors and windows, tucking iron nails into beams, teaching Vivienne and me to do the same. Caleb used to laugh at him for it, teasing about "salt in the corners and superstitions in the beams." But Dad's voice never lost its weight: "Keep the wards strong. Safer there than anywhere else."

Back then, I thought it was eccentricity — harmless habit.

Now, with the coin burning in my pocket and the air holding its breath, I'm not so sure.

CHAPTER 2

"Cal?" My voice carries into the mist — thin, uncertain — swallowed almost instantly by the silence.

He's ahead of me, moving with that steady stride I know so well, shoulders relaxed as though the weight of the world never quite touched him. He turns just enough for our eyes to meet — green catching mine — and his hand stretches out, waiting. Beckoning. Grounding me.

I hurry forward, breath catching, the fog clinging cold against my skin. When I reach him, he pauses at a crossroads — two paths stretching out in opposite directions, identical, endless. My chest squeezes.

"It doesn't matter which way, Cal," I whisper, my voice trembling. "As long as we go together."

He studies me — quiet, thoughtful — and for a heartbeat I believe he'll take my hand. Instead, he leans in, presses the faintest kiss against my cheek, and turns down the left path. His smile is faint. Almost apologetic.

I step forward to follow — and slam into something solid. Invisible. Unyielding.

Panic rips through me as I push, clawing at air that feels like glass. "Cal!" My voice cracks.

He doesn't stop. Doesn't answer. Just glances back once more, his eyes soft with something I can't name, before turning away.

His figure fades into the mist — step by step the faint echo of his shoes hitting the ground — until he is nothing but shadow, then nothing at all.

My throat burns. I keep calling — desperate, raw — but the silence swallows everything until the only sound left is my own heartbeat, frantic and hollow. Darkness, desolate, empty, that's all that remains. I crouch down making myself as small as possible willing there to be light again before I am swallowed whole.

The alarm shrieks.

I jolt awake, chest heaving, sweat trailing down my temples. My hand shoots out across the mattress, grasping for him — but finds only cool sheets, an expanse of emptiness where he should be.

That dream again.

I close my eyes, willing him back, clinging to the warmth that still lingers at the edges of my mind — the rough brush of his jaw, the slow press of his mouth, the way his laugh wrapped around me like sunlight spilling through morning windows.

For a moment, it feels real enough to believe. But even as I chase it, it slips through me like water through cupped hands, leaving only the ache and that raw, empty feeling inside my chest.

"Up, Lil," I mutter aloud, the sound rough in the quiet. "Come on."

My body resists. Heavy with the echo of the dream — but I force myself upright, rubbing the heel of my hand over my chest until the ache dulls. Grounding. Calming.

My fingers find the silver wedding band hanging warm against my skin, sliding along the chain until I catch it and spin it once, twice. The small ritual tucks everything back where it belongs — or at least pretends to.

Shower. Dressed. Coffee.

Steps that make sense when nothing else does.

In the bathroom, steam blooms across the mirror, blurring my reflection until I'm nothing but outlines. I braid my hair with damp fingers, pulling it out of my face. Nyxie pads in, claws tapping softly against the tiles, head tilted — those amber eyes always seem to catch too much. She watches like she knows where I've been in my dreams, what I've lost there and still haunts me.

"I know, sweetheart," I murmur, crouching to scratch the soft place behind her ears. Her tail thumps once, forgiving. "Eggs for you. Bit of cheese." Her huff sounds like approval.

I pass the wedding photo on the dressing table and pause, as I always do. Caleb's grin stares back through the glass — warm and alive in a way that slices through me every time. My fingers press against it, just for a heartbeat, like touching the memory might tether me to him again. "Morning, love," I whisper — and it feels less like a habit and more like a prayer.

Beside the frame, the crystal he found on one of our bushwalks catches the light, scattering a rainbow across the wall. It lands right over my chest, colours spilling like a benediction.

I close my eyes, let it wash through me, and take it as my sign to keep moving. Down the hall, the house begins to stir — doors creaking, pipes groaning, the muffled shuffle of feet. Oliver emerges first, hair still damp, school shirt half-done, toast clenched in one hand and socks in the other. Always half-finished. Always moving too fast.

"Eggs, Ol?" I call.

He shakes his head, already grinning. "Nah. Gotta be early, Mum. Got a second session this arvo." The grin is so Caleb it steals my breath for a moment. I always knew he'd be just like his dad. "You're at the café all day today, yeah?" he calls between mouthfuls of toast.

"Yep, just out the front if you need me. And try not to be home too late — make sure you call." I hesitate, my gaze lingering on him longer than he likes. "Where's your sister?" I ask, changing the topic, knowing he hates when I get too overprotective.

He shrugs, amused. "Pretty sure she's already over there."

"Of course she is," I mutter — and Nyxie barks, as if she too is laughing knowing at what we will find.

Outside, the morning carries the scent of damp earth and eucalyptus, with the sweet scent from the orange jasmine — sharp and clean after last night's drizzle. The cicadas sing their relentless, happy tune into the early air, no one around yet to disturb them, and the birds not quite ready to give chase.

I smile and wave to the regulars as I walk into the café — familiar faces, wide smiles, and friendly waves exchanged.

The bell above the café door jingles bright and familiar. "Morning, Dais," I call, my voice already curled into a smile. I don't have to fake or pretend with the kids. "Appreciate the help, but school first, remember. This is your final year."

Daisy pops up from behind the counter with a tea towel in hand, her grin wide enough to undo me. "Relax, Mum. I'm not ditching. Just thought I'd open for you."

I try for stern but lose the battle almost instantly. She's too tall now — all legs — her cheekbones sharpening into something older. But the eyes are mine: green, stubborn, unwilling to bend.

"You're trouble."

"No, just efficient," she fires back, dimples flashing like her father's.

She rattles off her work with mock seriousness, ticking points off on her fingers. "Float balanced. Beans topped. Muffins cooling. Grinder on,. Sal texted: 'On my way. Don't touch my banana bread.'" Daisy leans in with a conspiratorial wink. "That's a direct quote."

I huff out a laugh and set down the milk, wiping at a spotless patch of timber just to keep my hands busy. Then her grin slips — her hip shifting against the counter as she studies me with those too-perceptive eyes. "I can do more, you know."

"More?" I echo, slow, wary, pretending not to notice the thrum of seriousness beneath her voice.

"A heap more," she insists carefully, testing her ground. "I could open with you on weekends. A couple of afternoons after school. Learn the bank drops. Real shifts. Actual help." She hesitates, and it's the hesitation that cuts. "You're always tired, Mum. Let me help."

The pride hits first. Bright and sharp — followed by worry

that creeps in like a draught under the door. She's taking on too much, carrying more than I want her to. Then comes the crushing sense of failure — quieter, heavier — settling in my chest like stone. She shouldn't be worried about me. I haven't been hiding it enough. My thumb finds the silver ring at my sternum and spins it once.

"We can try weekends," I say, keeping my tone even. "Study first." Her smile unfurls like sunlight breaking through clouds. "Deal." She hesitates — the brightness dimming — and then: "Can I... borrow the car? Just today. Straight to school and back. I'll text when I leave, when I arrive. I know... about Dad."

The word falters on her lips, like it costs her something just to say it — and I know it hurts her as much as it hurts me.

I inhale — slow, deliberate — then let the air out through my teeth.

"You call before you drive off. You text when you park. Every time. I mean it."

"Promise."

She leans over the counter and presses a quick kiss to my cheek — a flash of affection that leaves my throat thick. "You taught me well, remember?"

The café stirs fully awake, stretching into its morning rhythm as locals filter through the doors — mums with prams, tradies in paint-splattered shorts, hikers chasing caffeine before the trail. The grinder purrs, steady as breath. The steam wand hisses and sighs. The air is rich with coffee and warm bread — the familiar heartbeat of my second home.

Sal breezes in with flour dusting her jeans, a scarf looped twice around her neck, and a grin that always reads like trouble.

"Morning, Lil."

Her eyes flick over me, cataloguing everything in a heartbeat — the curve of my mouth, the set of my shoulders, the shadows I think I've hidden.

"Was that Daisy opening? Miracles do happen."

"Don't scare her off," I warn, arching a brow. "And don't touch the muffins. She's determined to get on your good side."

Sal smirks, already drifting toward the cooling rack like a thief casing a vault. "We'll see."

Mr Fisher rolls up, the old Corolla pulling in crooked on the gravel like it always does — one tyre resting half in the garden bed. The engine coughs twice before he shuts it off.

He climbs out with the ease of a man who's done the same routine for decades — plaid shirt sleeves rolled to the elbow, work boots powdered with dust, his sun-bleached mullet tucked behind his ears.

He steps inside carrying the smell of earth and gum leaves with him, a smile already creasing his weathered face — the kind that feels more fatherly than neighbourly.

"Morning, Lillian. Morning, Sally," he rumbles, voice gravelly but kind. "The usual. Out the back by the fence."

"You and the sun," I say, shaking my head fondly. "Put on sunscreen today, or I'll book you in for a skin check with Dr Marose myself." Nyxie, the shameless traitor, abandons me immediately — padding over to claim her dues.

Mr Fisher, chuckling crouches to scratch behind her ears.

When he straightens, Nyxie stays rooted to the spot, watching him go with that solemn, measuring gaze she saves for the rare few — the ones she deems worth trusting.

The regulars return to their usual rhythms — prams, hi-vis, and one shared lamington like clockwork.

And then Mark Evans — right on cue.

He always arrives as if he's timed it: watch polished, teeth too white, shirt pressed within an inch of its life. His hair sits like it has its own publicist, not a strand daring to rebel.

"Flat white," he says with a wink. "And how about that *date*."

"Flat white," I confirm, my smile neat, polite, and firmly non-negotiable. "And a no."

It's our script — a dance he's been trying to lead for over a year. Never crude, never pushy — always packaged in charm. But charm doesn't hide everything. There's a flash in his eyes I don't like. Cat-like. Calculating. The kind of gaze that skims more than it should, lingers longer than it ought.

He drops a tip larger than sense, slides the saucer toward me with a flourish, and lingers just long enough to read the room before gliding back out into the mountain light.

Nyxie tracks him the whole way. Her hackles just barely rise — a ripple along her shoulders — before they settle again when the door shuts. Only then does she curl back at my feet, head resting on her paws, as if satisfied the unwanted attention has left.

I tuck the unease away — press it down beneath the rhythm of the café.

Sunlight creeps across the counter while my cloth traces timber already clean. The ivy along the back wall stirs — though the air is still — a leaf unfurling slow, as if reaching for something unseen.

"You're tired," I mutter under my breath, forcing the words into something solid. "That's all."

Sal swans past with a tray, hips cocked, hair pulled up in a messy knot dusted with flour. "You missed a spot," she teases, flicking at the timber I've already wiped three times. But her eyes catch mine — steady and sharp — and her voice softens.

"You okay?"

I nod, because the alternative is unspooling right here in front of the muffins and the mums with prams. My throat won't open for anything more.

Sal bumps my shoulder — light but grounding. "She'll be fine," she says, meaning Daisy without naming her.

"I know," I answer automatically, but the words don't feel like mine. My thumb finds the ring at my chest.

Time lurches. The tick of the clock grows louder. The café hum dips and swells, voices blurring like water rushing past stone.

And then the world rips. Tyres screaming. Gravel spitting. The violent sound cuts through everything, slamming into me like a fist. Silence follows a shockwave, heavy, ringing, too big for the room.

The bell above the door jolts. Mr Fisher fills the doorway, cap crushed in his hands. His boots leave a scatter of dust on the tiles, but it's his eyes that hold me — stripped bare of their usual warmth, carrying something I don't want to see. Concern. Fear.

"Lily."

My name lands rough in his throat. Final. Heavy. My stomach drops before he even says it.

"It's Daisy."

The words hit harder than any blow. "Up past the quarry turn-off." The tray in Sal's hands rattles. Nyxie is already up, ready to sprint. My heart is a hammer, a snarl, a prayer.

Gods. No.

CHAPTER 3

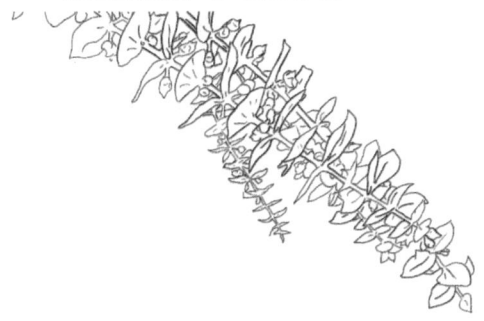

Everything freezes — steam, voices, my lungs — then flickers back.

"I've got the floor," Sal says, already moving. I'm running. Nyxie barks once and stays. Mr Fisher's Corolla coughs to life. As he drops the clutch, I dial triple zero with hands that only shake when they're allowed to. "Car accident," I tell the operator, voice steady because it has to be. It's the only thing it can be. I give the road, the bend, Daisy's name, my name. The operator's calm is a rope in a riptide:

Stay on the line. Check for danger. Don't move her if there's neck pain or head injuries. Help is on the way.

I say yes to all of it, holding onto their voice like a lifeline.

We crest the bend, and reality hits like a fist. The hatchback sits warped, front crumpled, glass crazed. Airbags collapsed like exhausted lungs. The road smells of hot rubber and fear. Daisy is on the grass under a silver blanket, blood stippling her hands where the glass kissed them, face paper-white, eyes too wide.

"*Daisy,*" I breathe.

Then louder, because my voice won't obey me.

"Daisy!" She looks up.

"Mum," she says — lost and far away — and the single syllable nearly drops me. I'm kneeling before I know how I got there, scanning pupils, shoulders, the angle of her spine.

"Head? Neck? Dizziness? Nausea?"

"Ringing," she whispers. "And my hands. I—" Her breath shudders.

"I think I killed someone." My heart stutters. "What?"

"He was just there." She shivers — the kind of whole-body shake shock brings. "In the middle of the road. I braked. He... he was there and then he wasn't. I don't understand."

"It's alright," I murmur, because that's the only thing I have. "I'm here. Help's on the way."

A figure leans against the crumpled bonnet like he owns it.

Tall.

Muscular.

The kind of look that would have most women weak at the knees. Dressed in dark, eyes like night that knows too much. His smile is a thin slice of amusement — and something like trouble. "Didn't expect my morning exploration to come with vehicular poetry," he drawls. "Your girl's reflexes are decent. Could've been worse."

"Who are you?" I ask, not bothering to make it nice.

"Maricus," he says — as if it's both answer and dare. "No need to thank me for not dying."

Mr Fisher stands to the side, shoulders squared, gaze tipped to the tree line as though listening to a frequency only he can hear. The hairs on my arms lift. The air... shifts Tightens like a pressure system rolling in without a cloud.

Sirens cut the bend. The ambulance arrives in a wash of red-blue. Paramedics move with that brisk competence that calms nerves.

"Hey, love. I'm Matt. I'm going to have a look at your hands and your head, yeah?"

He gets a tiny nod for his trouble and starts working, voice a steady tide. The other paramedic sweeps the scene. "Anyone else hurt?

"Not unless you count a bruised ego from this lovely creature not bothering to check if I'm okay," the stranger says, flexing his knuckles as if they're fascinating.

Despite the clear skies, a storm seems like it is brewing. Even the cicadas in the gum leaves hush, as though the mountain itself is waiting — tense.

A man steps out from the deeper shade, and the road seems to bend around him, making space it didn't have a second ago.

It's him.

The stranger from the café.

The one who moved like he owned the ground he walked on. The one who left the coin. The sun catches in his pale hair, throwing threads of gold into the air around him. The faint glow beneath his linen shifts like captured sunlight.

His eyes... god, those eyes. Even from this distance, the gold and silver at their edges are unmistakable.

Aodhan strolls forward, hands in pockets, looking like a mob boss ready to rein in his underling. I remember his face. Of course I do. How could I forget the way the air seemed to tilt around him? His gaze sweeps once across the scene. Daisy pale and trembling, the blood on the gravel, the mess of it all. His mouth hardens, that carved line of authority.

"Reckless."

The word is quiet, but it lands like stone dropped in water, rippling through everything. Aodhan's attention slides to Daisy for half a heartbeat, then pins me. Cold. Unyielding. Command woven into every syllable.

"You could have killed yourself. Human lives don't last long as it is. Why rush it with stupidity?"

The audacity knocks the air from my lungs. For a second, I'm nothing but disbelief — then fury flares, hot and fast, saving me from breaking apart.

"Excuse me?" My voice shakes, but with anger, not fear. "She's a child. My child. She's in shock, and you dare—" I grip Daisy's hand tighter, grounding myself. "If you've got nothing useful to add, keep walking — and take that nuisance with you." I jerk my chin toward the stranger leaning across the wreck of a car.

Something flickers in his eyes. Surprise. Annoyance. No — more than that. Sharp, something alive that collides with me like flint against steel. It sparks in the space between us, crackling invisible but undeniable, and my chest stutters like I've stepped too close to lightning. He feels it too. I see it, there in the minute shift of his jaw, in the way his gaze lingers a second too long, as if he can't quite tear it away. And then it's gone. Buried. Snapped shut.

He turns from me as though I'm nothing — as though the air hadn't just shifted between us. His focus locks on his companion, his voice snapping clean and precise.

"What were you doing in the middle of the road, Maricus?" The words aren't a question. They're accusation. But I barely hear them. My pulse hammers in my ears, my skin prickling with heat that shouldn't exist — with a pull I don't understand.

My fury trembles into something else entirely. Something dangerous. Because for one impossible breath... I wanted Aodhan to look back.

"Oh, look," Maricus purrs, voice sliding over the scene like oil. "He knows my name." He pushes off the bonnet with deliberate laziness, every movement a provocation, eyes bright with mischief edged in malice. "Stretching my legs. Thinking beautiful thoughts. Enjoying the sights. You know how it is."

Aodhan's jaw works once — the smallest tic of muscle betraying the control he wears like armour. Heat shimmers, subtle at first — the kind of shift that makes your eyes doubt themselves — until the day feels a fraction too sharp, the sunlight a fraction too bright. Power held tight, leaking anyway.

For a heartbeat, nobody breathes.

The pull from Aodhan sings against my skin like static — a second heartbeat I can't escape — and Maricus watches it all with the grin of someone who's just found a loaded weapon on the ground.

The paramedic cuts in before the air can split. "Give us a tick, yeah?" His tone is calm but iron, the kind of voice that's shut down bigger egos than these two. He tips a gentler look at me.

"Mum, she's shocked but okay. Hands are mostly superficial. We'll clean 'em up. Watch for nausea, headache, the usual. If anything worsens, bring her straight in."

"Thank you," I manage and mean it like a prayer my voice shaking despite myself.

Maricus flicks me a look that feels like being read and filed

— a glance sharp enough to cut. "Well," he says, mocking a bow, "since everyone's fine and no one appreciates my death-defying grace…"

His mouth curves, slow and dangerous. "I'll be off, but I'll be seeing you soon, I'm sure." He winks. The words are light, but the way his gaze slides from Aodhan to me before he straightens is anything but. It's a promise.

Aodhan still hasn't spoken. But the humidity in the air clings to my skin, and when his eyes meet mine for the briefest second, the world narrows to a single thread between us — sharp, unsteady, burning.

Maricus steps to the edge of the bend and is simply not there a second later — a sleight of presence that makes the hairs rise on my neck, though the paramedics' eyes slide right past it as if nothing happened. Fisher's mouth tightens — the only one unsettled enough to notice.

Aodhan — watches Maricus vanish with a flicker of distaste, the kind you might reserve for a fly you can't chase out the door. Then his gaze shifts back to me. The judgement is still there, sharp and unyielding, but something hides beneath it — something harder to name. Not exactly concern. Something rawer, buried under his façade.

"You need to take more care," he says at last. Stripped of tone, the words could almost be worry. But when he turns his gaze to Daisy, his restraint frays. "Next time, you might not get away with frightened and bruised."

His voice lands like a gavel — absolute. Anger — and the fear I've been suppressing — surge through me, quick and clean.

"Try speaking to people with some empathy," I snap, every syllable crisp as the mountain air.

"I would," he replies, crossing his arms and looking down at me from his impossible height, "if there were a need to be empathetic."

"Why are you still here? Go check on your friend. After all, he was the one strolling in the middle of the road. Heaven forbid another accident happens." I watch him glance toward the quarry, then down the road toward the café.

"He can take care of himself. You, on the other hand..." His gaze lingers — calculating, unsettling. "Can you manage all alone? You seem to be a bundle of nerves, stress, and lack of life." He's watching my every movement. Every breath.

"I am perfectly fine. And I am not alone. Mr Fisher is right here." I refuse to acknowledge how quickly he's seen through my mask. Mr Fisher glances between us, silent throughout the exchange, which is unlike him.

Aodhan hums, low and dismissive.

"Hmm. Yes, I can see how helpful he might be. An old, decrepit man."

My patience snaps.

"Next time, you might get a polite response — but I won't tolerate insults to friends. For now, I suggest you get off my property." My civility cracks. What does he want? Why hasn't he left?

For a heartbeat, his face falters. Something old, startled, and unguarded flashes there with recognition, longing, ache; I can't tell which before it shutters again. The gold beneath his skin dims to a muted thrum, like a fire banked but not gone.

"We're done here," he says voice low, final — before turning back into the trees.

One moment he is solid; the next, the shadows reclaim him, swallowing him whole.

The silence left in his wake hums — charged and unsettled. I exhale only when I'm sure he's gone — and even then, the echo of him clings like heat in my veins. The ambulance hums low, steady. My mind stores every word in some locked drawer for later — but my heart can only count her breaths.

One. Two. Still here. Still here. Still present. Still alive.

Mr Fisher, bless him, pulls out his phone and rings Sal before I can even think of it. "She'll cover," he mutters with quiet authority. "You stay put."

Daisy's fingers trembling through fresh bandages — reach for mine. "I'm sorry," she whispers. The words scrape raw. "I swear. I didn't see him."

Her breath hitches, catching in her throat.

My throat closes, my chest aching with the weight of her apology as if she's the one who needs to answer for a stranger stepping out of nowhere. "I know," I murmur, pressing my forehead to hers, swallowing back the break in my voice. "He shouldn't have been there." My jaw hardens. "What was he doing standing in the middle of the road?"

Her eyes close tight, lashes wet. I cup her face gently.

"We're going home. Tea. Couch. Nyxie's best blanket. That's the plan."

My phone buzzes in my pocket. Sal's text: Got the café. Don't you dare rush back. Relief settles like a fragile thread through the chaos.

But my gaze drifts, unbidden, to the tree line where he vanished, Aodhan. The echo of him still clings to the air, pressed into the day like a palm print cooling on glass. I don't know him. I don't want to know him. And yet — god help me — some stubborn, traitorous part of me keeps a lingering thought on him.

The drive home blurs.

Mr Fisher hums a tune in a foreign tongue, calming us all. Gravel spits beneath the tyres. Daisy sits silent in the passenger seat, staring out the window as if the trees might leap again into her path.

I keep one hand clamped around Daisy's, the other curled around the wedding band at my throat. I turn it over and over, until my thumb feels raw, the sting bringing me back to the present.

Inside the house, too much light pours through the glass walls. The rosemary and violets scent the air, jasmine spilling from the pots, Oliver's schoolbooks abandoned across the table — every detail ordinary, and somehow cruel in its ordinariness.

Normal feels like mockery when my daughter flinches at the creak of a floorboard. I guide her gently to the couch. Nyxie bounds up immediately, pressing herself tight against Daisy — her solid weight a shield. I pull a blanket over them both, smoothing damp hair from my daughter's forehead. Her hands, neat with the paramedics' tape, tremble against the fabric.

"You'll be fine," I whisper, even though the words taste thin. "You're safe. That's all that matters." I move through the ritual of making tea I won't drink, grounding myself in small motions.

The house folds around us like it remembers how — its walls cradling us with the familiar weight of silence. I brush my fingers over the crystal on the shelf — the one Caleb found years ago. Light fractures into a rainbow that strikes me in the chest.

I take it as a sign: time to breathe. She is home. She is safe. When Daisy finally sleeps, I stand alone by the window. The mountain looms steady, unchanged. And yet the air calls — faint and unsettling — like a note pitched just beyond hearing.

I press my palm flat to the cool glass, letting it leach the heat still burning in my bones. "Alright," I whisper — to the empty house, to Caleb, to the strange shape this day has carved into us. "We're still here."

Outside, the trees lean. And in their hush, I swear something listens.

CHAPTER 4

The knock came just as Daisy's lashes fluttered shut, her breathing finally evening out.

Emma swept in first. A whirlwind of perfume, jangling bracelets, and grocery bags cutting into her forearms. The mountain breeze had mussed her hair into a crown of chaos she wore with pride. "Emergency carb delivery," she announced grandly, dumping the bags onto the counter with a flourish.

"Also sugar. And possibly enough wine to drown a small horse. But we'll start with lasagne, because I'm not a monster." A laugh cracked out of me — jagged, half-broken. Relief disguised as amusement. "You didn't need to—"

"Didn't I?" Emma cut me off with one arched brow that could have out-argued a senate in Parliament. She tugged out foil trays and containers, slamming them down with deliberate drama.

"Best-friend contract, clause seven: in the event of trauma, drama, or mysterious, absurdly attractive men, I bring food and sarcasm. Don't make me get legal about it."

"You're ridiculous."

"Ridiculously the best," she countered, flashing a grin before turning her sharp gaze on the room. Then her eyes landed on Daisy — curled small on the couch, Nyxie planted like a sentry at her side. Emma's whole frame softened, her voice dropping into something quieter, steadier.

"Good girl. She's got the best guard dog in Misty Ridge. I'll handle carbs, Nyxie handles security. Division of labour." Before I could respond, the door opens again.

Vivienne stepped through the doorway, light catching in the neat braid over her shoulder. She didn't carry bags or make an entrance; she didn't need to. Her very presence shifted the room. Grounding it, stitching back seams I hadn't realised had come undone.

She crossed straight to Daisy, knelt, brushed a kiss across her forehead with the kind of reverence that made me feel like a child myself again. Then, as she rose to meet my gaze: "She's safe. She's unharmed," Viv said evenly. Her eyes held mine, steady as stone.

"That's what matters."

"See?" Emma muttered, shaking grated cheese onto the counter like it was a weapon of war. "We're basically an emergency response team. I do food, she does reassurance, Nyxie does intimidation-slash-protection. Lil, you—" She waved a spoon at me. "You can glower dramatically out the windows. Complete coverage. No one's getting through this fortress."

The corner of my mouth twitched, but my chest stayed tight. Their banter was balm, their existence an unbreakable bond — but somewhere beneath it all, another presence lingered.

A spark pressed into the day. A heat I couldn't forget. I kept seeing him at the bend in the road — tall, broad, sun caught in pale hair, golden tattoos lit from beneath as if they carried dawn itself. Those eyes: blue rimmed with gold, cutting through me, through everything, like he'd seen too much in a single glance.

I told myself I was being ridiculous — that exhaustion and adrenaline made ghosts out of strangers. But no matter how fiercely I clung to the normal — lasagne, laughter, Nyxie guarding

Daisy like she always had. I couldn't shake him. Aodhan. Even his name snagged in my thoughts like a thread I couldn't cut.

I forced myself back to the present, setting plates, pouring water, grounding in the weight of small, ordinary tasks. But the truth pressed in like a storm waiting at the horizon: he had taken up space in my mind, and he wasn't letting go.

Vivienne rolled her eyes but smiled, all calm efficiency taking in everything, already preparing to methodically sort and restore. Emma, meanwhile, was all noise and motion, stacking plates like a general preparing for battle, narrating every step as though the house itself needed distracting.

The kitchen filled with garlic, baked cheese, and Emma's running commentary. "Honestly, Lil, next time warn me if you're going to collect strays on the roadside. Gorgeous ones, sure — but the attitude? Ugh. Ten out of ten for bone structure, zero for bedside manner."

"Emma," Vivienne said — that single-word rebuke lined with patience — though even her eyes flicked toward me, sharp and searching. "Explain."

I hesitated, then told them, haltingly at first, then with the rhythm of someone who can't stop once they've begun. The accident. Daisy's shock. The man in the road who wasn't meant to be there. Maricus dangerous, mocking, danger wrapped in charm — totally Emma's type. And then him. Aodhan. His name tasted strange as I spoke it aloud, almost like a secret I should have kept to myself. His impossible presence. The way the air itself had seemed to hold its breath when he stepped from the trees.

Emma blinked at me, mouth parted, then snorted. "Of course. Mystery broody sun-god with cheekbones sharp enough to slice bread. Bloody typical. You always did attract the difficult ones — hot, but difficult." Vivienne ignored her, eyes narrowing. "And what did he want?"

"He didn't say," I admitted. "He barely said anything at all. Just... judged. Like Daisy's mistake was some kind of a crime." My throat tightened as I remembered his gaze.

"And then he disappeared — back into the trees, like he hadn't been there at all."

Silence stretched. Vivienne's mouth flattened, though she reached out to squeeze my hand firm, grounding. Emma let out a theatrical sigh and uncorked the wine with unnecessary violence.

"Well. Whether he's a king, a cult leader, or just some bloke with too much hair product, he doesn't get to come into your life and throw shade like that. Not unless he's good at grovelling at your feet, admitting he was wrong."

Despite myself, I laughed. But the echo of him lingered his eyes, that faint shimmer under his skin, the way he looked at me: a desperate and confused plea for something he was scared to admit even to himself.

Normality tried to stitch itself back into the evening: Vivienne's quiet questions, Emma's comic noise, garlic bread vanishing quicker than I could slice it. Oliver thundered in later, sweaty from soccer, muttered "Love you, Mum," kissed my cheek, and vanished into Daisy's room without waiting for food.

The sound of him made my chest ache in the good way, proof that some things, at least, were solid. Everyone home. Everyone safe.

But when night deepened, I found myself at the kitchen window again. The mountains loomed dark and watchful; my reflection in the glass looked pale and hollow, the ring glinting against my throat.

The air shifted, subtle and certain, like the same storm from the roadside had followed us home. Nyxie padded over and leaned her full weight against my leg, gaze trained on the tree line as though she, too, was waiting for something to step out.

"I know," I whispered, burying my hand in her fur. "I feel it too."

Weariness clung to me as I climbed the stairs, the day pressing heavy behind my eyes. I exhaled slowly as steam curled around me, rose-scented bathwater lapping at my skin. I let my head fall back, trying to let the day dissolve in the heat — but my mind betrayed me anyway, circling back to him like a moth to flame.

Those impossible eyes tracking me as if I already belonged to him. That restrained, immovable presence.

The way the air itself had seemed to change when he drew near. Sharp and charged — setting every nerve alight until I wasn't sure where my pulse ended and the humming began.

The bath rippled, though I hadn't moved. Tiny waves spreading from me like a heartbeat made visible. My breath hitched. The water stilled again.

I pressed my palms over my face, heat and scent rising around me.

"Ridiculous," I whispered to the empty room. "I'm going mad." But my voice sounded small and unconvincing against the steady thrum in my bones.

When sleep refused to take me, I rose and wandered barefoot into the garden. The potted herbs brushed my ankles, damp earth cooling the soles of my feet, grounding me in the present. Nyxie padded behind — a silent sentinel, her eyes catching glints of moonlight.

That's when I saw it.

New and impossible. Among the rosemary and daisies, a flower had bloomed overnight. Petals layered like a rose and a peony fused together, glimmering faintly in the last wash of moonlight. Threads of silver light ran through the petals as if spun from starlight, shifting with each breath of wind.

I reached out, fingers trembling, and brushed the velvet edge. Warmth pulsed beneath my touch — alive, aware. My heart lurched.

My mother once told me old stories of a flower that bloomed only for the reigning Queen of the Fae. Blessed. Rare. Said to mark bloodlines and legacy. She had whispered, almost shy, that her own mother — the one I never knew — once made one bloom.

Just a bedtime story, to get Vivienne and me into bed. The thought rooted cold and hot in my chest at once.

I drew back, heart racing, and left it swaying under the moon.

Nyxie's low huff rumbled through the garden breaking the silence.

When exhaustion finally dragged me under, I dreamed.

Caleb walked beside me along our favourite mountain track, sunlight filtering gold through the gums. His hand was warm in mine, his smile unchanged, steady and sure. We reached a fork in the path that had never been there before.

"It's okay, Lil," he murmured, his voice a balm. "Daisy's safe. Change is coming. You're stronger than you think. Don't hold your breath forever. Live. Open your heart again. Be strong."

I woke with his voice still in my ears, the ache in my chest bending into something I couldn't name. Outside, the first light of dawn slid across the hills, and in the garden, that impossible flower waited — glowing faintly as if it had been listening.

CHAPTER 5

Morning broke quiet, as if the mountain itself were holding its breath.

The usual chorus of kookaburras seemed muted, the air still heavy with the residue of yesterday.

I glance across into the lounge room to where Nyxie is sprawled across the rug, her dark coat gleaming faintly in the pale light. She refuses to move, chin anchored to Daisy's lap as Daisy slumps across the couch, as if she could pin the girl to safety with her sheer weight alone.

Daisy's bandaged fingers stroked her ears in slow, steady passes, her lips twitching into a smile — small, stubborn, defiant. A silent declaration: I won't break. But the bruises under her eyes betrayed her. They told a truer story — of shock that hadn't faded, of dreams shaken out of her hands too soon.

And still she sat there, spine straight, trying to look like herself when every line of her body said otherwise. I wanted to scoop her up, tell her she didn't need to be brave, that she could just be my child again for a while. But I knew her pride — the same iron thread I carried in my own bones. So I poured the boiling water, listened to the hollow clink of the spoon in the mug, and let her keep her armour, even if it was paper-thin.

Oliver perched at the edge of the table, his schoolbag slouched against his legs, one strap twisted as though he hadn't even tried to shoulder it properly. He wasn't rushing the way he usually did

— no toast clenched between his teeth, no last-minute scramble for socks. Instead, he sat unnervingly still, his gaze fixed on Daisy.

There was a weight in it — a steadiness older than his years.

His green eyes — steady and unyielding — tracked every movement of her bandaged hands, as though he could keep her from shattering just by watching closely enough. The muscle in his jaw ticked, subtle but there, like he was holding himself together by sheer will.

My stomach tightened. He shouldn't have to carry this. He should be worried about forgotten homework, soccer practice, and whether his boots still fit — not about the way his sister flinched at the scrape of a chair.

He was sixteen, not thirty. Guilt pressed in, sharp and cold. Caleb's absence had already asked too much of him. Now this. I curled my fingers around the warm ceramic of my mug, grounding myself, and made a silent promise: I would talk to him soon. Strip that weight from his shoulders before it rooted too deep.

The phone buzzed against the bench, sharp against the hush of morning. I snatched it up before the sound could rattle through the house — before Daisy stirred.

"Dad?"

Tom's voice rumbled down the line — warm and worn, the kind of sound that reminded me of his work boots on the porch after a long day.

"Lil. Just checking in. Heard about the scrape yesterday from Viv. How's my girl?"

I turned, glancing at Daisy where she sat curled into the couch. My throat tightened.

"She's shaken," I admitted, keeping my voice low. "But she'll be alright."

"And Ol?"

"He's okay — playing tough at the moment, but I see how worried he is. It's brought back Caleb." I paused, taking a deep breath. "Car accidents always shake him."

"And you?" Dad's voice shifted — softer now, lined with the weight of things he never quite said aloud.

"Holding together?"

A laugh escaped before I could catch it — brittle, too sharp, he won't like my sarcastic tone, never did. "As much as I can. Feels like life doesn't pause long enough to let you fall apart."

"That's because you can't afford to," he murmured. Then, quieter still — almost like a prayer he hadn't meant me to hear. "Keep those wards strong around the place, Lil. You're all safer there than anywhere else."

My hand tightened on the phone, nails biting into the wood of the bench. The words cracked something in me — the way they always did when he spoke of things no one else remembered. "What do you mean, Dad? What do wards have to do with protecting us from car accidents?" I asked sharper than I'd intended.

He cleared his throat, too fast. "Just an old man worrying and being superstitious, you know me." A pause. "You've got good people around you. That's what matters."

But the silence between us hummed — alive with the weight of what he wasn't saying. A half-truth lingered there, an unspoken promise in his voice that told me he meant more.

I wanted to press, to demand he tell me everything — what he knew, what he feared, why the air seemed to hum differently since yesterday.

But Daisy shifted on the couch, her eyes closing for a heartbeat, her face too pale in the light. My focus snapped back. "Thanks, Dad," I whispered instead, swallowing the ache. "We'll be fine. I'll add some salt and check the hazel trees."

"You be careful, and look after yourself," he said — rough as gravel. And then the line clicked dead.

The kitchen filled with silence again. Except it wasn't silent at all. The words still echoed, clinging to me like humidity slick on summer skin: Keep the wards strong.

What is he not telling me?

By mid-morning, we were at the doctor's. The clinic smelled faintly of disinfectant and bleach, the air-con humming too cold against skin that hadn't yet shaken the mountain's damp.

The waiting room had been crowded — coughs, a crying toddler, the low buzz of a TV replaying the same updates on loop — but now it was just us in a narrow exam room where every sound seemed too sharp.

Daisy sat stiff on the paper-covered bed, legs swinging, jaw set, her chin lifted as if bravado alone could hold her steady. The doctor — a kind woman with hair scraped into a practical bun and glasses perched halfway down her nose — peeled back the dressings with slow, careful hands.

Daisy hissed as antiseptic touched raw skin, her knuckles whitening against the edge of the bed. But she didn't cry. Not once. My girl. My brave, stubborn girl.

"Surface cuts," the doctor murmured, voice calm, efficient. "No nerve damage. You've had a lucky escape."

She glanced at me over the rim of her glasses, her look carrying both reassurance and warning. "She'll heal fine. Keep the dressings clean, change them daily. Watch for swelling, redness, fever — any sign of infection, bring her straight back."

Relief punched through me so hard I nearly swayed, loosening the steel that had gripped my chest since the gravel skidded under tyres yesterday.

I found my voice enough to say, "Thank you," and mean it like a prayer.

The doctor offered Daisy a coaxing smile. "You'll be back at school in no time. But today? No arguments. Rest, watch some cheesy rom-coms."

Daisy nodded once, lips pressed tight, shoulders squared. I recognised the battle flickering in her — the urge to argue, to prove she wasn't fragile, that she wasn't broken, that she could go back now and not fall behind before graduation. But instead of defiance, she swallowed it down and slid her hands into the kangaroo pocket of her hoodie, fingers hidden, restless.

The car smelled faintly of antiseptic and hospital paper as we pulled out of the clinic car park. The road stretched ahead — familiar bends and gullies dressed in morning haze — but every curve felt sharper today, as though the world itself wanted reminding how close we'd come.

I kept one hand clamped on the wheel, the other brushing the wedding band that hung on its chain — cold metal against warm skin.

Daisy sat curled in the passenger seat, the bandages bright against her hoodie. She stared out the window, quiet in a way that wasn't quite herself. When she finally spoke, her voice was small but steady.

"Guess I was lucky." Her mouth tilted — not quite a smile. "Just scrapes and bruises."

The words hit me like a second crash. Lucky. A word too fragile for what could have been.

"You're more than lucky," I said, my voice rougher than I meant. "It could have been so much worse, Dais. You don't just walk away from a car slamming on gravel like that."

I stopped myself before adding what neither of us needed spoken aloud — we know this; we've lived this once before.

She hesitated, fingers worrying the edge of her sleeve. "It... it didn't feel lucky. Not at first. I thought—" Her breath hitched. "I thought my hands were on fire. Everything hurt. I thought I was dying mum. Everything hurt until all of a sudden there was no pain. I felt weightless. But then Mr Fisher was there. He pulled me out, said he'd get you, and—" She glanced down at her bandages, as though surprised they didn't match the memory. "It was strange. The pain just... went like it was never there at all. Like it shut off the second he said it."

The wheel tugged under my hands, and I corrected too fast. My heart thudded unevenly.

Mr Fisher. Always there at the edge of things. Always knowing just when to step in.

I swallowed. "He was the first on the scene?"

Daisy nodded, almost matter-of-fact. "Yeah. It was like he knew it was coming. He didn't even look surprised. Just... calm. Like he already knew I wasn't really broken or that I would be fine." She frowned. "That makes no sense, does it?"

It made too much sense — in ways I wasn't ready to say aloud. Mr Fisher, with his kind eyes and quiet weight, his ever-calming presence in our lives, whether it be helping move boxes, or calming an aggressive customer. The way Nyxie trusted him without hesitation. The way his presence always felt grounding when the world threatened to tilt.

"You trust him," I said carefully.

Daisy shrugged, but the corner of her mouth softened. "Don't you?"

I gripped the wheel harder, the chain at my throat biting into my skin with each breath.

"Yeah," I admitted. "I do."

The road opened ahead, sunlight catching in the gums, and I felt it — a shift, subtle as a held breath — like the world was rearranging itself, and I was only just beginning to notice.

I dialled Vivienne on autopilot. She answered on the second ring — her voice brisk as ever, but with tension humming beneath it.

"Update?"

"Cuts only. No serious damage." The word damage scraped raw in my throat, cracking on its way out. I cleared it quickly, forcing steadiness. "We'll be home soon."

"Good," Viv said, firm and final — as if sheer willpower could keep us safe. "I'll swing by later. Don't argue."

I didn't. Not with Viv. She had a way of snapping me back into the present whenever I threatened to unravel. Caleb used to call it her iron spine.

"Bring her straight inside," she added after a beat. "I'll check the café before I come in."

The line went dead before I could answer — her efficiency, its own kind of comfort.

The road stretched out in front of us as I watched Daisy in broken flashes through the side mirror. The silence grew heavy in the car. She leaned her head against the window, the cool glass cradling her cheek.

"Aunt Viv's going to freak out, isn't she?"

"She'll worry," I said softly. "That's her job as your aunt. Same as mine."

Daisy gave a weary little laugh. "Feels like everyone's carrying me on a leash right now."

I glanced at her, at the neat bandages wrapped around her hands, and thought of Fisher's calm words — the way the pain had fled the moment he touched her.

A leash, maybe. Or a shield she didn't know she needed.

"You scared the life out of me yesterday," I whispered, the words meant more for the road than for her. Her eyes stayed on the trees flickering past. "Scared myself too. But..." She frowned, lips pressed tight, like she wanted to say more but didn't know how.

The driveway appeared ahead, winding like a ribbon through green. The sight should have steadied me. Instead, the band at my throat pulled tighter, the coin in my pocket heavy as a promise. "Well, you heard the doctor — when you get inside: sleep, rest, movies, and ignore your phone for a bit. But I know you'll struggle with that," I teased, trying to lighten the tone.

"Yes, Mum," she sighed. "I'll get Oli to be my personal swiper. How long do you think I can milk it before he cracks it?"

"Knowing Ol? As soon as you start watching anything with one of your favourite actors." Daisy laughed — real, unguarded. The tension eased.

Floral Beanz stirred to life as if the accident had never happened at all. The espresso machine hissed like an old friend; the grinder sang its steady song. The air thickened with the bittersweet perfume of beans, warmed milk, and the faint green tang of cut flowers from the vases lining the counter.

For a fleeting heartbeat, if I squinted, I could almost believe it was just another ordinary day.

Sal busied herself at the till, muttering about suppliers with her usual colourful commentary. Daisy, perched by the window with her bandaged hands folded in her lap, smirked faintly at Sal's theatrics.

She shouldn't have been here so soon, not with the tremors still in her fingers — but she'd crossed her arms at the very idea of staying home another minute.

"I'm not rotting on the couch, Mum," she'd declared.

So here she was with Nyxie curled tight under her chair, spine pressed against Daisy's legs.

The bell over the door jingled, and Emma blew in like weather — arms stacked high with a precarious tower of muffins in paper bags.

"Breakfast of champions, well would be breakfast albeit a tad late, sorry I got caught in a meeting, bloody old men too busy stroking each other's ego's." She announced to the entire café. "Also snacks for women who can't bake but know where the local bakery is for my favourite girls."

She plonked the bags onto the counter with a flourish. Daisy actually laughed — small, but real.

Oliver barrelled in not long after, leaning against the back counter and rolling his eyes so hard it was a wonder they didn't stick. Even Sal snorted and muttered something about retail espionage.

Emma grinned, triumphant, before launching into a tale about her latest disastrous date — hands flying, voice so dramatic the tradies at the corner table nearly choked on their wraps in laughter.

For ten blessed minutes, Daisy laughed and smiled like her usual self, as if yesterday's events had never touched her.

The café carried on: cups clinking, children squealing, Nyxie sighing under the table. But with Viv beside me, Emma filling the air with noise, and Sal bristling over her order forms, the balance of the day shifted.

For the first time since the bend in the road, I let myself breathe past the edges of fear.

The hiss of milk stretching into velvet foam. Friends talking over one another — Emma's laughter cutting bright against Sal's dry muttering. Customers orbited in their usual rhythms.

It almost felt normal.

And yet my mind wouldn't still.

Beneath the surface chatter, it dragged me back to the road — to Maricus's grin, knife-bright, cruel in its amusement. To

Aodhan stepping out of the tree line like winter sun — too sharp, too clear, a man shaped of presence and command.

His single word, reckless, still cut me open, replaying like a wound I couldn't close.

The memory burned through me, insistent.

The landline shrilled — loud, jarring. Everyone flinched. My heart thudded too fast as I snatched the receiver from its cradle. "Lily?" Mr Fisher's voice rolled down the line — gravel and warmth in equal measure. Always steady.

"Yes—" Relief punched out of me on the exhale. "Yes, we're alright."

"Just thought I'd check in. Figured you might be needing a steady word. How's Daisy?"

"She's fine. Cuts only. Doctor says rest — but you know Daisy, always rushing."

I swallowed, staring at my daughter curled by the window, stubbornly upright, bandages catching the morning light.

"Good girl." He chuckled, low and warm, but the sound carried an undertone — something older, heavier, threaded beneath it. "Stubborn, though. Like her mother." My lips twitched, but the ache behind my ribs didn't ease. "That she is."

"You need anything," he said, quieter now, his tone edged with something that felt more than neighbourly concern, "you holler. I'll be around."

"Mr Fisher..." I paused — so much I wanted to say, but the words caught in my throat.

"I know, Lily. I know." I could hear the warmth in his smile through the line. Then — the click of the connection ending.

But his words lingered like smoke, curling in the corners of my mind. Gentle, yes — but with an old weight behind them. Protective. Watchful. As though Mr Fisher knew more than he let on. As though he was guarding something. Guarding us.

Nyxie's ears snapped forward. The low ridge of hackles along her back bristled. A growl rolled up from her chest, so deep it vibrated through Daisy's chair legs into the floorboards.

The café stilled — as if the sound carried further than her throat. Even the grinder faltered mid-whirr, its hum dying into silence. A tang slid in beneath the scent of coffee and sugar — resin, ash, the sharp edge of something burnt too long in the fire.

It coiled down my spine like a drop of cold water, wrong against the warmth of the room. I drifted toward the window, trying for casual but feeling anything but. Beyond the glass, the gum branches stirred — restless — yet the breeze that moved them was ordinary, mountain-born. Normal.

But normal didn't explain the prickle on my skin, the way the fine hairs at my nape lifted, as if some unseen gaze pressed from just beyond the tree line. Watching and lying in wait.

For a heartbeat, I thought I saw it — a faint shimmer between the leaves, a flicker like heat off bitumen, like firelight trying to burn through from another place. When I blinked, it was gone, leaving only the ordinary green of the trees. Still, the image clung like smoke.

Emma forced a laugh, brittle at the edges. "Probably just a possum with indigestion," she said — too loudly, as if noise alone could push back the silence. Sal snorted but didn't look up from arguing with the delivery driver on the phone. Only Vivienne caught my eye — one brow flicking the barest fraction before smoothing into calm. But I saw the question there. Did you feel it too? Nyxie didn't ease. Neither did I. I walked towards Daisy and Nyxie a sense of unease settling into my being. My hand found her neck, fingers brushing the tight coil of muscle — her body taut as a drawn bowstring.

"We're just jumpy after yesterday," I whispered against her fur, though the words convinced neither of us. I stayed by the window, eyes fixed on the trees, holding myself steady. Unblinking.

And though nothing moved, the unease lingered — thin and sharp as a splinter, lodged just deep enough that when I finally dragged in a breath, it didn't feel like enough.

CHAPTER 6

It has been three weeks since the accident — three long weeks of worry and watching Daisy. I've been putting off my morning runs, but today I decide I need to move, to think.

Dawn pulls the mountains from shadow in slow strokes of grey and gold.

I lace my shoes on the back step and whistle once; Nyxie materialises from under the outdoor table, all liquid black and bright eyes, stretching like a cat before nudging my knee with her nose.

"C'mon, girl," I murmur, clipping on her lead even though we both know she never really needs it. "Just us and the lorikeets." I need some fresh air and to run, to clear my head.

The air is crisp, eucalyptus-sweet, cool enough to sting the lungs the first few breaths. We slip through the side gate and onto the narrow trail that threads along the ridgeline above the café. Dew silvers the grass; webs shimmer on the fence like tiny flags left by night.

Nyxie trots beside me, ears pricked, alert to everything—skitter of lizard, whipbird call, the far-off rumble of a truck winding up toward the pass. I run until my mind begins to empty, until the rhythm of footfalls and breath drowns the leftover noise of yesterdays—hospital soap and antiseptic, Daisy's small brave smile, Oliver's tight jaw when he thought I wasn't looking.

The track dips beneath a stand of stringybarks and opens

suddenly to a lookout that spills the valley at my feet: paddocks stitched in green, Crystal Hollow, a scatter of roofs, the mountains across the road wearing their usual blue haze.

It's the sort of view that makes you believe in second chances and peace. Nyxie stands at the edge, nose high, tasting the breeze. For a heartbeat she goes still, hackles lifting almost imperceptibly, and the hairs along my arms rise in answer. Nothing moves in the scrub. The world holds its breath.

Then the wind shifts, carrying the clean, ordinary scent of damp soil and warm stone, and she relaxes with a soft huff. I let out a breath I didn't realise I'd been holding.

"Show-off," I tell her, scruffing her ears. "Come on. Sal will mutiny if I'm not in by seven."

By the time we jog back through the gate, the house is awake. Daisy's voice drifts up the stairs and across the porch—bossy and bright, as if she can, will normal back into existence by force—and Oliver looms in the kitchen already in uniform, eating a bowl of porridge like it's a competitive sport ignoring Daisy's running commentary for the morning.

"Run?" he asks without looking up.

"Run," I confirm, stealing the corner of his toast and earning a look of theatrical betrayal. Daisy arrives to shove a banana at me with a you-will-eat-this face I recognise from my own mirror.

We move together, a small, practised dance of domesticity: mugs set, lunches checked, Nyxie fed, Oliver's boots located under the couch…of course, Daisy's bandages re-wrapped with clean gauze. The ache eases in my chest as the pieces click into place. Ordinary is a balm, even when it doesn't fit quite right anymore.

I grab my cardigan and my keys. "I'm opening. School. Text me before and after. Non-negotiable." Daisy rolls her eyes, smiling. "Yes, Mum. I can't wait to get back and socialise." Oliver leans in to kiss my cheek, his voice soft. "Love you."

"Love you more," I say — our daily battle over who gets the last word.

Floral Beanz breathes warm when I push the door open. The little cottage café always seems a fraction brighter than outside, as if light gets caught and softened on the white boards and the jars of gum leaves.

I flick the lamps on and the room lifts at once: honey pooling across the counter, the chalkboard menu a smug list of our best ideas, window boxes spilling nasturtiums like confetti. Nyxie does her usual circuit—back door, pantry, cool room, bins—before stationing herself at her preferred sentry point beside the cake cabinet. If there were a badge for Head of Security, I'd pin it between her shoulders.

I grind the first beans and the scent rises—rich, bitter, comforting. There's a rhythm to opening that steadies the hands. Sal arrives as I'm chalking pear and ginger muffins — fresh in deliberately wonky lettering. She shoulders through the door in a spray jacket, hair in a messy ponytail, a scarf looped around her neck — my lovely, eccentric manager, chaos and all.

"Thought you'd sleep in for once," she says, already washing her hands like a surgeon — her foreign accent stronger in the mornings when she's been talking to her mum back home.

"Ha," I say. "I tried that once. Didn't take. How's Mum going?"

Sal sets to with her favourite theatrical sigh. "Same old. Says I'm looking too thin, not eating enough. Why am I not married yet. When is she getting grandkids…the usual. Wants a visit back home in the New Year. You can only imagine what that will be like." She huffs out a long sigh, "Also, supplier's stuff-up — milk'll be an hour late. I'll be on the phone to them, but we'll do a rationed opening: push long blacks and batch brew until the delivery rolls up."

"I'll sweet-talk the tradies," I say.. "They pretend to be tough but cry over black coffee, and you know I wouldn't survive without you."

She grins. "You do the convincing, I'll do the steaming," She comes over and hugs me tight, "It would be great if everyone was as easy going as you Lil."

Mr Fisher appears at 7:12 exactly, mullet tucked behind his ears, boots faintly dusted with clay, that gentled, fatherly smile softening his weathered face.

"Morning, Lil," he says, lowering himself into his usual seat by the fence. "Another day, eh?"

"Another day," I echo, and his eyes crinkle like we've shared a joke. It is, for a blessed stretch, just coffee and chatter and the hiss of steam.

But there's been a different kind of customer lately—faces too perfect, stillness too deliberate. They sit a fraction too straight. Watch a fraction too long. Today, one of them drifts in with the first wave: a man in slate trousers and a white shirt, umbrella he doesn't need hooked over one arm. He scans the room without moving his head, smile politely empty. When he glances at the vines threading the front window, something sharp leaks through his expression and is gone.

"Can I get you anything?" I ask, the picture of hospitality. He lifts a brow.

"Your house speciality."

"We specialise in everything," I say sweetly. He orders a long black. Drinks half. Stays too long. Leaves without a crumb out of place and the faintest smell of rain-on-stone that doesn't match the day. I pocket the unease, no time to look at that now.

I take the empty moment and the card long overdue. My handwriting is small and fiddly, never quite equal to the weight of what I want to say.

Mr Fisher, Thank you for helping at the accident.
The words look flat.
For always knowing when to appear like magic.
I hesitate.
For being a constant presence—

I can't finish the sentence. My pen drags to a stop, leaving a thin score in the card. I cross the line out, hard enough to crease the paper.

My hand lifts to my forehead. I close my eyes. Why is this so damn hard? It shouldn't be. He's been here through everything — school plays and broken bones, flat tyres and late nights. He is steady where my world has cracked. A grandfather in all the ways that matter. Quietly there. Always there.

My throat tightens.

I turn the card over and start again.

Thank you for always being there.

The sentence trembles under my pen. My hand stills, hovering, as if the next words might break something if I let them out. The café feels too quiet. My chest feels too full.

I draw in a slow, careful breath and write anyway.

Thank you for always being there when I need you... when the kids need you... and when Cal needed you.

The name lands like a bruise. My vision blurs. I blink hard, once, twice, until the words steady again.

You were a massive help again.

It feels small for everything he has been, everything he still is. At the bottom of the card, I add the practical things, because I need the anchor of them.

Enclosed are some of your favourite brownies from Sal.

My mouth tilts into a sad, familiar smile. I'll add homemade shortbread too.

My fingers pause as I imagine his reaction — the way he'll grunt and pretend he hasn't noticed, the way his eyes will soften all the same. The way he'll never say he needed it.

He'll pretend not to notice.

And I'll pretend this doesn't still hurt as much as it does.

We will both lie gently.

Nyxie lifts her head before I hear anything — the low rumble in her chest vibrating through the timber floor. I know that sound now: warning, not alarm.

My fingers still on the pen.

A laugh rolls across the room — low, rich, unmistakable. The air shifts with it, warmer by a degree, like the moment before summer rain.

I look up.

He stands at the counter like he belongs there. Pale hair tied loosely at the nape of his neck, a few strands catching the light as if the sun itself his halo— gracing him alone.

White linen shirt rolled to the elbow, and along his forearms those not-ink markings shimmer — light trapped under skin.

A prickle runs down my spine. Nyxie doesn't growl this time. She simply gets to her feet and stands between us, head high. A silent, cautionary warning.

"What," I say, sharper than I intend, "are you doing here?"

Aodhan doesn't flinch. An almost-smile tugs at his mouth, infuriating for how little it gives away.

"Stopping by," he says. His gaze flicks to the board and back to me. "And to see how you were recovering from your scare."

"I'm fine." Bristling at his nonchalance.

Something changes behind his eyes at that — small, quick — then smooths back into nothing.

"And your daughter?" he asks, tone careful, pitched for me alone.

"Why?" The word lands flatter than a slap. "Is there a reason you're here — in my café?"

"Besides watching how you react to every little thing I say?" The line is soft, not unkind, but unquestionably a test.

The quiet thickens until I reach for the cloth and wipe a clean patch of counter just to move my hands. "Is there a reason you're here?" I repeat, steadier.

"Yes." His eyes are the thing it's hardest to look at — deep blue ringed with molten gold and silver that brightens when he leans in across the counter.

"I'm looking for something. Something lost." His head tilts, the smallest acknowledgement that he's about to push a line. "By all accounts, it led me here."

"Have you checked the lost-and-found?" I ask. "We're amassing quite the collection of reusable cups and umbrellas." I raise a brow and point to the box near the front door.

His laugh is low and warm and curls around places I'd rather keep closed. "Not that sort of lost." The edge returns to his voice. "Something that should never have been broken or brought here."

"What..."

The bell rings and a couple stroll in, and the moment shifts and is gone. By the time I've taken their order, whatever was there between us has faded. The only sign he was there is the thin ribbon of invisible heat left behind, and the way my chest feels too tight for a few breaths.

Sal materialises at my elbow like a crow with excellent timing. "He's the one from the bend," she says out of the side of her mouth.

"Mm."

"Want me to spit in his coffee next time?"

"Tempting," I say. "But we're a reputable establishment."

"We are...but I can make an exception," Sal mutters, but her smile is fond.

I take a moment to message Oliver. He worries me more — quieter now, running harder, training until his legs shake. When I try to bring it up, he says he's fine — in that steady, unbudgeable way his father used to, which somehow makes it harder to argue with.

I text him: *Ol, if you need to talk, I'm here.*

A simple response comes back: *k.*

Teenage brevity — an art form of its own.

Sal taps my shoulder, shrugging with a sympathetic smile. "Boys..."

The kids swing by for smoothies and to corner Mr Fisher about his new calf. Daisy parks herself at the window with a glass of water; Oliver pretends to study and fails in a way that keeps him close to his sister; Nyxie dozes at their feet with one eye open. The bell chimes.

Aodhan returns.

The atmosphere shifts the way a room does when the weather breaks.

He doesn't loom or swagger — he doesn't need to. Stillness can take up just as much space as noise. "A long black," he says. Not a please. Not a smile. Every day he's been coming in — getting a coffee, lurking at the back, leaving.

Not one bit friendly or approachable. But there is something that draws me to him like a moth to a flame.

I set the shot running and reach for a second cup. The milk pitcher feels heavier than usual in my hand.

"Name?" I ask, pretending I've forgotten who this man is, as if his very presence doesn't pull the air taut.

He blinks once, as if he hadn't expected the question.

"Your memory must be failing you," he retorts, dragging his gaze up and down my body, like I'm the one who just had a fall.

"Reckless," I say lightly, using his own word from the road — pettiness is free.

"Is that what we write?"

"Aodhan," he replies.

Then, dry as a paper cut

"Your Highness will do in a room that insists on titles."

"I insist on decency," I say, and pass him the cup. "You're in my café. Don't frighten my daughter on the way out."

"At the moment," he says, looking past me to the window, "your daughter is frightened by the echo of her own memory." Nyxie rises, a ridge of dark along her spine. His gaze meets hers; something unreadable moves behind his eyes.

"She's a good guardian."

"She has a name," I tell him.

"I know it," he says.

"She knows mine." I look between Nyxie and Aodhan, wondering how on earth they've reached an impasse.

The lights above the pass flicker — once, twice — then hold. The temperature tilts, a fraction warmer than it should be. Aodhan's head cocks, listening to something I can't hear.

"What is it you want?" I ask, because pretending we're not having this conversation won't make him leave faster. "Did Maricus say anything about Fire at the accident?" His tone is neutral; the word itself isn't.

"Fire like... bonfires? Or fire like a lighter?"

"Fire Court." The vowels land like they've been sharpened. "Did he use the word? Did he scent like smoke and resin?"

"You think I'd know what that smells like?" My eyebrow arches in answer.

His eyes warm a degree. "You already do."

A muscle jumps in my jaw. "He said nothing useful. He bled on my car and vanished like a stray cat chasing a mouse. Odd one to be friends with. The only thing that smelt was the tyres burning."

Aodhan's mouth almost curves.

"He is not my friend. More family."

"Pity for him," I say. "And for you, if you've got to herd him."

He smirks — a dimple pulling in the corner of his mouth.

He sets the cup down, untouched. "Keep your family inside the wards after dark. Don't make bank drops alone. If something watches you from the hedgerow, do not go to meet it. Send your guardian." His gaze flicks to Nyxie, whose amber eyes haven't left him.

"You sound like Dad. We run a café," I say. "We make muffins. We water plants. We don't generally specialise in the fairy-and-magic side of things. That's just old tales."

"You live on ground that remembers more than muffins," he answers. "And you are not... ordinary." His gaze skims — my hands, my face, the vines, the line of salt I haven't told anyone I laid under the mat last night. "Pretend not to believe if you need to. But don't be careless."

"Is that a threat?"

"A request," he says. "For you and your child to stay safe."

Before I can pry open the request with something sharp — as is my right in my own café — Daisy rustles at the window. Nyxie shifts, muscles setting like wire. Aodhan's attention snaps that way, all the softness gone.

"Answer me straight," I demand. "Why?"

He meets my eyes like a vow. "Because the accident has caused intrigue. Because the magic is not a myth. Because when power stirs, it tugs on everything tied to it." His voice drops, silver flecks in his irises brightening. "Because you are already on their radar."

"Who's? Get me off it," I shoot back. "We didn't ask to be pinned on your map of crazy." He nods once, as if I've said something he agrees with.

"Then protect yourself. Don't let them use you or take advantage. Play it safe." He leaves before I can decide if that was advice or an order.

The café exhales after him. Sal swears softly into the milk jug. Oliver brings me Daisy's empty glass without being asked — his version of I'm here, Mum.

Daisy back at the house now, asleep upstairs with Nyx curled tight along the back of her legs like a living brace.

Vivienne sends me a photo — Daisy's hair fanned across the pillow, Nyxie's dark shape a watchful crescent at her feet — as if the image itself might stitch my nerves back together. I stare at it longer than I should, letting the simple miracle of rest settle my breathing.

Oliver doesn't stop moving.

He stacks chairs with careful precision.

Wipes tables in slow, methodical circles. Lines the sugar jars just so.

The kind of focus that belongs to a boy trying to keep his thoughts contained by keeping his hands busy. I let him work. The soft scrape of wood on tile, the whisper of cloth over laminate — small, steady sounds anchoring the room.

"Ol," I say, chewing at the inside of my cheek.

"I know Daisy's accident gave us all a scare, but if anything's stressing you… let me know, okay?" The scraping of chairs pauses.

For a moment, there's nothing but silence.

Then Oliver murmurs, quiet and careful, "I'm fine, Mum. Just… you know. Dad's anniversary is coming up. And then Daisy…"

A loud knock cuts the moment short. Sal shoulders through

the door, already announcing,

"Emma's care package has arrived — in sugar and foil."

A box lands on the counter with a solid thud. Inside is an offensively large block of chocolate — the good kind. Rich. Dark. Unapologetic. Tucked beneath it is a note in her looping scrawl:

for medicinal purposes only

I huff a weak laugh that catches in my chest before it can become anything like relief.

Sal leaves the offering quietly.

Later, I notice a scrap of paper beside the register, the heading underlined twice:

Things we can fix that aren't the past

Three bullet points sit beneath it. Practical. Achievable. Ordinary — in the way only deliberate kindness ever is.

My throat tightens as I read them again and again, until the words blur.

I lock the door, slide the bolt, and step onto the garden path toward the house as dusk stretches long and blue along the mountain. Rosemary brushes my jeans; the jasmine has put out a handful of starry flowers like hope.

A scorched, sweet smell — chemical and resinous — threads the air. I pause at the gate. On the jasmine closest to the fence, one leaf is crisped to black at the tip, as if someone touched it with a match and pinched it out again.

I touch it. The leaf is cool. The heat prickling under my fingertips is not.

"Nyxie." My voice is a thread. She's already at the house door, head high, body low. When I move, she flows down the steps and sets herself between me and the fence, eyes on the hedgerow. She doesn't growl. She watches hackles raised in silence.

"Inside," I tell her, as steady as I can make it. We go in together. I throw the bolt and turn the porch light up two clicks.

The house breathes its usual evening sighs — dishwasher ticking, a distant thud from Oliver's room, a soft exhale from Daisy's. I stand in the dim hall and listen until the beat of my heart stops drowning everything else.

My phone buzzes. *You home? Lights on out front? — Dad.*

Home. Lights on, I type back.

Then, after a breath:

Something at the fence. Just a smell. A leaf burned without fire.

The wards, he sends. *Let me know if you notice anything else.*

Dad, I write, *one day you're going to tell me why you know these things — and why you're so superstitious.*

One day, he replies. *For now, keep your head. Keep the kids close.*

I lay a fine line of salt where no one will notice it and wipe the excess away with the heel of my hand. It feels foolish and necessary at once.

In the lounge-room window, my reflection looks back: tired, yes, but no more than usual. I rub my thumb over my ring until the metal warms and glance at the coin on the kitchen bench. I need to return that to him.

Outside, the hedgerow rustles without wind. Inside, I flick off the hall light and climb to check my children, one by one, like I did when they were small. Oliver, sprawled, one arm flung over his eyes. Daisy, turned to the wall, Nyxie's breath ruffling her hair.

I kiss my fingers and touch them to their door frames — ridiculous, superstitious, but just as my mother did with me.

Back in my room, I sit on the bed and let the silence gather.

Somewhere down there, beneath the floorboards and the soil and the stones that remember other houses and other women who locked their doors at dusk, something hums with its own patient heartbeat.

I turn out the lamp. The house listens. The vines keep growing — faster than normal — wrapping themselves around the beams as though they, too, remember what it means to protect.

CHAPTER 7

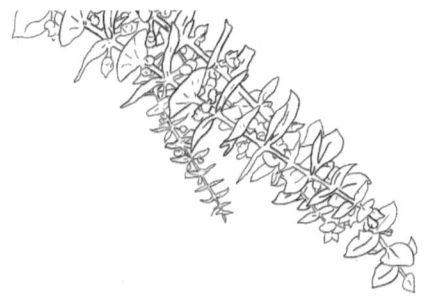

Saturday at Floral Beanz always carried a rhythm of its own, less predictable than weekdays, more like a tide that surged and receded in waves.

The space hummed with sound — cups clinking, incessant chatter, Sal's "order up" booming from the kitchen, Oliver's laughter threading through it all. The air swirled thick with roasted beans and sweet vanilla syrup, layered with the clean tang of damp eucalyptus carried in from the mountain road.

Every inhale tasted like comfort and work all at once. Oliver worked at my side with the kind of ease that warmed me. There was something of Caleb in the way he moved — the tilt of his grin, the way humour slipped into his words like sunlight through clouds.

Customers leaned closer when he spoke, pulled in by that quiet gravity. The older regulars chuckled at his quick quips, while the girls from the local high school lingered longer than necessary, pretending to debate frappé flavours when really, they were drinking in every flash of his smile.

He didn't notice or pretended not to — but I did. I caught myself staring at him too long, tracing Caleb's shadow in the line of Oliver's jaw, in the cadence of his laugh.

For a moment, the past and present blurred — the sound of my husband's chuckle echoing faintly beneath my son's voice. His charm was effortless. Like his father, he'd be breaking hearts soon enough.

The bell jingled, and my body went rigid before I even turned. Mark arrives like clockwork — polished shoes tapping against the timber floor, that too-bright smile built for boardrooms and wine bars rather than cafés tucked into mountain folds.

He comes in with the same buoyant skip in his step, the same rehearsed charm, the same confidence of a man who believes today might finally be the day his joke lands.

"Morning, Lily," he drawls, sliding up to the counter as if he owns a piece of it.

His cologne arrives before he does — sharp, synthetic — clashing with the warmth of coffee and cut flowers. He leans in far too close, his gaze skimming down and across, everywhere but my eyes.

"Flat white. And maybe... dinner? You keep saying no, but I'm nothing if not persistent."

I feel Oliver's eyes snap to me across the machine, the joking curve of his mouth gone in an instant. He straightens, shoulders squaring — the resemblance to Caleb so sudden it knocks the air from me. Protective. Watchful. Ready.

"No chance of that happening," I say crisply, stepping back just enough to put space between Mark's hand and my skin. My voice is polite, professional — but laced with steel. A finality that should have ended it.

For a heartbeat, his smirk falters. Then something flickers in his gaze. It isn't attraction. It's the thrill of pursuit. The challenge of a closed door he thinks he can pry open. And still — every time — he seems faintly surprised by that. Then the moment slides right off him.

Reset.

He laughs, a little too loudly, already pivoting to the next attempt, the next angle, the next hopeful invitation that history has already declined a dozen times over. It's as though the memory of every no evaporates the moment it leaves the air between us.

I watch him go, unsettled by the hollow space where recognition should live. Can a person really forget that many refusals? Or is forgetting easier than remembering being told no?

The hum of the café dips, like the room has exhaled all at once. My skin prickles — that same high-altitude taste of ozone and fire threading the air. Nyxie stirs beneath Daisy's chair, ears twitching, a low vibration building in her throat.

Mark doesn't notice. But I do.

And my pulse tripped faster, because whatever had just crossed the threshold — it wasn't Mark. That aura again — subtle, insistent — pressing at the edges of the room until the fine hairs at the back of my neck rose like they'd been touched by static.

I didn't need to look. I felt him. Aodhan filled the doorway as if the mountain itself had shaped space to make way for him. Hair threaded with fire and sunlight. Power radiated from him — leashed so tight it vibrated in the air, coiled and waiting.

His gaze swept the café once, sharp and surgical, noting every face, every corner, every exit. When his eyes found me, my breath hitched, as though the pull between us had tightened another invisible knot.

He was right. I am reckless.

Then his attention slid — to the regular. To Mark's hand, still lingering too close to mine, fingers curved on the counter as if he had some claim. For a heartbeat, the air turned hot, hard to breathe.

The shimmer beneath Aodhan's skin flared brighter, glowing like embers fed a sudden rush of oxygen. His jaw tightened, muscles working with the kind of restraint that looked like it hurt. A dangerous heat rippled through the room — subtle enough no one else noticed but I felt it, pressing against my ribs, demanding I see him.

Possessiveness burned in the blue-and-silver depths of his eyes. Raw and uncompromising. And yet he held himself in check. A soldier on a leash.

A king behind glass. Controlled. Contained — for now.

But the air around him whispered what he wouldn't say aloud: one wrong move, and he would not hesitate.

Mark, oblivious — or perhaps foolish — lingered. He leaned closer, his breath brushing the space I refused to give him.

"See, Lily? Even your other customers know you deserve better company than this busy café. Now, how about that date?"

The slyness in his tone grated like grit in my teeth. But as the words left his mouth, his confidence faltered. Because he finally noticed Aodhan's stare.

The silence stretched — taut and dangerous. The weight in the air grew almost unbearable, pressing down until even the vines strung along the café's back wall curled tighter, leaves twitching as if bracing for fire.

Aodhan didn't move.

His stance loomed, muscles taut, barely restrained. The fury in his eyes said everything. He was a storm contained in flesh, a blade held just before the strike. Mark swallowed, his smirk slipping into something thinner, his eyes flicking anywhere but that searing gaze.

And then —the balance shifted.

The bell over the door chimed again, softer this time, almost drowned out by the tension in the air.

Maricus stepped through with a kind of grace that mocked everyone present — smooth, deliberate, calm. His presence rolled through the café like a tide, unnoticed until it was already dragging everyone under. He cut a figure both elegant and dangerous: tall, angular features, and a grin curling his mouth that never quite reached the cold calculation in his eyes. His short dark hair, tousled and messy as though he'd just rolled out of bed, added to the air of effortless danger.

That same rip-current energy bled into the room, subtle but suffocating, pulling the easy hum of chatter and clinking cups into his undertow. And then, his gaze found me.

Satisfaction flickered there dark, knowing as if he'd been waiting for this exact stage, this exact collision of players. Aodhan's simmering restraint. Mark's faltering bravado. And me, caught at the centre.

The pulse in my throat beat harder, my hand spinning the silver ring on its chain, attempting to coax calm back into my body.

"Aodh," Maricus drawled, letting the nickname spill like poison wrapped in silk. Mockery dripped from every syllable. "Didn't realise you'd found yourself a new favourite haunt."

Aodhan's posture sharpened — subtle, lethal — though his voice, when it came, was cold, cut through with restraint. "Maricus. Why are you here?"

"Relax," Maricus replied, laziness feigned, but every movement calculated. He lounged against the back of a chair like he owned the room, eyes burning with the sharp edge of someone waiting for a slip.

"Just meeting the owner of Floral Beanz." His smirk widened as his gaze slid back to me — deliberate, lingering far too long. "Charming place," he added smoothly. "And charming company. You do know how much I enjoy a little play amongst the... shall we say, common folk."

The air grew heavy — a storm gathering charge. The same electric pressure I'd felt yesterday clawed at the edges of the café again, pressing down like the stillness before lightning split the sky.

Even the plants seemed to sense it, their leaves trembling and curling inward, though no breeze stirred.

Before I could speak, Oliver moved. My son — tall, unflinching — stepped squarely in front of me. His shoulders squared, jaw set, green eyes hard in a way that startled me with their familiarity.

"If you three want a pissing contest," he said flatly, his voice cutting through the tension like a knife, "take it outside and leave the staff here, out of whatever it is you're trying to do. We don't care for people who think of us as *common folk*, or leering where they shouldn't." The words landed sharp and impossible to ignore. He was furious, and it showed. For a heartbeat, everything slowed to a standstill.

Aodhan's gaze flicked to Oliver, the faintest crack breaking through his steel mask — something unreadable, something almost... like jealousy.

Maricus, by contrast, leaned back, a low, amused laugh spilling from him, though his eyes glittered with that predator's calculation — as if he were already filing my son's defiance away for later.

I placed a hand on Oliver's arm, steadying him even as pride and fear warred in my chest. My son should never have to stand between others like this. "Oli, I'm okay," I said quietly. "But I need you to step back. Let me handle this." My hand tried to guide him behind me, to shield him from the three of them.

Maricus chuckled, low and entertained, as though our exchange were nothing more than kindling for his private fire.

He leaned into the moment, his grin sharpening into something wolfish.

"Didn't realise you liked them young, Ms Beanz. Aodh..." His gaze slid deliberately to Oliver, lingering just long enough for the insinuation to sink its claws in. "Thought the café owner here preferred more... seasoned company. But perhaps you do like them younger Ms Beanz..I myself know someone else who likes them in their better years too."

He tilted his head, mockingly thoughtful.

"But I do think he seems a bit young for you — but he certainly looks fiery. That your type?" The words sliced through the room like ice water. Chairs creaked as customers shifted, sensing something wrong without quite understanding it.

Aodhan's jaw flexed, his control fracturing for the first time. His gaze snapped to me — sharp, raw, unguarded — something burning there he hadn't meant for me to see. "He's your lover?" The words were quiet, barely more than a thread of sound, but they carried the weight of betrayal — heavy, demanding, impossible to ignore. Then his voice broke, edged with fury that wasn't entirely his own. "No wonder he smells of you," he said harshly.

"The way you soften for him. It explains everything." Rage flared in his eyes, molten gold sparking hot beneath his skin, twisting tight with what appears to be jealousy and yet couldn't stop.

"What the actual—" I choked, heat flashing through me, half fury, half disbelief.

"She's my mum," Oliver snapped, fierce and unflinching, his voice ricocheting through the café like a shot. His green eyes blazed, his disgust and fury mirroring my own.

"He's my son," I bit out, my voice laced with a fury sharp enough to cut the air clean. My hand tightened on Oliver's arm.

For a heartbeat, silence swallowed the café.

Maricus's grin only widened, satisfied.

Aodhan watched me hold onto Oliver's arm as if the touch itself were burning him. His chest rose and fell, like he was keeping himself tethered by force alone. Shame flickered in his gaze — colliding with fury, with something deeper, rawer. Something that looked a lot like fear. He had let Maricus bait him. Now every eye in the café was on him. On me. On Oliver. As if the three of us had been stitched into some grotesque display no one but Maricus had signed up to watch.

Maricus's smirk widened again — slow and poisonous — the grin of a man who'd tossed a spark into dry kindling and stepped back to enjoy the fire. He didn't need to gloat aloud; the satisfaction in his eyes was enough.

The silence cracked with nervous laughter — sharp, brittle, too high-pitched. Customers desperate to shake off the tension. To pretend they hadn't just felt the weight of something far larger than themselves press down on the room.

Cups clinked too loudly. Chairs scraped too fast. The ordinary rhythm of the café stumbled back into place. And then Mark — ever the opportunist — saw an opening. He leaned closer, his hand reaching as though to brush my arm, staking some pathetic claim while the air was still heavy with the aftermath.

I stepped back instantly, my glare cutting him off cold. "Don't." One word. Flat. Sharp and final.

Aodhan's gaze followed the movement. His face was carved from stone — unreadable — but the burn in his eyes betrayed him.

Possessiveness. Regret. For a heartbeat, I thought he might snap — unleash whatever fire lived beneath his skin, scorch the smirk off Maricus's face, reduce Mark to ash for grabbing my arm. And for a fleeting moment, I almost hoped he would.

But instead, he turned on his heel, every line of him rigid with fury he refused to loose. The door swung shut behind him, and with it the heat bled from the air, leaving only a hollow chill in its place.

Maricus lingered one beat longer, watching me with that sharp, knowing grin — a predator's promise — before sauntering after him. "A pleasure, as always, Ms Floral Beanz," he called lightly. "But do let me know if you'd prefer someone a little more experienced. I'd be happy to show you a good time."

Smooth. Deliberate. Leaving exactly how he entered. Like a wolf who knew exactly when to bare his teeth — and when to walk away, leaving only unease in his wake.

The vines along the back wall slackened, leaves settling as though some unseen fist had unclenched. Only then did I realise I'd been holding my breath.

Oliver's voice broke the quiet, low but steady, carrying more rage than his years should hold. "Mum. If those two show up again, you call me. Got it?" I forced a nod, the word scraping out in a whisper. "Got it." But we both knew it wasn't true. I wouldn't drag him into a storm. Not one I barely understood myself.

That night, the estate should have been safe — warm light spilling from the windows, the air thick with rosemary and lavender, the steady hum of our home alive around us. And yet Nyxie stood rigid at the gate. Her hackles bristled, a low growl vibrating deep in her chest. Amber eyes locked on the tree line, unblinking. The air sharpened — brittle and wrong — static prickling over my skin as though the night itself had joined the hunt.

I felt it. A weight. A stare. Someone out there in the dark — too patient, too deliberate. Waiting. But for what?

Nyxie didn't move, every muscle strung tight, until the presence slipped back into the trees. Even then, she prowled the fence line, circling once, ears pricked to every rustle. When she finally returned to my side, she pressed her solid weight against my leg — a silent shield. A warning I couldn't ignore.

We walked the garden path together, gravel crunching beneath our feet, the estate looming ahead — warm, familiar, home. But the night vibrated with certainty.

We were not alone.

I spun the ring on its chain, the silver biting into my skin, and the vow rose fierce as iron in my chest. Whatever comes. Whatever hunts us. I'll keep them safe. Even if it breaks me. I won't lose anyone ever again.

CHAPTER 8

Dawn came soft and pink, the valley holding its breath the way it always did before the heat woke the cicadas. The ridge line caught the first light, painting the gum trunks in rose-gold bands.

I laced my runners, slid into gym tights and a long-sleeved tee, and whistled for Nyxie. She appeared at once a black ripple of muscle and intent ears high, eyes molten amber in the thin light, tail flicking with anticipation.

We took the lower track that looped around the property before spilling toward the old fire trail. The air was sharp, washed clean overnight, carrying the cool bite of damp bark and the mineral tang of cold earth. Dew jewelled the wire fences in neat, glimmering rows; spiderwebs slung between rosemary spikes flashed silver when the sun caught them.

My breath fogged faintly. Nyxie's paws made no sound at all — each step silent. She kept to my left knee, her rhythm so precise it looked trained, though no trainer had taught her. She simply knew.

At the bend where the gums thinned, the world always felt different. Not cooler. Not warmer. Just... different.

The bird chatter fractured into silence, abrupt as a curtain dropping. The cicadas faltered, as if holding their breath. Every hair on my arms rose, tingling — my skin prickling like it had brushed a live wire. My lungs forgot how to draw a full breath.

I slowed. Nyxie didn't.

Her body sharpened, muscles ridged beneath her coat like a bowstring drawn back. She lifted her head, nostrils flaring, ears pinned, drinking the breeze as if it carried a looming threat. A low sound rattled in her chest — half growl, half rumble — eyes narrowing toward the tree line where the fire trail vanished into shade, her coat bristling along her spine.

It was nearby. Something was out there.

Watching. Waiting.

The ordinary morning suddenly felt staged, as though the mountain itself were holding back a truth it didn't want me to see.

"What is it?" I murmured.

She didn't growl.

Silence followed. That was somehow worse.

Nyxie just watched. The way a thing with bite will watch when it already knows distance and intent.

The feeling of being seen without seeing slid cold along my spine. I forced a breath, then another, and carried on, lengthening my stride until my lungs burned and my legs found their usual rhythm.

Halfway down the trail, it came again.

A footfall that wasn't mine — or the impression of one. A subtle hitch in the silence when my shoes slapped grit. My heart lurched, pulse kicking hard. I glanced back once, twice nothing but gums and grass and the long spill of morning light.

Still, the prickle stayed, threading into my skin like needles.

Nyxie pressed tight against my leg, her flank urging me faster.

I listened.

We ran.

By the time the property roof lines appeared through the trees, my lungs were burning and terror had already tipped into rage, adrenaline snapping everything into sharper focus. We cut across the last paddock, vaulted the fence, my muscles screaming at the extra push as I forced myself to keep moving faster, harder until I hit the café's garden path too fast to recover my usual calm.

The bell over Floral Beanz's back door jittered against its hook as I shouldered inside, chest heaving, one hand braced at my side as a stitch bloomed sharp and insistent. I made it as far as the office before stopping, grabbing my spare change of clothes with hands that wouldn't quite steady.

The familiar scent of coffee grounded me — roasted beans, vanilla, the clean bite of lemon oil on the benches — and I focused on it, forcing my breath to slow, my pulse to follow.

Nyxie padded to her corner, curling into her usual post where she could command the doors and windows with a single sweep of her amber gaze. Her hackles were still raised, her body coiled and alert.

I wasn't alone.

Aodhan sat at the table by the far window, broad shoulders caught in the spill of morning light. His cup sat untouched, steam long faded, but his attention wasn't on the café — it was fixed beyond the glass, sharp as a blade turned toward the tree line.

Beneath his skin, the faint shimmer of gold pulsed once bright, answering, as if something out there had called to him.

For a heartbeat, I was certain he would rise. That he would stride into the trees and drag whatever lingered there into the open. Instead, his jaw tightened. Heat rolled faintly from him in a controlled wave — restrained, leashed — and then vanished as he pulled it back under.

Our eyes met. For the briefest flicker, naked fury crossed his face before the mask slid back into place. The weight of it dropped through me like a stone into deep water. I looked away first.

A Corolla coughed into the gravel outside, right on time. Mr Fisher's step creaked on the porch before he appeared in the doorway. Two knuckle taps on the frame, always the same, a habit older than both of us. Then his head poked in. "Morning, love."

His grin was the familiar one — fatherly, warm — but his eyes lingered longer than a coffee order ever required. They tracked the tremor in my hands, the faint sheen of sweat at my temple. Measuring. Weighing. His brows pinched, concern flickering there before he smoothed it away.

"You right?"

"I'm fine. Just a bit out of practice with my running."

The lie slid out smooth — years of necessity had made it second nature.

I reached for a mug, letting the soft clink against the saucer fill the space between us. "What's your poison?"

"Flat white. And a brownie the size of me head." Then, gently, "And you don't need to hide from me, love. Something's got you spooked." The corner of his mouth twitched, but the humour didn't reach his eyes. He squinted past me toward the back door — the one I'd slammed behind me not ten minutes earlier.

"Something stirred the roos early. Track felt jumpy." I steadied my hands on the saucer and let out a breath I hadn't realised I'd been holding. "Wind, maybe."

"Mm." It wasn't agreement. Just a sound that left room for things unsaid. He adjusted his cap, gaze drifting back to the door I'd entered through — then, almost imperceptibly, to the same strip of tree line Aodhan had been watching moments earlier.

"You sing out if you need anything," he said quietly. "And keep ya dog with you on your runs. Might be wild dog out on the tracks. Or a boar. You never know."

"I will."

And for the first time in a long time, I meant it. Because the world didn't feel ordinary anymore. And Mr Fisher — steady, quiet, ever-present Mr Fisher — suddenly felt less like a neighbour...and more like someone who knew far more about what was shifting beneath the surface than he ever let on.

By the time the first trays of muffins came out, blueberry, lemon–poppyseed, and a token savoury batch because Sal insisted civilisation might collapse without them — my pulse had finally slowed, tricking me into thinking the world had returned to plain and ordinary.

I chalked Pistachio croissants — be kind on the board, and counted the float from the safe with hands that no longer trembled.

Daisy arrived for her coffee and muffin before heading off to school. Mark Evans slid in straight after her, taking his usual corner table. "Morning, Lily." Oil-smooth. He dragged the syllables, tasting them. "You're looking bright."

"The usual?" I kept my tone brisk. Clipped.

"You know me." He winked, mock-easy, like persistence was

something to be admired.

Nyxie stiffened — ears flat, hackles whispering up. The low growl that rumbled from her chest had weight, the kind that made the café itself pause. She had never liked him — never — and animal instincts are reliable.

Daisy's hand found her fur, stroking slow, coaxing calm. "Easy, girl." Her voice was stronger this week, colour back in her tone, fewer nightmares — and it eased something tight in my chest. But Nyxie's gaze never left him. She tracked him with the same cold, measuring patience she reserved for whatever lingered in the treeline. And for the first time, I wondered if Nyxie knew something I didn't — if the prickle I'd felt on my morning runs, the sense of a footfall just beyond mine, belonged less to ghosts... and more to men with smiles that never touched their eyes.

Emma breezed in with a wicker basket of "homemade" pastries — stickers flashing when she bent too far — planted a loud kiss on my cheek, and announced she was now in charge of my social calendar whether I liked it or not.

Vivienne arrived moments later in a neat plaid shirt with the sleeves rolled, dropped a container of last night's stew on the counter without comment, then crouched to fix a wobbly chair with a single twist of her wrist.

Between them, they held the day together in their usual way — Emma with riotous noise, Vivienne with quiet order — chaos and calm balancing like two halves of a scale.

Aodhan rose from his seat, his stride cutting cleanly through the chatter as though the air itself deferred to him. Presence rolled off him like heat before a storm — subtle and undeniable. Sunlight followed him, sliding along his shoulders, catching threads of white and gold that pulsed faintly beneath his skin.

He paused once, just inside the threshold, gaze sweeping the café like a soldier taking stock — the exits, the tables, the distance between Daisy and the windows. Only after that measure did he cross to the counter.

"Long black," he said, voice low, vowels worn like stone.

I fitted the handle into the machine with more force than necessary, refusing to meet those impossible eyes — blue rimmed with molten gold, eyes that made my lungs forget their purpose.

"You could say please," I said crisply. Steam hissed around us, the machine masking the tremor in my hands. "This is a café, not some royal court with me at your service."

Something flickered at his mouth — the ghost of a smile, dangerous and fleeting, like a blade catching light. He didn't argue. Instead, his gaze cut across the room, snagging on Mark. A flash of distaste passed through his eyes — sharp, searing, gone before anyone else could notice — but I caught it, and it unnerved me more than Mark's entire smirk-ridden existence ever had.

From Mark, Aodhan's attention shifted to Nyxie.

For a breath, time paused. Nyxie rose to her elbows, hackles half-raised, amber gaze locked on him. Not quite hostile. Not submissive. Wary. The kind of stillness that spoke of instinct — predator recognising predator.

The air went taut as wire. Nyxie huffed once, low and dismissive, then sank back down, though her gaze never left him. Neither did mine.

I slid the coffee across. He didn't touch it. His eyes stayed on me — blue rimmed in molten gold, sharp enough to peel back your darkest secrets. "Still as fiery as ever. I can't imagine you bending for anyone." A pause. "But thank you for the coffee." He studied me for a heartbeat longer than necessary. "You're exposed," he said quietly. Not a warning — a statement. "Those wards... the cracks in your boundaries widen by the day. You need to be ready."

A cold shiver traced my spine. I lifted my chin. "This is a café," I said, voice steady. "Not a battlefield. And I still have no idea what you're talking about — or why you insist on speaking in riddles like some walking prophet or tarot reader."

"It's more or less both," he replied calmly, though a storm coiled beneath the words.

His gaze flicked down, catching the chain at my throat — the wedding band spinning against my collarbone. For a breath his expression fractured. Hurt. Something raw, almost human. Then the mask returned — that relentless control that made you want to either yield or defy him.

I chose defiance.

"If you've come here to play oracle, you're wasting your time. My battles are coffee orders and keeping my kids alive and happy — not... whatever this is."

Something in his jaw tightened, as if I'd struck too close to the truth. He leaned in a fraction — close enough that the air between us sang, close enough that my pulse betrayed me.

"You're already in it," he murmured. "Whether you choose to believe it or not."

My mouth went dry. Heat prickled beneath my skin where his gaze lingered. I wanted answers. Wanted distance. Wanted to drag him closer. Every instinct collided until all I could do was grip the counter and breathe.

Emma, of course, shattered the moment like a hammer through glass. She leaned in, chin propped on her palm, shameless grin aimed straight at him. "If you're going to brood like a superhero, sunshine, at least buy a muffin. We've got lemon. Very bold flavour."

For the briefest instant, the corner of his mouth curved — light flickering through the storm in his eyes. Almost laughter. Almost.

Then it vanished, as though humour were a luxury he couldn't afford.

He turned, finally reaching for the coffee.

Before his fingers touched the cup. A glass slid by itself to the edge of the shelf and shattered on the floor. Ferns by the window stirred in a wind that hadn't come through the door. A woman at table four swayed, her chair tipping beneath her.

Aodhan crossed the room in three strides — faster than my eyes could track. He steadied her with one hand, and for a single breath the air shimmered around his palm — gold brightening, searing, then gone.

The woman blinked, confused, straightening as though nothing had happened.

No one else seemed to notice. No one but Vivienne.

She stood near the counter, arms crossed, eyes narrowed like blades as she tracked him. When her gaze finally found mine, it was sharp with questions.

"Who is he?" she murmured, low enough that only I could hear.

"I don't know," I whispered back. "Seems to be becoming a regular, though."

The words scraped my throat. It wasn't a lie. Not entirely.

But my heart knew what my head refused to name.

Whoever he was, the moment he walked in, my world had already changed.

I carried a tray of cups toward the back hall where we kept the spare milk and takeaway lids. The café's hum softened behind me, replaced by the muted creak of floorboards and the faint chill of brick walls that never quite warmed.

Mark was there before I could blink, cutting the corner like he'd timed it.

That too-smooth smile stretched across his face — the one people mistook for charm if they didn't look closely enough to see the calculation behind it.

"Let me," he murmured, reaching for the tray. When I shifted to pass, he didn't move aside. He moved into me. His chest pressed against the edge of the tray, pinning it between us. Painted brick chilled my back. His hand hovered far too close to my hip.

"You can't stay frozen forever," he said, voice dropping into something low he probably thought persuasive. "It's time to move on. To say yes. To me. To us." His mouth curved. "I could help with those little kids of yours — after all, they won't be around much longer anyway."

Heat flashed across my face, then drained just as fast, leaving only the cold, razor-edged clarity of anger. My voice cut clean. "I have tolerated your behaviour for a year. Do not mistake my politeness for weakness. Move. Now."

He didn't. His smile warped into something thinner. Hungrier. His hand drifted closer to my hip, my thigh. The hair on my arms lifted. Every instinct screamed to smash the tray over his head and run. "Come on, Lily," he coaxed. "It's been a year of asking nicely. I've been patient. You and I—"

A shadow fell across us.

The corridor contracted, the air thickening until each breath scraped. The tray grew lighter in my hands, as though some unseen current had taken hold of it. The wall at my back burned — no longer brick and paint, but heat, tightly contained in a human shape.

"You'll take your hands off her. Now." Aodhan's voice was quiet enough to be heard. Cold enough to cut bone. "Unless you want them removed."

The air pulsed — one sharp shift, like pressure before a storm. For the barest instant, something unfurled behind him: not wings, not quite, but the seared outline of raw power — a shimmer like heat off asphalt, edges sharp enough to cut — and then it was gone. It couldn't have been real.

Mark's smirk collapsed. Fear slackened his features before he tried to lacquer it over with indignation. He peeled back, palms lifted, as though the gesture alone could erase what I'd seen. "Mate, we were just talking."

"You were trying to corner her. Intimidate her. Pressure her." Aodhan didn't raise his voice. He didn't need to. Each word landed with the finality of a gavel.

"And if I hadn't arrived," he continued evenly, "who knows what other lines you would have crossed. I know your type." His lip curled in disgust and something sharp flashing across his face.

"You're done. And this will not happen again."

"This is public," Mark sputtered, fumbling for bravado — for anything that might cover his retreat. "You can't—"

Aodhan's gaze cut to him, flat and lethal as a drawn blade.

It was enough.

The rest of Mark's protest dissolved into nothing. He backed away, muttering about service, about standards — his indignation too thin to hide the panic underneath. He all but fled, the bell over the café door jangling hard behind him.

The sound of retreat. The air loosened, dropping a degree.

I hadn't realised my hands were trembling until I set the tray down on a crate before I dropped it. Anger and humiliation ricocheted in my chest, sharp enough to draw blood.

"I didn't need you," I said. My voice was steady. Inside, I was not.

"You didn't," Aodhan agreed. His eyes — blue rimmed with molten gold — didn't soften. They fixed on me, unyielding. Watchful.

"But I needed him to know he was seen," he said quietly. "That what he was doing was not acceptable. The harassment. The stalking. The leering."

That pull — the one I hated, the one that felt like a thread stitching me to him against my will — throbbed in the silence between us.

Infuriating. Dangerous.

And yet some traitorous part of me — the part that hadn't felt safe in a very long time — recognised something in his stance, in the way the world bent around him, that whispered of protection.

It unsettled me more than Mark ever could.

I shouldn't be reacting to him like this.

I have Caleb.

I hated that it helped. That his presence, heavy and immovable — steadied something in me I didn't want steadied by him.

He glanced down the hall toward the front, then back again. Shifted his stance. Not towering. Not blocking. Leaving me a clear line out either way.

The gesture was small. Deliberate. My breath caught anyway. "May I—" His jaw flexed, the word catching, reshaped by restraint. "May we talk? Here. Or there." He nodded toward the two-seater hidden near the counter — the one I always used when I needed to watch the room without being in it. He'd noticed. Remembered.

I went first, needing the distance. He followed but didn't take the opposite chair. He slid into the one beside me. Close enough that warmth spilled between us, close enough that my pulse betrayed me.

Bergamot and rain threaded the air — not cologne, not anything bought — something woven into him. An impossible scent that tugged at places I kept locked and buried deep.

"I wanted to apologise," he said. His gaze never wavered. He didn't deflect, didn't soften the words with charm. They landed raw. "For what I said about your son. It was out of line."

"You think?" The bite in my voice was armour — brittle but sharp.

"You owe me for future counselling bills. Poor kid will dine out on that trauma for years. And I honestly don't know why you let Maricus bait you like that — or why you'd ever think I'd be with someone that young."

I gestured to myself. "Look at me."

"I'm, looking." Something flickered across his face then — brief, clean, unguarded. Shame, yes. But something else too, as raw and dangerous as an open flame. Possessiveness. His, not mine. As if even the thought of me belonging to another burned him from the inside out. He shuttered it fast, that perfect control slamming back into place, but I'd seen it. And worse — I'd felt it.

I leaned back in my chair, crossing my arms, because distance felt like the only shield I had left.

"So you can apologise when you feel like it," I said coolly, "but you still talk like you own the place. Like you know me — and in riddles about protection from mystic beings."

His jaw worked once, the muscle there ticking. "I don't know you," he said carefully. "But I know enough."

"That's comforting." I rolled my eyes, but my pulse stuttered anyway. "You've been here, what — every day for a month? Ordering coffee. Glaring at the walls. Frightening half my regulars. And now you sit there acting like—"

I stopped, shaking my head.

"Like what exactly? A bodyguard? A jealous lover? A king?"

His gaze cut sharp to mine — blue rimmed with that impossible gold and silver, bright enough to feel as though he saw through every word, every hidden thought.

"More than a month," he said evenly. "And I act like a man who recognises danger when he sees it." His eyes raked over me — slow, assessing.

"I may not be a bodyguard, or king. But I do not like how that man looks at you."

The words stripped the air between us bare.

"Danger?" I repeated, my laugh brittle and forced.

Heat curled low in my stomach anyway, traitorous and unwelcome.

"This is a café, not a war zone. The most threatening thing that happens here is Sal's banana bread disappearing before lunch."

For the first time, something broke in his composure — a sound that might have been a laugh if it hadn't been dragged through fire first.

He leaned in, voice low. "Are you really going to say you haven't been in danger? Look at what just happened. You came in terrified after being on a run. You tell yourself nothing's amiss because it's easier than admitting you feel it too — the cracks, the way you sense the air and what it carries, the way things that should not be, are beginning to change."

My skin prickled. I hated it. "I was fine. I had it. I don't need protection. And you're talking in riddles again." I lifted my chin. "Maybe you should get a muffin with that lecture."

He didn't move. Didn't blink. "You might be strong," he said evenly, "but you need to keep your wits about you." His hand lifted to his temple, rubbing once, as though the thought cost him. "Keep the wards strong. You've let them slip."

His gaze dropped to the faint shimmer at the windowsill — the rosemary in the planter, wilted overnight. "That's how they'll find you first."

The words punched straight through me. My fingers stilled on the ring. My breath snagged. "How do you know about wards?" I demanded, heat flooding my chest. "That's my father's nonsense, not yours. He used to salt the doors — old superstition. That's all."

"Not superstition," Aodhan said softly. "I just want you safe, even if you think I'm talking nonsense." He sat back then, as if the moment had cost him, as if staying closer was fire against his skin. "You don't have to believe me," he said. "But you'll remember I said it, when the time comes."

"Is that why you left that coin?"

"Yes. It's imbued with something that will strengthen the wards." He hesitated. "Keep it close. It will help keep you safe." He tipped his head, almost wary. "What should I call you? I can't keep thinking of you as 'the woman from the café' — or Ms Floral Beanz, as Maricus so helpfully pointed out."

"Lillian," I said — because Lily takes a second. "Ah... or you can call me Lily. Everyone calls me Lily."

"Lily," he repeated, slower this time, as though he'd known it all along and was only now permitted to speak it. Something in his expression softened — not a smile, but a quiet recognition that made my breath catch. "It suits you."

My heart raced and skipped beats at the sound of my name on his tongue. Deep, captivating, sending a chill down my spine. My gaze skittered anywhere else: the potted herbs trailing from the rafters, the chalkboard where Sal had drawn a cartoon possum making off with a croissant. The vines above the counter shifted a fraction, though no door had opened, no draft stirred. It was as if the air itself leaned closer, like it too found everything about this man alluring.

"You like plants," he said — not a question, but an observation, as though he were gathering pieces of me.

"They make the air cleaner, and bring a sense of I don't know...peace?" I answered, searching for the right words, grateful for the gentle shade of his voice. "It's like the place breathes with you if you give it enough green." I gestured vaguely around us.

He studied the ivy too long, as though he recognised something I didn't. Then the flicker in his eyes was gone, replaced with the same relentless composure that both steadied and infuriated me. The tether — whatever this taut, thrumming thread was — pulled tighter in my chest. I hated it.

Yet...I wanted it.

And the wanting terrified me most.

"I wanted to ask you something." His tone shifted, precise and careful, like a knife finding a seam.

"Has anyone mentioned finding gemstones nearby? Shards. Anything unusual in the soil?"

"Gems?" I blinked at him. "We're not in opal country. I haven't heard a word." I tilted my head, raising a brow, suspicious. "Why?"

The calculation in his gaze didn't sharpen so much as condense — storm clouds thickening without moving. Then, just as quickly, he shuttered it. "Curiosity. If you hear anything, you'll tell me."

"That depends." I let the words hang between us, edged. "On whether you're actually helpful again — and use manners and maybe stop talking in riddles?" For a moment, a spark slipped through his composure. The corner of his mouth tugged upward — a flash of wickedness I had no business enjoying. "Then I'll endeavour to be helpful," he said, voice low. "In all the ways you need me — whenever you call for me."

"Start by buying a muffin," Emma cut in, sweeping past with two plates, her voice carrying with theatrical authority. "House rule: brooding men pay the taxe de sunshine."

The faintest sound rumbled in Aodhan's chest — half amusement, half disappointment at the interruption.

"Lemon," I said, because daring him felt safer than ignoring him. Then, before he could vanish into silence again, I added, "And if you're that curious about local gossip, talk to Mr Fisher. If anyone's heard about odd rocks or people poking around, it's him. He's got a nose for things others miss."

Aodhan's gaze sharpened at the name, but his answer was only a nod, deliberate and unreadable. "I thought it might be."

He rose in that smooth, way of his — as though even standing carried purpose. Then he paused, the smallest flicker of uncertainty breaking through his usual armour. When his gaze returned to me, the café blurred away until there was only the weight of it, heavy as heat on bare skin.

"And you, Lily," he said, pitched soft enough that only I could catch it, "smell like jasmine. And rain."

My breath snagged. "What?"

"My new favourite scent. I have a nose for things too." From anyone else, it would've been arrogance — a line, a trick. From him, it sounded like truth. Fact. My pulse stumbled, traitorous, and I hated the way it thrilled me. "Just remember what I said. Stay safe...please."

Just like that. No goodbye. No farewell. He left the coffee untouched, steam still curling off the surface as the door swung shut behind him.

I sat frozen, staring at the cup, every nerve lit with the aftershock of his words. I wanted to laugh, to dismiss him, to tuck it away with my father's salt and iron nails.

He left me there — heart hammering, throat scorched where his gaze had lingered — as the bell chimed and the café remembered itself.

I watched as he stopped at Mr Fisher's table. No handshake. No smile. Just the weight of two men measuring one another. Mr Fisher tipped his chin, subtle as a nod to the weather, and for the briefest moment something like respect passed between them — uneasy, fragile, real.

Aodhan's eyes cut toward the tree line, narrowing on the very bend where dread had chased me at dawn. He walked to the edge of the clearing, and it felt like the trees closed over him, erasing his presence like water smoothing over stone.

A thread of fire licked up from the herb bed. Bright. Quick. Gone. No scorch. No smoke. Just absence where flame had been. A woman at the nearest table gasped, crossing herself before muttering about faulty wiring.

"In a garden?" Vivienne murmured, dry as drought.

But when the lull came — the school-run quiet and the vines trembling overhead as though in a wind I couldn't feel — I found myself whispering to the beams, the leaves, the air itself.

"This place is mine," I said quietly. "It stays safe". The same promise my father taught me to keep — to the land, and to those within it. Nyxie looked at me then, eyes gleaming, as though she'd heard every word.

I locked the café with its familiar click and walked the jasmine-lined path toward the house. That's when I saw it: a single leaf blackened at the tip, crisp as if touched by a flame unseen.

I brushed it. Cool. Harmless. But the jolt that shot through me screamed otherwise.

CHAPTER 9

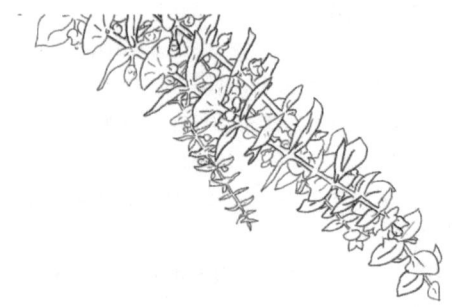

Morning broke heavy and close — the kind of mountain morning where mist clung low to the gums and the air tasted damp, as if the night hadn't quite let go.

Light crept slowly into the kitchen, brushing pale gold across the worn timber table and the ivy trailing along the window. I moved through it with quiet determination, body following the choreography of habit: kettle on, plates stacked, mugs lined like soldiers.

Oliver came down early, footsteps quick and restless. He fussed with his schoolbag — unzipping, rezipping, checking again, as though preparedness could anchor the unease that had haunted them since the accident. His jaw was set, the shape of Caleb's resolve wearing itself too young.

Daisy trailed after him, Nyxie glued to her side. "You don't have to watch me every second," she muttered, shoving her hair into a loose braid with more force than necessary. Oliver ignored her, shouldering his bag with deliberate calm.

"I'm walking you to the café for your morning muffin. And I need one of Sal's protein muffins." He shot her a look. "Stop being annoying and just accept that I'm the best."

Daisy groaned, rolling her eyes skyward. "Nyxie has already volunteered for that, and she is the best." As if on cue, Nyxie's tail thumped once a slow wag of approval, her amber gaze fixed like a sentinel's. She pressed closer into Daisy's hip, the picture of a creature who would rather starve than abandon her post.

The tension between the siblings hummed like static, but beneath it ran something steadier — loyalty stitched tight where words failed.

I caught myself smiling despite the heaviness in my chest. The small rituals of family life — the teasing, the fussing, the unspoken protections — held us together. Fragile in places. Imperfect in others. But strong enough to carry us through the dark. I lifted my coffee, pausing to take it all in as I watched them walk down the path toward the café together.

I looked around the house, letting the quiet settle. With Sal covering today, and the kids off with Dad I'd stay here. Tend to the small things, set the house back to rights, remind myself that there was comfort to be found in order and no brooding men in sight.

"Hey, girlfriend!" Emma's voice ricocheted up the stairs just as the front door slammed shut hard enough to rattle the photo frames.

Oh, hell.

I groaned, glaring down at my flannel pyjamas patterned with little coffee mugs. Tonight had been supposed to be mine — quiet, soft, predictable. Maybe a glass of wine. Maybe a book I'd read halfway and abandon on the nightstand. Maybe, if the universe was kind, a stretch of proper sleep.

Definitely not... whatever this was about to become.

"We're going out!" Emma bellowed from the bottom step, her words marching up like they owned the place. "Live music at Crystal Hollow square. Dinner. Drinks. It's not our twenties, but it'll bloody do!"

I raised my voice, aiming for weary but firm. "What if we just stayed in? Netflix, wine—"

"Nope!" she cut in, merciless. "Get your arse ready, unless you want me dress you." Her tone dropped into wicked glee. "And you know what happens when I play dress-up."

A vivid memory of sequins, leopard print, and a neon feather boa flashed uninvited through my brain. I winced. "You wouldn't."

The answering silence was far too smug I sighed. "God help me."

My gaze drifted to the wedding photo on my dresser — Caleb's easy grin frozen mid-laugh, his arm looped around me, both of us lit from within in a way we hadn't even realised then. My chest ached, that same deep pull I'd learned to carry but never quieted. "She hasn't changed, love," I whispered to him, fingers tracing the cool glass. "Still bossing me around."

For a heartbeat I let the ache rise, crest, and pass. Then I squared myself in front of the mirror and drew a long, steady breath. Lipstick — a soft rose, not daring but not invisible. A shimmer of gold on the lids to lift the tiredness. Mascara to open my eyes wider.

My hands hesitated at my collarbone, at the thin chain where his ring still lived. I tucked it beneath the neckline, then tugged it back out again. Older, more worn, Shadows carved beneath the cheekbones — but still me. Still Lily. Tonight, Emma wasn't going to let me pretend otherwise.

When I turned, she was already in my wardrobe, muttering like a general counting artillery. Hangers rattled.

"Oh, no," I groaned.

"Oh, yes," she fired back, spinning on her heel and brandishing her selections like weapons: a black pencil skirt that promised shape, a white bralette, and a sheer, sparkly blouse that looked like it had escaped from a nightclub's VIP booth. Sequins winked under the overhead light.

"Tonight, Lil," she declared, "you're done hiding behind flowy cardigans. You are hot, and Crystal Hollow needs reminding."

I arched a brow, unimpressed by the idea that anyone needed reminding of anything. "This is a terrible idea."

Her grin was pure sin — the kind that could rally armies. "You love me," she said. "And you're going to thank me."

Crystal Hollow's square pulsed with life. String lights stretched from awning to lamppost, casting the cobblestones in a wash of honeyed gold. Music throbbed from the bandstand — a bluesy guitar tangled with a drumbeat that got under the skin — stitched with the rise and fall of laughter, the clink of glasses, and the heady scent of wood-fired pizza laced with summer rain. The whole place smelled like warmth and want.

Emma wove through the crowd as if she were queen of it, balancing a tray of margaritas with reckless grace. She thrust one into my hand like an order. "Four," she declared, raising hers in salute. "Hydration. And courage."

I arched a brow, smirking despite myself. "You're going to regret this tomorrow."

"Future Emma can file a complaint," she sang, already shimmying to the beat. "Tonight is for fun. And maybe," she added with wicked relish, "a little trouble."

I sipped, cautious. "And who exactly are we here for?"

Her grin sharpened into something feral. "A Taurus. Reliable. Stubborn. Hung." She winked. I nearly spat my margarita across the table. "Emma!"

"What?" She tossed her hair, hips already swaying like she'd been born to command the rhythm. Sequins winked from her blouse with every turn.

"Don't give me that look. You've been locked in widow mode for six years, Lil. Six. Years." She jabbed a finger toward me, perfectly dramatic. "It's time to remember you've still got a pulse — wants and needs included."

I did look then, really looked — and it was the pinch in her brow, the worry tucked just beneath the sparkle, that landed first in my chest. Warmth flared, chased by a twist of guilt.

"Nothing wrong with owning a vibrator," I said, arching a brow back at her. "At least it doesn't need emotional coaching. Unlike someone's ex, if I recall correctly."

Emma barked a laugh — startled and delighted. "Oi, rude!"

"Factually accurate," I shot back, grin tugging at my mouth despite myself.

Emma snorted into her margarita. "If the job ends with that, the job wasn't satisfying!"

"Em," I said, leaning in just enough to test the ground, "you've complained plenty that your ex needed all the coaching in the world."

"Ugh," Emma groaned — fondness threaded through the sigh. "Fair." We laughed then — real, unguarded, a brief truce brokered by noise, and the ridiculous glue of friendship.

The music swelled, bass thrumming through the square like a heartbeat.

Emma became a blur of glitter and laughter, spinning and swaying, strangers falling into her orbit as if gravity itself had shifted. People cheered when she twirled, drinks sloshing, the night bending to her will.

I lingered at the edge, half in shadow, nursing my margarita and sipping slowly. The lime bite was sharp on my tongue, the tequila a hum in my blood. For a moment I let it carry me — the press of bodies, the scent of sweat and stone warmed by day, the way the air itself seemed alive. But then the crowd surged tighter, hotter, the laughter sharper, the music too loud. My throat closed. I ducked toward the bar, desperate for space, for air — for the quiet of something that wasn't so much.

"Ahhh, I know you."

The voice slithered across my skin before the man stepped from the crowd. He didn't stumble, didn't sway. He placed himself in front of me, body angled just enough to block my path. His smile loose and ugly. The whiskey on his breath was deliberate camouflage, but his eyes. His eyes were sharp, calculating. They belonged to someone dangerous.

My spine locked. "No. You don't."

"Don't be like that." His tone was coaxing, mock-gentle, like a man luring a stray animal closer. "You smell... strange." His nostrils flared as though he were testing the air. "Not human."

Fear cracked through me. He leaned in, brushing my arm with two fingers, and I couldn't stop the shiver that shot down my spine. His grin sharpened.

"Where's your friend, hm? Tell me, and maybe..." His lips brushed too close to my ear, cold and wet. "...maybe I'll let you walk away."

I shoved him, fury rising to mask the terror. "Get off me."

He caught my wrist — hard, locked in place. Mocking. Like he wanted me to know I couldn't shake him. His thumb traced the inside of my wrist, slow as a threat.

"Oh, I *like* you," he whispered. "The fire. The fight." His eyes gleamed, cruel amusement dancing there. "Pretty thing like you... I'd enjoy the chase and putting out that fire."

My pulse thundered, fear slamming through me before I could think. The crowd was only steps away — laughing, talking, oblivious.

No one saw. No one would hear me scream. My heart stutters.

His other hand braced the wall beside my head, boxing me in. The space shrank. My breath came shallow, sharp in my chest. I folded inward, instinct dragging me smaller, quieter.

I knew this moment.

I knew what came next.

Then heat rolled through the space, cutting straight through the noise of the square.

The stranger's grip faltered, just slightly. Enough to draw his attention.

And his voice — low, smooth, laced with quiet fury — broke the world open.

"I've been looking for you, mo draganín." The words curled through me like smoke and fire, my pulse jolting so hard it hurt.

Aodhan.

He stepped out of the press of bodies, and for a heartbeat the world seemed to pull back — making space for him.

Gods, he was impossible. Tall. Broad. Built with soldier's precision. Pale blond hair threaded with gold, tied loosely at the nape, his ears hidden beneath it. His linen shirt clung to his chest and arms, sleeves rolled to reveal muscle and veins — tattoos shimmering faintly beneath his skin, alive.

His face was too masculine to be called beautiful — sharp cheekbones, straight nose, a strong jaw shadowed with the faintest scruff that sent a ridiculous urge flickering through me: to touch.

And his eyes. Blue threaded with molten gold and silver — bright, sharp, searing. The kind of gaze that felt capable of stripping me down to bone and rebuilding me in the same breath.

I couldn't look away.

The man faltered under that gaze, muttering, "Found you. See you soon, darlin," and slunk into the crowd with a crooked grin. The promise in it made my stomach twist, but he didn't look back. Not with Aodhan standing there.

Aodhan didn't spare him a glance. The space around us hummed — charged, coiled — like thunder before lightning.

His hand found the small of my back — firm, steady. Heat flared beneath his palm, deeper than touch alone, thrumming into my bones.

I tried to tell myself it was just the chill, but a shiver climbed my spine anyway — a reaction that betrayed the lie before I could swallow it. "You attract trouble," he murmured, voice low — barely there, meant only for me. "Or perhaps trouble just knows where to find you."

My laugh slipped out, shaky around the edges. "That's rich, coming from the man who seems to have brought the trouble to the cafe and..."

"Only the café?" His mouth curved — that faint, crooked almost-smile again. The words should have tasted arrogant, but instead they landed easy — banter, familiar, almost natural.

I should have pulled away. I knew I should. Instead, I leaned closer — as if his warmth were the only thing anchoring me in place. A safety I didn't know I needed.

"Thank you," I whispered. The words felt foreign on my tongue. I didn't say them easily — not like this, not when I should have handled it myself without anyone stepping in.

His eyes softened, just barely — silver flaring when the strobe lights caught them, lightning trapped in human form.

"Don't thank me, Lily," he said quietly. "You shouldn't have to thank anyone for stepping in like that — especially not me." His gaze sharpened again, the softness folding away. "But you need to be more careful. He was only a fool. The true danger hasn't arrived yet." A chill trickled down my spine, even as his hand stayed warm at my back.

"What kind of danger? And what happens when it does?" I managed, forcing calm, not wanting to show how shaken I was — by both his words and the man before.

His gaze dropped to my mouth, then lifted again, pinning me in place. "Then I'll be there. Whether you want me to be or not." His jaw flexed. "I don't want you hurt — not in a fight you shouldn't be in." The words carried a weight I couldn't name. Instead of letting myself process what he meant, I looked back toward the bar and across the dance floor, mouth suddenly dry.

"I was just getting a drink," I managed, though my voice came out softer, thinner than I wanted — as if the music and the crowd had swallowed the air around me.

His gaze dragged over me slowly, deliberately — the sheer blouse, the curve of my waist, the rise and fall of my chest. My knees nearly buckled under the weight of it.

He didn't leer. No. He looked like a man who'd found something he'd been searching for — something he never wanted to lose again. Something that was his, and his alone.

"You look..." His voice dropped, rough, husky, velvet and heat. "Irresistible. Though this—" his knuckles brushed the sleeve, dragging slowly up my arm to my neckline "—doesn't leave much to the imagination."

The brush of his skin was fleeting, but my whole body lit up — traitorous and alive. My pulse stuttered, my knees weakened, my heartbeat raced. Heat twisted low in my belly, sharp and insistent.

Desire. Need. And beneath it, a fear I couldn't name — not of him, but of myself. Of what this pull between us meant, and everything it shouldn't.

I laughed, breathless, trying to hide the pull he has over me.

"It's... not something I've worn in years."

His eyes darkened, drinking me in. The look in them made my chest ache and my thighs press together instinctively — desperate and ashamed all at once.

"A shame," he murmured, voice like smoke curling around me. "That you've hidden this for so long. You really are stunning."

Gods, why does his voice sound like that? Like he already knows how my body would arch beneath his touch. Like he's sure of it. And worse — I want to believe him. Believe everything he says.

My fingers twitched against the glass, the urge flaring before I could cage it.

I told myself it was the margaritas, the lights, the music — but even that lie felt thin.

Get it together, Lily. I cleared my throat, the attempt at casual cracking in my voice. "What were you doing before you came over?" I asked and hated how much it sounded like I cared.

"Watching you," he said simply. No shame. No disguise. "You looked magnificent on the dance floor. I don't think I've ever seen you look so free."

The words struck deep and sharp as an arrowhead. My stomach twisted, heat flaring hot and wanting. The crowd surged around us, laughing and spinning, but he'd peeled the world back to nothing — no sound, no colour, only this pull, this impossible gravity binding me to him.

"You okay?" he asked, his voice softening — like a hand brushing the back of my neck.

"Yeah," I whispered, though it was a lie. My throat was too dry, my pulse too fast. I had far too many thoughts about this man — and the things his voice was doing to me. I swallowed. "I... need to check on Emma."

He didn't move to stop me. But the way his gaze lingered as I slipped from his touch made my skin burn hotter, as though his hand still rested at my back, guiding me.

As though even when I left, he wasn't letting me go.

His gaze flicked to the dance floor. "Short, brown hair — dancing with the man who doesn't know the word no to a good time?"

I blinked, startled by his accuracy. "Yes... most likely."

"She's with Maricus. His tone wasn't explanation, it was a statement.

My stomach knotted. Emma was laughing, glitter in her hair catching the lights, leaning into him like the danger wasn't dripping from his smile.

Maricus's dark hand sprawled low across her hip, his grin all cheek and predatory. He looked past her shoulder, eyes locking on mine.

It was a look that hooked sharp, cold, and deliberate. A silent reminder that he knew exactly what game he was playing, and he planned to win.

I pushed through the crowd, pulse racing. Aodhan stayed steady behind me — a wall of heat and presence that parted people without a word. Men stepped back instinctively; women glanced, watching him move, hoping he'd inch closer their way.

"Ready to head back?" I murmured, voice pitched low, hoping Emma would hear the urgency beneath it.

Emma twirled, carefree, oblivious — or pretending to be. "Nope."

"What about the Taurus?" I tried, desperate for levity.

"Forget the Taurus. I found myself a Pisces." Her chin tipped toward Maricus, sly and daring. The words hit— sharp, disbelieving, heat and panic colliding in my chest.

"Promise I'm fine," she added, already pulling out her phone. "I'll share my location. Call before I leave." Her grin turned wicked, voice dropping into a tease edged with dare: "Unless you want to be on the call during—"

"Em," I cut in, breath snatching, cheeks flushing hot. "Do not finish that sentence."

The room seemed to lean in just to hear her scandalise herself. I refused to look at Maricus at all. The refusal felt necessary. Not jealousy. Not of how free and uncontained Emma is.

I kept my eyes forward, because looking back at the man who had my core performing acrobatics felt like inviting commentary, I didn't have the bandwidth to survive tonight. She cackled, spinning back into the crush of bodies like she was untouchable. She stopped before Maricus, turning back toward me and mouthing, go have fun with Mr Broody.

Maricus's hand tightened at her waist. His grin sharpened — eyes never leaving mine, as if he knew this was coming. Aodhan brushed the back of my hand — deliberate, grounding — a faint spark chasing up my arm. Without looking at me, he guided me out of the square, his presence shielding, his silence louder than any jet engine roaring to life.

"Let me escort you home."

His fingers closed around mine as we moved away from the town centre toward the waiting cabs. I hesitated, tightening my grip for a heartbeat before letting go.

"Only if it's convenient," I said softly. "I don't want to pull you out of your way." His hand found mine again — firmer this time, possessive without apology. "It's exactly what a pushy reckless man like myself should do."

The ride home was thick with quiet — heavy with the heat rolling between us, relentless in its certainty.

The engine hummed low beneath us, but it couldn't drown out the uneven cadence of my heart — a pulse that thundered loud enough I was sure he could hear it, feel it, claim it.

His hand rested on my thigh, thumb tracing slow circles through the fabric — deceptively casual, painfully deliberate. The touch carried weight, staking territory, taking space I hadn't offered but couldn't bring myself to pull away from. Sparks chased beneath my skin, traitorous and electric, the warmth of him bleeding through the layers, sinking deeper than touch alone should reach.

He smelled of bergamot and smoke, of salt-tanged rain and storm-washed air — a scent I craved like breath itself. My body leaned into it first, hungry, aching, alive — before my mind could form a single objection. Every nerve was awake. Every cell attuned. I felt the pull low in my belly, coiling tight and undeniable, twisting into the part of me that remembered need, remembered want, remembered him.

I hated that it steadied me. Hated that it awakened me more. But god. I felt it all the same.

I stared hard out the window, counting headlights, gum trees flicking by — anything to distract my mind. His reflection wavered in the glass: a carved jaw, faint stubble I ached to touch, eyes fixed on the road like it was the only thing keeping him from looking at me.

"You really shouldn't have been alone in there," he said finally, voice quiet but taut, roughened by something sharp.

"I wasn't," I snapped, though the tremor in my chest betrayed me. "Emma was—"

"Emma was on the dance floor," Aodhan cut in, jaw flexing. His eyes flashed in the dashlight. "You were prey in a square full of predators tonight — and looking like you do, a delicious one at that." The words hit — brutal in their simplicity. I spun the ring at my throat, the metal cool against my burning skin. "I'm not weak. And it wouldn't be the first time I've had to tell someone no."

"No," he agreed instantly, fierce and unflinching, but it wasn't the agreement that stole my breath. It was the way his hand tightened around mine as he said it, dragging me into the moment, forcing my eyes upward. I met the concern in his gaze — a thing etched into his face with painful sincerity. "You're not weak," he continued, voice a low spark striking flint. "You're fire. A dragon." His jaw flexed once — composure barely leashed — before he added, quieter now, "But... I still don't like to see you preyed upon."

The words hit me like a physical blow, heat flaring through my ribs before fear could swallow it whole. My throat went desert-dry. The air between us felt molten, thick with a tug-of-war between dread and that reckless, furious wanting I refused to name.

Then he moved.

He turned his palm up slow, deliberate, permission offered in the gesture alone. And slid his fingers between mine, threading us together with steady precision. Grounding. Claiming. A bond forged in silence first, choice second.

"Tell me to stop," he murmured, his voice velvet-deep — intimate, warm, iron-strong. "And I will." I didn't speak. The silence answered for me instead electric, alive, thrumming with everything unspoken that coiled between us like fate itself had tied the knot and dared either of us to loosen it.

Outside, the mountain loomed dark and watchful. Inside the car, I was burning. I glanced at him, at the hard line of his jaw.

The perfect control etched into every angle of his posture. The faint scruff shadowing his throat. The strong vein running down his forearm where golden ink glowed faintly beneath his skin, alive, as though carrying fire instead of blood. He looked carved for war, for command, for power — untouchable.

But right now, all I could think about was what those hands would feel like if they weren't holding back.

"Oh." The sound slipped out before I could bite it back. His arousal pressed against the fabric of his pants — unmistakable, straining with the same tension vibrating between us. Heat flooded me, fast and merciless. Shame and hunger tangled until I couldn't tell one from the other. I shouldn't look. Yet, I couldn't stop looking. Have I really caused that?

When my gaze jerked up, his eyes were waiting molten, knowing. He'd seen. He knew. The air tightened, charged until I thought it might combust. My skin felt too tight, my chest too shallow. I wanted him — with a need so sharp it hurt. But I couldn't. Because if I gave in, I didn't know if there would be any of me left to gather back up again.

His thumb dragged higher on my thigh, deliberate, slow — each stroke a promise and a threat. My pulse stuttered. My knees shifted — instinct, surrender, invitation. I didn't know which.

His inhale cut through the silence, sharp and guttural, like restraint had become all too much. For a heartbeat, the world held its breath. Just us, the dark road, and the fire we were both pretending not to feed.

"Aodhan..." My voice trembled, fragile as glass.

The heat rolling off him, hotter, like his very skin was aflame. The dashboard lights flickered, shadows leaping across his jaw as his control frayed. For one unbearable moment, I swore the car itself might ignite with the heat radiating between us.

Then headlights swept across the gravel, cutting through the spell. The world snapped back into motion. His hand withdrew, leaving my skin cold and too aware of its emptiness.

I fumbled for the door handle, legs unsteady, lungs tight. His low laugh curled after me, soft and rough at once. It wasn't mocking. If anything, it was release — his attempt to disarm what had nearly consumed us both.

At the gate, I forced my voice steady. "What were you doing at Crystal Hollow?"

His gaze sharpened, catching the moonlight, his eyes shifting shades under it. "Looking for my lost item," he said simply, each word measured. Then, softer — a flicker of honesty slipping past the armour: "False lead. And... not in their lost and found." The corner of my mouth twitched despite the tension still coiled low in my belly. A sound escaped — a laugh, sharp and nervous. But it felt good to laugh, even for a moment.

He studied me. Not the way Mark stared, or strangers glanced and dismissed — but saw. The way I tucked my hair behind my ear when rattled. The faint ache in my smile when I spoke of Caleb. The unconscious spin of the ring I forgot I was even doing. He noticed it all, every detail I'd spent years hiding. And somehow, instead of feeling exposed, I felt... seen.

"I should really be getting in," I said, my brain stumbling over words and what to do next.

"Sure. How about I walk you to the door?" he asked, glancing toward the house.

I hesitated before whispering, because anything louder might unravel me — and because if he walked me to the door, I wasn't sure I'd be able to turn him away.

"Goodnight, Aodhan."

"Goodnight, Lily."

My name in his mouth wasn't casual. It was a vow, a tether. A promise I shouldn't want. But how my body wanted him.

A shudder runs down my spine at where the night could have ended and how Aodhan was there again. Nyxie pressed close as I stepped onto the porch, her solid weight grounding me where my thoughts wouldn't. I rested a hand on her head, the warmth of her fur steady beneath my palm. "Yeah, old girl," I whispered into the quiet night. "What a night." She leaned harder, as if she knew how thin the ground felt beneath me.

He stood at the gate, watching until I reached the door, staying until it clicked shut.

Later, steam curled against the bathroom mirror, softening

the edges of the woman reflected there. I slid into the bath, water lapping at my collarbones, rose-scented heat wrapping around me.

It should have soothed. Instead, the memory returned unbidden — his hand on my thigh, the rough pad of his thumb circling, the way his gaze burned with gilded fire when I said his name.

The thought sparked through me again, raw and dangerous. Heat unfurled low in my belly, traitorous and sharp. My hand drifted lower, chasing the echo of that phantom touch, as though I could summon him back through memory alone. Pleasure built, tight and unbearable, until it crashed over me — sharp, blinding, Aodhan's name caught in my throat, bitten back before it could escape.

When it ebbed, silence crashed in — heavy as stone, cold as the mountain night pressing against the windows. My breath came uneven, my skin still flushed, yet my heart ached with a different hunger — the hollow absence of the man I should still be tangled with, the one whose ring rested against my chest.

My fingers closed around the chain — the silver band cool and immovable. Caleb's ring. My anchor. My wound. I pressed it hard enough to leave a dent in my skin.

"Damn it," I whispered to the empty room, voice breaking. I didn't know if the words were meant for Aodhan — for the need he'd woken — or for myself, for letting it take root.

CHAPTER 10

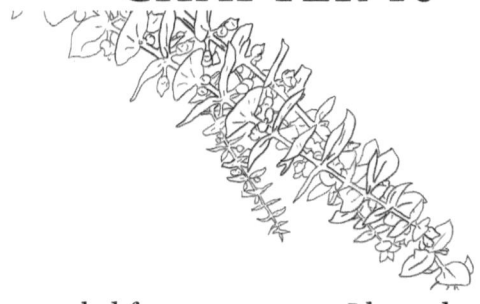

Steam curled from my mug as I leaned against the black railing of the balcony. The air carried the damp scent of dew-soaked earth and eucalyptus sap. Below, the hedge and dense shrubs shielded the café from view, though a thin curl of smoke from Sal's early baking already spiralled above the roofline.

It was almost enough to pretend things were ordinary. Almost.

The thunder of feet shattered the quiet, and I jumped, sloshing tea down my shirt.

Oliver barrelled down the stairs, hair sticking up at odd angles, school bag half-zipped and threatening to spill everything—including what looked suspiciously like yesterday's half-eaten sandwich. Daisy trailed after him, Nyxie glued to her side, bribed by the promise of treats. Daisy's colour had improved, but the careful steadiness in her smile remained.

She was coming back to herself, slowly, though in the quiet moments, the unease still flickered through.

"Morning, Mum," Oliver said around a mouthful of toast he'd scavenged from the bread box, kissing my cheek on his way to the fridge. "Daisy's decided she's not an invalid anymore. She's planning her dramatic return to the café to make some cash before graduation."

"I'm not fragile," Daisy muttered, pouring herself juice. She squared her shoulders. "I can carry a tray without fainting. And I want to help Mum too. Besides," she added, shooting him a look, "since when were you allowed to question your elders?" Nyxie huffed softly, ears flicking as if disagreeing.

My chest ached. I reached out, tucking a strand of hair behind Daisy's ear, fingers brushing her temple. "You're always welcome to help," I said gently. "But that doesn't mean rushing back before you're ready. You could always do some odd jobs around the house if you want to make quick cash."

Daisy ducked her head, embarrassed. Her hand covered mine briefly before she shrugged. "Sitting here makes me bored. I need to move. I need to do something, and I miss the regulars and the babies that visit."

"Bored? Even though the café is just out the front." I teased, trying to ease the tension tightening her shoulders.

"Mum…" Her tone made it clear there would be no arguing.

I let it go. I understood. Silence had a way of lingering, long after the pain should have faded.

I reached Floral Beanz to find the café already alive. The garden path wound through lavender thick with bees, roses climbing the cottage walls and glowing faintly pink in the morning light. From the outside, it was all quaint charm — the kind of place that belonged on postcards. Inside, the air smelled of cinnamon, espresso, and polished wood.

Locals crowded the tables. Hikers with dusty boots grabbed takeaway coffees before vanishing into the mountain trails. A pair of cyclists clattered in, helmets swinging from their fingers. The morning chorus — chatter, clinking mugs, cutlery against plates — filled the space like music. The sound grounded me. I took a slow breath and stepped inside.

Sal worked the counter in her usual brusque way, flour streaking her dark forearms, braids swinging as she danced around the kitchen. Mark Evans slid in — right on cue — heading straight for his usual corner. His smile, polished and practised, stretched just a fraction too wide.

"Morning, Lily," he said smoothly, his gaze lingering in a way that no longer bothered to disguise its intent. "Busy as ever. Don't know how you manage it all."

"The usual?" I asked, my tone brisk — a reminder that he was here as a customer and nothing more.

"You know me," he said with a wink. "Creature of habit."

"I'm well aware of the creature you are," I replied, irritation sharpening my words as I noted the complete lack of remorse in his return. "And this is a reminder — you are not to enter staff areas."

Mark's gaze drifted across the room, something dark flickering there before he looked back at me. "As you wish, Lily."

The café moved with its usual rhythm, but something in the air made me restless. A faint hum beneath my skin, that prickling sense of awareness that something was coming.

I thumbed out a quick message: Fresh coffee and muffins at the counter.

Within minutes, Daisy and Oliver spilled through the front door, their laughter bright and easy as they raided the tray. Vivienne followed soon after, heels clicking, phone pressed to her ear as she mouthed a distracted good morning before disappearing into the back.

The bell jingled again as I slid another tray of muffins into the display.

"Order up, Mum!" Daisy called, balancing cappuccinos with infuriating grace.

"Careful with table six," I warned. "They'll flirt with anything if it means a free coffee."

"Please." Daisy scoffed. "I'm not the one giving extra marshmallows to the regulars."

I shot her a look, but the customers only beamed, as if Daisy had hung the moon herself. That glow she carried — how easily people gravitated toward her — reminded me painfully of myself when Caleb and I first met. A smile tugged at my lips. Then my pulse shifted — that faint thrum, like the breath before lightning splits the sky.

He was there.

Leaning at the counter beside Mr Fisher. Tall and broad in a rolled cream linen shirt, golden hair tied high today in a loose, messy knot, sunlight catching in the pale strands. The faint shimmer of tattoos pulsed beneath his skin, barely restrained. His muscles were taut as he leaned across Fisher's table, fingers tapping lightly against the timber.

Those hands.

Hands that had only yesterday traced slow circles along my thigh — and in my mind, very deliberately, far more than that. I snapped my gaze away, dragging myself back into the present before the thought could finish forming.

Aodhan didn't need to move to command a room; his presence bent it around him regardless. Today he looked calm. Collected. As though last night hadn't unsettled him nearly as much as it had me.

Then his eyes lifted.

Locked with mine.

Heat licked up my throat — from memory. His hand on my thigh. His thumb circling. My name in his mouth. The way I'd fallen apart later, alone in the bath.

My stomach dipped hard. Shame tangled with a flare of want I couldn't smother — not with him standing there now, gaze branding me like he knew exactly where my thoughts had gone.

"Morning," I said — sharper than I intended, my voice cracking against the tension.

"Morning."

His reply was velvet. Quiet. Low. Curling straight into my chest and every place I refused to acknowledge.

I turned too fast, handing Mr Fisher his coffee with more force than necessary, willing my hands to steady. But every movement felt watched — tracked — as if Aodhan were still touching me, mapping me, memorising the slope of my wrist, the bow of my shoulders, the hitch in my breath when I reached for a cup.

What would've happened if I hadn't pulled away last night? If I'd let his hand climb higher — leaned into that dangerous look instead of running?

The thought struck like a spark. My thighs pressed together beneath the counter. A traitorous echo. When I glanced up again, he was still watching.

Not smug. Not gloating. Just... seeing. Like he knew exactly where my thoughts had gone. Like he'd been thinking about it too.

"Hold up there, love — you're in such a rush I nearly wore my coffee," Mr Fisher laughed, dusting his shirt in mock offence. "Don't let my good looks go to waste. I wore my good boots for you today."

He winked, lifting one foot just enough to show them off. My cheeks burned. I spun Caleb's ring at my throat — harder than I meant to — forcing a brittle smile. Anything to hide how undone I already felt.

"You're always handsome, Mr Fisher," I said lightly. "Good boots or not."

I still couldn't bring myself to look at Aodhan, heat rushing to my face. Then I heard his scoff — half laugh, half cough — his hand rising to cover it.

"Looking lovely as always, Lily," he said, amusement threading his voice. "Glitter or not."

He winked. And just like that, I lost myself for a heartbeat in his careless smile.

The bell jingled again. Breaking the spell. Trouble. Maricus prowled in, all sharp edges cloaked in confidence. Dark hair deliberately tousled, tawny skin gleaming, his shirt unbuttoned with intent rather than care. His grin cut quick and cruel. When his gaze found me, it latched on like a hook.

"Ahhh," he dragged, voice like silk. "Morning, Lillian..." The temperature spiked. The quiet warmth of Aodhan's restraint sharpened — wary.

"Morning," I managed, though my pulse rattled against my ribs.

Maricus let his gaze roam, slow and insolent, like he wanted me to feel every inch of it. "You looked... stunning last night. Quite the treat compared to your usual Ms Floral Beanz look." Aodhan's jaw flexed, the gold under his skin thrumming brighter. Heat thickened the air until my own skin prickled.

"Maricus," Aodhan said — his voice cut like tempered steel. Maricus smirked wider, leaning one elbow on the counter, all mockery and charm. His cologne curled around me — spice, smoke, sin — and my pulse betrayed me.

"What's the matter, Aodh? Getting territorial over a coffee shop?" His eyes slid to me, deliberate and knowing. "Or... someone in it?"

The air went brittle.

Aodhan's body drew tight as a bowstring, control stretched thin. "Careful with what you say aloud."

"Oh, I am." Maricus's grin was all teeth. "But isn't it funny? All those years of ironclad control, discipline, restraint — and here you are. Undone by a mortal woman with flour on her cheek."

I blinked, catching my reflection in the espresso machine — a smear of flour. Perfect. I groaned softly and brushed it away with the back of my hand. Silence follows. Awkward. Heavy.

Aodhan leaned closer, voice low. "You looked fine. Like you. Don't let him rattle you."

My breath hitched. Heat tangled inside me until I couldn't tell where embarrassment ended and something darker began. A dangerous thrill threaded through the fear — realising Maricus had noticed. That he was baiting Aodhan. That I was the reason Aodhan's composure cracked.

"What would your court say?" Maricus purred. "The mighty Sun... distracted."

My pulse tripped. Court? It sounded like some inside joke, but the tension in Aodhan's shoulders told me otherwise. Before I could speak, Emma barrelled in, heels clacking like a war drum, perfume sweeping ahead of her.

"Lil!"

She stopped dead, taking in the scene — me pinned behind the counter, Maricus lounging, Aodhan rigid as carved stone. A grin bloomed, wicked and merciless.

"Well, well," she drawled. "This is delicious."

"Emma—" I hissed, but she was already moving.

"Oh, hush." She slid an arm through Maricus's like she'd been waiting her whole life for this performance. "If you're serious about her, handsome, you'd better up your game. Lily's a popular lady these days."

Aodhan's jaw clenched. Gold flickered beneath his skin. Maricus laughed, low and delighted. "Competition, then." His eyes glinted darkly. "Better make a move, old friend. Before someone else does." The café lights flickered once.

"She's not a game," Aodhan said, voice quiet but carrying like thunder. His gaze locked on Maricus, white-hot and unyielding. "She'll never be a game. She deserves only the best and I will…" He stopped, heat rushing to his neck. "Don't cause misunderstandings here, Maricus. You have a job to do."

The words landed like a strike. Even the tradies froze mid-bite. Emma's grin faltered into awe. Vivienne, mid-sip, lifted her brow with new calculation.

Maricus's grin sharpened. "Ah," he murmured. "So he does care. Good to know." And god help me — I didn't know what scared me more: Maricus's satisfaction, or the dangerous truth burning in Aodhan's voice when he'd alluded to being that best.

Vivienne smirked over her cup. "Well, Lil, if you don't want one, I'll take one."

"Oh, don't worry," Emma cut in, wicked as sin. "I'll save you both the trouble. I already had a go with this one."

Vivienne choked mid-sip. "Emma!"

Emma only grinned wider. "What? Maricus is obscene. The stamina? Unreal. And the… size?" She held her hands indecently wide, half the café snickering into their cups while I prayed for the floor to swallow me. "Lil, that man could make a saint sin. If my neighbours didn't hear me last night, they're deaf."

Maricus clutched his chest in mock swoon. "Sweetheart, you'll make me blush."

"You?" Emma purred. "Never. But Lily's gone redder than a Shiraz." I dropped my face into my hands, mortified heat crawling up my neck. The regulars tittered — scandalised but amused. Through it all, Aodhan said nothing. But silence had never felt so heavy. His storm pressed harder with each heartbeat, his gaze on Maricus burning enough to turn the air molten.

And then I caught it — the acrid tang. Smoke. My head snapped toward the door. One leaf on the rosemary hedge was blackened, curling inward as if touched by invisible flame.

Mr Fisher stepped forward, his eyes sharper than usual.

"Smells off out there. Not like bushfire. Like something's smouldering, something foreign."

"Yes," I said, keeping my voice tight. "Found a burnt leaf by the door this morning. Another near the orange jasmine. They're showing up more often now. Weird. Kid's pranks?"

Aodhan's head turned sharply toward the hedge. His whole body coiled, gold light flaring beneath his skin. For a heartbeat, he looked less man, more weapon. Maricus chuckled, low and taunting. "Ah. It's begun."

"Maricus." Aodhan didn't look at him. "We need to go. Now."

Aodhan moved sharp with determination and purpose.

The kind of movement that made my chest lock tight, that told me he could have crossed the room and vanished into the trees in a single breath if he wanted to. He didn't look at Maricus. Didn't look at me. He headed for the door, the heat of him brushing past like a scorch, and then he was gone. My chest tightened — hard, sudden.

For one wild, ridiculous heartbeat, I thought it was Emma's jokes or Maricus's taunts that had driven him out. That he couldn't stand being teased about me. About wanting something he refused to name. The thought twisted sharp and hot inside me, equal parts infuriating and impossible to ignore.

Because the truth was... I wanted to know what it was he truly wanted.

That evening, the property carried an unusual hush, as though one thing unseen lingered just beyond the shadow. Dinner was simple, comforting — roast chicken, salad, bread pulled warm from the oven. The kind of meal meant to settle a household after days that hadn't been kind, too long, too heavy, too much and needing a restart for the next day.

Daisy twirled her fork idly, mischief curling at the corners of her mouth. "So... that blond guy. The one who keeps showing up. He's... intense. Hot — and I mean, really hot. But intense."

Oliver looked up immediately, expression flat, jaw setting like steel.

"Intense is one word. Creepy's another. Have you seen how he looks at Mum? Like she's his reason for breathing." He grimaced. "Hard pass."

"Excuse me," I cut in, sharper than meant. "He's not creepy."

Three pairs of eyes snapped. Silence stretched, just long enough. Daisy's grin widened, slow and victorious. "Ohhh. Not creepy, huh? Interesting choice of words there mum…"

I felt the heat crawl up my neck. Vivienne swirled her wine lazily, gaze cool but amused. "She's right. You were flustered this morning. I saw it." Her eyes flicked pointedly to my face. "And you're blushing now."

"I was not flustered — and I'm not blushing. It's just hot."

Oliver snorted into his plate. "Mum, you dropped the tongs. Twice." He glanced at the open window. "And it's autumn." I flushed again. "I was distracted."

"Yeah," Daisy sing-songed, spearing a cherry tomato. "Distracted by his eyes. Blue, right? And muscly. Very… dreamy."

Viv chuckled into her glass. "Don't forget tall, intense, and smug — Maricus." She tipped her head, smirking. "Lil, you've got yourself a love triangle forming."

I groaned, dropping my head into my hands. "I am not in a love triangle. I'm running a café and raising two teenagers. That's it."

"Sure," Viv said lightly. "But the whole of Crystal Hollow can feel it. Men are circling you like moths to a flame." She raised her glass. "And honestly? It's about time."

Daisy giggled, nudging Oliver. "We should start taking bets on which one Mum ends up with."

Oliver's glare cut sharp as glass. "Neither. She deserves better than both."

My throat tightened fast, painful, unexpected. Heat pressed behind my eyes. I reached across the table and squeezed his hand before I could stop myself.

"Thanks, Ol."

Later, the house fell into its night-breathing rhythm. Daisy disappeared behind her headphones. Oliver kicked a ball down the hall until Vivienne threatened him with a lecture. I stood at my dresser, brushing out my hair, their words looping back with every stroke.

Not creepy. Distracted. Flustered.

I set the brush down. My fingers drifted to the silver band on its chain, rubbing the cool metal until it steadied me — or tried to. When I finally slipped into bed, Nyxie curled at my feet, her familiar weight grounding, soothing.

It didn't help. I could still feel him. Aodhan's gaze — heavy, electric — lingered like a brand beneath my skin, as though he'd left some invisible imprint behind. I tried to push it away. I failed.

Sleep came in fragments, dragging me under like a tide that never let me surface for long. The mountain track unfolded around me, familiar, and yet wrong. Gum leaves shimmered silver in the moonlight, shadows stretching farther than they should. My feet knew the ground instinctively, even as my chest tightened with the certainty that this wasn't quite real.

Caleb walked ahead.

The easy roll of his stride was unchanged. He glanced back, green eyes warm, that smile still piercing me the way it always had — sunlight through the clouds. His hand lifted, reaching for me. Waiting...

The path forked. One trail curved toward the house and cafe, its glass walls glowing softly in the dark, a lantern against the night. Home. Safe. Comfort.

The other path pulsed with something stranger. Wild grass brushed my calves, illuminated by a bloom I both knew and didn't — iridescent petals layered like rose and peony, threaded through with silver and green, starlight caught in a flower. The one from the garden. The one that shouldn't exist, merely old stories.

Caleb stopped.

"You know which way is safe," he said gently, nodding toward the house. His voice wrapped around me like it always had —

steady, anchoring. But this time, he didn't take my hand. He let it fall back to his side, just out of my reach.

My heart thudded hard. "Cal I... I don't want to lose you again."

"You won't lose me." His certainty was quiet, unshakeable. He touched his chest. "I'll always be here." Then his gaze shifted — toward the flower-lit path. "But you have to keep walking. Even if it's not with me." The words cut deeper than fear. "Especially if it's not with me," he added softly. "You're far more important than you realise."

The air humming — alive. That pull I knew now. That presence. I turned. The dream sharpened, colours vivid and bright. The flower pulsed faint. Beyond it, the shadows waited — patient. Jasmine and rain drifted on the breeze.

I reached for Caleb. My fingers brushed his sleeve — and passed straight through smoke. His smile lingered as he dissolved, his voice echoing through me:

Don't hold your breath forever, Lil. Live.

I woke gasping, chest aching, the ring clutched so tight in my fist the chain had cut into my palm. Tears streaked my face, hot and unstoppable.

CHAPTER 11

Aodhan POV

Fuck.

I should leave. That's always the first thought — leave. Turn my back. Step through the veil before the pull tightens and I forget why I swore to keep my distance.

But I'm an idiot. A glutton for punishment. Instead of staying hidden, I walked in — straight into the gravity I've spent months pretending doesn't exist. Pretend I never felt the thread snap taut between us the moment I stepped through that cafe door — the moment my eyes locked with hers. Those impossibly green, defiant eyes.

The second thought crushes the first: stay. Watch. Breathe. Remember her scent, her presence. Because if I don't, the world tilts wrong — as though a constellation has been moved and the sky can't find its true north.

She moves through her café as if it were built around her pulse. Every motion unthinking. Perfect. The scent of earth and roasted beans. Light spilling through the windows, clinging to her like worship. Vines lean toward her. Steam from the milk wands curls as if trying to steal her scent. Even the noise softens around her. It's absurd and impossible.

It's her.

A mortal, I remind myself. A small sun in a fragile body,

drawing everything into her gravity — and I, Air Prince, heir to storms and lightning, and the sky am the one who bows to her every whim.

I don't mean to think of her as sacred. The thought simply arrives, the way breathing comes naturally. Goddess — not of crown or altar, but of small mercies and stubborn will. A mortal divinity stitched from laugh lines and calloused hands.

I catch myself and recoil, but it makes nothing better. I shouldn't be here.

And then she looks up green eyes bright as wet leaves, mouth curved in a distracted half-smile as she passes a mug across the counter, and my resolve disintegrates like frost in sunlight.

The bond thrums once, low and steady, a pulse beneath my ribs. She feels it too; she must. Her fingers falter, a tremor so slight no one else notices. I drink my espresso like it's an anchor and tell myself I'll leave after one more heartbeat. Then another. And another.

But the first time I stepped onto that mountain road after Maricus's message "a complication," he'd called it, as though a single word could smother what I felt — the world had gone quiet.

And then she turned. Later, on the road, her scent hits me before the scene does. Jasmine. Rain. Blood. My magic hisses up my spine like a storm breaking. She's on her knees in the gravel, hair wild, hands pressed to the girl — her girl — as if sheer will alone could hold the world together.

I should stay back. Interfere and you bind yourself, my father's voice warns. Stay out of mortal storms. But the bond roars like a gale through a canyon. My feet move before thought. She turns at my shadow. Those same green eyes, wide now — fear and fury and love all tangled in a single breath. And my world realigns again — not north, not south, but to her.

Maricus is there, of course. Always at the edges of ruin. His grin is a blade, his words sharpened to provoke. I taste copper under my tongue. I shouldn't care. I shouldn't burn at the idea of her. But when she steps between him and the girl, voice trembling but unbroken, something inside me locks.

"*Reckless*," I hear myself say. The word lands heavier than intended. It's not accusation. It's prayer. Plea. Promise. All the things I shouldn't let myself feel. She fires back fierce, protective and goddess help me, even then she's luminous.

Humans don't feel mate bonds. Not like we do. Among the Fae, the bond itself is rare — a half-myth even to us. Among mortals it's unheard of, a bedtime story whispered to soften loneliness. No threads of power coil in their bones, no ancestral hum to draw the knot tight. They choose those they feel safe with and call it love.

Green eyes. Hair curling loose from its braid. The scent of oil and jasmine — and something warmer that had no name. Her gaze caught mine. Something under my skin rose — sharp, instinctive, like a hawk startled from a branch.

Mine.

The word didn't come from thought. It came from bone, my very being, all senses claiming her. A surge followed fierce and undeniable — the need to take her, shield her, give her everything I'd sworn I would never need.

I rejected it outright. I am my father's son — trained to read politics from a single breath, to bury instinct beneath duty, to carve weakness out of myself with ritual and steel. The prophecy that caged my childhood promised the Sun Prince would walk alone — no mate, no heir. An empty throne room. A dynasty reduced to echoes.

I once called it peace. Now I know it for what it is: habit. A cold, tidy habit shaped like a life. And then came her — everything the prophecy said I was not allowed to have.

She told me to leave her property, her voice sharp as a drawn blade. I should have obeyed. I didn't. I stood there, hungry, noticing things no warrior should: the dusting of flour on her wrist from the morning bake, the freckle at the corner of her mouth, the way her fingers kept finding the chain at her throat, as if it tethered her to the earth.

My control snapped shut like a sprung trap. So, I left. Jaw locked. Hands shaking.

Coward.

Since then, I trace the pattern of my weakness the way a

tactician studies a map: dawns spent hidden in the gum trees across the road; shadows stitched into the hedge line; two steps inside the café door when the bell sings my poor decisions. Each moment another fracture in my discipline.

I hold distance like a shield. Practise the only mercy I can still claim — coldness, aloof a mask.

Because I know the truth: if I let the warmth in, I will claim her. And if I claim her, I will mark her as mine. If she is marked, I will paint a target on her back large enough for an entire court to aim at if not the realm. The bond isn't a tether. It's a brand. And I will not do that to my goddess who happens to be mortal.

"Still haunting her doorway?" Maricus ghosts to my shoulder without a sound — because he enjoys reminding me I'm not the only thing that moves in shadows. He's my Fíralen when I'm wise, my ruin when I'm not. We've bled together for centuries; I know the rhythm of his breathing in battle better than my own, just as he knows mine.

He stands easy now, hands buried in his pockets, smile lazy. Only his eyes tell the truth — too sharp, too knowing, catching the scent of weakness-like blood on water.

"Never thought I'd see you like this," he murmurs, voice low enough to slide between the ribs slicing deep. "The great Sun Prince, orbiting a mortal. If the courts knew..."

I don't turn to him. "They won't. And they can never know." My voice is the blade I wish I could draw. Maricus chuckled, low and knowing.

"You always believe you can hold the line. But no one holds a storm forever, Aodh. Sooner or later, lightning breaks — and it rarely strikes where you think it will." His smile sharpened, eyes flicking toward the doorway.

"And your presence alone is enough to draw attention. The Sceptre, perhaps... or something much more tempting."

His words slide under my skin, but I keep my eyes on her window — the light spilling through it, the shadow of her moving past. My shield. My weakness. My impossible.

"Report," I say, voice flat, unwilling to give him the satisfaction of curiosity.

"I sent it to Ellisar already — nothing but circles. Sightings, shifting hands. Humans would have auctioned it if they knew its value," he drawls, every syllable a lazy hook. "Or were you asking about the Sylvari I dragged out of her hedgerow last night?"

Heat flares under my skin. "You told me he was gone."

"I told you he would be," he says lightly. "He is — for now. But he's not acting alone."

"The Fire Court?"

Maricus's mouth flattens. "They're sniffing. And they're patient, which I hate. Patience means a plan, and intent." He slants me a look, eyes glinting dark as oil. "You sure you want to keep playing statue out here? Because your restraint's starting to look like an invitation. Any Fae in your position would've snapped by now — or combusted."

"It's protection," I bite out. "For her."

"For you," he says, quiet now. "Don't dress it prettier than it is. She's not as breakable as she looks."

He shifts, shoulder brushing mine. "You think hiding her in plain sight will work forever? You think the bond you're choking down isn't a beacon? You're the Sun Prince — the courts gossip like crows. The prophecy's been sung since before your mother's first war. They'll smell you on her skin before you even touch her. And then?" He shrugs. "Then she's a pawn. Or bait. A trap you set — willingly or not."

I don't answer. Because he's right. And he's wrong. And I don't bother telling him which parts. His smile cuts sideways. "She's beautiful, though, isn't she? All that stubborn fire wrapped in mortal skin. No crown. No court. She doesn't even know what she is to you. That's the worst of it." His voice softens — turns dangerous. "You sure you want to leave that unclaimed? Because if you don't claim her, someone else will."

My hands clench. "No one will touch her. Not even you."

Maricus laughs, low and delighted at the slip. "I don't have to. Others will try. You've made her a story now, Aodh. You've made her a myth before she even knows the word for it." He watches her through the glass with me for a moment, though he knows better than to push further.

Inside, she laughs at something the barista says. The café's noise folds around that sound like hands around a candle. I feel it in my chest — a knot loosening. For a dangerous heartbeat there is no court, no sceptre, no father's voice. Only the shape of her mouth as it curves. Only that. My own mouth betrays me, lifting in an echo of hers.

"She's human," Maricus murmurs, as if he can smell the line I'm about to cross. "And you're an idiot."

"I know." The words taste like ash. "That's why I stay out here."

He huffs — something between laughter and disgust. "For how long?"

"As long as it takes."

"To do what?" he presses. "Prove your father right? Or prove the prophecy wrong?"

I don't answer. Because I don't know. Because if I open my mouth, I'll say the word my blood screams every time she looks my way.

Mine.

Maricus's smile is sharp as a blade's edge. "You'll choke on restraint before you starve the bond out of you." He clapped my shoulder once — too sharp to be comfort, too familiar to be insult — and then slipped back into the hedgerow. He left words behind like shards: Sylvari. A plan. Be patient.

Then, softer — amused. *Restraint never lasts forever, Aodh.*

A trail of unease, laid deliberately, waiting for me to trip over it later. I should be the storm. I should move. Instead, I stand and count the beats between her breaths.

The café empties slowly, the midday crowd dissolving into the mountain roads. Through the glass, she leans a hip against the counter and rubs the spot beneath her ribs. She doesn't know she does it. No one notices — except me.

My feet take two steps closer to the door before I stop them with a general's command. I remember my father's lesson: Want nothing. Need nothing. Love nothing you cannot afford to lose. He taught it with a blade in one hand and a leather strap in the other, the wind rattling the palace glass like bones in a cup. The

Air Rívaran loved his speeches. He could speak of war like it was a hymn — just as he could punish those who doubted his gospel.

I loved very little. And yet here I am — outside a mortal café, training my heartbeat to slow while the girl inside laughs with flour on her wrist, and every part of me that isn't steel moves toward her anyway.

But the bond doesn't care for lessons. It's old magic — older than courts, older than crowns — wild as the first lightning to kiss a mountain. It moves under my skin like a living thing, gnawing at marrow, threading through sinew until every pulse is hers. It's changing me in ways I can't name.

My magic — a lattice of storm-script — heat when she's near, lines glowing faintly under the glamour like molten filigree. I grind my will against them until the shine dulls. She hasn't seen. Thank the goddess, she hasn't seen.

Yet restraint costs me. The bond flares each time I turn away, pain sparking through my chest like cracked glass under pressure. It feels like denying air, like strangling myself on silence. Every time I resist, it carves deeper.

And then she tilts her head. The light catches faint scars at her wrist — human scars. Work. Carelessness. Survival. I shouldn't want to map them with my mouth. I shouldn't want to know each story carved into her skin. But my thoughts kneel anyway — a blasphemy small and absolute.

A cup rattles on a saucer. Another tremor. The veil is thinnest around places built on welcome and repetition — cafés, homes, cemeteries, thresholds. Someone presses at this one from the other side, testing the seams. The air tastes briefly of scorched resin. Nyxie — the dog with night in her coat — lifts her head, staring at the rosemary bush as though it stared first. My hands ache to draw wards, to burn the threat back into silence.

I don't. Not yet. The instant I stake ground here, I brand her as mine. Our enemies would see it as proof written in fire. So I stay at the edges, swallowing the fury, swallowing the ache that claws from the inside.

She turns, and the simple arc of her body drags heat across every raw nerve I own. I am half-wild with the need to walk in —

to ask for nothing, take nothing, just breathe beside her. Instead, I turn my back and carve the need out of myself with discipline. Again. Again. Again. Until my chest feels hollowed with knives.

Night finds me at the ridge line above her property. I hold the sky until it steadies me, until the quarrel inside my ribs lowers its blades.

Maricus finds me, because of course he does. He's not just any Fíralen. He's the second Fíralen — the one who taught me the cruelties that kept me alive long enough to wear a title.

He stands where I can see him — and where, if I need to, I can push him off the cliff. That's how we speak love to each other.

"Explain," I say again.

"Two scouts from the Fire Court in the gully after sundown," he answers, voice casual. "They're keeping a respectful distance from your temper. Either smarter than they look, or ordered to watch — not poke."

"Orders change."

"Mm." His gaze drops to the house lights below. "You should tell her."

"Tell her what?"

"That you're a crazy stalker who's fallen deep," he says, mouth curling. "That magic is real. That gods play games with mortals."

"She doesn't believe in gods or magic." The words snap out before I can stop them. "She believes in getting the pastry case stocked before the morning rush. She believes in making sure her son eats breakfast."

Maricus cackles. "You mean the same son you mistook for a lover?" I groan, heat flaring at the memory. Humiliation burns sharp and fast.

"She believes in checking the alley twice after close," I continue, voice tightening, "because a man in town won't stop lingering near the bins. Waiting. Watching." My hands clench against the wind. "She believes in not breaking."

Maricus goes very still. For all his ruin and mockery, there are lines he does not cross — and men who stalk women are one of them.

His voice drops to flat steel.

"Name?"

"Evans," I say. "Human. Thinks he's subtle."

I let the next words sharpen until they cut. "He's careless. I've warned him already."

Memory unfurls — cold. Precise.

I'd caught him outside at dusk, skulking near the rubbish bins where the security lights stuttered and failed more often than they should. Watching. Waiting. Too close to the house. Too close to Lily.

I wrapped myself in glamour before he ever knew I was there, bending the dying light so it slid off me like glare and dust. I stepped into his shadow and whispered his name straight into his ear.

He jolted like prey.

I told him exactly what would happen if he lingered again. If he watched her. If he unsettled her — or anyone under her protection. Each word was shaped with magic. Not enough to bind him. Not enough to brand him. Just enough to lodge deep, a splinter he would never quite reach.

His eyes went blank as I spoke, the memory dissolving even as it formed — recognition stripped clean by the glamour. Then I leaned closer. I told him that the next time I saw his face near her home, there would be no warning. Only the sound of his last breath, and flesh torn from bone.

He forgot my face. He did not forget the fear. I smiled as the wet stain spread down the front of his trousers.

Maricus's eyes narrowed, the corner of his mouth ticking with interest as the present snapped back into place.

"Do you want him gone?"

For a moment, the thought tempts me — quick, brutal, efficient. The kind of solution the Air Court would favour. The kind my father would expect.

The answer tears free before I can leash it. "Yes." The honesty shocks me — burns in my throat. "But not by your hand. Not yet.

If he's a leash for a Sylvari pack, I want the hand that holds it." A snarl forms in the crook of my mouth.

Maricus hums with approval low and pleased. We stand in silence, two predators with centuries of blood on our blades and hands, both learning the new scent of fear curling from Misty Ridge below.

At length, he says, almost kindly, "You can't keep her at arm's length forever, Aodh."

"I can try."

"And what of the storm brewing, Aodh?"

"I'll contain it."

"I wasn't talking about yours." His gaze tilts downhill, toward her light. "I was talking about hers."

The words hit and keep hitting— sinking under my armour. He's right. She's changing. The earth leans toward her when she walks. Vines turn. Leaves shiver. Blossoms open out of season, as if they remember her. She's human, and she's not. A contradiction that shouldn't exist and yet every law I know buckles in her presence.

The last time I felt something this old stirring in mortal skin, an empire burned. A war followed. I taste the ash of it still, remnants burnt into every Fae. I let the dark take my face. My voice comes rough as gravel. "We find the sceptre fragment. We move it before Fire does. We keep her name out of every mouth that might whisper it to a crown."

"And if the fragment's tied to her?" Maricus asks, too softly.

"Then we cut the rope," I snarl. "Or we hang whoever tied it — and keep her safe."

His grin cuts wide, teeth bright in the dark.

"There he is — my love-sick, violent bastard."

"Shut up." The words are a growl, but the bite steadies me. Resolve is a crude drug — it leaves you shaking, but it works.

Maricus shifts, stepping into the wind beside me like the commander he's always been. "Come on. You've been putting off the inevitable. If we're going to ground this without setting the sky on fire, we need the Earth Court."

I do not flinch. But my magic does. It writhes in my veins

at the name, storm light uneasy, as if the bond itself recognises where she belongs before I will admit it aloud.

Buried halls. Root and stone. Damp, heavy air where sunlight dies. The opposite of my blood, my birthright. I was made for sky and storm, not the earth's slow pulse. I'd rather fight blindfolded on a glass bridge in a gale than crawl beneath a mountain and call it mercy.

But the Earth Court keeps the oldest records — the ones written before crowns. If there's a way to sever a bond, or bend it without breaking the one bound, they will have the myth of it, if not the method. And if there isn't — if there has never been — then the truth I've been avoiding will stand up and name itself: that I am already lost.

"To the mountain, then," I say, trying not to sound like a man walking into a tomb. The wind doesn't bother hiding its hiss of amusement at my expense.

Maricus claps me on the back hard enough to stagger me a step, his grin a blade. "Shall I obtain a photo of you, so you can continue your creepy wistful stare?"

"Bring a shovel."

He snorts. "For the bodies or your feelings?"

"Both," I tell him, and for once the sound that leaves my throat is almost a laugh. It rings hollow in the dark. He grins wider, but his eyes flick to the house below and then back to me. We both know why we're joking — Fíralen' humour before a bad march.

When I look down again, the laughter tastes like surrender. The café's windows flare gold as she moves through the rooms turning out the lights, and that glow catches in my bones like a hook.

It's the only hearth I've ever wanted. Mine, the bond whispers again — inexorable. A drumbeat under my skin.

CHAPTER 12

Aodhan POV

The mountain swallows light. It doesn't matter that the Earth Court's seeds glow, moss spilling luminescence into the cracks of its halls, or that lanterns burn with bottled lightning strung along the passages. The dark here is suffocating. It clings to the skin—heavy, pressing—tasting of mineral and rain and the copper tang buried deep within clay.

The stone hums with memory. Roots twist through the ceiling like ribs, gnarled and pulsing faintly with sap and dew. Water moves in unseen caverns not trickling, but speaking to the earth — in an older tongue than crowns, steady as heartbeats, certain as time.

Every instinct I own recoils. I am air and fire; I crave the open sky. I am built for speed, for height, for flinging myself into the gale and daring gravity to catch me. But here, the earth presses its hand over every nerve, squeezing my magic down until it thrums low and contained. And I do not like to be confined.

"Breathe through it," Maricus murmurs — he, too, longing for the open sky. He's walked these roads before. He knows me too well. He also knows that if he smirks now, I'll plant his teeth in the nearest stone. "In through the nose. Think of why we're here, or shall I bring out that photo now..."

"I'm thinking of how fast I can be out of here," I mutter.

He chuckles, the sound echoing through the cavern, and gestures toward the arch ahead. "Then don't annoy our host. Just ask what we need so we can leave — you know how Varyn can drawl."

Before I can respond, the inner gate unfurls like a fern in spring. Vines peel back from the stone, revealing a doorway veined with quartz and etched in filigree — crowns, leaves, antlers. A scent rolls out: not perfume, not spell-work, but life itself — green sap, crushed herbs, rain striking warm soil. For a heartbeat, my shoulders ease despite myself.

This magic is like hers. And a pang strikes deep. Earth magic is strongest here, in the depths of its court. How much do they know of her?

The hall beyond widens — deceptive from the narrow entrance. Pillars the size of towers rise from floor to ceiling, carved not by hand but by root and stone, then claimed and infused with Fae magic until veins of crystal glimmer like lightning frozen in rock.

Gardens unfurl in terraces along the walls, lush with impossible growth: lilies blooming in shadow, vines heavy with fruit that glow faintly like lanterns, trees bowing their boughs to whisper into the ears of those who pass.

Statues line the way, their faces softened by time. They are not Kárith's with swords or kings with crowns, but farmers, healers, gatherers — mortals and Fae alike — immortalised in stone, as though the Earth Court worships not conquest but the ordinary work that binds its people together.

So different from the other Courts, who rule through pride and fear, and would cast out the weak. We walk in silence, Maricus huffs out a breath, folding his arms as he watches me from the corner of his eye.

"Aodhan," he says — half a joke, not entirely. "She's a mortal. Her life is a blink compared to ours. Yet here you are, thinking of her again. What do you even see in her? Yes, she's attractive but you've seen attractive, been with attractive. So what is it? What's the allure?"

Silence settles between us before I answer. I don't rush it. My thoughts drift instead to Lily — not what she represents, not what the bond demands, but the woman herself.

A faint smile tugs at my mouth before I can stop it. "She works," I say finally. "Relentlessly. Up every morning, seeing to the children first. The love she gives them… it isn't something we cultivate in the Fae realm. Not like that."

I glance away, my focus turning inward. "And it's her kindness. The quiet kind. The way she treats strangers as if they matter. She pauses to check on the elderly couple who come into the café every day. Helps a mother carry groceries to her car without being asked. Kneels to hug a child who's tripped and skinned their knee — like the world hasn't just ended for them — and does it with a smile she doesn't realise is rare."

My jaw tightens. The air shifts. "I've heard the whispers about her husband," I continue, slower now. "How she lost him. Brutally. Sudden. Even for a human, it was… wrong. Too violent. Almost as brutal as one of ours seeking retribution." The words leaves a bitter taste. "The kind of death that leaves damage behind."

Something old and sharp coils in my chest. "And yet, with all that grief pulling at her, she still stands. She hasn't lost her light. She hasn't hardened or turned cruel." My gaze lifts, steady now. "The resilience she shows — especially to that bastard Evans — isn't weakness. There's fire in her." A pause. "Controlled, patient" I add. "She's dangerous. A fire."

A breeze curls around my shoulders, air responding to my honesty, to the freedom of speaking these thoughts aloud. My magic hums, lighter than it has any right to be.

"She radiates something," I murmur. "Something I can't look away from. Yes, she's stunning — enough to steal my breath when I least expect it. But there's more to her than that. Depth. Strength. A quiet defiance." I exhale slowly. "I want to know all of it. I want to unravel her not because the bond demands it… but because she's her…Lily."

For a moment, Maricus says nothing. A shadow crosses his face — not mockery, not quite amusement. Then he snorts. "Wipe that ridiculous, lovesick look off your face before you make me nauseous." But the bite is gone. "I didn't think I'd ever hear words like that come out of you, I regret asking."

Neither did I.

Somewhere ahead, the throne room waits — not glass and marble like the Air Court, but carved straight from the mountain's heart. Earth's honesty and humility show even in its simplicity.

"Prince Aodhan."

Varyn steps forward from the shadow of a root-pillar, the mountain's silence parting for him like mist at dawn. The Earth Court emissary is shorter than me by a head, but he carries a kind of weight that makes height irrelevant. Built like an oak that has learned to bend without breaking, his presence is steady and immovable.

His hair is the grey of river stone, braided tight against his skull, threaded with flowers, twigs, and small antlers. His skin is the warm brown of sunlit soil after rain; his eyes, a muted green that sees everything and gives nothing away. He bows — hands open, palms stained with the black of loam that still carries the scent of root and earth.

"Varyn," I return, offering the bow his rank and reputation demand. My voice is flint against granite. "I need your discretion."

"You usually do not ask so politely — so typical of Air to demand answers without a proper tribute," he replies. His mouth curves, though the lines at his eyes suggest laughter is no stranger to him. "Come. The mountain listens better when we walk. It will decide if you're worthy of answers."

We move side by side through halls carved along the grain of the rock, never against it. That is the first law of Earth: build with, not on. The walls ripple with the centuries, untouched save for the shaping hands that coaxed the natural veins into pattern rather than cutting them away — their magic strengthening the earth as the earth fuels theirs.

The floor beneath us is a mosaic of river stones, flecked with mica that catches the lantern-light and scatters it up the walls like fragments of fallen stars. Somewhere deeper, someone sings — a low work-song, guttural and steady, carried along the tunnels not for ears but for roots. To help them remember where to grow, where to stop. To remind the mountain that those who dwell in its bones mean no harm. The sound threads through my ribs, strange and hollow.

I crave the voice of the wind, the freedom of the sky.

We pass a curtain of hanging vines that breathe dampness into the air. Children laugh behind it — bright, quick notes of joy — and the vines sway with them, shaking their leaves in rhythm, echoing that laughter like a secret passed back and forth, protecting their most vulnerable.

My chest tightens, unwillingly, with memory. Her laugh. Light falling through her café windows. The way ordinary things bend toward her without knowing why. The sound of her smile when she speaks to her children. How I was a fool to assume her son was a lover. I groan quietly at my own stupidity and glance at Maricus, wanting more than ever to punch him square in the jaw.

"You walk like a hawk in a cave," Varyn observes mildly, drawing me back. "Everything in you wants to lift, to strike, to fly. But you will find no sky here."

"You know exactly how Air feels when it's trapped," I answer. "But I'll endure. I need answers."

He inclines his head, expression unreadable. "Answers are like mantle, Prince. You don't take them, you dig for them and earn it. And mantle does not yield quickly." Patience. Always patience. Earth wears down fire and air alike with that word. I grit my teeth and keep walking. Patience I do not have.

"Your timing is poor," Varyn says, not as censure but as fact. Earth rarely judges; it endures, and its truths are layered, much like this court. His voice carries that same patience. "The Fire Court pushes West. They have no respect for borders or balances. Should you not be watching their advance toward the sisters of the verdant veil and the wyvern territory?"

"The witches and wyvern were a distraction," I reply, the words grinding flatter than intended, tasting of iron. I force my jaw to ease. "I have people watching them. I'm here for something else — something older."

"You always are, when you arrive without an army or courtesy." He tilts his head, and the stone-grey braids shift; petals unfurl and fall to the ground. "What do you seek this time, Sun Prince?"

"A story that could lead to truth," I say. The word itself is harder to speak than any battle order. "Older than politics. Older than courts. I need to know what kind of magic could hide something that should never have been hidden."

At that, a flicker of interest bends his mouth — small, but genuine. "Ah. All stories hold a form of truth, Prince Aodhan. We just need to find the one that remembers correctly."

He leads us down a passage that slopes like a root toward deep soil, no entrance in sight. Trees unfurl at Varyn's touch, and we enter the Archive Grove. Maricus sucks in a breath beside me. The deeper we go, the more our magic recoils. It is no library — not as Air keeps one. No rigid stacks of vellum or chained tomes. No scribes hunched and muttering over ink. Air's libraries are clean, sterile. This place is alive.

The chamber opens like something grown, not carved. Roots rise from the floor in spirals and loops, some as thick as trunks, others fine as hair. Moss blankets whole swathes of wall, its surface patterned with glow-worms in shifting constellations. If you press your ear close, you can hear them — whispers caught and kept, old voices murmuring to the patient listener.

"Leave your weapons," Varyn says, gesturing to a shallow basin carved from a single boulder. The stone is wet, dark as spilled ink. "Earth does not favour those who spill blood—or those who cut the ground unnecessarily. These will be your tributes to the mountain."

Maricus sighs, unbuckling three blades I can see and two I can't, dropping them into the basin one by one. They vanish soundlessly into the stone, swallowed as though the mountain itself has claimed them. My hand lingers on my sword. Setting it down feels like scraping the skin from my ribs. Every nerve screams: a Kárith without their weapon is careless. I force my grip to loosen, finger by finger, and lower the blade.

The stone accepts it with a heavy silence. Varyn's eyes soften; there is no mockery in the tilt of his mouth. "You can keep the little one in your boot," he allows, voice dry as shale. "So your pride survives the visit."

Maricus smirks and whispers, "Good. One of us should keep a knife handy—even if it's strapped to your ego."

I ignore them both. Yet when the runes along the nearest root brighten faintly — as though acknowledging me — the bond to Lily in my chest tugs harder. Her face. Her voice. Even here, deep beneath stone.

"My pride thanks you," I mutter, though the corner of my mouth betrays me, tugging up despite myself.

Earth will decide whether it answers. We kneel before a root older than maps, older than crowns. Its bark is ridged like scar tissue, veins of crystal running through it as though lightning once kissed the grain and was trapped there forever. Varyn lays his earth-stained palm against it and hums a note so low it thrums in my chest before I hear it. The root warms beneath our touch. Runes flare, slow and deliberate, until flickering images rise from the grain—

A woman with vines braided through her hair, eyes alight with verdant fire.

A man with storm-light in his gaze, wind coiling at his heels.

A sceptre, whole, burning with balance.

Then the fracture — a sound like stone splitting under frost. Six shards scatter like fish slipping through a net into four rivers of power. They vanish: into mud, into salt, into fire, into cloud.

"Rívalis Ailith and the Sceptre of Elemental Unity," Varyn murmurs, reverent. "Every court keeps its version of this tale. Ours is the least pretty, I'm told."

"Because yours doesn't distort the truth," Maricus says dryly, arms folded.

"Because ours remembers the cost of history — and what it means if repeated," Varyn corrects, gentle but firm, like a teacher smoothing a reckless child. His moss-dark eyes find mine, unblinking. "You did not come for history. Say it plain, Prince. My mountain appreciates honesty — do not waste its time."

The words stick in my throat. I am heir to Air; we do not speak plain. We obscure, deflect, cloak truth in riddles. But this mountain has no patience for masks. And I... no longer have the luxury of deception.

"There is a human woman on the mountain," I say at last. Human. The word feels like a bluff. "Since the accident months past, magic bends around her — as though it knew her name before I did. Plants lean. Portals hold for her. Even the air listens." My chest tightens. "I need to know what that means."

"Ah." Varyn's eyes sharpen, the patience of stone cutting clean. "Then the rumours are not merely Fire's."

The ground stills. My pulse does not.

"What rumours?"

He does not hurry in response. "Whispers," he says — and that is worse than reports. "Of a mortal who walks like the heir of a living court. Of trees and earth bowing when she passes. Of a guardian's presence — old magic like no other." His gaze holds mine, steady as bedrock. "And of a prince who lingers where he should not."

Maricus coughs a laugh into his fist — the bastard. I do not look at him. My control barely contained.

"If you have something to say, speak plainly," I tell Varyn, voice sharp as sleet. "Ask what you want and be done. Do not waste my time."

Varyn smiles — gentle, kind. "You asked for honesty." He presses his earth-stained palm back to the root. "Then listen." The wood shivers beneath our hands. Light ripples through the grain and pulls us in.

A child — mortal, fierce — laughing at a dog black as midnight with eyes lit with fire and amber.

Her joy rings against stone until even the roots seem to lean in.

A woman bends presses a kiss to the child's brow, and the air hums as if the mountain itself has taken a vow.

Then a man steps forward. Old. Power overwhelming. Extraordinary in the way only guardians are. He lifts the child, holds her as though she is an oath. The moss-voice whispers: guardian. His face is obscured — but familiar all the same.

Power nets around the girl a weave of light — sinking into

her bones like water into soil. The vision shudders, skips. Years turn like pages. The girl grows, unbowed: childhood, teens, then adulthood. She refuses to yield to anything but love. I see her in a wedding dress, kissing a man, a child born. She's in her café and then she looks up. The net holds — until it snaps.

A flare of iridescent light races down an unseen line, tearing silence into the dark.

Lily. My mind names her before I can stop it. Everything tilts. A thousand choices I have not yet made lean toward ruin.

The root goes quiet under our palms, pulsing as though catching its breath.

"Sometimes," Varyn says softly, "a guardian will oversee a family for centuries a line that remains pure—."

"Don't say her name." The snarl tears free before I can stop it. My voice cracks the air like a whip. "Not to the roots. Not to the moss. Not to anyone. She must be kept safe. This is not her fight."

Varyn does not flinch. Earth does not fear storms; it outlives them. "Then do not make me say it," he replies mildly. "Tell me instead why you came without invitation. Why you sought this information about this human."

"Because I don't want another to learn this first." The words scrape raw. "I need to know if a bond can be coerced. If a sceptre fragment could warp fate. If someone could tie two souls never meant to be bound."

"And if the answer is no?" Varyn's voice is steady as bedrock, his eyes piercing.

"Then the answer is worse." My throat tightens. "Then the bond is true, and she was kept from me." The silence that follows isn't empty — it grows. Roots creak overhead as if listening, the moss at our knees pulsing once in time with my heart. The mountain holds its breath.

Varyn studies me as though reading a chart. "You do not want it," he says at last. Not accusation, just fact. "You fear what it will make of her."

"I...I fear what I will make of her," I answer, the words falling like stones. "I was forged into a weapon. I grew up with my prophecy for a lullaby and war councils for lessons. Everything

I touch becomes a lever in someone else hand. If Fire learns her name, they'll use her throat as a scabbard for their power. If Air learns it"—I bite down on the word father until it tastes like metal—"they'll use her as a lesson to me."

"And you?" Varyn asks quietly. "What would you use her for?"

"Nothing. Just to let her live. To see her move through that café like sunlight through storm clouds—to hear her laugh, watch her smile at her children, feel her temper spark when she looks at me. To embrace..." The confession rips free before I can stop it. I shut my eyes, disbelief twisting through me that I've let the truth slip—raw, exposed, and far too real. Maricus' hand lands on my shoulder—a blow that steadies rather than comforts.

The emissary exhales, and the grove exhales with him. "There are stories," he says at last, "of bonds that should have been but were not. A coercion. A trick. A correction yet to be made, some called it — as if the world remembered something kings tried to make it forget." His smile is small and tired. "But Prince, your magic is powerful; the guardian was there to protect, not to hide her power. She was intentionally blocked from you — that is a deep and dangerous spell of old."

"Sisters of the Verdant Veil?" I hiss.

Varyn looks at me; a sigh forms. "Possibly. But we cannot confirm unless we capture the spell maker."

I pause, breathing heavy, rage coiling like iron in my gut. "Can it be hidden?" My voice is raw. "Not broken — hidden, so she walks free of the target."

"Hidden," Varyn repeats, tasting the word. "Perhaps. But hiding is not safety. We could muffle the bond beneath your skin so Fire doesn't taste it on the wind. We could weave you both inside a slow-growing seed until the world forgets to look. But it will cost."

"What?"

"Time," he says simply. "And choice. When the seed blossoms and breaks free, all that contained power could be unleashed at once."

Time. Choice. Two things I've never been granted — two she still has. To steal either from her feels like carving into my own palms. "No," I say, hoarse. "Not if it takes that from her. She must choose."

The moss pulses — agreement. Varyn's gaze goes cold.

Maricus' hand tightens once, then drops away. His silence speaks all the truths he won't voice: she's already marked; they're already moving; you're already too deep.

"I'll find the fragment," I say. "Before Fire does. Before anyone else finds her, I'll have the Sceptre whole or destroy it completely."

Varyn inclines his head. The plants coil as though they have received too much sun.

The weight of stone presses down — ancient, knowing. I clamp my jaw until the ache swallows the threat of tears. "You want me to make the choice for her," I say.

"I'm telling you," Varyn replies, gaze unblinking, "the war already chose *you*."

A gong sounds — stone against stone, deep and resonant. The air shivers through my bones, a summons older than language. Varyn rises, loam still on his palms. "Come. There's someone you should meet."

We follow him. The corridor narrows, roots curling overhead. The smell shifts — less moss, more river, sharp mineral that clings to the tongue. The space widens again, my magic stirring beneath the surface.

The passage breaks open and the sight drives the air from my chest. A cavern vast enough to house a kingdom yawns before us. Stalactites glazed in mica scatter lantern-light like stars dragged underground. A river runs the length of one wall, its bed threaded with glow-worms in ribbons of blue light.

And trees. Great oaks and slender birches, roots sunk into sacred soil, trunks wrapped in moss that glows faintly where roots kiss stone. Earth magic hums here — ancient, potent. I recognise the runes carved into the rock. Between the trees, a platform rises from polished blackwood, lanterns shaped like seedpods casting amber light.

On the platform, a woman waits.

Shit.

Her hair is dark as tilled soil, threaded with copper. Her skin, the deep brown of rain-warmed earth. Her eyes — steady purple, unblinking as the mountain. Draped in a gown the colour of lichen and shadow, she radiates a power that makes even Maricus — smiling bastard that he is — shift his stance.

Varyn inclines his head. "High Warden Nivara. She will decide your next move."

Her gaze settles on me, slow and thorough, as if peeling back every layer of glamour and magic. "Sun Prince," she says, voice like roots splitting stone. "You've dragged the sky beneath the mountain. Let's see if you can stand without it."

Nivara doesn't bow. Her small, sharp smile is utterly unthreatened. "You smell like the Sun," she says. "And bad decisions. Same as a century ago."

Maricus laughs loud enough to wake ghosts. "Oh, fuck."

Nivara only shrugs. "Don't flatter yourself, Sun Prince. What we had was a season, not a sentence. You were meant to make me your consort, remember? Instead, you made excuses. And now — " she flicks her fingers as though scattering ash " — I aim higher than a boy hiding from his crown."

Maricus grins. "Intimate once, ignored after — and she still sounds every bit bitter."

"Shut up. Don't give her anything," I warn, voice flat as thunder.

Nivara laughs, low and certain. "Please. I've had lovers since who could shatter mountains with a kiss. I'm not in the habit of mourning what's outgrown." She steps closer, roots shifting aside. "You didn't come here to relive old bed-talk. You came because you're bleeding magic where you shouldn't be, and Fire can track it — which will ruin all our plans."

Her eyes drop to my forearm where, sigils pulse faintly, betraying me. "You need a silence-wreath. It won't mask you forever, but it'll keep the bond from humming every time you think about touching her." The corner of her mouth crooks. "Which, judging by that twitch, is often."

"I don't — "

"Save the denial," she cuts in, tone sharp as ever. She takes my wrist, uninvited, pinching the inside where storm-script thrums. Magic snaps under my skin like a stretched band, then releases. The bond's hum dulls; the ache in my chest loosens. I exhale, realising I'd been holding a breath. Then Empty.

Realisation hits.

"What the fuck did you just do? I said she should decide!" I spin to Varyn; rage slams into me like a physical thing — betrayal first, then a cold, animal panic as Lily's presence thins to a whisper. For the first time in months, the air around me doesn't vibrate with her name.

"Better?" Nivara says, releasing my wrist as if she's only straightened a cuff. Magic peels off me in ragged waves. Varyn steps forward, hands low; stone answers him, rising at his command to pin the spill. I look at Nivara and taste blood—a hard, bright promise. I have never wanted to tear a body limb from limb, throat-open and raw, and shove what's left into the earth, as I want to now.

"You've betrayed my trust, Varyn." The words leave me like a blade. My wings ache to burst free; power claws under my skin, hot and vicious.

Maricus's voice threads through the hush — low, unamused, and deadly. "Not allies, Aodhan. Not yet." The warning is a blade against my teeth. The urge to kill roars, absolute and immediate. I clamp down on it until my jaw aches, until the mountain might split beneath me.

Nivara's smile thins to a blade. "It's dulled. Don't feed the bond." Her voice is silk and sickening. "But you'll bring her here — not now, not soon. When she's ready. When the earth calls. You'll bring her. And you'll do the one thing you hate most." She savours the scowl—slow, deliberate. "You'll ask for help."

My wings cleave forth. Power surges, raw and hot, flaring from me until the soil at my feet blackens. I taste iron. I taste intent. "I'd rather die than hand her to you." My voice is low and hungry. The next words come like a knife. "Parasite. Every word from your mouth is poison." Rage is a living thing under my skin. I could peel her open. Strip her to bone. Feed the dirt on her blood. I could drag Nivara by the hair and watch the mountain drink her.

Images strike fast — scouts in the gully, a Sylvari's grin like a blade, my father's voice a ledger of punishments. And Lily — always Lily — twisting her ring, pretending she is not a hair's breadth from falling. "If she's hurt because of this, I will take your head."

The words are measured. Cold as the back of a blade. "I will stake you and set your Court to ash. I will make the Sun Prince's name a curse on every tongue that once bowed to you. It will be slow. And I will relish in it."

For the first time, Nivara's smile wavers. Fear slips through the cracks — not of a prince, but of the bloodied one standing before her.

"Get out of my mountain," she says, voice thin as steel. "Before your magic burns the trees."

I do not lower my hands. I do not temper my magic coiled tight in my chest. But the promise settles under my skin like a lit coal. I will not forget. I will not forgive this betrayal.

Maricus laughs as we leave. "A consort scorned, a betrayal, a broken prophecy — Aodh, your past outshines any Fire Court spectacle."

"She was a parasite then," I spit. Rage tastes like iron.

Varyn comes forward slow, hands open. "Only the useful are unbearable. This will help — learn each other without the bond, Sun Prince. You might not see it yet; she matters far more than you think. And this will teach you to love her as a human without the Bond."

"My threat stands." I close on him, voice a blade. "If she is harmed because of this, I will take Nivara's head from her shoulders and watch your Court burn around you. I do not take back my words."

The sky cut with stars — the kind you only get on a ridge where the air bites. I rolled my shoulders for the wind and felt the silence under my skin like a muted string. Nivara's wreath held. The bond's hum was dulled; my magic had seared part of the wreath. Relief should have come. Instead there was a hollow I couldn't name.

Maricus eased like a cat freed from a cage, grin dragging across his face. "Gods, I've missed her. Nivara hasn't lost her edge — or her mouth. Did she remind you of your bed habits, or spare you the shame?"

My look was cold enough to cut. "Nothing happened. You know that." He laughed, amused and clean. "Don't pout — it suits her more. Watching you threaten a Court was worth the climb."

I stop long enough to let him feel the weight of my words. "You can't compare them. Nivara was nothing a choice born of duty and distraction, one I couldn't commit to. She was insufferable. But Lily — " My throat tightens. "Lily is everything. She makes the air easier to breathe. She makes simplicity feel like peace. I can't imagine a realm without her in it."

For once, his grin falters. Then it creeps back, slow and wicked. "That silence-wreath must be slipping. You're sounding downright sentimental, Aodh. Careful — another speech like that and I'll think you've gone soft."

My jaw clenches. "Soft is the last thing I feel when it comes to her."

Maricus laughs, sharp and pleased. "That's better. Obsession disguised as restraint. Noble words wrapped around filthy thoughts — all while you imagine exactly how you'd take her in that cosy little café she thinks keeps her safe."

I start down the ridge path, wind tugging at my sleeves. He keeps pace, too amused to shut up.

"She's right, you know," Maricus goes on. "You can't smother this thing forever. A silence-wreath's just a patch on a dam that's already cracked. What happens when you finally let yourself feel it again—full force? What happens when she does? We also can't make them an enemy now, not when we are so close Aodhan."

I don't answer. My jaw ticks, teeth locked until the muscle jumps. The question lodges under my ribs like a thorn.

He smirks. "Ah. That's the real terror, isn't it? Not Fire finding her. Not Air claiming her. Not even the sceptre. It's her. What she'll do when she looks at you and doesn't see a prince or a prophecy — just a man. Not human, but Fae."

I stop. Night pulls taut around us. My voice is rougher than I intend.

"That's what I fear most. Because if she sees me — really sees me — she won't stay." For once Maricus doesn't laugh. He slaps my shoulder hard enough to jar bone.

"Or she will. And then you're fucked."

He straightens: the Fíralen sliding out from under the jester. "And what now?"

"Now I hunt." The words fall — sharp, final. "We monitor the café. We watch the hedgerow. We move the fragment if it's here. And when we find who wrote lies into my prophecy—" I bare my teeth. "—we take their court."

My eyes are already caught on the ridge below. A single square of golden light glows against the dark — her window. She moves across the room in silhouette, loose hair catching the lamplight. Even from this distance, the sight knocks the air from my chest.

The silence-wreath around my wrist dampens the bond's song, muffles the way it wants to scream her name into the marrow of the world. But it does nothing to touch the worship. It never will.

My Lily. My goddess.

CHAPTER 13

Lily POV

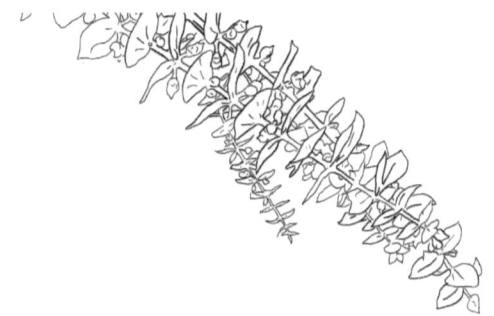

Sleep doesn't come easily.

When it finally does, it feels... quieter. The thread in my chest — that constant, maddening feeling, I've tried so hard to ignore — disappears. For the first time since the accident, the air doesn't feel like it's pressing against me, waiting, demanding I notice something just beyond reach.

I should feel free. Instead, I feel... hollow. Empty. Nyxie stirs at the foot of the bed — a ripple of muscle and fur, ears flicking restlessly.

When sleep drags me under, it doesn't give me the forked road this time. No Caleb walking toward the estate. No iridescent flower glowing like a beacon. There's only warmth. A hand brushing the inside of my wrist, where the scars live. A rough thumb pausing, as though memorising them. A voice I shouldn't crave — low, steady, inescapable, a sound that sends chills to my very core.

You're not alone, Lily.

I wake with my cheeks wet, breath caught halfway between a sob and a laugh — my whole body filled with the ache of something lost. It's the echo of a storm that never broke — restless, wanting, wrong.

Cups stack in neat towers, the milk wands gleam, and I wipe the counter, rotating condiments as the playlist drifts softly from the speakers — fading beneath the gentle scrape of cutlery from the last table.

Normal. Quiet. Safe. That's how it should feel. It doesn't. The air sings with an unfamiliar tension, like something unseen has decided to wake. Since the accident, very little has felt safe — especially now, with strangers slipping into town one by one. Their gazes are sharp as talons, testing boundaries, measuring who might move first. They sit too still — backs straight, shoulders angled like soldiers at rest. They sip once or twice, then linger, eyes too smooth, faces too careful. Far too beautiful to be real. Patient. Waiting.

Earlier this week, I caught one of them staring at the vines threading along the café's front window. His head tilted, lips curling in something that wasn't quite a smile before he leaned toward his companion. The two murmured in low tones, the cadence a language I didn't recognise. Their eyes flicked to me, and my skin prickled as though I'd been pulled into a secret I wasn't meant to hear.

I force myself back into motion — stacking cups, wiping the bench again, letting work drown out thought. Then the door opens. Two figures step in, and the air rearranges as though a storm has slipped through the threshold.

One is dark, poised — quiet and coiled, a weight that settles in the corner of the room. The other is light — handsome, magnetic — every gaze in the café drawn to him.

I always feel him before I see him — the way heat usually

slides over my skin, subtle but insistent, raising the fine hairs along my arms. A tide pressing against the shore, impossible to ignore.

But today... nothing.

Just the hollow ache where it should be.

Maricus. Dark hair cropped and messy, a smile tugging toward a smirk. Eyes sharp, sweeping the café as though assessing threats. He moves like a tiger stalking its prey — confidence oozing from every step. He leans against the far wall, casual as sin, but there's a soldier's patience in the way he waits. When his gaze finally finds me, there's confusion there. Concern. Guilt. But beneath it all, calculation — the kind that belongs to a man who keeps lists, remembers every debt, and always intends to collect.

But when my eyes lift to Aodhan, something inside me shifts — an ache low in my chest, a hollow tug as though something vital has been pressed just out of reach but refuses to vanish. I don't know what it means. I only know it hurts. He fills the doorway — one shoulder braced against the frame as though the building itself might shift beneath his weight.

I shake the thought away just as Caleb's ring spins along its chain, glinting under the café lights. My hand catches it automatically, tucking it back beneath my cardigan — but not before the metal flashes once, and Aodhan's eyes flick to it.

Just a glance. But in that heartbeat, the world tilts. And I know he saw. His eyes find me. Unblinking. Unrelenting. Knowing. The café blurs at the edges; the playlist drops into a hush — as if even the air is holding its breath, waiting for mine.

"Lily," he says, and my name sounds like a quiet prayer.

My heart clenches.

"Afternoon," I manage. The word comes out thinner than I intend. He steps closer, boots whispering over the tiles.

"Lily," he repeats — softer this time, like he's tasting my name to see what it does to both of us. The sound that once sent chills down my spine now falls flat. My hands seize the first thing they can find — a clean towel — and fold it once, twice, eight times, like a ritual. It's a useless motion, but it gives my fingers something to do other than tremble.

"What will it be today?" I offer, because my brain can't function — because it's safer to stick to simple conversation than to delve into the feelings warring inside me.

His smile is small, not reaching his eyes. "I'm here to make sure you're all right."

I blink. He shouldn't be able to unsettle me like this — with a glance that seems to see too much. Yet my chest stutters anyway, and the faint ache under my ribs — that strange pull that's lived in me since the accident — shivers, as if recognising him. I tuck my hand to my side, as though hiding the motion might hide the truth it betrays.

"I'm fine," I say, my voice a pitch too high. It's a lie. One I hope he doesn't notice. He lifts one neat brow, unreadable, and his voice drops low — meant for me alone.

"You don't have to pretend with me," he says. He's stepped back a pace, but his presence hasn't moved at all.

"Whatever this... thing is—" I gesture vaguely between us, too afraid to name it. "You don't have to—"

"I know," he cuts in, quick. "But I want to. I...need to. Being near you..."

He swallows once, as though the confession costs him something. "I feel more at ease."

The words strike like a comet — sudden, brilliant, impossible to ignore. My breath catches. I freeze, because that admission is too large, too intimate to be meant for me.

"That's not—" I begin, but the rest dies on my tongue. Because what else am I supposed to say? That I shouldn't crave his nearness? That the only time this ache quiets is when he's in the room? That his presence both steadies and unravels me?

For a heartbeat, the café ceases to exist. It's just us — his restraint, my confusion, and the air between, alive and waiting. Then the tension snaps. "Well, well." The voice drips satisfaction. "If it isn't my favourite barista. Morning, Lillian."

The room's temperature shifts. The quiet warmth of Aodhan's restraint sharpens — searing and volatile. He doesn't move closer, but his control frays at the edges. "Morning," I manage, though my pulse betrays me, fluttering like a trapped bird.

Maricus takes his time — gaze dragging over me with deliberate insolence.

"You look lovely as always. Although, nothing compares to the other night."

He winks, taunting. "You really ought to wear more sheer and glitter."

Heat rushes to my cheeks. Aodhan's jaw flexes, the faint shimmer beneath his tattoos flaring brighter. "Maricus." Aodhan's voice cut through the air like a blade — quiet, controlled, and sharp enough to still the room. Maricus only smirks wider, closing the gap between us until the spice-laced edge of his cologne tangles with the coffee and citrus.

"What's the matter, Aodh?" Maricus drawled. "Are we feeling? Or is it more..." His gaze slid to me — deliberate, intimate, cruel. "...empty today?"

The storm inside Aodhan became a living thing. Heat pressed sharp against my skin, the air thickening as his entire body went taut — drawn steel held a breath from striking.

"You should be careful what you say next," he warned, voice low.

"Oh, I am." Maricus leaned back against the counter as though nothing in the room could touch him — as though he hadn't just poured oil onto a waiting fire. "It's just amusing, isn't it? Especially after seeing your ex..." His smile sharpened. "And here you are again, ignoring your father's summons. The mighty Sun Prince... distracted." He tilted his head, eyes glinting. "Earth has a lot to answer for." A soft chuckle. "Not even hours have passed, and already you can't keep your distance."

Sun Prince.

Earth.

Ex.

The words hooked into me — foreign, sharp. I frowned, caught between the violence simmering in one man's stillness and the mockery dancing in the other's smile. Some private joke between them, maybe. Or something far more dangerous.

Nyxie pads in from the back, slipping through the swinging door with the quiet confidence of something that has always belonged. She's all night in a coat — coal-black fur, eyes like turned opals, a tail that flicks once, twice, then stills.

She stops dead between us, a living wall, and emits a low, rolling rumble that vibrates under my ribs like a second heartbeat. The café hushes around the sound. Even Maricus's smirk stills for a breath. "She doesn't trust easily," I say, crouching on instinct to scratch behind her ears, "and she doesn't appreciate taunts aimed at the café owner." Her fur is warm beneath my fingers, familiar and grounding. She leans into my hand like a tide finding stone, gaze never leaving Aodhan.

"She's smart," Aodhan replies quietly, his tone softened — not dismissive, not indulgent. Watching. "They tend to notice what others overlook."

My head lifts, the words catching before I can stop them. "And what's that? A stranger hanging around somewhere he shouldn't, who is also seeing his ex?" I ask, trying — and failing — to sound indifferent.

"Nothing you need to worry about," he says simply.

I huff, sarcasm spilling before I can stop it. "That's very specific. Thanks."

He doesn't smile. The gold at the rim of his eyes flares faintly, and for the first time, something hesitant slips through his control. "I'll explain when I can," he says at last.

"Oh yeah? When's that?" My voice snaps sharper than I intend. "Because you seem to be the reason my life is—" I break off, exhaling hard. "Twisted. Strange men staring into my shop. Strangers sitting for hours. And you—" My voice wavers. "You stand there like you know something I don't. And won't elaborate on and leading me on."

He steps closer. Close enough that I can feel the direction of his breath — close enough to smell him. The scent of storm and bergamot on a hot day hits me, overwhelming, muddling my thoughts. His presence is a tide I can't brace against.

"I want you safe," he says, quiet but fierce. "Safe enough that you don't become tangled in other people's greed, and I did not see her willingly. She is nothing to me."

For a moment, I can't look at him. My palms press flat to the counter as if the wood could steady me. "I don't need to be kept safe," I tell him, though the words taste hollow. Because what are we? Not friends. Not lovers. Too far gone to be strangers.

"No," he says slowly — then, lower, the sound darkening. His hand finds my chin, tilting my face up until our eyes lock. "But you deserve someone who'd destroy the realm, and rebuild it for you if it meant your happiness and safety."

I swallow, throat tight.

Shit.

The ache in my chest twists. Caleb's absence flares — that quiet domestic ghost that lingers in every morning without him. Aodhan's words bury themselves deep, dangerous things that feel like they could take root and bloom if I let them. He watches me for a moment longer before stepping back, breaking the tug between us. Then he takes a seat, his fingers leaving behind a tingling trail along my jaw — the echo of a promise I'm not ready to name.

For the rest of the afternoon, he's there — sometimes standing near the hedgerow that borders the path, sometimes at the edge of the garden, moving with quiet, deliberate purpose. Maricus comes and goes like a nervous breeze, surveying, measuring, and I feel his gaze more than once. I still can't tell if he's friend or foe. He's a man used to probing and provoking — one who hides his true intentions behind that easy, jovial facade.

When the sun dips and I reach for the lock, his voice stops me. Low and certain.

"I'll walk the fence line."

"You don't need—" I begin.

"I'm doing it anyway," he says. There's no force in it, no raised voice — just certainty. His gaze holds mine, gentle and immovable, like a decision already made.

I should be annoyed. I should tell him to leave. I should remind him that my life is mine, that I don't need his protection.

Instead, my voice comes out quieter. "Fine," I say — because

I'm tired of being brave on my own. Because there's a small, foolish comfort in letting someone else hold the worry, even briefly. Because I'm bone-deep weary. From work, from pretending everything's fine with Viv and Emma, from maintaining my father's wards that mean little to me and everything to him. And beneath it all lies a deeper exhaustion — the kind no sleep can touch. The quiet guilt of still breathing, still standing here, when Caleb isn't.

Aodhan's a silhouette cut against the last of the daylight, the heat shimmering around him like a halo. He moves with a soldier's precision, eyes scanning the hedgerow, murmuring to himself like a sergeant giving quiet orders. I catch fragments — "nothing to the west... to the east, in the hedge... something's been camping."

The words hang like a snagged curtain. Something among the leaves watches us — patient, deliberate. A twig snaps further along the track, soft and careful. Nyxie bares a tooth, hackles lifting, a low warning rolling from her chest. I step closer to him, even though every sensible part of me lists the reasons not to. His nearness pulls like gravity. The small ritual of spinning the band on my finger is as natural as breathing, and I choke back the urge to tuck my hand into my pocket where no one can see.

"You spun your ring," he says — not looking, but noticing all the same, as though he's been cataloguing the smallest things for longer than I realised. His tone isn't mocking; it's the observation of someone who sees detail.

I stop. "Habit," I say — too sharply. The lie tastes metallic, old. "A stupid habit."

"It grounds you," he says simply. "If it helps, don't hide it. Don't be ashamed of what you have survived."

There's something in the way he says it — no judgement, no pity — that makes my chest unfurl a little, cautious as a new leaf. He's composed and ridiculous all at once; impossible to read. He stands like a man trained never to yield, yet undone by the smallest human things. "You could tell me what you are sooner," I say — half a joke, half a challenge.

"Or at least who sent you. People are whispering about a handsome man hanging around my café. While I appreciate the extra business, it's becoming a little... distracting." His gaze darkens. "Handsome?"

There's a pause — deliberate. Then his voice drops, rougher, lower. "There's only one person in that café whose opinion I care about."

Heat skims my skin.

"And I'm a man," he adds, brushing his hand lightly against mine as we walk, the touch brief but unmistakable. "A distracting one, apparently. I'd have thought that obvious by now."

I snort softly. "Are you sure the handsome one, was you?" I glance at him sidelong. "You're certainly beautiful — but you're not the only handsome man to visit my café. Tall, dark, and cocky sets the mum club aflutter every time he shows up."

His mouth quirks. "As long as it's only the mums he's setting racing, I can live with that." His laughter follows — low, rolling, a sound that curls through the dark and settles somewhere under my ribs. My gaze drifts to the hedgerow. Maricus ghosts along its edge — a shadow with intent. He steps into view with casual menace, like someone who's been given a task and intends to enjoy it.

"Maricus is one of my Fíralen," Aodhan says at last. "We work together."

A beat. "Think of it as a private army."

"You'll stay until you find your item?" I ask.

"For as long as you'll let me — without kicking me off your property again."

His voice carries a promise and threads deeper to something more. Nyxie leans in as I run my hand through her coat, and she closes her eyes, the rumble in her chest settling into a steady purr that vibrates through the soles of my feet.

I glance at him again — at the clean line of his jaw, the faint glow beneath his skin — and a dull ache blooms behind my ribs. Attraction shouldn't feel like this: not for someone I barely know, whose world I don't understand, whose name sits on my tongue like a secret. Yet here I am, his quiet steadiness pressed against my chaos, and it feels like the first breath after holding it too long.

"I look forward to greeting my new regular royal army, then," I manage with a smirk. "Emma will be by tomorrow with more of those lemon muffins," I add. "She's on a mission of cheer and annoying customers with citrus out of season — calls it whittling out the sad sacks. Annoyingly good at it, too."

Aodhan's expression softens — the smallest shift, almost missed. Behind him, Maricus lets out a low, private laugh before muttering under his breath, "She would know all about whittling out the bad eggs."

There's more to come. I can feel it in the way the air cools, unnaturally still for the season. But for now — for tonight — I feel safe.

CHAPTER 14

Lily POV

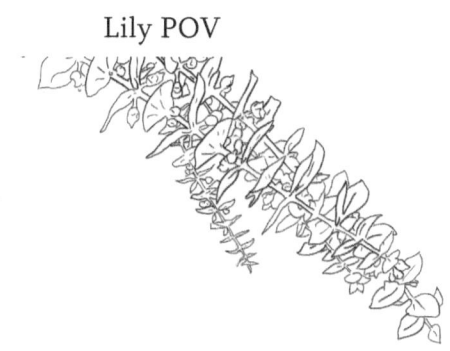

I should've known today was going to be hell. Emma would've blamed the stars, muttering about Mercury in retrograde — which, in her dictionary, translates to chaos, caffeine shortages, and customers with the patience of wet tissue paper.

The signs were all there.

First, the overhead light blew in the storage room, plunging me into a dim, flickering half-dark while I rummaged for a carton of oat milk. I stubbed my toe on the ladder, dropped an entire sleeve of takeaway lids, and emerged looking like I'd survived a skirmish with a particularly vindictive poltergeist.

Then both terminals crashed — a special kind of torture in an age when nobody under seventy carries cash. One man actually tried to pay in coins fished from the bottom of his gym bag. They smelled like sweat and despair.

The complaints rolled in like waves, sharp voices cutting through the whir of the grinder.

"Too hot."

"Too cold."

"Too much foam."

"Not enough foam."

Each one a reminder that apparently I was personally orchestrating the downfall of civilisation, one imperfect latte at a time.

By noon, my nerves were strung thin. My smile had the brittle shine of glass about to crack; my voice was sandpaper from repeating the same half-dozen apologies; my whole body thrummed with the frantic rhythm of trying to hold everything together with nothing but willpower and caffeine.

When Vivienne breezed in — calm, serene, polished as ever — I could have kissed her. She had her phone tucked between shoulder and ear, arguing softly with a client in that honeyed, unshakable voice that never cracked. Her heels clicked once on the tiles, her eyes cutting straight to me: my grip too tight on the cloth, the twitch betraying itself in my jaw.

"Walk," she said, lowering the phone just long enough to pin me with that steel-and-silk look. "Five minutes. I've got this."

I didn't argue. Out back, I leaned against the cool brick wall, dragging in a breath that scraped my lungs raw but never quite found its depth. My hand went to my waist, squeezing tight — attempting to centre myself by force alone, to hold the fragments from scattering.

I tipped my head back, drawing in a ragged breath once more. A bead of sweat rolled down my spine, even though the shade was cool. Then an "ahem" startles me from reverie.

"You look like you could use a hand," he said finally. His voice was low, quiet. My pulse stuttered — caught like a record skipping. Damn it, I didn't notice him. How did I not notice him? Relief warred with irritation, colliding so hard it felt like sparks under my ribs.

"Uh, what are you doing here?"

He looked me over with one brow raised. "It seemed like you were needing a hand, just thought I'd see if you needed a little help?" I laugh to myself, imagining this giant of a man standing behind the counter.

"Why do you want to help?" I ask, needing to know what he wants from me — why he keeps hanging around, why he wants to protect me from dangers I can't even see.

"Because you need it," he said simply. Then a pause — a flicker of hesitation I'd never seen from him before, and the rarity of it made my breath falter.

"And because..." His jaw flexed, control bending for a heartbeat. "I can't seem to stay away."

For a heartbeat, all I could do was stare, my lips parting with no words to fill the space. My chest ached with something dangerous. So I did the only thing left — I deflected.

"Well," I muttered, tucking a curl behind my ear, "if you don't mind lending your height, there's a light bulb in here that's been mocking me all morning." A corner of his mouth lifted — not a full smile, but the suggestion of one. "Show me the way."

The storage room was narrow, dim, cluttered with boxes. His heat filled every inch of space. I passed him the new bulb without meeting his eyes, which was pointless; even without looking, I could feel him watching my every move, a knowing smile playing on his lips.

The first attempt ended with a sharp crack of glass. He cursed under his breath — low and foreign — the kind of word that felt crude. He tried again. Another brittle snap, another muttered expletive. By the third, I lost it.

Laughter punched out of me, sudden and wild, until I was doubled over against the shelving, cheeks aching, breath hiccupping.

"You're—oh God—you're terrible at this," I gasped, wiping at my eyes. The sight of him — the so-called Sun Prince, this man who radiated impossible control — defeated by a light bulb nearly killed me with hysterics.

His head tilted, expression flat. But under the steel I caught it: the faintest flicker of embarrassment. "I've never had to replace one before," he muttered, clipped, annoyed at my laughter.

That only made it worse. "Clearly," I teased, grinning like a fool. "Sit down before you burn the whole place down. I'll handle it — just hold the ladder for me."

He crouched without argument, cheeks and neck reddening further. His gaze tracked me while I climbed the step stool — steady, relentless — like I was the only thing in the room worth noting. My heart hammered with every second of it. I twisted the new bulb into place. The light flared back to life, warm and steady. For half a heartbeat, triumph bubbled in my chest — until I turned and realised how close we were.

The space was too small. The air too thick. His presence too much. He leaned in, hands braced on either side of the ladder, framing me in place. I licked my lips before I could stop myself, bracing for what felt inevitable as he closed the distance. Too close. Breath-close. His mouth hovered near enough that I felt it — warmth, promise, restraint.

"Smoothie?" I blurted — the first word to tumble out, desperate to puncture the silence. My voice came out thinner than I wanted.

His mouth curved. He knew exactly what he did to me. "Sure."

He paused — deliberate — like he wanted me to feel the lack of space between us. "I'll move those boxes first," he said, flicking his chin toward the stack in the corner. His tone dipped sly, velvet over steel. "I promise I'll be gentle… "

Heat curled low in my stomach at the implication. I spun away quickly, my face darkening to a crimson shade. My laugh came too fast, too brittle.

"Please. The café insurance wouldn't survive you."

He chuckled — soft, dangerous — as though amused by my retreat as I closed the door.

The front counter went silent.

The temperature dropped. Nyxie was on her feet before I even turned — a low, guttural growl pouring out of her chest, hackles raised. Her whole body bristled, the kind of instinct that needed no translation danger.

The café froze with her. Conversations cut mid-sentence, laughter caught in throats. Even the hiss of the steam wand stuttered out, as though the room itself understood what had just walked in and knew to be afraid.

Mark entered first.

His smile had always been wrong — too practised, too polite. Now it stretched wider, feral at the edges. His eyes glittered with something sharper than interest. He moved with purpose, no longer pretending.

And behind him came the real danger.

He was taller, broader — presence like a wraith given flesh. Dark hair threaded with white. Skin the colour of old ash. His smile wasn't human at all; cruelty etched into every line of it. His eyes black, rimmed red and hollow — locked on me, and my chest clenched.

He didn't bother with civility.

"Well, well, well," Mark drawled, slipping into his role with a sneer. "Our pretty little Lily." His gaze dragged down me like a knife. "I knew you were hiding something."

The stranger's smile deepened — savage. His voice was lower, rasped with menace, every word deliberate. "Ahhh... our little widow. And here I thought you were lonely..." He paused, scanning the café. "And now," he said, eyes never leaving mine, "I hear you're spreading your legs for an Air-y. You could have spent that time with someone who enjoys your fire."

The word spat from him like venom.

The café went deathly quiet. Customers sat rigid, wide-eyed, instinct warning them not to breathe too loud. Nyxie snarled, stepping forward, teeth flashing white. The Stranger tilted his head, enjoying the reaction — enjoying me. "Tell me, little widow. Where is it?" His tone sharpened, cruel. "The shard. The piece that doesn't belong to you. Give it up, and maybe you keep your children — and you'll only bleed a little."

My blood iced.

Fear surged up, hot and choking — but it burned away almost instantly, replaced with something sharper.

I looked to Vivienne and nodded. She moved quietly through the room, guiding the customers out one by one — fast, efficient. Within moments, the door clicked shut behind the last of them. The silence that followed was suffocating.

His smile spread, slow and ugly. "You've got spirit. I like that." He stepped closer, and with every pace the air thickened, pressing down on me like invisible hands. My knees trembled as though the floor wanted me on them.

Mark leaned against the counter like he owned it, voice smug. "Told you she was hiding something. You should tell the Sylavri now. He will find out sooner or later. You don't want him to extract the information he wants. It won't be pleasant, and I would rather you be in one piece as promised."

He pauses licking his lips, "We were always watching. Always waiting. You never fooled me, Lily." He dragged out my name, twisting it into something dirty. "And now? Now you're his little whore you could have bed me instead, at least I am human."

"Shut your mouth," I spat, finding the bat located under the counter, the hilt biting into my palm as I gripped it tighter under the counter.

The Sylvari chuckled. "She's feisty. I'll enjoy breaking that." His gaze flicked past me, catching on Vivienne as she gathered her bag by the door. His grin sharpened, cruel. "And if the widow doesn't want to play nice... the sister will do. She looks fun. Pretty mouth. Pretty bones. I wonder—" His eyes gleamed black. "Would she scream like you... or beg first, she strikes as the type to beg."

Vivienne froze, hand tightening around the strap of her bag. Her chin lifted, but her throat betrayed her — a tiny flicker, pulse hammering.

The bat trembled in my grip. Rage boiled so fast I thought it might eat me alive. The vines across the window shuddered, leaves trembling.

A blossom burst open, unnatural — and a cloud of fine pollen spilled into the air, golden dust motes catching the light.

"Run, Vivienne!" I screamed, lungs tearing raw. Mark coughed, doubling over, swiping at his face as though the air itself had turned against him.

"What the—?" His voice broke in a rasp.

The Sylvari snarled low, eyes flashing almost catlike—power pressing harder as though trying to smother the plant pollen, to smother me. My lungs tightened, each breath heavy, but I refused to break first.

"You will give me the shard," he said, voice dropping into something darker, older. His words vibrated like grinding stone.

"Or I will take apart everyone you love, one piece at a time.

And I'll make you watch, and I will…" he shivers "relish with your every scream."

My vision blurred at the edges; the air felt harder to breathe.

"You don't know what you're holding," he continued, low, nearly a growl. "The shard belongs to my people. If the Fae get it first, we're finished. I'll kill anyone and anything to stop that from happening." His eyes glittered with animal hunger. "Do you understand me, little widow? Blood is cheaper than waiting."

Before I could reply, he moved—smooth, predatory. His hand slid across the counter, fingers brushing my shoulder, tracing deliberately down the line of my arm. The contact was light, almost mocking—but it made every muscle in my body lock. I froze in the wrongness of his touch, the weight of him pressing in until the walls felt too close.

My fingers twitched for the bat but they refused to move. The bat clattered out of reach, the sound loud and damning, and my stomach plunged. Then he leaned further across the counter; his other hand snapped out with brutal precision. He caught my wrist, yanked hard, and dragged me forward over the polished wood as if I were nothing more than an object. Pain flared as my hip clipped the edge; my feet scrambled uselessly until he shoved me down into a chair.

He bent close, breath grazing my cheek—hot, sour. The stench of whiskey, iron and smoke filled my nose thick enough to taste. His lips hovered too close, the heat of him prickling over my skin, each fine hair lifting in warning.

Realisation hits me like a road-train. It's him the creep from the bar.

"Sit still," he murmured voice dragging with, cruel delight savouring the moment of fear. "Or I'll start with your sister. She looks softer. Easier, like she has been through this before. Nice and easy to break. Maybe she'd even taste prettier than you."

The words were poison, deliberate and slow. My pulse hammered. Rage twisted with terror. The plants were vibrating, like an aftershock from a quake was taking place within the café, a sweet fragrance permeated throughout the room. The room thickened.

The sylvari inhaled and coughed—once, twice—as though the air itself had turned against him. Glasses rattled on the shelves; the pendant lights flickered hard.

I gripped the chair edge with white knuckles, every instinct screaming to lash out, to hurt this man to put him down where he stood, before he touched Vivienne.

Nyxie now finished with Mark lunged before I could even breathe her name. One moment she'd been crouched, keeping him at bay; the next she was a streak of black muscle and fury, jaws snapping with a sound that ripped through the café like tearing steel.

She hit the Sylvari so hard he staggered back, shock flashing in his eyes. For an instant he looked smaller, caught off guard by the size.

Nyxie seemed to grow in her rage—larger, darker, a beast with teeth like razors ready to destroy and hunt its prey. Mark—coward, rat, spy—yelped and scrambled for the door. He tripped over a chair in his haste, palms smacking the floor, then hid behind a table. The Sylvari growled, recovering from the shock, and turned his fury on Nyxie. His lip curled, teeth bared, muscles coiling as if to strike her down.

I ran for the bat.

My fingers closed around it where it had skidded across the floor, the metal warm like it recognised me — or answered me. Something primal surged up my spine, sharp and hot, drowning out every other thought except — hit him.

I swung. All instinct. All terror. All the rage I'd buried since the moment my world split open.

Green sparks flared before the bat even connected, slipping through my fingers like static, like something trying to escape me. Pollen shimmered off my skin in a faint, trembling halo — uncontrolled, unintentional — a pulse of wild magic that felt too big for my body.

Then the bat struck. The impact cracked across his shoulder, loud as gunfire. A brutal, bone-deep sound that vibrated through the walls. Pain jolted up my arms, white-hot, rattling my teeth until they ached. My wrists buckled. My breath tore out of me in a gasp.

But my hands didn't let go. I wouldn't let go, I refused. Because some part of me — the part that had been quiet for far too long — snarled that stopping meant dying. That if I didn't finish this, he would finish me or hurt someone I loved.

He grunted, stumbling back, his face flickering from shock to white hot wrath. Good. Let him be pissed off. Let him know I will not be taken down easy.

"Who the fuck," I spat, breath heaving, voice shaking, "do you think you are? You walk into my café—my home—and you think you can threaten me? My sister? My kids? My customers?"

Nyxie prowled back to my side, shoulder brushing mine, body low and taut as wire. A rumble rolled through her chest, deeper now, darker. And then I saw it: a glow clinging faintly to her coat, subtle but real, as though the night itself bent around her and gave her weight.

The Sylvari's eyes narrowed, his shoulders shifting as if something dislodged.

"I don't know what the hell you're talking about," I hissed, fury scraping my throat raw, "but you will not stand here and threaten anyone I love."

The rage whipping around, I can taste the iron in my mouth. The need to destroy this man taking over. Something in his eyes changed; he began to shuffle back.

The vines along the walls rustled again, sharper now; blossoms tore open with a hiss like silk ripping. The scent of jasmine and peonies filled the room, thick and sweet, clinging in my lungs until my skin tingled.

The lights trembled overhead; wooden boards creaked. Heat surged through me—not just anger anymore, but something else. Something ancient and powerful.

I advanced, dragging the bat along the polished floorboards. The scrape was deliberate, grating, a sound that made him flinch despite himself. I stopped just close enough to touch him, the tip of the bat resting between his legs. I tapped a threatening rhythm against his knee—once. Twice. Slow. Steady.

"I hear these balls don't fare too well when hit," I said softly, every word laced with venom. "Want me to test my aim? I'll happily see how loud you scream for me, when they *pop-p*." I smiled, menacing.

Something flickered in his eyes—instinct. He knew I wasn't bluffing. It wasn't just rage that carried me. It was power. The Sylvari's lips peeled back in a snarl; his body shifted, ready. Before I realise it, Aodhan is there. I step back the look on his face terrifying, his eyes flashing like silver and gold fireworks, his scowl deadly.

He emerges from the back hallway — every line of him cut from fury and unbridled rage. His gaze sweeps the room once, lands on me — and for a heartbeat, the whole world stills.

Concern and hurt. Both raw, unhidden, etched into the tight clench of his jaw and the flicker in his eyes as they track every inch of me, searching for blood, for bruises, for anything he wasn't there to stop.

"Are you hurt? Did he touch you? Why did you not call for me?"

His voice is low, meant only for me, roughened by something that aches. I shake my head, breath shallow. My fingers tighten on the bat, sweat beading in my palms because the trembling won't stop.

His hands glide up and down my body, skimming my wrists, tracing along my sides. I wince when he finds the bruise blooming across my hip, another on my wrist where I'd been grabbed. His gaze lingers a moment longer, as though he doesn't quite believe me, then slides past — all kindness gone in an instant.

The Sylvari sneers, feigning bravado, but I feel the shift in the room. His confidence frays at the edges, unravelling under Aodhan's stare.

"I'll take it from here," Aodhan murmurs, brushing a curl back behind my ear with surprising tenderness. "You were so brave." His forehead lowers to mine briefly, like he's grounding himself, breathing me in to prove I am real and upright and alive.

But his restraint is more frightening than any outburst. It carries the promise of destruction. The Sylvari straightens, trying to mask the tremble in his stance. "This isn't your fight, Airy." A fatal mistake.

"You," Aodhan says. Not shouted. Not raised. But the word lands like a command. The stranger freezes. Aodhan's eyes ignite — molten bright — and before I can blink, he moves.

He grabs the Sylvari by the collar and hurls him upright with effortless strength. The temperature spikes. Heat licks the walls. A tang of scorched earth floods my throat — bitter, metallic and sharp. The sylvari hisses, clutching his arm as angry welts rise across his skin, not burned, but branded, as though the very air had marked him at Aodhan's command.

He staggers back, spitting curses, but the swagger is gone. Fear blooms in its place — real, choking fear — as the truth of the predator in front of him finally sinks in.

Aodhan doesn't give him time to recover. With a flick of his wrist — casual, almost bored — he hurls the Sylvari through the café doors. Wood splinters. Glass rattles in its frame. The man hits the gravel outside with a pained, broken grunt.

"And you, Mr Evans," Aodhan adds, not even bothering to look at the cowering man by the entrance. "You will follow me outside. Or share his fate." A squeak. Then frantic footsteps scrambling out the door.

Aodhan follows Mark Evans without haste — every step measured, controlled, disturbingly calm, like this is not the first time he has walked a dangerous man out of a café and into a reckoning.

He looks back once. A single nod. A single anchor.

"I'll be back, Lily. Lock the door. Mr Fisher will be by soon."

Then he is gone. The bell above the café door gives one soft jangle — a delicate sound out of place in the wreckage of adrenaline — before the door slams shut on a breath of wind. Silence floods in after him.

A heavy, shuddering silence that seems too large for the room.

My hands shake so violently the bat nearly slips from my grip. I tighten my hold until my knuckles burn. Nyxie presses herself into my leg, solid and warm, a living weight leaning her certainty into my trembling body. Her growl fades into a low, protective rumble — a sound that feels like a hand on my spine, steadying me before I come apart.

"Good girl," I breathe, though my voice is barely sound. Vivienne appears from the hallway a moment later. Her face tries for composed, but her eyes — wide, glassy, shaken — tell the truth. She places a trembling hand on my arm, trying to ground me. Trying to ground herself.

"You're all right," she says, steady despite the quiver in her fingers. "He's gone."

But the truth settles thick and cold in my chest. He isn't gone. Not really. Men like him don't disappear. And moments like that don't fade. This is only the beginning. My breath stutters. Something hot and furious twists under my ribs — not fear anymore, but a rising vow. I turn and pull Vivienne into my arms, holding her tight. She's shaking worse than I am, her breath hitching against my shoulder.

This hit her harder than it hit me. And I hate that she was here to see it. I hope — fiercely, quietly — that Aodhan puts the kind of fear into Evans, and into that Sylvari, that they'll never forget for as long as they live. The front door bangs open again.

Mr Fisher barrels through with more speed than his age should allow, his gaze sweeping the café, cataloguing everything in two heartbeats — the overturned chairs, my shaking hands, Vivienne's pale face. "Girls," he says firmly, stepping inside like a shield. "Nothing will be known about this incident. So, you can relax and be rest assured." His eyes flick to Vivienne, softening. "And Vivienne — he isn't coming back. You have my word." A pause. A certainty. A promise sealed with something ancient in his tone. "I'll be out the front if either of you need me." He disappears as quickly as he arrived — but his presence leaves a rush of safety in his wake, as if the café itself takes a steadying breath.

I do too. Still, a hollow ache pulses through me.

With Aodhan gone, a want rises — sharp, instinctive — pulling at me like gravity shifting direction. I want him back. Here. Beside me. And the truth is undeniable now.

The world isn't safe anymore.

But with him... I might be.

CHAPTER 15

Aodhan POV

I drag a near-lifeless Mark Evans by the foot; my blood is boiling. I can smell his skin burning as we walk. The coward passed out the moment I drew my blade. Little does he know what's in store.

The scrub presses in close at this hour, branches knitting shadows thick enough to strangle light. Good. Darkness means privacy. Darkness means no witnesses.

I should have known. Should have felt the prickle sooner, caught the stench in the hedgerow before he ever stepped across Lily's threshold. But the silence-wreath dulled the bond, pressed it down to an ache instead of a tell-tale, and for that sin alone I wanted to rip the wreath from my skin and grind it into ash. She had been threatened under my watch. Touched. Dragged across her own counter. And I had not felt it.

That would not happen again. The Sylvari leans against the carcass of a dead gum, arms folded like a man who isn't about to have a hand thrust through his chest. His grin is the same one he'd worn inside—thin, feral. The sight of it makes my stomach coil. How dare he threaten her.

I let heat roll off me, slow as sunrise, steady as a tide. My magic burns gold against my skin, every line of storm-script alive with power. The ground hisses faintly where dry grass meets the warmth; a crackle sounds like flint ready to form a flame. "You should have stayed hidden in your territory," I tell him, voice low enough to make the leaves still. "Instead, you touched what's mine."

He laughs, sharp and ugly. "She's mortal. Weak. A vessel at best. And you—" he sneers, showing teeth too long, "—you're too late. I've already scented her."

That sentence breaks whatever restraint remains in me. I take a step, deliberate, the earth sears underfoot. The Sylvari falters—takes a step back. My fury sharpens into focus. Torture first, then death. I will strip the skin from his arrogance inch by inch. Break his fingers one at a time so he remembers each bone. Burn the breath from his lungs until he begs for death. No clean kill. Clean is mercy. And this Sylvari will not get my mercy.

"She is not yours to scent," I say, words molten. "She is not yours to threaten. She is not yours to touch or be in her presence." My jaw tightens. "But she is mine, and what's mine deserves divine retribution."

I raise my hand, and the air shimmers around it — a veil of heat, of promise, of storm barely contained. "Where did you touch her? I may show mercy if you tell me where and how...," I tell him, though in truth I care for none of it. His screams will be the only prayer I require.

He spits his poison without shame. "Didn't realise she was yours to play with," he sneers. "A widow untouched for six years? Taste must be sweet."

The words drive in and twist. They land where family and honour sit like old armour, and for a moment all I hear is the echo of my father's voice in a hall of glass: Want nothing. Need nothing. Love nothing you cannot afford to lose. I had already lost to that rule.

Power surges — wild, reckless, honed. Vengeance and wrath braid together as phoenix fire blooms along the edge, white-gold flames licking steel that did not exist a heartbeat ago.

There is no warning. His hand leaves his body so cleanly he doesn't realise it's gone until I throw it back at him.

He reaches for it — a grotesque, instinctive scramble — fingers clawing at empty air as understanding crashes through him too late.

The scream that follows tears loose from his chest, raw and animal, loud enough to stir the fields below. Even Mark Evans startles. Excellent. The bond under the silence-wreath surges once, hard enough to make my magic glow faintly through the glamour. The word tears out of me without permission, naked and violent: "Mine."

He laughs, wet and ugly, but there is a tremor under it. "Protective, are we? Cute. Think you scare me, Sun Prince?"

I move.

One step and I am inside his guard. My palm hits his throat, not gentle, fingers closing with the precision of a trap. The look in his eyes telescopes—surprise, then fury, then the dawning horror of realisation. The air screams where my skin meets his — Fae power rejecting Sylvari corruption on contact.

Half-breeds. Witch-blood spliced with stolen Fae magic. Creatures that crawl between courts, feeding on unseelie rot and calling it strength. An abomination of bloodlines that should never have mixed. Welts erupt along his neck and arm, skin blistering red-gold as my power burns the corruption straight to the surface.

He chokes, gurgling. "You'll—pay—" he hisses, but the sound is small now. I bend my head closer, the heat building between us until sweat slicks his temple. My voice stays low, dangerous, controlled. "You put a hand on her shoulder. You dragged her over her own counter. You tossed her through the air like she was a toy."

"Tell me," I whisper, thumb pressing just enough to steal his breath, "which part of you I remove first. The hand that touched her. The mouth that spoke her name. Or the leg you'll crawl away on." Flames stir under my skin, hungry for permission.

He makes a sound between a growl and a cough, trying to shift, but the power rolling off me pins him like a nailed Shadow. "You—don't—get it," he rasps. "She's—just—a—"

I tighten my grip a fraction. "Finish that sentence," I murmur, "and you won't need a tongue to regret it." His eyes flicker — fear now. I can scent it in waves rolling off him.

Mark Evans stirs beside me. Realising he's no longer in the café, he tries to run. Stupid. I grab his arm and throw him in front of the Sylvari, my sneer widening. "Perfect timing. I need one of you to talk."

Evans scrambles, babbling apologies, trading anything for his life. He has no information. I glance at the Sylvari, smirking. "Well... I don't need both of you, do I?"

Relief washes over Evans — for a single heartbeat. Right before I plunge my arm through his chest.

Bone's part. Flesh yields. The heat of his life collapses around my forearm as if his body itself is shocked I dared to enter it. Blood erupts in a fine mist, warm against my face and chest, flecking the Sylvari standing in front of me. His eyes go wide. Too slow. Too late.

"This," I breathe, my lips brushing Evans's ear as he gurgles on his own shock, "is for terrorising Lily. For harassing her. For stalking not just her... but her children."

His pulse stutters against my wrist. My voice drops lower. Deadly.

"You would have taken her daughter by force if Lily kept rejecting you. I know your kind. I know your plans. And I warned you."

I withdraw my arm slowly. Deliberately. The sound is wet. Muscle and flesh falling to the ground in a thud. Evans crumples at my feet, all weight and silence. Mouth frozen mid-plea. He never finishes it.

The Sylvari shifts uneasily. His aura spikes with fear — scenting truth in the rumours he'd once scoffed at. The Sun Prince. The one who burns without flame. The one who hunts like light itself.

I let him smell the truth. Blood and flame kiss my fingers as I turn toward him. Not rushing. Walking. Behind the rigid line of my spine, plans coil — sharp and patient.

Not if he breaks. But when.

Whether to drag him back to Maricus for extraction. Or break him here and purge the ground so nothing of his lineage ever grows again. Perhaps I'll remove an item for each strike he used on Lily. Let him learn what pain feels like when inflicted by someone who doesn't tire. Let him scream in the dark of my dungeons. Let him answer to the Fae he thought he could toy with. Let him understand what it means to threaten what is mine.

I step closer, the blood dripping rhythmically onto the gravel. The Sylvari swallows hard.

"Get up," I say, kicking him where he huddles, clutching the mangled arm. "Because you're going to tell me who sent you, who's leash you're on, and how far the Fire Court has already come." I step closer, and the clearing grows hotter still. "And then," I add softly, "you're going to pray I'm merciful."

The Sylvari coughs, smog curling faintly from the welts on his arm. His eyes flick toward the ridge — toward the café, toward Lily — and I see the thought forming. I let my smile show teeth. "You might want to focus on me," I say, "or I'll take the eyes too."

He looks away. He gags, trying to form threats that melt under the heat. My magic burns him slowly, circling. I use Air to contain it — cooling slightly for short reprieves before sending another wave. Each jerk of his body makes his skin hiss where magic brushes it, thin spirals of smoke rising and vanishing.

Killing would be clean — no loose ends for the Courts. The beast in me wants that, wants to silence the mouth that dared speak her name. But death is silence, and silence tells you nothing. I need names. Routes. Courts. I need to know who to hunt first who to destroy and who to kill.

Maricus's voice threads through my mind, cool and wry: *Don't melt the bastard before I get there. Interrogations work best when they can still speak.*

"Well, you'd better hurry," I mutter aloud, "or I'll be the one doing your job."

"*Calm down, Aodh,*" he replies in my mind. "*Not all of us can portal wherever we like.*"

I ignore him. I ease the pressure just enough to let the Sylvari breathe in shallow, burning gulps.

Maricus steps through the trees, stalking forward, ready to join the hunt. He glances from the bruised, handless Sylvari to me, grin splitting slow and satisfied. "Really, Aodh," he drawls. "Do you always have to be so theatrical?"

I don't answer. I let silence do the work. Let the heat press against the Sylvari's ribs. Let him feel how quickly the world can unmake him when it chooses to. He spits blood, red and dark in the dark. Maricus crouches opposite him, close enough for the Sylvari to see the predatory amusement on his face. He picks up a stick and taps it against the stump of the missing hand. "Start with a name," he suggests. "Preferably sooner rather than later. I've a mortal to play with, and her temper rivals mine. Best not be late."

Silence stretches — even the crickets hush. The Sylvari's eyes roll white with pain and fear before locking on the distant café light. He swallows, lips cracked.

"Chaser," he croaks. "Called himself Chaser. Pays in coin and women. Sends masked men, those of the elite. Said to look for Air's weakness. Said the shard would be with the mortal. Said the café woman's land had old roots. Said bring it."

"Chaser," Maricus repeats, tasting the name. "A middleman, then. Not the Fire Court themselves — too careful for that. Someone trading in the Shadows."

"Who hired Chaser?" I press.

He spits again, blood flecking his lips. "A sigil. A hand with three prongs. Said the shard called to those who couldn't see it — would make them kings. More powerful than any Fae or court."

The sheer arrogance of it sickens me. People always want dominion, even if it means burning the world to claim a throne.

"Get Ellisar to look into the sigil," I say. "Find out who they are."

Maricus nods. "Where did you last meet this Chaser?" Maricus asks, voice calm now.

"Beyond the old quarry," the Sylvari wheezes. "Three nights ago. Blue caravan, sigil in Fae ash and wyvern blood. They come with lanterns that smell of sea-salt. Speak in the court tongue when they think no one hears. The human was bait — flirt, watch. We used him for information, not that he was useful. Everyone sent to the widow came back with their memory wiped."

Maricus rises, dusting off his hands, satisfaction flickering. The Sylvari is spent. His body will be a scar of memory; his oath will devour him soon. Chaser will know he's been found.

I straighten, night air cooling the fire in my veins. The silence-wreath hums at my wrist like a caged thing. Fuck Nivara and Earth. I'll break the wreath if I must. I will protect her.

I have a list now, a map: the sigil, Chaser, whoever he serves the hunt will begin, and it will start with Water. Maricus's voice is dry with amusement. "You heading back to Ms Beanz — or are we hunting?"

"No." I draw the heat back, let rage settle into something sharper. Air is a storm — but storms wait. They gather.

"First we watch. Then we hunt. Cut the dog from its leash. Then we take the master. Prepare the elite." Maricus lets out a short, approving laugh. "Careful. The man of wind sounds like a planner."

"I'm ready for war," I reply. "And they should know better than to provoke the winds — or me." I turn toward the ridge. Below, the café window glows — a warm square against the dark. I draw an invisible vow around it with my gaze.

I will not let their hunger turn her into a hinge for the Courts. I will find the shard, if it exists — and I will destroy it. And anyone who reaches for her will burn. "Take him," I say, voice low and absolute. "Alive. Karlen holds the cell. Keep him breathing until I return."

Maricus's grin sharpens. "Alive, for now. You didn't say anything about intact. But we'll have answers by the time you're back."

I leave him to it. He falls into step beside me, amusement giving way to something more wary.

"What are you doing now, Aodh? You're warring — I can feel it." His gaze flicks to the air around me. "Phoenix fire's rolling off you in waves. You'll need to rein it in before you see her."

"Nivara," I say. The name tastes like ash. "I want her head. Varyn too. The Earth Court needs a reminder that my promises are not hollow."

"Alliances," Maricus cautions. "Aodh—"

"Fuck the alliance." The words snap clean. "They were warned." I don't slow. Rage simmers, tendrils of fire claiming. Burning, for vengeance. "Send Harrid. Purge the old oak. I want proof the debt is paid."

Maricus stops. For a moment, he only studies me — measuring, recalibrating. Then he inclines his head, slow and deliberate. "As you command, my Prince."

Fisher is waiting on the path as I head back toward Lily — boots planted, jaw tight enough to crack. His face carries a rage he's not even bothering to hide.

When his eyes slice toward me, they gleam with something older, more dangerous, than mere mortal anger. "You protect her, boy," he mutters, voice gravelled with promise. "Or I will end you faster than you did Evans."

The threat hangs there — heavy, absurd, and yet... not.

I shrug it off, but the old man's warning digs under my skin in a way I don't admit.

When I enter Floral Beanz, she's exactly where I knew she'd be — hands occupied with the small, human rituals she uses to stitch herself back together. Wiping the rim of a mug. Aligning teaspoons so they sit just right. Moving with the fierce, stubborn precision of someone forcing her world back into order piece by fragile piece.

She looks up when I enter. For a heartbeat, the worry she's worn like a halo all morning softens — its edges melting at the sight of me. That tiny shift spears straight through my chest. It aches in a way that isn't just hunger and isn't just need. It's something older. Truer. Dangerously close to home. Safety.

"My fierce little dragon," I murmur, the words brushed with something ancient. Mo draganín.

The word leaves me before I can stop it — mine, soft and raw. "Lock up," I say next, gentler than I've spoken to anyone in years.

Her fingers fumble on the bolt. The tiny clink of metal betrays the tremor she's trying to hide. I lean in, covering her hand with mine, guiding the lock home with a soft click.

She flinches — not from me, but from the residue of danger still clinging to her skin.

The tremor in her hands makes my whole chest seize. "I'm

sorry."

The words scrape out too blunt, far too small to hold everything inside me.

"I should have been there. Should have known. If you'd only called for me—" My voice cracks. I hate the sound of it — the weakness, the truth in it. If only she needed me. If only I'd known. I will never forgive myself. My gaze catches the bruise blooming on her wrist. My insides twist. I should have taken his entire arm.

She draws a breath, steadying herself. "I don't scare," she says, though her voice frays at the edges like worn lace. "I'm used to people yelling if they don't get their coffee."

Humour as armour. A shield forged from routine. For a heartbeat, it works. Something in me unclenches. She hasn't broken — not entirely.

She pulls back, swallowing whatever shakes inside her.

"Could you... please bring in the chairs from out the front?"

I nod. Words feel too heavy, too sharp for my mouth.

I gather the chairs, the mundanity almost sacred after the violence outside.

When I find her again, she's in the back office, shrinking into familiar motions — aligning receipts, straightening pens, tidying what is already tidy, mundane human tasks.

The light is soft here. The air warm. I step close and place my hands on her shoulders, slow enough she could stop me. Her spine goes taut under my palms — the way a young mare stiffens before deciding whether to bolt. "Breathe," I whisper. "Relax. I will never harm you. You're in your space. You're safe."

She exhales — ragged, fraying, barely held together. The sound cuts me open. My hands move instinctively, easing tension from her neck and shoulders. Just clumsy gentleness from hands made for war, not for comfort. Yet here she is leaning into my touch.

Her soft, involuntary sounds as the knots loosen... They shiver through me like threads pulled tight in my chest.

I want to lift her. Hide her. Drag the whole world to its knees for frightening her.

The impulse to do more is a physical ache — sharp, consuming, unsteadying. I bend, lips brushing the pale curve of her throat. Not a kiss. A benediction. Her breath hitches. And then—

"Aodhan."

My name leaves her like a prayer she didn't mean to say aloud. Heat surges under my skin. Magic stirs. Every instinct I have — Fae, phoenix, prince — rises in a roar to claim, to mark, to make her mine. But I don't. I hold the line.

Because she hasn't chosen that path yet — and whatever this becomes, she will decide when, where, and how we cross it.

So instead, I wrap my arms around her, pulling her against my chest, my heart racing in uneven, frantic beats. I hold her. Quiet. Steady. Fiercely. Hoping this small, fragile moment is enough to keep her nightmares away... at least for tonight.

CHAPTER 16

Lily POV

The room feels too small. Too warm and too charged. Every surface seems to close in, like the space itself has become aware of us. Even the light feels thicker, honeyed, suspended between our bodies. His fingers find a knot just beneath my ear — one I didn't even know I'd been carrying — and he works it gently, deliberately. Heat spreads under his touch, something unclenching in me with every slow, sure pass of his thumbs.

I exhale, shaky. His hands slide lower, circling tension at the base of my skull, easing it open. My shoulders drop without my permission. My body leans into him — instinctive, drawn, as if gravity has chosen him as its new centre.

The steadiness of him — the quiet strength, the patience, the restraint — makes my chest both tighten and loosen at once. Like I'm coming undone and being put back together in the same breath. His hands come to rest lightly over mine, his warmth wrapping around my fingers. The simple contact steals the breath from my throat.

Nothing about this is casual. Nothing about this is safe. And yet...

I notice small things because noticing small things has kept me sane — and keeps me from turning to face him. The rough callus along the pad of his thumb. The way his pressure always stops a hair before a flinch. The faint shimmer at the edge of his tattoos. The warmth of his breath angled near my ear — deliberate, measured, never quite touching enough to cross the line into taking.

I should stop this. I should pull away. But... I don't.

Instead, he embraces me — and what do I do? I lean back. I feel the tension leave me in waves as I relax into his chest. A firm wall of muscle, his heart racing. My body leans before my brain catches up — traitorous and grateful all at once.

The warmth of him seeps into the cracks I thought I'd sealed shut. It is terrifying. It is steady. It is a tide pressing against a door I've held closed for too long. And for a moment, I let it.

"Aodhan," I whisper before I can swallow the name.

His hands still. For a single heartbeat the heat sharpens — a flare, like a stove turned up too high, like lightning coiling behind a cloud. My pulse trips and hammers. He must feel it the way I do.

"Relax," he murmurs, voice low and rough at the edges. The word falls between us like a plea and a kindness all at once. "You're safe."

Safe. The word lands in my chest like a stone dropped into deep water. It ripples outward, stirring things I've kept still for too long — grief, hunger, fear, something more dangerous than all three. I don't know whether to lean into it or run. My breath catches. I let my eyes close.

I should joke. Apologise. Deflect. I should say I'm fine. I'm not. I should do what I've done every year since Caleb — swallow it down until the ache turns quiet. Instead, his breath ghosts across my neck. Careful. Steady. So warm it stings behind my eyes, like the first tears after too long dry. My thoughts scatter like ash caught in a draft.

"Lily."

My name in his voice is a paradox — prayer and profanity, reverence and ruin. It drags out of him as though he can't hold it back, as though speaking it aloud is a mistake he means to keep making. And the sound of it in his mouth makes something deep in me twist sharp and sweet, an ache so startling it feels like being split open and put back together all at once.

I open my eyes. The office is the same as it always is — battered couch pushed against one wall, shelves stacked with invoices and boxes of takeaway cups, the scuffed skirting board I've been meaning to paint for three years. Ordinary. Familiar.

"Thank you. I didn't realise how much I've come to rely on you," I breathe, softer this time, surrender threaded into the syllables.

The world collapses to its smallest sounds: the faint whirr of the café fridge beyond the wall, the tick of the clock marking each second like a held breath, the twin cadence of his inhale and mine.

"You have no idea what you do to me," he murmurs. His voice is low, measured, but there's a ragged edge where restraint has begun to fray. My throat tightens. Logic claws for footing, but what spills out is pure instinct. "I think I do. It's the same for me."

His breath snags. A sharp inhale catches between us, the sound of control slipping. For a heartbeat, neither of us moves. The air swells, tight as a drawn bow, aching for release. One spark — just one — and the whole room would burn. Maybe that's what we both want.

Then his fingers fold around mine. Warm. Grounding. A tether I didn't know I wanted until it was there. His thumb strokes once, deliberate, and he leans closer. An unspoken question in the line of his mouth, in the patience woven through his every movement.

He gives me all the time in the world to pull away. To make this decision on my own. And so, when we finally close the last breath of distance, it isn't a kiss so much as ignition. A spark striking tinder, fire racing the line before either of us can second-guess. Mouths crash together, breath tangling, and everything I've braced tight for six long years — grief, guilt, hunger, want, need — shatters into thousands of pieces.

His lips are hot, unyielding, a claiming deep within — vibrating against my mouth, down my spine, into the hollow places I thought had gone numb. I fold into it, desperate, fists knotting in the linen of his shirt as if that alone could keep us suspended in this tiny circle where the world cannot intrude.

When we part, breathless and flushed, our foreheads fall together, slick with sweat, panting like runners stumbling across a finish line we never trained for. His eyes darker than I've ever seen them, need written in a script my body understands without translation.

"Not here," he rasps.

His voice is torn, roughened, as if each word costs him. "Not like this. I want you to choose — not in a moment of fear, but for it to be meaningful."

The hollow space inside me twists at the promise beneath those words. Not here. Not rushed. Not careless. Something in me nods before I can find speech, a silent agreement that feels bigger than language.

"Now let me get you home, safe and sound." He smiles, the corners of his eyes softening.

That night, I do not sleep.

I lie on my back and track the fan's gentle hum.

I count the slats of light through the curtains. I think of the way he said safe — and meant it.

Memory is a traitor; it plays me back slices I didn't ask for: his hands — the steadiness, the strength; the Shadow of his breath along my throat; the stunned, greedy relief that poured through me when our mouths met. I touch my lips, ridiculous and tender. They are swollen, not much, but enough to know I've crossed a border with no map for getting back.

"God," I breathe into the dark, because there is no one to hear it but Nyxie and whatever old thing still listens in this house. "What am I doing?" I roll, tangle my leg in the sheet, untangle it. The need coiling within me keeps returning, strong enough to knock me off my feet.

I haven't wanted anyone like this since Cal.

The thought is cold water — Cal in the garden riddled with spiderwebs, Cal swearing when he dropped screws down vents, Cal letting Daisy paint his nails because she asked without looking at him, and he understood the kind of decisions that mattered. I exhale so slow it barely counts and the ache folds up from my chest to my throat.

"I know," I tell the ceiling. "I know."

I don't think the dead hear the living, not really. But I speak to him anyway because I need him to know. "I met someone who feels dangerous — but the kind of danger I want around. I'm trying to be brave without being stupid. I'm trying to keep everyone safe.

I miss you," I whisper.

CHAPTER 17

Lily POV

I wake just before dawn, groggy and exhausted, nightmares on my mind. I pad barefoot through the quiet. The big panes of glass Cal once called impractical, hold a picture of the world in soft layers — grey paddocks, darker gums, sky blanching at the edges with coming heat. The plants along the banister tilt toward the window, leaves glossy, sated from last night's watering. The hanging pots throw shadows shaped like crowns.

"High ceilings? For your plants?" Cal had teased the first week we moved in, laughter tucked into his voice because he already knew the answer.

"Yes," I'd answered with my chin high, as if I'd invented the concept of light. "And for the vines. I want them to reach and not hit a ceiling."

The memory fades as I walk to the kitchen. I make coffee quietly so as not to wake anyone, the kids upstairs sleep like stones — and I stand at the window with the mug warming my hands. I drop the teaspoon. The clang shivers up my arm in a way that makes me want to cry. I crouch, pick it up, and press my forehead to the cool tile for three counts. When I stand, my hands shake, and I can't find an honest reason why.

My eyes drift, as they always do, to the photos on the wall. Cal's easy grin is frozen there — sun tangled in his hair, arm slung around me, the kids climbing over him in the garden like he was a tree built just for them. For a moment, it feels like if I roll over, I'll find him there, warm and laughing, smelling of coffee and grass.

But reality creeps in like a slow poison. He isn't here. Hasn't been for years. And each time that truth hits, it feels new and raw — and I relive the phone call I received that day.

The guilt is always worst in the mornings. Like waking up is a betrayal, proof that I kept going when he didn't. And every time, some part of me whispers: traitor. I think about two truths that want to fight: I am a widow, and I am a woman who has found someone she is drawn to. I don't know if they can coexist without tearing me open. I know that yesterday, they did.

"Oi! Mum!" Oliver's voice breaks the silence, sharp from upstairs, threaded with frustration. His tone yanks me out of the hole I'd fallen into.

I drag myself from the bench and the memories that ache and take myself away from further thoughts. Daisy barrels into the kitchen before I can reach the last step, arms crossed and smirk firmly in place. "Don't look at me," she says, rolling her eyes. "He's losing his mind because he lost again."

"You cheated!" Oliver yells up the staircase, indignant as only a sixteen-year-old boy can be. Daisy's grin widens, sharp and smug. "It's called strategy, little brother. Try it sometime — and don't be such a sore loser."

"You're the loser, Daisy!" He sticks his tongue out as if that ends the argument. Watching them like this, so alive, makes me think the same thing every time: I'd do anything to keep them safe.

But when their voices fade, the house quiets too quickly. The silence presses down, heavy as lead. It makes the walls feel closer. Nyxie pads to my side, silent as ever, a constant presence. She knows. I let my hand fall to her head, fingers brushing over velvet-soft ears, grounding myself in her warmth. I force myself into motion.

On days like this — when the grief swells too sharp, and nightmares linger — I have to move, or I'll drown in it. I walk Nyxie through the garden, check the fences, water the plants — the small rituals that make up survival. Distraction. If I keep my body busy, maybe my mind won't catch up. The morning air is crisp, tinged with damp earth and wildflowers, dew clinging like diamonds to the grass. But none of it touches the knot twisting in my chest.

Ah, damn it — my thoughts have strayed too far. The ache rises fast, brutal in its suddenness, and my knees buckle. I sink to the floor, hands braced against garden path, palms slipping with sweat. My breaths come short and jagged, chest too tight, vision hazing at the edges. Panic — sharp, merciless — a predator that never gives chase but always catches up.

"It's okay," I whisper, though my voice trembles so thin it barely sounds like mine. "Breathe. Just… breathe." Nyxie presses her full weight against me, steady as an anchor, her warm flank a wall between me and the abyss. In. Out. Her warmth. My breath. Earth beneath my palms. And then the ground rumbles.

At first it's subtle — a low tremor threading through the ground, rattling the pots. Then it deepens — a rolling growl, like thunder dragged through the earth itself. The trees sway; the basil pot on the windowsill shivers. A pot topples from the stand and shatters in a spray of jagged shards.

My head snaps up. My pulse leaps into my throat. "What the hell…" The vibration fades as suddenly as it began, but the echo clings. Is this what Aodhan warned me about?

His words coil back, steady and terrible: *Trouble is coming, and you're standing in the centre of it.* Nyxie watches from the doorway — ears forward, eyes gold as candlelight. "Let's head to work, hey, pup." My phone buzzes.

Viv: *I'm okay, Lil. I mean… I will be. I'll be back in tomorrow. I know you said take as much time as I need. He wasn't Deck — just memories.*

I type back without hesitating.

Me: *Deck will never hurt you again. And that stranger is*

gone — Aodhan saw to it. But take all the time you need, Viv.

Another buzz.

Emma sends twelve knife emojis and a heart. I laugh out loud in the empty kitchen and feel human again — for three whole seconds.

By the time I reach the café, I've plastered a calm mask over my features. Inside, my nerves fray. My chest feels too tight; my hands tremble even as I force them still. Sal's already behind the counter, resumes spread in neat surgical rows, her pen tapping in rhythm. She doesn't look up when I walk in — small mercies.

"We need to shortlist three before ten," she says briskly. "First impressions matter, and I'd like another casual as soon as possible."

"You need to meet them before you cull, Sal," I reply, tying my apron. My voice sounds steadier than I feel — thank the gods. She shrugs, eyes still on the paper.

"How I weed them out. Excellent instincts." I snort softly. "Okay, Sal." I keep walking, heading for the back.

The bell chimes. Aodhan's expression when he sees me is threaded with concern — and something softer, more dangerous: the look of a man who slept as little as I did.

"Morning," I say, and the word feels too small.

"Morning," he returns, just as gentle.

We don't speak about yesterday. But when he orders a long black and I hand it over, our fingers brush — the briefest pass — and heat licks along my palm like memory.

"Later," he says under his breath — a promise, not a question.

"Later," I say back, because it's all I can promise.

Outside, the mountain breathes. Inside, the café fills. Between those two spaces, I decide — not with logic, but with the tired, stubborn part of me that has survived worse — that I am allowed to have this. Not the whole of it, not yet. But this: a safe word said in a dark office; a kiss that was offered, not took; a man who will stand at my boundary and keep others back without stepping over it himself.

I breathe, finally, and the room exhales with me.

The morning rush hits fast and merciless. I smile, nod, pour coffee with the precision of muscle memory. My body's coiled tight, sensing a storm before it breaks.

That's when a group walks in. Too perfect. Too still. Beauty so sharp it borders unreal — cheekbones precise, eyes too symmetrical, movements too smooth to be human. They don't shuffle. Don't stumble. They glide.

My skin prickles. The vines along the window twitch, leaves stirring though no breeze moves them. I sense it straight away. Trouble. I cross the floor, voice warm, professional. "Afternoon. Just checking in — can I get you anything?"

The tallest woman rises, unhurried, eyes sweeping over me like a blade. She's striking — dangerous — her gown draped like molten silk. Her pale eyes are glacial, lightless, and her smile doesn't touch them. The smaller woman beside her flinches before smoothing her face into composure.

"Everything's fine, thank you," she says softly — accented — but her gaze betrays her, flicking anxious toward her companion, as if waiting for permission to breathe. "Everything would be better," the tall one purrs, voice a knife wrapped in silk, "if you offered us some entertainment. A song... a *dance,* perhaps." Her gaze drifts over me, slow, deliberate, predatory — as if I might perform for her amusement.

My stomach knots, but I square my shoulders, drawing a steady breath. "We don't do live entertainment here," I say, even. "Crystal Hollow half an hour down the road has a pub. You'll find what you're after there." For a fraction of a second, surprise cracks her mask. Then fury floods in its place. The air tightens, sharp as glass, hairs rising on my arms.

She lifts her hand — poised to strike with those perfectly manicured nails — when the door swings open.

Maricus strolls in first, loose-limbed, a grin that would make most women weak at the knees. Behind him follows Emma all sunshine with teeth. Where he radiates menace wrapped in charm, she radiates the danger of a blade disguised as warmth.

The tall woman freezes. Her head turns, eyes snapping to Maricus as if realising she's no longer the most dangerous thing in the room. "And what," Maricus drags, smooth and lazy, "is a Fire Court princess doing so far from home?" His head tilts, voice calm but edged. "Erif."

The name lands like a slap. Her spine stiffens, fury coiling in her posture — hot enough to scorch. "None of your business, Prince's pet," she spits, every syllable dipped in venom. Her gaze slides back to me, and the weight of it makes my skin crawl. Danger there. Calculation. A promise that tastes of blood. "Though perhaps..." Her smile unfurls, menacing. "I've found something more interesting than I expected."

My pulse stutters. Emma steps closer, jaw tight, ready. Nyxie shifts at my heel. Maricus moves first. In a blink, he's in her path — loose grin still carved across his face, but his stance betrays him "Careful, princess," he says softly, a threat curling under every syllable. "Your mother would be most displeased if she knew where you've wandered. Or who you've been seen with." His grin sharpens, humourless now — a weapon instead of charm. "And you know me. I do so love gossip."

The air crackles, heat brittle and dangerous, their stand-off filling the café until it feels like the walls might cave in. Erif doesn't flinch, but her fingers twitch once — a spark skitters across her palm before dying.

"I'll be back," she promises finally, lips curling into a cruel smile. "And next time, your little pets won't be here to protect you." She snaps her fingers. The group dissolves in a shimmer of fire and smoke, the scent of scorched air hanging heavy where they'd stood. Silence slams down in their absence.

What the hell was that?

Maricus clicks his tongue. Emma exhales slow. Nyxie's growl fades. And me? I realise only then that my hands are trembling, white-knuckled around the cloth I hadn't even noticed I was still holding.

The door creaks, and Mr Fisher pokes his head in — plaid shirt dusty, boots scuffed with red earth. His cap sits crooked,

Shadowing his weathered face. His eyes crinkle, the lines of a man who's seen more than he ever says, as he frowns. "What'd I miss, love?"

I summon a smile with every bit of restraint I have not to show how I feel inside.

"Nothing. Just a rude customer, who somehow specialises in magic."

His gaze lingers a moment too long, sharp and knowing — like he can smell a lie as easily as petrol on his hands. Then he nods, satisfied enough to let it go, and slips away, the door closing behind him with a soft thud. Emma blows out a breath, running her hand through her hair until it sticks out in dark, messy waves. "Bloody hell," she mutters, laughter bleeding through her nerves. "Dramatic much?"

I laugh, trying to break the tension. "So... you and Maricus, then? A thing?" Her cheeks flush, but her grin is wicked, teeth flashing. "Maybe. Maybe not."

Maricus smirks from where he leans — lazy as a cat, sharp as a blade.

"Oh, it's a thing. She burns brighter every time I touch her." Emma arches a brow, lips curling. "Touch me? If I recall correctly, you were begging last night. Twice."

He leans in closer, Shadows at his heels coiling like they enjoy the banter as much as he does. His eyes gleam "Strategy, sweetheart. Had you ready to combust at a breath."

I groan, dragging a hand down my face. "Too much information. Please." Sal snorts from behind the counter, trying and failing to hide her laughter behind a mug.

Later, I catch Aodhan at the door. He stands like stone — shoulders drawn tight, jaw cut hard. Unease radiates off him, quiet but sharp. Maricus had told me earlier that he'd let Aodhan know what happened, grinning like the cheshire cat as he said it.

I walk over as calmly as I can. "Erif?" I ask, my voice steady though my hands are not. "Another of your... friends?"

His eyes snap to mine. "She's no friend," he says flatly. "She's a pampered brat who wields words like weapons. Dangerous. Volatile." His voice drops lower, rougher, threaded with something that sounds almost like fear. "Don't go near her. And if she appears again, call for me."

The finality in his tone is a wall, and part of me wants to push against it — to demand more, to pry open the storm locked tight behind his ribs. But I see it: the strain in his posture, the shadows of fury barely leashed. I swallow the urge. Some truths aren't ready to be spoken. Not yet.

Then again, I think, how do I call someone if I don't have their number?

When I finally lock up for the night, the weight of it all presses in — Cal's absence, the strangers circling closer, the way Oliver has been watching me lately like he's waiting for something to break.

The café smells of cooling bread and coffee gone bitter with the hour. Outside, gravel crunches under tyres.

Oliver pedals up, his bike rattling over the stones. His hair is damp with sweat, his jaw set too tight for a sixteen-year-old. He doesn't even put a foot down before blurting, "Mum. Why didn't you tell me?"

The words throw my mind into chaos. "Tell you what?"

"Emma said." His voice is rough, cracking at the edges. "You've got people hanging around — dangerous ones. And you didn't call me, didn't tell me." His fingers clench on the handlebars, white-knuckled. "I heard Viv talking to her about it. And you—" He swallows, the next words tearing out before he can stop them. "Dad would've—" He cuts himself off, jaw trembling, eyes bright with the pain of saying his name.

The blow lands deep. A reflex rises — to tell him everything so he knows to protect himself. But he's sixteen. He should be worrying about soccer boots, about making the team, about a girl at school who smiles at him — not about me. I step closer, keep my voice soft. "I'm your mum," I say, though the words shake. "You don't need to protect me. *That's not your job.*"

He shakes his head, anger sharp in every line of him. "It's not a job if it's family," he mutters, and then he's gone — pushing off hard, tyres spitting gravel, his back a stiff line as he pedals into the dark. Tears sting. My chest aches. The echo of his wheels fades down the road, leaving only the night. The ground trembles again — sharper this time, like a warning threaded through the cool mountain air. The leaves on the hedgerow shiver without wind, blossoms shedding a faint, metallic-smelling pollen.

A hand lands on my shoulder — warm, steady, anchoring. "Breathe," Aodhan murmurs, his voice low, close, a rumble that settles under my ribs. "Everything will be okay. He's just trying to look out for you."

And for the first time all day, I lean into him, grounding myself and take a long breathe.

CHAPTER 18

Lily POV

I decide to take a few days off — not the usual stay-at-home break of washing, errands, and half-working through emails, but a real one. A clean cut. Just silence, if only for a moment.

Sal doesn't argue. She's been watching me fray for weeks — the way I press my palms flat against the counter too long after closing, the way my eyes track the door for danger, the way I forget I'm still holding the milk jug until steam curls past my wrist.

When she tells me she'll run the shop, there's no hesitation. "Finally hired a casual," she announces with exaggerated triumph, "someone who can operate an espresso machine without causing an incident. Miracles happen. So you don't need to be here every day — you can actually just... you know, Manage from home."

Relief moves through me, a weight lifting off my shoulders. She winks. Her grin is sharp, but her eyes are soft. Then she tosses me the toasties she insisted on making — one so overloaded with cheese it might qualify as a hazard. She hands it over with a mock flourish. "For the road. Don't choke boss. And relax today will ya?"

I pack as if afraid my resolve might vanish if I wait too long: a picnic blanket, a thermos of coffee strong enough to wake the dead, the toasties, and finally, the book Emma swore would change my life. She'd pressed it into my hands with that relentless gleam of hers "Read it," she'd said. "Life-changing, this one."

The bag sits ready at my feet. My chest feels both lighter and heavier — as though permission to rest is a luxury I'm not sure I've earned.

Nyxie scrambles into the passenger seat the moment I click the door shut, claws scratching across the upholstery and tufts of fur flying. She circles twice, pawing at the picnic blanket with all the dignity of a queen rearranging her throne, then collapses with a huff. One paw drapes over the edge of the seat as though she owns not just the car, but the whole road ahead. Her tail thumps the dash in a steady beat.

I text the kids and Vivienne in one breath, thumbs flying: *Taking a drive. Nyxie's with me. Back for dinner.*

Viv's reply pings almost instantly: *Take all the time you need.*

Oliver: *k*

Daisy: *Jealous, Mum! Send pics of the valley. And if you drive past Frosty's, grab pistachio and salted caramel!*

A laugh slips out. "Some things never change."

The asphalt winds through green so dense it feels painted — the kind of green that makes you believe in old stories, in fae and dragons and magic tucked between gum trees. Mist clings low at first, veiling the trunks in silver gauze before lifting in soft puffs that snag on spiderwebs and scatter into the tops of the shrubs. The air grows rich with eucalyptus, sharp and sweet, until I can taste it.

The mountains roll out slow and endless ahead, their backs curved against the sky like something ancient and unchanging. I park at our lookout. The tyres crunch over gravel and settle into the same scraped patch of ground where a dozen picnics have landed over the years — summer lunches with the kids, Cal's guitar propped against the rail, afternoons that smelled of sandwiches and sunscreen.

The grass rolls out like a green sea, folding down to the valley where Crystal Hollow lies tiny and fragile: houses no bigger than ants, the creek glinting silver as though stitched by an unseen hand, paddocks flattened into quilt squares.

I spread the rug with more care than it needs, lay out the thermos, the toasties wrapped in foil, and the book Emma pressed into my hands. Lush words, lovers set apart only to be found again later. For the first hour, I lose myself in the pages. The characters bleed and burn and kiss with the urgency of people who don't know what they'll lose. I read until my pulse matches theirs, kicking my feet and giggling aloud.

Nyxie occupies herself with her usual mischief — digging a hole she has no intention of lying in, then sprawling belly-up on the rug, all four legs in the air, ignoring me completely.

Time drips slow and gentle. Sun warms the back of my neck. A soft breeze skates across the valley, stirring the grass until it shimmers like water. Insects buzz a lazy chorus. Birds call from somewhere down the slope, the sound rich and echoing between trees.

Then they hush mid-note. The air stops moving. The silence is too clean. Every hair along my arms prickles awake. I set the book down, eyes searching the tree line.

Then the voice comes — low, careful. "I didn't mean to interrupt." The sound is unmistakable.

I look up, squinting against the sun's glare — and there he is. Aodhan, all silhouette and sunlight. "You really shouldn't jump out like that," I mutter, blinking back the sting in my eyes.

"I apologise," he says softly. "I didn't want to frighten you."

His shirt clings where the breeze presses against him, and beneath the linen I catch the shifting glow of those lines carved into his skin — gold and amber tattoos alive with their own quiet weather, like dawn has learned how to breathe beneath his flesh. The sight knocks something loose in me, folds my chest in half, then lets it drop all at once.

"Bloody hell," I mutter before I can stop myself, and then laugh — because what else does one do when they've just caught themselves drooling. "Oh. Uh—no worries." My voice sounds thinner than I am, embarrassed and fragile in my own mouth. Heat crawls up my throat. I reach for the book as if hiding the page will erase what I've been reading — words meant for fantasy, not reality.

His gaze — that impossible ring of blue and molten gold — fixes on me like a hinge, pinning me open. He bends, fluid, and before my fingers can close around the cover, the book is in his hand.

"You seemed... preoccupied," he says, glancing at the title, then back to me.

I want to die. Or at least burrow six feet under the picnic rug and let the valley fold over me. Instead, with the deliberate calm of a man who knows the weight of what I was imagining moments before, he lets the pages fall open and begins to read.

His voice lowers, deliberate and unhurried, and I feel every word before I understand it. *"He skims her thigh, fingertips brushing the edge of her heat, drawing slow circles until her breath hitches. He lifts her leg, bends low, and kisses a path inward, tasting every—"*

"Stop!" The word bursts out of me like a fire alarm.

My face burns hotter than the sun overhead. I lunge for the book, snatching it back and clutching it to my chest like a shield. "You—no. Absolutely not."

He straightens slowly, watching me. Amusement flickers at the corner of his mouth. The silence stretches, charged.

"I..." My throat locks. My heart beats itself against my ribs like it's trying to escape. "That was... fiction. Emma's."

Sorry, Emma.

"Was it?" he murmurs. The question hangs there — heavier than it has any right to be. Then, teasing, he snatches the book back, looking at the cover once more.

"Aodhan!" My lunge is pure reflex, ridiculous — half-laugh, half-panicked gasp — as I grab at the book clutched in his hand. His hands find my waist, steadying me as I half-fall into him. He doesn't let go. Of course he doesn't. The corner of his mouth curves — that almost-smile that knows exactly how much chaos he's just unleashed.

"You surprise me more, Lily," he says, voice low and deliberate. His gaze holds mine until my breath stutters. "Is this what you like?" My legs knot together in a reflex of decorum, an instinct to contain myself, to shut the door on everything his question cracks open.

It fails spectacularly. My cheeks burn, my pulse trips, and a small, traitorous part of me answers to the rhythm of the line he read aloud — the cadence of his voice threading through me like fact instead of fiction. The thought of his mouth forming those words again, for me, leaves a low, insistent heat curling tight in my core.

"Do you mind if I join you?" he asks. Simple. Easy. As if he hasn't just set my world spinning. His tone is casual, but the look in his eyes ruins the act — molten edges, patient and coiled, like something caged and choosing not to strike. "I could keep reading to you, if you like…"

My inner voice shrieks — don't you dare let him. Another, softer voice murmurs back — *don't you dare stop him.* When I look at him, I realise I'm still in his arms — steady, warm, safe. Near enough to feel the pull of him, the heat rolling off his body like weather shifting the whole valley to make room for him. Even the breeze feels different, skimming my skin, tilting toward him as though it, too, has no choice.

"Sit," I manage, pointing to the far end of the blanket as I step out from his arms. The cold hits me immediately. "But Nyxie's claimed this spot." My attempt at humour lands, then dies a miserable death. I shrink inward at the terrible dad joke that just left my mouth. "And absolutely no… play-by-plays. Thank you."

He grins — cheeky, dimples tugging at the corners of his mouth — and lowers himself with deliberate care. Every movement is unhurried. I can see each muscle contract and tell myself to swallow the drool forming. I look elsewhere, pretending to admire the view, but I see his hand hover in the space between us, fingers flexing once — like a man fighting his own inner battle. Like he wants to touch but knows that if we cross that line there will be no going back, no casual jokes, no pretending this is simple.

For a minute we simply exist inside the same sliver of light.

No conversation. Just the blanket, the smell of cool air, and the line of the horizon brightening in soft orange hues. The valley below lies hazed in eucalyptus and pine, the greens darkening beneath the shifting light.

He watches me watch the world — quiet, steady — like a question is forming, like he doesn't quite understand why I'm so entranced. There's a gentleness to him I didn't expect. Softness at odds with the incendiary sweep of him. He's so many things at once — arrogant, assertive, protective, and kind. I wonder which face is truly his, and why his very presence sends my thoughts into turmoil.

I turn to look at him, pause, and decide to muster courage later. "How did you find me?"

"Emma mentioned you were taking the day when I stopped by the café earlier. I was worried about you, considering everything you've been through these last few weeks." His eyes flash with anger before softening again. "I didn't want you to be alone, and she told me where to find your favourite spot."

Emma. I groan inwardly, rubbing my temple. Of course. I can already imagine her smirking to herself. "What were you doing up here?" he asks at last, voice quiet, almost blending with the wind.

"Thinking," I say, eyes fixed on the silver thread of the creek. "Trying to remember what silence used to feel like. And because I needed to get away from life for a day."

His gaze stays on me, patient — like he can see the words I don't say hovering between us. Sometimes I wonder if he can read minds.

"And are you any better for it?"

"Not really." The laugh that leaves me is small and brittle. It tastes like chalk. The sound flares with a memory: Cal, face streaked with mud; Daisy's hair tangled with creek weeds and that grin — the kind that made you feel you'd done something right just by existing. Oliver, proud on a rock with a scraped knee and a heroic story. The images are bright and sharp as glass lodged under my ribs. "But," I add, swallowing against the ache, "I can reminisce. Enjoy the quiet and the memories before chaos changed my life."

He lifts his head slightly, eyes softening, and I know he understands exactly what that means. He listens like every word matters — like the air itself was built for hearing without judgement.

"So much has changed since you showed up," I continue. The words spill easily here, in this open valley with no interruptions. "Everything's shifting faster than I can follow. The kids growing into their own lives. Daisy graduating, Oli is nearly in senior year. Money, mornings, the café. And now..."

My throat tightens, the weight lifting even as I say it. "You. Aodhan."

His jaw works at the sound of his name — a small visible pulse along the muscle in his neck, a flex beneath his skin. For once I see him not as myth or pedestal but as a man, with Shadows of his own. He looks away briefly and the gold ring in his eyes flickers like an old coin catching sun.

"I'm... sorry for the instability I've brought," he says slowly, each word measured, the honesty raw. "I didn't mean to turn your life upside-down."

"You did," I admit, because it's true. "In a way that's complicated. Dangerous. And opening old wounds I didn't want to face." I can't stop the words; they tumble out faster than sense can catch them. "You made me realise I haven't been living, just you know...moving through the motions."

Between us, this connection hums — a vibration, a song tethering him to something inside me. He reaches, and my heart stutters, unsure. His fingers brush the necklace at my throat — the wedding band sleeping beneath my collarbone. Cal's once; something older now that remembers roots and earth and vows.

"You're not alone," he says softly. "You won't be. I won't let you be — not when you're sad, not when you need a shoulder, or someone to fight beside you. Or, in your case, maybe hold your bat, mo draganín."

The admission blooms like a flower in a cave — gentle, defiant of its lack of light, a truth he shouldn't say but does anyway. For the first time, we trade small, private confessions — sins that shouldn't be spoken.

He gives me his in fragments: his father's long illness, the relentless expectations of a royal line, the way his childhood wasn't the shining world I'd imagined but a corridor of glass, watched by voices waiting for him to misstep. His words are quiet but heavy, and with each one he seems lighter.

"They laid out my path from birth," he says, voice low, edged with bitterness. "Every step planned, no deviation allowed."

"You don't look like someone who does as he's told," I tell him, and I mean it. I've seen that glower in the café — the way his eyes and posture change when threatened.

For a second his mask shifts. He gives one of those small, crooked half-grins — knowing, reckless. "You don't look like someone who hides in the mountains when she needs a break," he counters softly.

Something stirs in the scrub down the slope — just a rustle, a shift of dry leaves — and my pulse jumps. We both turn at once, twin instruments tuned to the same pitch. For a second I'm ready to bolt to the car and drag him with me. But it's only a wallaby, skittering past, oblivious to our complicated human lives. I sigh in relief. "Thank God for that.

He laughs, softer — a crack opening in stone. "You looked ready to take on a bear. His head tips back, laughter rough and unrestrained.

"Well, if you must know, I was ready to grab my bat." He laughs harder, snorting behind his fist as if I can't hear him.

"Yes, I can imagine," he says finally, eyes gleaming. "I still recall your swing the other day. Magnificent to watch." His laughter fades, replaced by something gentler — appreciation, awe. The tension unravels... then recoils somewhere deeper. Heat pools low and heavy. He shifts closer, just a fraction, and the space between us disappears. I feel his arm brush mine.

"You make me feel safe," I say at last — a truth I didn't expect to speak aloud. The words hang between us like a secret never meant to exist.

He looks at me as though I'm a constellation newly discovered. "And you make me feel... human," he replies, voice rough, almost a confession. "Which is a dangerous place for me to be." The last words slip into the hush of the valley and stay there, echoing. His gaze holds mine, unguarded, and for a heartbeat we're both just people — no titles, no café — breathing the same thin air and wondering what happens if we stop pretending the seam between us isn't already a line we've crossed.

We both know the meaning behind the words. We both know the consequences — my children and his world, planets in opposing orbits. Yet there, in that green quiet, the weight of it feels a thousand miles away.

I lean, almost without thought, and let my head come to rest against his shoulder. His arm lifts, drawing me closer until I'm folded against the warmth of his chest, the crook of his arm a perfect fit. Beside me, he doesn't speak, doesn't move — just breathes in rhythm, as if he's content to be a man in the quiet instead of a prince, a weapon, a storm.

Eventually the sun disappears behind the ridge. Shadows lengthen, slow and drawn, and the birds trade their bright calls for softer evening notes. We pack away slowly, dragging time out for a few moments more. Leaving feels like shutting a book before you've read the ending.

Nyxie bounds into the car with all the grace of a baby gazelle — awkward, knocking everything off the passenger seat. Aodhan helps make sure everything's loaded, then brushes a loose curl behind my ear. "I'll see you soon, Lily, I know you have questions. And I will answer them when your ready to ask," he murmurs, before leaning down to press a soft kiss to the crown of my head a small goodbye that promises more tomorrows.

The drive home feels different. The road is the same — winding and green — but the colours are sharper, as if the world itself has turned a dial. The air tastes clean, the scent of the trees sharper, the sky layered with quiet promise. Somewhere on the ridge I know his palace gleams — towers of glass and gold, roads that shimmer like heat haze on a dry summer's day — but it feels far away, like a story meant for someone else's lifetime.

When I pull into the drive, the house looks smaller and softer, as if it's calling me home. Oliver sits on the porch, guitar slung haphazardly, making faces at the neighbour's dog until Daisy shoves him with her hip. She waves, broad and bright, a grin splitting her face.

Viv meets me at the door, tea in hand, eyes sharp with knowing. She doesn't waste time. "And?" she says. And everything.

And nothing. I melt into the kitchen, the time with Aodhan sealed away in a quiet corner of my mind, something meant only for me — just for tonight. "It was what I needed," I say softly.

That night I sleep in a way I haven't in months. I wake and swear I can still feel his fingers anchored at my shoulder. Sometimes, in those deep, merciful stretches where the dream is only the house — safe and whole — I hear his voice again, reading the lines from the book.

Awake, the burn inside me doesn't extinguish; it settles instead into something steadier. A fire. A need. An urgency. And for the first time in nearly six years I haven't dreamt of Caleb.

CHAPTER 19

Lily POV

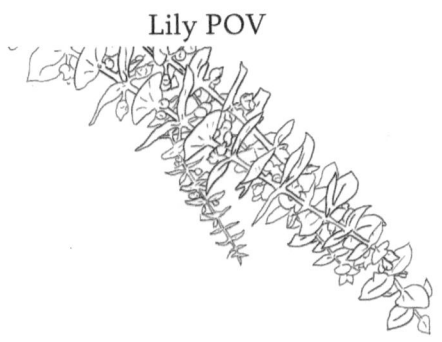

Vivienne and Emma ambush me before I've even had my first sip of coffee for the day. "You've got one more day off," Viv says, arms folded across her chest, her voice sharp enough to slice bread. She looks every inch the bossy older sister, chin tipped, daring me to argue.

Emma leans against the counter like she owns the place, her wicked grin already curving, eyes bright with trouble. "Your sister's right, babe. Dad's taking the kids tonight — pizza, footy, the usual chaos. And we"—she gestures extravagantly between the three of us—"are going out."

I squint at her, mug halfway to my lips. "Define 'out.'" A sense of foreboding washes over me.

"A night out," she sing-songs, practically bouncing. "Girls only. No boy talk. And before you even ask — no saying no."

I arch a brow, suspicion lacing through my fatigue. "Or Maricus, or was it ... an Aquarius now?" Emma throws her head back and laughs, loud and unashamed.

"Especially no Maricus." She pauses for dramatic effect, her grin sharpening into something downright feral.

"Although... if you're desperate, I could call him, get him to perform a strip tease. That man loves an audience almost as much as he loves his cock."

Vivienne groans, pinching the bridge of her nose like she's

already regretting this plan. I choke on my coffee, sputtering into my sleeve. "God, Em," I manage, heat climbing my face. "I don't need the mental images. Can't you filter?"

"Not when it's true," she fires back, utterly unabashed. "Besides, someone needs to keep things interesting around here—or should I say, someone needs..."

"Do not finish that sentence." Viv's sigh is long-suffering but her mouth twitches like she's fighting a smile.

"Ignore her. Tonight's about you, Lily. Not kids. Not work or Crystal Hollow politics. Not bloody weird customers. Just... us. One night where you're allowed to laugh without looking over your shoulder, or forcing a smile."

Something inside me softens — the care of being seen in a way I hadn't realised I needed. I nod slowly, letting the corner of my mouth tilt. "Fine. One night. But I swear, if this ends with me singing in a pub, I'm never forgiving the both of you."

Emma's grin is pure mischief. "Oh, sweetheart. You'll be lucky if that's all it ends with." Vivienne snorts, shaking her head, but the amusement in her eyes is impossible to hide — she's just as excited.

"Tonight," Emma continues, voice dropping to faux-serious, "is about us. Cocktails, dancing, forgetting every ounce of crap that's been weighing you down." She pokes me with a manicured finger, then softens so quick it's theatrical.

"And if you show up in one of those tragic boho maxi dresses, I will set it on fire. Don't test me, Lil."

"Tragic?" I echo, affronted.

"Yes, tragic." She beams, triumphant as a child who's stolen the last cookie from the jar. "This is a rescue mission. Wardrobe intervention is step one." Vivienne folds her arms, all playful readiness. "Something that says you could run a business and also make someone's jaw drop. Not 'I couldn't be bothered, I'd rather be in pyjamas.'"

I glance down at my cardigan, the one I've worn so often it's showing holes — more character than most of Emma's dates. The idea of parading myself out of habit and into attention makes my stomach do a small, traitorous flip. "What if I don't want to be stared at?" I ask, genuinely.

Emma's usual cheeky smile fades, replaced with gentle kindness. "We don't want strangers staring, love. We want admiration that comes with an awkward compliment and a drink bought in your name. Different breed. Harmless... mostly. But I'll fend off any unwanted attention with my wit."

Viv steps in like the diplomat sister she is. "We'll start simple. Neutral palette, structured cut. One bold accessory. You can still be you — just the version that pops. We'll build from there."

They already have it planned like a well-structured operation: Vivienne on logistics, Emma on aesthetics, me on reluctant compliance. The three of us move through my bedroom like a well-rehearsed troupe. Emma raids my closet with more enthusiasm than I can muster.

"Wow, where was this hidden?" Viv mutters, nodding to Emma like the conspirators they are.

"Try this," Emma says, holding up an emerald-green dress that somehow reads party. It catches the light, showing all the right curves.

"You can move in it. You can kick a chair over in it and still look like you, just shiny."

I hold it at arm's length, feeling ridiculous and oddly exhilarated.

"This was a gift," I tell them.

"From who?" Viv looks over, intrigued.

"Mum, but I never had a reason to wear it."

In the bathroom mirror it's chaos. My dress hanging behind us over the door, gleaming like it's finally getting its time to shine. It draws the eye and refuses to let go. Emma fusses with my hair like I'm a wild horse needing to be tamed and groomed — pulling, brushing, tightening — my scalp tender under her hands. Viv applies my makeup with every bit of care, a steady hand painting a masterpiece. She looks over my face one last time before blowing a soft breath to dust away the excess powder. They step back, nod, and smile like they've achieved all their goals before setting to work on themselves.

I step into the emerald-green halter maxi — silk that pours

over my skin like liquid. The slit runs high — near my thigh — every step whispering scandal. My curls fall loose around my shoulders, the faint shimmer Viv dusted along my cheekbones catching every stray beam of light.

"You look amazing," Viv says softly.

"Every bit the young woman I remember running amok in Rivertide in our younger years. Someone who didn't leave until the sun had risen and walked out of the club barefoot."

Emma adds, wicked as ever, "You look like someone who could absolutely make a prince lose his composure in public. Bonus."

Emma is temptation incarnate — her fitted black dress clings in all the right places, kitten heels clicking a rhythm that promises trouble, lips painted the precise shade of sin that makes heads turn without effort. She knows it too, her dark hair bouncing around her in loose curls.

Vivienne, usually the calm in any storm, is a revelation in crimson, making her red hair pop in the light. The dress is sculpted perfection — neckline daring, hemline ruthless. Paired with heels sharp enough to draw blood, she carries herself like a queen who doesn't need a crown.

"Perfect," she purrs, snapping a picture before I can register the flash. Her grin widens at my horrified look. "Now, let's go remind the world what we're made of — and why women run it."

I roll my eyes, but the words stick somewhere between my ribs and my throat. Maybe it's the dress, or maybe it's the way their confidence bleeds into me, but I feel less like a shadow of myself and more like someone capable of stepping into the light again. My laugh this time is real, the edges softened — those words ringing truer than ever.

"Promise me you'll text if you feel uncomfortable," Viv says, suddenly fierce.

"One word: Weird. Two words if you need an escape – Home now."

"Or call Aodhan," Emma says, half-jest, half-genuine. Her mouth quirks: we both think of the way he has a habit of showing up when trouble's near. I feel the thread of tension pull tight for a second, then loosen. There's no saying his name aloud without every hair on my arms remembering the warmth of his embrace and the tenderness of his kiss.

I tuck a stray curl behind my ear and meet their eyes. "I'll go. For one night. Because you two are amazing. And Em, Viv — the texts apply to you too."

Emma does a tiny victory dance. Viv reaches across and pats my hand, steadying, just as she always does. "Tonight," Viv says, "you let us handle the drama. You just be you."

Outside, the evening air feels purposefully ordinary, as if it doesn't know the mischief we're carrying in with us. The stars burn bright, a knowing gleam across the sky. Our laughter skims over the ridge, measuring the possibilities of a single evening — excitement thrumming through every nerve, anticipation for the night to begin.

The rooftop bar is alive with summer. Golden string lights criss-cross overhead, glittering against a City sky painted in twilight hues. Music thrums low and smooth, a rhythm you can feel reverberating in your bones. The scent of wood-fired pizza, charred rosemary, and spilt cocktails laces the air.

The first rooftop bar is a dream — a scatter of fairy lights strung like constellations; the City sprawled below in ribbons of gold and silver. The music hums smooth and low, a rhythm designed to make you sway with every beat.

"To us," Emma declares, lifting her cocktail high. The glass catches the light like a shard of captured flame.

"To us," Vivienne and I echo, glasses clinking as the summer breeze washes over the rooftop, sending a shiver down my spine.

Each drink loosens the threads we've tied too tightly around ourselves. Vivienne — always the steady hand, the voice of reason — shocks us both by ordering shots. She slides the tiny glasses across the table with a grin from ear to ear.

"Viv," I laugh, groaning as the liquid inside shimmers an alarming neon. "We don't do shots anymore. We're responsible adults, remember? What even is this?"

She shrugs, unapologetic. "No idea. But we do tonight — because we are not that old yet." The burn sears down my throat, igniting a bloom of heat low in my belly — coiling into something reckless.

By the time we spill onto the dance floor, I'm a live wire. The bass doesn't just play — it takes over, thudding through my veins until the edges of the world blur. My body moves fluidly with the music.

Emma is a goddess in black, hips swaying with the lazy, dangerous grace of someone who knows she's performing for an audience — one completely enraptured but too intimidated to close the distance. Vivienne melts into the rhythm, lashes lowered, mouth parted, her body moving like she's made of sound itself — every sway and spin effortless, a silent warning that says look, but don't touch. There's something about them tonight — a freedom in their movements that's intoxicating.

I stop holding back. The silk of my dress clings as I move, the slit flashing thigh with every turn, curls sticking damp to my cheeks. I laugh — unguarded, raw, free. For a handful of songs, I'm not a widow or a mother or the keeper of too many burdens. I'm just a woman, alive, alight, burning at the centre of a night that feels infinite.

I let go. My shoulders roll back as realisation hits — the tension that's lived in my bones loosens and slips away. The rhythm claims me, hips rolling slow and sinuous, my body winding to the heavy pulse that rattles through the floor and straight into my soul. Each beat tugs me deeper, stripping thought, stripping control, until I'm nothing but breathless motion.

The air shifts — thickening, charged with something that prickles across my skin. Every sway of my hips, every arch of my spine draws invisible eyes like moths to a flame. It feels like the whole room is watching me. No — it feels like he's watching me.

Even though I know he couldn't be here, the weight of that imagined gaze sparks across my skin as if he's standing at the edge of the dance floor, burning me alive with nothing more than focus.

Song after song bleeds together. My laughter turns reckless, spilling with the music as my pulse races faster, sharper, hotter. My mind tries to tell me something, but the words are lost — distant, fogged. My body demands I forget and move — a promise of what's to come.

By the time I stagger off the floor, breathless, my skin glows as if lit from within. My cheeks ache from smiling, curls damp with sweat, chest rising and falling like I've run a race. The glass of water in my hand trembles; my fingers can't quite stop shaking. I catch sight of my reflection in a window and barely recognise her — flushed, fierce, alive, alluring. And then I feel it. That pull. That hum beneath my skin — low and primal, vibrating like the air before lightning strikes. It coils around me, electric, dangerous, inevitable. My breath catches as sparks dance across my skin.

When I turn, the air ignites.

He's there. At the edge of the crowd — the sun around which the whole room tilts. Tall, broad, every sharp line of his body carved from power and control. The strobe cuts across his face, gilding pale-gold hair until it gleams like fire and shadow. And those eyes — merciless — find mine like a weapon and a vow.

Every muscle strains against the fabric clinging to him, taut as if one wrong breath could tear it apart. My body betrays me, imagining the feel of that strength beneath my hands instead of the useless glass I clutch. The thought is a spark, and I am already a flame.

The crowd disappears — no music, no lights, just him. The world contracts to the brutal simplicity of him. His gaze pins me — possessive, claiming. I am his.

My pulse stutters. Heat races through me. I want him. God, I want him like air to drowning lungs, like water in a desert. Every nerve leans toward him, frantic with need, craving the gravity only he creates.

Before thought can catch up, before I can move. He's there. Close enough that his heat radiates in waves, thick and overwhelming. The crowd presses around us, faceless, irrelevant; all I know is the strength of his body a breath from mine. His hand slides to my hip, sure and unyielding — a touch that steadies and claims in the same motion. My body answers with a shiver; his touch burns.

"You look..." His voice is a low rumble against my ear, husky enough to tangle with the bass. "...ravishing. The things you make me want to do to you right here, right now." A groan slips from him — dark, restrained. The words slide over me, leaving goosebumps in their wake.

I swallow hard, pulse jumping, but when I speak my voice betrays me — soft, breathy. "You don't look too bad yourself." His chuckle is dark, sinful, threaded with a promise. Then we're moving. Or maybe I'm moving and he's guiding me — my body no longer mine, his hands unyielding, directing every subtle shift of my hips as though the music itself bends to him.

I roll my hips back, deliberate, pressing into the hard line of him. The effect is instant. His breath hitches. His grip tightens, fingers biting into my waist, restraint fracturing just enough to make my stomach flip and my thighs tremble.

"Careful, mo draganín." he murmurs, voice low, rough — a warning edged with hunger. My lips curve — reckless, emboldened by heat, alcohol, and the ache of wanting. "Or what?"

The challenge hangs between us, a dare wrapped in smoke. His chest presses flush against my back, all muscle and heat. I feel every inch of him — the rise and fall of his breath, the sharp control vibrating through him like he's one breath from losing it. His mouth hovers near my neck, ghosting my skin with heat. Each exhale is a brand — hot, rough, hungry.

"Or I'll stop pretending I'm a gentleman," he growls, "and show you exactly what I want to do to you — in that little dress." The sound goes straight to my core. My knees nearly buckle, heat flooding low and deep until every thought scatters. Images flash — his hands pinning, his mouth claiming, his body pressed over mine, leaving no room for escape.

I tilt my head slightly, reckless — offering the barest sliver of throat. His breath catches, and the gold in his eyes flares when I risk a glance back. "I don't think you could," I whisper — but my voice trembles, betraying me. His lips skim my ear, teeth grazing my skin without marking. "mo draganín," he murmurs, velvet and sin, "you don't want to know how wrong you are."

The beat drops. My heart stumbles. I realise this man could command me with his voice alone. I tilt my head, catching his gaze over my shoulder. The look in his eyes obliterates what's left of my control — hunger, raw and unrestrained, locked on me like I'm the only thing left in his world.

The song slows — deeper, sultry, rolling like a heartbeat through the floor — and he doesn't let go. His palm slides from my waist, fingers dragging deliberately, possessively, up the curve of my body until they hover just beneath my breasts. The heat of his touch sears through the thin emerald fabric; my nipples tighten painfully against it. I shudder, a broken sound catching in my throat.

His mouth dips, lips grazing my ear, breath a sinful rasp that drips like honey. "You want this," he murmurs. Not a question. A claim. A truth written in the slow grind of his hips against mine, in the way my body arches to meet him. I can't think. Can't breathe.

There's only him — his heat, his scent, his power threading through every inch of me until I'm drowning in it.

"Lilian," he breathes — just my name — but the way it leaves his mouth, a prayer, a plea, unravels me completely. The line we've walked so carefully trembles. His thumb strokes a small circle beneath my breast; my hips shift back into him, answering without permission. His control shakes; mine is gone entirely.

He eases back just enough for air to slide between us, though his hand remains anchored at my waist, thumb dragging one last, deliberate stroke across my hip bone. My skin burns where he leaves it. I spin to face him — unsteady, flushed, chest heaving. The look he gives me is worse than his touch, devouring, unreadable, molten with things I'm not sure I can survive.

Words hover, but before they form, Emma barrels in — laughing, glowing, drunk on the night. She hooks an arm around my neck and nearly knocks the breath out of me. "Well, well," she declares, wicked amusement sparkling in her eyes as she flicks her gaze between us. "Looks like our Lil finally remembered she's ready to mingle. Took you long enough, babe."

"Emma—" My protest is weak.

"Nope. Don't ruin this," she cuts me off, wagging a finger. "Do you know how long I've waited? Six bloody years to see that look on your face." Her grin sharpens as she turns it on Aodhan. "And you — Blondie." She pokes him square in the chest, utterly unafraid of the seven foot man in front of her. "Don't hurt her. If you do, I'll kill you. And trust me — I won't need much to do it." Emma spins away in a whirl of black silk and wicked laughter, tossing something obscene at the DJ that makes Vivienne choke on her drink and bark laughter.

When I finally find my voice, it's barely a whisper. "Why are you here?" His mouth curves — faint, dangerous, like a blade catching light.

"Why else?" His voice is low, steady, lethal in its simplicity. "To watch over you. And I'm glad I did — watching you tonight, you looked free, breaking away from what's been keeping you caged. You were mesmerising." The way he says it sends heat trailing across my skin, like flames licking the surface.

Sparks turn to fire. My blood ignites. And gods, how I want this man to stoke the flames within me.

CHAPTER 20

Aodhan POV

I should have been thinking of the Earth Mountains, where a rogue Sylvari had slipped from our palace prisons and now prowled too close to the portals. A Sylvari who belonged to the same group that were targeting mortals, my mortal. I should have already tracked him, burned him where he stood, erased the threat before it could touch her.

I should have been thinking of the sceptre — the fractured weapon that could unite or destroy the Courts.

Rumours had circled for decades, whispers hidden in half-burnt scrolls and old war songs. But now I had confirmation: two fragments located, one locked in the Air Rívaran's vault, another hidden within my keeping. Four more remained — one rumoured to be buried deep within Fire Court territory, the other lost, a mere ghost of whispers hidden amongst the archives, only in the cryptic words of a half-mad seer. Water hiding theirs and Earth refusing to part with it until the rightful heir were to be found.

Each piece had the potential to shift the balance of our entire world, and every rival court knew it. Whoever wielded the Sceptre would hold more than power. They would hold dominion, a prospect so concerning all heirs and Royals alike were watching the other, lying in wait to see who would make the first move.

That should have been my only focus. But even as I forced my eyes across the ink on the report, her image slid between the lines—unavoidable.

Lily.

Centuries of training. Of holding power steady under my blade and crown — and still my thoughts drifted to her. My father's voice echoed like a hammer: You will never have what other heirs have. No mate shall temper your fire. No heir shall bear your name. You are the weapon. You are the crown, you will retrieve the Sceptre pieces to unite and prevent chaos from breaking.

I'd worn that fate like armour so long it was part of my very being.

Until her. A hum beneath my ribs, deep and relentless, answered every breath I took. The bond sang whether I acknowledged it or not. The silence wreath dulled the sensation, but it never silenced it. Each time I accepted my fate, accepted the bond, it weakened and frayed. And still I wanted a way to break free.

To claim her. To keep her close.

I shoved the parchment aside, moving to the balcony above the club floor. From here I could see them all: emissaries cloaked in glamour, Fire and Water Fae playing at human decadence, witches passing charms beneath the neon glow, and humans who thought themselves predators — blind to the true predators already circling them. The air was thick with smoke, magic, and need, the mingled scents clinging like perfume to the skin.

Then I scent the rain, tinged with jasmine and my pulse races, she shouldn't be here, not here, not in this place.

Emerald-green silk hugged every curve, the fabric sliding over her body like it had been spun with the intention of tormenting me alone. Her hair spilled loose around her shoulders, wild and untamed, catching the low light like strands of molten gold.

She laughed — not the careful, guarded sound she used in her café, not the polite one she wore with strangers, but something free, unarmoured, pure. I couldn't help but marvel at the freedom on her face. That sound cut through the haze, slicing sharper than any blade, impossible to ignore. My chest constricted with the ache of wanting to hear it again.

Duty dissolved. The fractured Sceptre and its cursed fragments, the rogue, the politics of Courts circling like vultures — gone. There was only her. And goddess, the way every eye in the room turned to her. Humans with hunger in their gaze, like wolves scenting a lamb they had no right to touch.

Fae, sharper still, their attention predatory, knowing on some primal level that she was rare, priceless, something powerful enough to tempt even them.

Jealousy spiked through me, molten and vicious. My power stirred with it, magic flaring, my marks heating under my skin until I could feel the glow pulse against the collar of my shirt. No one should look at her like that.

No one should see the delicate line of her throat, the curve of her hips swaying to the rhythm of the music, the soft flush in her cheeks from the drink in her hand. That was mine. Every stolen glance felt like a blade pressed to my throat — and every instinct in me wanted to turn this place into ash until no eyes remained but mine.

She didn't even see it. Didn't see what she was doing to me — or the danger in the way other men, mortal and fae alike, devoured her with their stares.

I wanted her pressed to me, her laugh spilling only into my ear, her beauty burning only for me. Every part of me screamed the same truth — raw, primal, unrelenting.

When she drifted onto the dance floor, hips swaying to the rhythm, instinct took over. I was moving before thought could intervene, cutting through the crowd like a blade, lethal, absolute. A human dared to step closer, his gaze sliding over her like a dessert he was ready to sample.

My blood burned.

One second, he was moving toward her. The next, I was there — a wall of heat and power, blocking his path with a look that promised violence if he so much as breathed wrong.

And then she turned — close enough to breathe in. Her scent branded itself into me, every breath sharpening the bond until I felt it vibrate in my bones.

From across the crowd, I caught the shift of shadow. Maricus. He wasn't watching Emma at the bar. Not monitoring the Sylvaris. His eyes were locked on Lily — sharp, unreadable, edged with that calculating darkness he never quite concealed. And he saw me. He saw the way I moved closer, the way my hand slid around her waist like I had a right. His mouth curved into a predator's grin, silent mockery gleaming in his eyes.

The bastard knew. He'd seen it from the beginning — every fracture she carved into my armour. He'd read me, watched me, calculated my weakness, a knowing she was my only weakness.

If the Courts discovered the truth — if they learned she was my mate — they would use her against me. They would use her to break me. To chain me. To bleed me dry for power. I tightened my grip on her waist, a vow threading through the contact: Mine to protect. No harm would come to her.

Her eyes widened when she saw me, lips parting like she wanted to speak, but I didn't give her the chance. My hand found her hip — firm, claiming, aching with wanting more.

"You look..." My voice came out low, a need and desperation to my own ears, "...*ravishing*." She shivered. Just slightly. Enough to unravel another thread of my control.

The music slowed, the bass pulsing like a heartbeat as her hips rolled back against me, deliberate, testing. My body responded instantly — too instantly — hardness pressing against her as my fingers dug into her waist. "Careful," I murmured, though the word was a growl, no warning at all. She tilted her head, eyes catching mine, fire in their depths.

"Or what?" Or what? The question seared through me, tearing at the last of my restraint. Images slammed into me — her pinned against the wall, my mouth at her throat, her hands tangled in my hair, her cries echoing against the stone of my chambers. I bit back the growl crawling up my throat, leaning down until my lips brushed the curve of her ear.

"Or I stop pretending I'm a gentleman."

She froze. Just for a breath. Then moved again, grinding back into me, slow and deliberate, and my vision went white-hot. I couldn't do this here. Not with strangers watching. Not with rivals calculating every shift of power.

From across the floor, Emma caught my gaze. Vivienne too. Both women wore the same look — sharp, protective, daring me to remember who I was and what I meant to Lily. I mouthed one promise: I'll keep her safe.

Emma's brow arched — a warning, plain as steel: Hurt her, and you'll answer to me a continuation of her threat from earlier tonight.

Vivienne's arms folded, her stare just as fierce. I gave them both one nod. Then I guided Lily from the floor, my hand never leaving her waist. She followed without hesitation, cheeks flushed, lips parted, like she'd forgotten how to breathe.

The portal waited in the shadows outside, its hum concealed from human ears. I'd sworn never to use it for anyone but my kin, but tonight I broke that vow without hesitation. She stumbled as the magic folded around us, her fingers clutching at my shirt — small, trusting, my body tensing under her touch. Heat rolled under my skin as the portal's shimmer tore open, folding reality back on itself in a rush of light and scent — earth and sun-warmed stone, metal and sky.

The moment we stepped through, every part of me expanded; the tether to my power snapped taut and then surged, bright and intoxicating. And then we were in my chambers.

Glass walls rose around us like a cathedral built of crystal and air, open and endless, high above the clouds.

The night below was a living map: a lattice of glowing bridges spanning between spires of pale gold and pearl, towers tapering into the sky like spears of frozen lightning. Thousands of tiny lights shimmered along the avenues, moving in silent constellations.

The currents of power that ran beneath the city — my city — glowed faintly in the veins of the streets, pulsing like a heartbeat. The air itself was different here, rich and electric. Every breath carried the scent of sun-warmed quartz and storm-cooled metal, threaded with something floral from the gardens suspended far below. It hummed against my skin, alive, thick with the quiet, steady pulse of the Air Court.

Beneath our feet, the floor was carved from a single sheet of pale stone shot through with veins of molten gold, warm to the touch as if it remembered the sun's warmth from mere hours ago. Beyond the far wall, the horizon was a sweep of star-dusted clouds; their edges blazed faintly with auroral fire where the ley lines crossed.

Even the ceiling sang — a faint vibration, a low chime — the sound of the Court breathing with me. She blinked, dazed, laughter spilling softly from her lips, cheeks flushed.

"Wow... I think those sparkly shots are kicking in. This... this feels unreal."

Her voice was small against the vastness. A note of wonder.

She didn't know that here, in my element, every sense of mine sharpened.

Power thrummed through me, glowing faintly under my skin.

This was where I was strongest — where the pulse of the realm rose up to meet me, heir to the air and all those within it — and still she managed to be the only thing in my focus.

I should explain. Should have told her she wasn't dreaming, that she was standing in the heart of my world, in the place built of my magic and my bloodline. That the entire palace — the bridges, the spires, the golden pulse of the City below — bent to my command. But I didn't. Not yet. I only watched her. Let her take in what she thought was a fantasy.

"Lily," I rasped against her lips, my forehead pressed to hers, my breath ripped from me. My voice was wrecked, a plea hidden inside a command. "Tell me you want this. Tell me you want me." It was everything. Not just a question. Not just hunger. It was the core of me laid bare, stripped of crown, stripped of war, stripped of prophecy. The words were a blade to my own throat, because if she turned away now, if she said no, I didn't know if I could rebuild myself from the ashes.

Her answer was a whisper, breathless but sure. "I want you, Aodhan. I've wanted you since the first moment you walked into my café." The sound of it hit me like thunder.

Not just want, but choice.

She wanted me.

Me.

Not the prince, not the weapon, not the heir.

Me.

The growl that rumbled from my chest was primal, raw, unrestrained; it felt like centuries of restraint snapping all at once, like iron chains giving way. She wanted me.

I was so caught up in the very notion that I was her choice that when she leaned in, when she sighed into my mouth, I forgot how to breathe — forgot the centuries of control, the throne, the Sceptre fragments, the prophecy that had chained me to solitude.

All of it burned away until there was only her and the searing rightness of her mouth on mine. The faint burn of fae liquor lingered on her tongue.

I should have thanked the bastard.

It stripped away her walls, baring her desires, every hidden thought laid open for me to feel through the bond. Every pulse of her magic tasted like truth, like something that had been waiting for me just as long as I had been waiting for it.

Her hands slid up my chest, fingers trembling, then fisting in my shirt, tugging me closer — a desperate, unguarded pull that unravelled the last threads of my control.

Yet with her, I didn't want to hold anything back.

I let her — goddess, I let her — as I deepened the kiss, my tongue sweeping over hers with slow, deliberate precision, claiming, tasting, branding.

I poured every word I couldn't speak into that kiss — mine, wanted, chosen, always. The bond hummed sharper and louder, an unrelenting drumbeat that drowned out reason.

She is the missing note in a song, I had been forced to sing alone for centuries. Finally found. My magic roared to life, surging beneath my skin like a living sun.

Heat bled into the space around us, curling in gold and white, restrained only by the thin, fraying thread of control I still clung to.

One wrong move and I'd burn this entire place down just to keep her close, keep her safe. And the truth was, I would. Every oath I'd ever sworn, every piece of the crown I'd been forced to wear, every fragment of Sceptre I'd hunted — all of it meant nothing compared to this moment, to her.

She deepened the kiss again, tugging at my shirt, pulling away to grunt slightly as she fumbled with the buttons before forgoing them entirely, instead lifting the shirt and gliding her hands across my back and down my side.

A low, guttural sound broke from my throat as I lifted her, her legs wrapping around my waist like they had been made for it, like they had always been meant to fit around my body. That small, instinctive motion shattered — not just my control, but the brittle wall between need and devotion. And I knew — I knew — there was no coming back from this.

CHAPTER 21

Aodhan POV

Her lips taste like sin and salvation — a paradox I never knew I'd crave until this moment. Dark sweetness and burning light all at once. And I know, with a bone-deep certainty, I'll never have enough of her. Not in a night. Not in a lifetime. She is everything and even more than I could have wished for.

I need her to tell me this isn't just the Fae juice talking — that she truly wants this sober not high and intoxicated free of consequences and after thought. I break away, looking her in the eye, reaching into my pocket for a small pouch of arrowroot powder and herbs, I keep for emergencies. I dust some into the air; it glitters faintly.

"Lily," I pause again, my voice rough. "I want you to tell me if you want me to continue. I won't go any further — not now — not if you aren't ready." Her brilliant green eyes, sharp and unwavering, meet mine.

Her voice is clear, sure. "Aodhan," she breathes out a maddening huff, "shut up and take off your clothes. Now." Slowly, I do. My gaze never leaves hers as I pull the fabric over my head, watching the way she drinks in every movement.

I press her down against the soft sheets — every motion slow, careful, reverent — as though she's something holy I've been forbidden to touch. Yet the restraint in my muscles tremble, stretched thin under the weight of the bond thrumming between us — an electric pulse beating in time with my heart.

My power hums beneath my skin, gathering like a storm. My magic burning faintly, sparking to life along my arms and shoulders, casting flickers of light across her skin. Heat radiates in waves, curling around her, rolling off me like sunlight over stone — claiming, needing, worshiping. The chamber responds to her presence: the glass walls glint brighter, the air thickens with the scent of sun-warmed quartz and storm-cooled metal — a quiet testament to the magic I can barely hold in check.

"Lily," I murmur, my voice rough, cracked around the edges like it's been forged in fire. Her name tastes like something sacred on my tongue — a prayer, a plea, a vow.

Her green eyes meet mine — wide, soft, yet impossibly sure — despite the stutter in her breath, despite the tremor that travels through her body.

"Don't stop, Aodh… please." My heart races, thundering around my chest, as if the syllables themselves are a promise. As if she's already claiming me as hers. And in this moment, I am — completely.

I lower my forehead to hers, breathing her in. Jasmine, lilies, rain, and now me — and I realise the truth like a blow to the chest: I would burn down the sky for her. Everything I have been waiting for is here — her. She is my future, my present, and will forever be my everything. All that I could ever need or want.

The kiss deepens — slow, unhurried at first, a brush of mouths that feels like reverence rather than hunger — until it isn't. Until every fragile thread of my control snaps like a bowstring under strain. My lips drag over hers with growing insistence, tasting every sigh, every soft gasp she gives me, until the edges of the world blur and all I know is her.

Her body trembles beneath mine, a shiver that travels from her mouth to my hands, into my chest. Her fingers slide into my hair, fisting there like she's afraid I'll disappear — like she's anchoring herself to me.

The bond hums louder, a low, thrumming ache under my

skin, matching the wild beat of her pulse against my mouth. A sound escapes me, torn from somewhere deep in my chest — a growl, low and raw, primal and broken all at once. It vibrates against her lips.

I need more. All of her. Her taste. Her breath. The sharp, unguarded sounds she makes when she forgets herself. It's not just desire; it's a hunger that claws at the inside of my ribs, threatening to devour me if I don't take her, hold her, become part of her.

The thought drives me deeper. My mouth moves against hers with a new intensity — a claiming heat that has nothing to do with royalty or power. The kiss turns molten, our tongues clashing in a fierce, breathless rhythm that leaves no space for air or reason.

All I feel is her.

Heat coils low in my spine, spreading through my ribs, tightening every muscle in my body. The marble beneath us warms from the press of our bodies, slick beneath my palms where I brace myself above her. Her breath fans across my throat — a small, soft exhale — and it shatters whatever control I thought I had left.

Every point where her skin touches mine burns.

Every movement she makes draws me in closer.

Every sound she gives pulls something primal loose inside me.

The bond is still there —thudding, a heavy pulse that matches mine, heartbeat to heartbeat. It feels maddeningly physical: the drag of her fingertips at my hips, the arch of her body meeting mine, the stutter in her breath when I trail my mouth along her jaw.

My world narrows to the shape of her beneath me. Her legs tightening around my waist. Her fingers curling into my shoulders. Her lips parting my name — not in power, not in magic, but in need.

I lower my forehead to hers, breathing her in like I've been starved of air for years. The room, the palace, the entire realm could fall away and I wouldn't notice. All I know is the way she trembles when I touch her. The way her breath catches. The way she looks at me like she's choosing me in this moment and every one after.

The sky beyond the glass glows faintly with streaks of auroral light, the colours of my power bleeding into the night. The sky relishing in my release. Her need is intoxicating. It rushes through me like wine poured too fast, sharp and consuming, flooding every sense until I can't tell where she ends and I begin.

Her tremble against me is a prayer, a plea, a spark to the dry tinder of my restraint. I'm barely holding the leash on my control, fingers digging into her hips as my power claws at me — demanding release, demanding that I claim what the bond already knows is mine.

I lower myself, slow as a prayer, my breath brushing over her skin before my lips do. I start at her calf, pressing a kiss to the smooth curve of muscle, then another just above, letting the taste of her skin ground me. Her pulse flutters beneath my mouth — delicate and frantic. I drag my lips higher, to the delicate line of her ankle, my tongue flicking out to taste the faint salt of her skin, the warmth of her blood thrumming just beneath the surface.

My mouth traces up her leg in slow, reverent worship — a path of heat and devotion. Each inch of her is mine to savour, to learn, to map with my tongue like a cartographer tracing the edges of a new world. Her skin shivers beneath my lips, goosebumps lifting in a reverent wave, and her breath falters a soft, breaking sound that feels like she's offering herself to me without a single word. I lift her thigh, spreading her gently, pressing my mouth higher, kissing, tasting — the soft inside of her knee, the sensitive crease where thigh meets hip — every spot that makes her gasp or arch a little more.

My hands anchor her hips, fingers digging lightly into her skin — to steady her, to hold her together as I undo her piece by piece. And then I reach the place I crave most — the heat and scent of her desire flooding my senses before I even touch her. I hover there for a heartbeat, breathing her in, my self-control hanging by a single frayed thread.

The moment my mouth meets her, her hips jerk — a soft, desperate moan spilling free, half gasp, half plea. Gods, that sound wrecks me. It's raw and unguarded, a sound only I plan to hear for the rest of our lives mortal or Fae.

Her need is intoxicating — a heady, unrelenting current that coils through me like fire under the skin. It burns away everything else until there's nothing left but her. Her scent. Her trembling. Her pulse fluttering wild beneath my hands. Her. Always her. Trembling with want.

And me — barely holding the leash on my control, the thin thread threatening to snap with every breath she takes. I do exactly what I've imagined since that first time I caught her blushing, shifting in her seat, thighs pressing together as she read that damned book — wet, flustered, unaware of how she undid me even then.

All those nights I pictured this, every detail etched into my mind, and now she's here.

Open beneath me.

And I'm the one shaking.

I lower myself, slow and deliberate, kissing her calf first. A reverent press of lips to soft skin — then another, higher, tasting the faint salt of her, the warmth of blood thrumming just beneath the surface. My mouth trails up the delicate line of her ankle, teeth grazing, tongue flicking out to soothe where I've nipped. Each touch a vow, a plea, a worship, a mark to claim.

"Now, Lillian," I murmur, my voice low and deliberate, "shall we continue where we left off in the valley?"

Her breath catches as my mouth traces higher along her leg, unhurried, reverent. My hands slide over her thighs, easing her open as though unveiling something sacred — something I've hunted my entire life.

"This is where you stopped me," I whisper against her skin, "before I could read any further." She shivers beneath the words alone. "But I know where he continued."

My lips follow the memory, drawing a gasp from her as I linger where her pulse betrays her. Her body answers me instinctively, breath quickening, skin alive beneath my touch. I lift her thigh, pressing my lips higher, tasting, teasing — the soft skin of her inner thigh, the edge of her hip. I roll my tongue across her inner thigh where her pulse beats strongest — until I'm exactly where I've been craving to be, the heart of her scent flooding my senses.

I can't help but swallow, salivating; my heart races, my body tightens. I can hear every breath between us — her scent intoxicating, mingling with the faint trace of alcohol on her skin. She's wet. The slick heat of her arousal rolls off her in waves, thick and sweet, drowning me in it. And my need — the primal, unholy hunger to have her on my tongue — burns just as fiercely.

I breathe her in first, just hovering, my lips so close that my breath ghosts over her. She stills at the contact, that sharp, shaky pause right before I give in. I hear her breathy, impatient moan — a silent plea to connect. "

And then my mouth meets her.

The taste of her explodes on my tongue — salt and sweet and wholly hers. Her hips jerk instantly, a soft, desperate moan spilling free — raw, unguarded, breaking against the silence of the room like thunder. It vibrates through me, wrecking me, pulling a low growl from my chest as I press my mouth deeper, tongue moving with slow, deliberate strokes that make her gasp and arch, already coming undone beneath me.

She writhes under me, helpless beneath the steady press of my hands pinning her hips to the mattress, every tremor feeding my hunger. Her body arches, seeking more, and I give her exactly what she wants — a torment of slow strokes, the kind that have her gasping and shuddering, caught between desperation and surrender.

"Fuck..." I growl against her, my voice rough, reverent, breaking with the force of it. "You taste so fucking good. I'll make sure you won't be thinking of any other man again after this, Lily — you'll only think of my tongue on your body and how you taste on it."

I drag her higher, shifting her until her thighs lock around my shoulders, until my face is buried between them. I devour her — with worship, with hunger born of centuries of longing to be seen, to be loved. Every movement of my tongue, every flick and press, is a vow carved in flesh and heat: she will never doubt how wanted she is.

I press deeper, tongue sliding inside her — slow at first, coaxing, teasing, drawing out broken little gasps that pierce straight through me.

Then harder. Faster. Relentless. Until she's panting my name, clawing at the sheets, thighs trembling and tightening around my head as if she never wants to let me go. I can feel the wild magic under her skin humming louder with every stroke of my tongue. It vibrates against my mouth — faint sparks of earth and storm — like the world itself is holding its breath with her, waiting for her to break and come undone.

And when she does — when she finally shatters — it's with a broken, breathless sound that sends waves of satisfaction through me. She cries out my name, back arching off the bed, thighs clamping tight as waves of pleasure roll through her.

I drink her in greedily, lapping at every drop of her release like a dying man finally given water in the desert. I don't stop — not until I've had every taste. She quivers, still sensitive, and I kiss her again, flicking my tongue over her bud. I put this very taste and scent to memory. How have I not had this before now? She is everything.

My goddess. *Mo draganín.*

I look over her — the rosy tint to her cheeks, her hair matted across the mattress, her eyes greedily taking in my body. Everything about her is stunning. My cock swells again at the very sight of her.

"Ready?" My voice is raw, broken — more plea than question.

Her eyes — wide, glassy, molten — lock on mine. She nods once, the smallest movement, yet it sends waves of euphoria through me. Her breath stutters as she whispers, "Yes."

"Tell me if you want me to stop," I rasp, forcing the words out even as every instinct screams to lose myself in her. My gaze holds hers, golden light flickering between us. I know I'm too big; I know she'll need to take me slowly — carefully — inch by inch.

I take my time. I want her to feel every inch, every claim. I want her to enjoy every moment. Pressing the head of my cock against her slick heat, I tease the entrance — circling, sliding just close enough to make her gasp. Her hips lift in wordless demand, instinctive, desperate.

A groan tears from my chest as I finally push — the roaring heat of her gripping me before I've even moved. The way her body welcomes me — tight, wet, perfect — makes my vision blur, my marks burning brighter in response. I pause, letting her adjust.

Her lips part, her voice trembling but sure. "I want more. Please, Aodh... need more."

I press forward, stretching her slowly, carefully, until I'm buried to the hilt. Her cry punches through me — raw and exquisite. I grip her hips, holding her still, giving her time. The feel of her around me — the wet, silken tightness — steals the breath from my lungs.

"Fuck... you feel so good," I groan, the words spilling out, unsure if I can manage another coherent thought.

For a moment, I still, forehead pressed to hers, forcing control. Then I move — slow, deliberate strokes, drawing out soft whimpers and sharp gasps. Each shift of her body drags me deeper, tighter, until restraint frays with every roll of her hips.

And when she moves against me — urging, demanding more — I lose it. Her nails rake down my back, sharp enough to sting, and the pain only fuels me. My thrusts deepen, rhythm building — raw, unrelenting. The smell of her — wild, sweet, intoxicating — clings to the air, mixing with the faint crackle of magic bleeding from my skin, gold threads sparking across the walls like starlight.

She clings to me, her moans sharp and broken, and I know with absolute certainty: I will never survive her.

Each thrust drives harder, deeper, until the sharp, rhythmic sound of our bodies colliding fills the chamber, echoing against glass and stone, blending with her soft, broken moans.

I shift and lift her easily — she weighs nothing. Her body fits against mine, weightless in my arms, and I hold her pinned to my chest as I drive into her, hard and deep. Her head tips back, a sharp cry of my name tearing from her lips.

She comes again, shuddering in my hold, her body gripping me so tight I nearly come undone. But I'm not done. I can't be. I need more — her, this, everything.

I carry her across the room, still buried deep inside her, each step a deliberate test of control. The chamber shifts around us, light rippling in gold and white like sunlight on water, my power answering the rhythm of our bodies. She answers in kind — the air thickening with earth and sky, our magic twining as one.

I set her on the edge of my desk, the polished surface cool against her heated skin. She sprawls there, hair wild and spilling over her shoulders like molten gold, skin flushed and glowing, eyes glazed with heat and something deeper — trust, want, belonging.

She looks at me like I'm everything she's ever wanted. Like I'm the only thing she's ever needed. Before glancing away embarrassed.

"Look at me," I growl, my voice rough and ragged — a plea dragged from somewhere deeper than breath. I hook one of her legs over my arm, the smoothness of her skin hot against my palm, and slam into her — deep, hard — claiming every inch of her as mine.

She does look at me — that look destroys me. Desire, trust, need — all tangled into one blazing stare. Her eyes hold me, binding and freeing me in the same breath.

It has me teetering on the razor edge of control, a breath away from breaking apart completely.

My pace becomes relentless, every thrust harder, deeper, each with her name on my lips. The world narrows until there's nothing left but her — her sounds, her scent, her body moving with mine in a rhythm older than any crown or court. Her moans rise and fall like music I never want to stop hearing, a litany of devotion I never thought I'd earn.

When I finally spill inside her, it's with a guttural sound I can't suppress, my entire body trembling, her name ripped from my throat. I hold her close as the force of release tears through me, the bond between us snapping taut, sealing itself in light and heat. Silence wraps around us like dawn.

Hours blur together — her breathless sighs, the soft, broken moans, the way her body arches into mine, hungry and unashamed. There's no beginning, no end — just the unbroken current of us. She's perfect — my perfect match — moving with me in sync, every shiver and gasp a response to my touch, every brush of my hands answered by the way her body trembles and yields.

I lose myself in her again and again. Every time I think I can't want her more, she looks at me, touches me, whispers my name in that soft, breathless way — and I'm worshiping her with my hands, my mouth, my magic. Making her mine over and over until the night itself feels endless.

When it's finally over — when we're both spent, tangled together in the quiet aftermath — I gather her against my chest, breathing her in like my reason to live. Jasmine. Lilies. Rain and now, me. Her scent mingles with mine, my claim etched invisibly into her skin, into her magic. I feel whole.

I press a kiss to her temple, my lips lingering against her warm skin, and murmur soft words I know she doesn't hear — not with the way sleep has already claimed her, heavy and deep. Still, I say them anyway, low and reverent, as if speaking to my own goddess: promises of safety, of devotion, of a future she doesn't yet know is hers.

Gently, I lift her from the bed, cradling her against my chest — something fragile, precious. The glow of my power fades to a muted gold as I guide her to the adjoining chamber.

Steam curls from the bath I'd drawn earlier, scented faintly with crushed herbs and roses from the high gardens, with a healing oil for any lingering swelling.

I lower her into the water with care, my hands slow and reverent as I wash her skin, cleansing away the remnants of our passion. She rests against me, her head tucked beneath my chin, breath soft and even — trusting in a way that tightens something deep in my chest.

When she's clean, I ease her into one of my shirts. It hangs off her small frame, swallowing her in pale fabric that still carries my scent and warmth.

Seeing her like that — wrapped in something of mine — my cock swells again.

The portal hums to life at my gesture, its shimmer bending reality around us like liquid glass. Magic coils up my arms, warm and alive, as I step through with her held close. We emerge in her room, and the shift between worlds is like stepping from sunlight into candlelight. The house is quiet, still, except for the soft clicking of a gecko in the hall and the faint hum of her plants, their leaves stirring as though recognising her return.

I lay her down on her bed, tucking the blankets around her with a care I show no one. My fingers linger along the delicate line of her jaw, tracing the soft hollow beneath her ear. Her curls spill across the pillow, her lips parted slightly, cheeks still flushed from what we've shared. She looks at peace.

A Kárith's heart asleep in a mortal's body.

I lean down and press a soft kiss to her forehead. The sound of it — the small exhale she makes even in sleep — lodges itself in my chest. What this woman does to me. I brush a curl from her cheek and whisper, "Mo draganín."

My little dragon. Mine.

For a moment, I just stand there, watching her — committing the sight to memory: her in my shirt, curled in her own bed, surrounded by the life she built. And in the quiet, I know. Everything has already changed. We have changed. We've pushed past the boundaries we were keeping and tomorrow will be the start of something new. And then my gaze catches on the photograph on her bedside table.

Him.

Caleb. Her husband. The man she once told me was her everything. The man who held her first. The image is simple — her smile softer, his arm around her waist, the both of them framed by sunlight. But it feels like a blade twisting under my ribs, my heart breaking at the very sight of it.

Jealousy rips through me, sharp and ugly, a violent spark I don't bother to contain. My power flares hotter beneath my skin, golden light flickering through the dim room like sunrise breaking, and my jaw tightens until it aches.

I drag my gaze back to her — sleeping peacefully, oblivious to the storm tearing through my chest. Her lashes rest against her flushed cheeks, curls spilling across the pillow, lips parted in a soft sigh. She looks untouched by the war inside me. I take slow, steady breaths, reining in my power.

I know I'm being unreasonable. Jealous of a dead man. Jealous of a life she built in a world where I was nothing but myth. Jealous of a family she created without ever knowing I existed — without knowing what we were meant to be. The rational part of me knows this. But it doesn't matter. The ache doesn't lessen.

"I should have found you sooner," I whisper, the words low and fierce, rough against the stillness. "You were mine long before this, Lily. Before him. Before all of it. This should have been ours."

My voice cracks on the last line as I imagine the children we could have had — what was meant for us, what was taken. "And whoever kept you from me — whoever tried to bury what you are... will pay," I murmur, the words rolling out like a curse, a promise, for a false prophecy.

I stand there for a long moment, watching the steady rise and fall of her chest, fighting the irrational urge to crawl back into that bed. To pull her into my arms. To stay until morning. To claim the eternity that should have been ours from the beginning.

Her scent clings to me — now mixed with the warmth of my skin. It's all I can do not to drown in it. Not to brand her again with my hands, my mouth, my magic, until no wisp of another man remains between us.

Instead, I straighten, pulling the mask of the prince back over my features like armour. Quiet as a whisper, I turn and step through the portal into the trees near the café. Magic hums against my palms, restless and sparking, mirroring the storm in my veins.

And my thoughts — every single one of them — are full of her. Her sleeping face. Her soft moan. Her scent on my skin. And the promise of reckoning to come for those who denied me of her.

CHAPTER 22

Lily POV

I wake slowly, as if surfacing from a dream I'm not ready to leave. The morning light spills across my room in long, pale-gold and pink strokes, turning the walls into soft watercolour. For a moment I don't move. I just lie there, cocooned in warmth, wrapped in sheets that smell faintly of clean linen and something darker, richer — a scent that makes my breath catch. Sunlight on a hot summer's day in the mountains.

The fresh scent of earth after a storm. Bergamot... Aodhan.

Memory crashes — a wave of heat, hands, breath, voice. The way his mouth caressed mine, my body bending, the way he whispered my name like a vow, like a secret he wasn't supposed to tell. My skin prickles at the ghost of his mouth, his tongue, the reverent weight of his palms.

I kick my legs, trying to outrun the heat still humming under my skin. God. What have I done? I press my burning face into the pillow, but it's useless. The scent clings. My body hums like it remembers him, like some quiet fuse has been lit beneath my chest and hasn't gone out. My fingers curl in the sheet as if it might steady me, anchor me to the present.

When I sit up, the sheet pools at my waist, cool air brushing across skin still sensitive from everything that happened.

That's when I see it — the bouquet. Sitting on the bedside

table like it's always belonged there. Lilies and peonies, lush and impossible for this time of season, petals still damp with morning dew as if someone plucked them from another world. The lilies almost glow in the slant of light, white and green and gold edges, their scent curling around me. The peonies are a flourish of blush and cream, a softness that feels like something stolen from a dream.

For a second, my chest tightens at the gesture, flowers, his reminder he is thinking of me after everything we shared. But tucked into the ribbon is a note.

My fingers shake when I pull it free. The script is elegant, looping — a hand used to signatures on decrees and notepaper, not post-its on café counters.

For my Mo draganín,
You are everything.
I will wait for you as long as you need.
— A

The breath catches in my throat so hard it hurts. "Mo draganín" — the name he uses in his head, the one he's called me in jest, want his name for me. Everything. The word; it's like a shot of electricity straight into my veins, awakening my every thought all at once. I don't know whether to laugh or cry.

To tear it up or press it to my heart. So I do neither. I just sit there, frozen in the quiet, the scent of lilies rising around me as the reality crashes down — sharp, merciless, unforgiving.

My gaze snags on the dresser. The photo sits where it always has, framed in worn wood. Our wedding day. His arm is slung around me, sunlight catching his hair until it looks spun from copper. His smile is wide and unstoppable, his eyes so green they seem to hold entire forests. Full of life. Alive. Us. My chest caves, aching with every breath.

What have I done? How could I?

The words slice jagged, and cruel.

My hands fly to my face, palms pressed hard against my eyes, as if pressure alone might hold the tears back. My voice fractures in the quiet.

"You'd hate me for this," I whisper, raw, shaking. "Or maybe you wouldn't. Maybe you'd just... laugh at me. Tell me to stop being so bloody stubborn. To stop being so scared."

But the guilt doesn't ease. It coils tighter. Suffocating. A noose drawn slow around my throat. Because no matter how right last night felt — how safe I was in Aodhan's arms, how easily I wanted to stay there, to drown in him, to imagine something real — it still tastes of betrayal. Every kiss feels like a chisel striking Cal's memory. Every breath I draw near Aodhan carries a sting, a reminder that wanting him means loosening my grip on the man I swore I'd never let go of.

And worse — it feels cruel.

Cruel to Cal, who should still be here.

Cruel to Aodhan, who deserves more than this fractured, jagged version of me.

He deserves sunlight. Joy. Someone whole. Someone who doesn't choke on guilt every time he looks at her — someone not carved hollow around the memory of a man she cannot let go of.

Not me.

Not this.

And yet... I care. Too much. For the man who tore into my life like a storm breaking a drought. Who unsettled everything I thought was unshakable. The thought of him turning away one day — finding someone better, someone unmarked by grief, untouched by fear, someone who could give him everything I cannot — guts me. It leaves me raw. Bleeding. Burning with a jealousy I have no right to feel.

I fold forward, burying my face in my hands. And for the first time since last night, I admit the truth I've been too afraid to touch — too afraid to say aloud. I don't just want him. I need him.

My phone buzzes on the nightstand, loud in the hush. I jump like I've been caught doing something wrong. Emma, of course she would be checking in. I swipe before my courage can second-guess me. Her voice bursts through the speaker, bright and unapologetic despite the turmoil raging within me. "Well, good morning, sleeping beauty. So... was he everything I told you it would be?"

My stomach twists hard enough to hurl. "Emma..."

"Don't 'Emma' me, Lil." Her tone is playful, relentless.

"I saw the way he looked at you. That man didn't just watch you on the dance floor — he devoured you. Like you were the only woman in the room and the rest of us were scenery. He looked at you like you hung the damn stars. Don't you dare deny it. I saw it. Everyone saw it and hell no one was going to get close enough to you to question it."

I squeeze my eyes shut. Tears prick, burn. My voice is a scrape. "I... I can't do this." A beat of silence. Then her voice softens, teasing stripped away instantly, worry in her voice. "Lil... what's wrong?"

"Everything," I choke. It bursts out like a dam breaking.

"I— I let this happen, and it felt..." My throat closes. I drag in a ragged breath. "It felt like the first time I could breathe in years. Like I was... loved. Cared for. Adored, worshiped even. And then I look at that photo of Cal and I just—" my voice fractures "—I feel like I've cheated. Like I'm erasing him. Like every touch, every second, was wrong when it felt so damn right."

"Lil—" a sigh resounds.

"No." The word slices out of me, sharp enough to cut Emma off. My head shakes even though she can't see. "And what about the kids, Em? How do I even explain this to them? What if they look at me and think I'm replacing their dad? What if they think I don't miss him anymore? What if..." My breath splinters. "What if they hate me for it?"

The tears come hard, hot, relentless — blurring the room, making it small and airless. The weight presses on my chest until it's hard to breathe. I clutch the sheet in a white-knuckled fist as if it might anchor me.

"I hate myself for this," I blurt. "For wanting him. For craving him so much it feels like my bones ache. For letting him touch me, kiss me, make me feel things I swore I'd never let myself feel again. God, I'm furious with myself because I can't stop."

Tears roll down my cheeks, scalding. "I can't lose him. Not even now. And being with Aodhan..." My voice trembles. "It terrifies me. Because I think I want it — no, I know I want it. I want him. There's something there, something so raw, so magnetic it's pulling me under. But wanting him feels like betrayal. Like I'm cutting away the last piece of Cal I have left. Like I'm rewriting us. Erasing him and I can't lose him Em, I can't. He's already fading."

On the other end there's a shuffle, a muted curse, then Emma's voice — steady now, stripped of everything but unwavering loyalty. "We're coming over - don't move."

What feels like minutes later, I hear the familiar rumble of Vivienne's car in the driveway, gravel flying under her tyres. The front door opens, and then they're there — sweeping into the room ready to take on a battle I didn't know I needed them too.

Emma, usually the jester, is silent this time. No smirks. No biting one-liners. She just crosses the room in three strides and folds me into her arms, tight and grounding, her chin pressed to the top of my head. She doesn't let go, not even when my tears start again, hot and humiliating. She just holds on like she's daring the world to try and pull me apart.

Vivienne sits beside me on the bed, her presence quieter but no less fierce. Her hand settles over mine, steady, warm. "Lilian," she says, her voice soft but firm in the way only she can manage, "you don't have to be so strong all the time. You've carried more than anyone should. You've given everything — to Cal, to the kids, to the café, to us. But who looks after you?"

Her thumb brushes the back of my hand, and for a moment, I almost burst into tears again. "You're allowed to want happiness," she continues, her gaze steady on mine. "Wanting someone doesn't erase Cal. Missing him and needing to love and connect again aren't the same thing. He loved you, we all saw it — and you loved him. But love doesn't end just because you're still here. He'd want you to keep living, not turn yourself into a shadow of the person you once were out of guilt. Letting someone love you now... that isn't betrayal, Lil. That's living."

The words spear straight through me, but the guilt still sits heavy, immovable, pressing like a weight on my heart. My head shakes, helpless.

Emma pulls back just enough to look at me, her eyes glossy

but her jaw set. "And if anyone dares say otherwise, you send them to me. I'll flatten them before they get the words out." She swipes at her cheek quickly, almost angrily, as if denying the tears there. "No one denies my friend her shot at happiness. Not even you."

A broken laugh slips through my tears, surprising all of us. Emma's mouth quirks, triumphant in that small victory, but her voice is steady, low, when she leans in again.

"Listen. I know I joke a lot, Lil. But this? I'm deadly serious. That man. Aodhan. He doesn't just look at you. He sees you. Like you're the air in his lungs. And you…"

She shakes her head, eyes narrowing with something fierce and protective. "You're different around him. You're lighter. You laugh again. You don't even notice it, but I do. I see my best friend clawing her way back from the dark, and he's the one pulling you toward the light. So, stop punishing yourself for feeling it. Stop convincing yourself it's wrong." Her grip on my shoulders tightens. "You deserve this. You deserve him. You deserve to be worshiped, Lil. Every inch of you." My gaze drops, snagging on the band at my neck — Cal's wedding band— its edges catching the light like a quiet reminder. The sight slices through me, sharp and aching.

No matter what they say, no matter how fiercely they love me, the guilt lingers. Heavy. Relentless. But beneath it, curling deep in my chest, is something else. Something that frightens me even more than grief. Hope.

The thought of a new beginning and with that thought I hug Emma a little tighter and hold Vivienne's hand grounding me more, hoping their love and resolve seeps into me a little more.

CHAPTER 23

Aodhan POV

The room still carries her scent... Jasmine. Lilies. Rain. The faint salt of her skin. Her scent has bled into mine, tangled in every breath I take. It's not just in the sheets — it's in me, sunk down into bone and blood. I breathe, and she answers, even when she's not here. I close my eyes and it consumes me — the way her body bowed into mine, desperate and defiant. The broken way she whispered my name as if it were salvation. The trembling when I told her what she already is — mine. Centuries of control, of being forged into discipline and steel, shattered in a single night. A leash cut. A dam broken. All for her.

My cock hardens again at the memory, painful and relentless. I snarl under my breath, raking a hand through my hair as if I could tear the want out. Useless. She's under my skin, carved into me, more than lust — need. I glance around the room, my magic coiling. I can feel the hum of hers left behind — vines crawling across the glass ceiling, still glowing faintly.

And the bond — Fuck. The silence band forced upon us by, the thing meant to mute the pull, to smother the tether between us — it's failing. It failed the moment I touched her, tasted her, buried myself in her heat. I can feel her now, more than ever. Every flicker of thought, every curl of emotion slides beneath my ribs and anchors there.

Her grief is sharp, threaded with guilt that tastes like ash on my tongue. It cuts through me because she hides it from everyone else.

Her strength hums, steady and bright, though she doesn't believe it. And I feel the quiet, trembling edges of her love — the way she wants but resists, yearns but fears — like a storm that's been building too long, finally straining at the sky, ready to break and bring the world down with it.

It drives me mad. I can't separate her heartbeat from my own. I can't breathe without tasting her sorrow and her stubborn determination to keep me at arm's length.

I don't want to cage her. I don't want to take what she's not ready to give. But every part of me wants to be the one who carries her grief so she doesn't have to. The one who holds her until the fear fades. The one who gives her back her breath.

She was married. She is a mother. She built a life that should have been mine if fate had not conspired to keep her from me. That thought festers like a wound that will not close. If I had found her sooner, she would never have known this kind of grief. She would never have carried the weight alone. The bond is awake now. So am I. She can run. She can deny it. But I will feel her — in every breath, every distance. I will wait. As long as she needs.

I stalk to the portal room, leaving behind the Sun Palace, power sparking at my fingertips like sunlight trapped under skin. With a sharp flick of my wrist, the shimmering arch ignites. A tear of light in the air — and the pull hits instantly.

The cool expanse of the Air Court swallows me whole. Gone is the scent of coffee and damp earth. Here, the air is all marble and glass.

Towers cutting through the sky, the faint hum of currents winding through the clouds. My father's domain. His empire. Air's Court. The weight of duty drops over my shoulders the second I cross the threshold. The easy facade I wear in the human realm peels away, leaving only the mask of the Sun Prince — Kárith, heir, the blade poised between Courts.

The one who must hold the Sceptre, the one sworn to keep the Air Court's supremacy and still avert war. The heir to a crown that grows heavier by the hour.

I don't get the luxury of losing myself. Not here. Not when the balance between the Courts is tipping toward chaos, and every flicker of vulnerability is an invitation for a blade in the back.

"Report," I snap as my inner circle assembles in the war chamber. Sunlight filters through panes of skyglass, throwing fractured light across the floor like scattered wings. The few I trust beyond question stand at attention, their magic pulsing faintly with restrained power.

Kaelen, my third, takes his place at my right. Broad-shouldered, steady, his amber markings flicker as he bows. "My prince." His voice is even. "The Earth Court remains stable. No signs of aggression. Varys still withholds further intelligence on the Sceptre and its piece and Nivara's whereabouts. But the Fire Court..." He hesitates. The shift in the air tells me more than words — my temper spiking, heat blooming in the chamber.

"What of them?" My voice comes out quiet.

"They've doubled their patrols along the southern border. And the princess—" Kaelen's gaze meets mine without flinching. "She's left their territory more than once. Alone. So far, her visits seem limited to the human realm, but some of her close associates have been reaching out to the witches."

The image hits me unbidden — her in the café, her arrogance, the calculated smile she aimed at Lily, the lingering hunger in her eyes. My jaw tightens, heat pulsing under my skin like an echo of sunlight. "Keep eyes on her," I say, voice honed to steel. "I don't want her anywhere near the human realm without me knowing. If she so much as breathes wrong, I want to know instantly. And dig into her associates — find out who they're speaking to and why. If the witches are moving again, this may be our chance to take the upper hand."

"Yes, my prince," Kaelen replies, clipped but calm.

I stand there for a breath longer, fingers flexing at my sides, aware of how close I came to burning through the marble. Duty first. Always duty. And yet, behind my eyes, Lily's face still lingers — the feel of her pulse under my hands, the bond thrumming now like a live current I can't silence.

I dismiss them one by one, my voice clipped and impersonal until the last echo dies against the marble walls. Orders given. Loyalties reaffirmed. Masks re-secured. The chamber empties like a tide going out, leaving only stillness and the faint crackle of restrained power under my skin. Only Ellisar remains. She doesn't bow. She never does. Instead, she leans one hip against the long table, arms crossed, her pale hair braided down her back. Eyes like cut crystal fix on me — sharp enough to catch the smallest tremor of movement. There's always an edge to her — honed and quiet — a hunter's stillness that makes courtiers avert their gaze without knowing why.

"You've been pacing since you came through the portal," she says at last. Her voice is soft but carries a knowing edge. "Talk to me, Aodhan. What have you done that has you so shaken? Don't think I haven't noticed Maricus walking around with an extra spring in his smug step. He knows something, I don't. Now spill it."

I hesitate. Ellisar has been at my side since we were children — my blade-sister, my shadow in battle, the one who steadied me when the politics of this Court tried to cut me to pieces. She has seen every fracture in my armour and kept every secret that could have destroyed me. Like me, she lost a parent in the last war; grief and vengeance forged between us something tighter than blood ever could.

I drag a hand down my face, fingers trembling once before I master the movement. "Something I can't lose," I murmur, eyes fixed on the window where the winds race like white banners across the horizon. "Someone I can't afford to lose."

Her head tilts slightly. No pity in her gaze, just understanding. "The human you've been watching," she says. Not a question. A statement. I don't answer. But my silence is answer enough.

Ellisar pushes off the table, stepping closer. "Stop pacing — and stop rubbing your head. You'll end up with a bald spot, and you can't afford to get any less attractive if you've found someone you care for," she says, voice low and measured, a smirk tugging at her lips. "Breathe. Think. If you're going to break the pattern of centuries for her, then for the goddess' sake, look around and pay attention to what's happening in front of you."

For a heartbeat, I almost tell her everything what happened just mere hours ago — the scent of lilies in my sheets, the way Lily whispered my name, the way her fear and hope echo inside me even now. But I don't. I just stand there, the mask slipping for one beat too long while my oldest friend watches the man beneath the prince claw his way to the surface. Ellisar cocks her head, eyes narrowing with that blade-sharp scrutiny she saves only for me. "Just spit it out, Aodh. You're pacing like a caged wyvern and looking constipated. It's unseemly."

The corner of my mouth twitches, but the sound that leaves me isn't laughter. It's a low, rough exhale that drags something jagged out of me. "Fine." So I tell her. Everything.

From the first moment I saw Lily — to the way my world tilted when I realised what she is to me — my mate. The bond. The undeniable, unrelenting pull tying her to me in ways that defy logic or reason. And last night — the way every wall I've built crumbled the second she let me in, the second she looked at me like I was hers. How she had a husband. How she has children. How, despite the sharp, relentless jealousy that coils in me when I think of the man she loved, she is all I want. How my heart craves her. How all I want is to put back her broken pieces and make her whole. How I want to protect her children as if they were my own — to give her a world where she never has to carry everything alone again. I tell her how every Fae instinct in me screams to take what's mine — but that all I want is to let her set the pace, to let her take me too, in her own time. And I tell her about the band. The ancient binding around my wrist, meant to temper the bond's call, to keep my instincts in check. How Nivara used a silence wreath — and how it worked, until it didn't. Now it's useless, sparking, searing against my skin — every heartbeat amplifying her inside me.

When I finish, the silence between us is deafening. Ellisar blinks once. Twice. Then she shakes her head, disbelief etched in every line of her face. "No. That's... impossible. The prophecy—"

"The prophecy was wrong," I bite out, my words harsh and clipped. "Or someone made sure it was."

Her expression hardens, the strategist surfacing. She recites the old verse like a curse:

"He who shall unite the Fae,
He who shall bind the realms as one,
Shall walk ever in shadowed solitude.
No mate shall temper his fire,
No heir shall bear his name.
Death shall follow in every step,
whispering of ruin.
The Sun Prince shall claim no heart,
For his power shall be all the realm
will ever need —
And all it will ever fear."

She exhales sharply, pacing once before turning back to me, eyes flashing like cut ice.

"Why would anyone hide this from you? Mates are rare, Aodh — reverent — something sacred. Only a few are ever blessed to find one. Why keep her from you, when the bond could amplify your strength? When accepting her could make you unstoppable? All they've done..." she pauses, anger colouring her tone, "...is isolate you. Strip you of the chance to have heirs. To prevent you from embracing your full power."

I pace the length of the chamber, fists curling, heat flaring under my skin. "I don't know. But I've come to the same conclusion. Someone had a hand in it. Someone didn't want me to find her. Didn't want me to know. They wanted me powerless."

Ellisar straightens, her gaze like shards of ice. "Then we find out which court."

I stop pacing, meet her stare head-on. "Quietly. This doesn't leave you, Ellisar. No one else can know. Search the records. The archives. Every seer who's ever touched the prophecy. And find out why I was told I didn't have one, be wary of the sisters if they are working with fire..."

She studies me for a long moment, sharp and calculating, then nods once — crisp and certain. "Consider it done. But Aodh..."

She steps closer, her voice dropping low, laced with quiet warning.

"If someone hid her from you — if someone tampered with your bond. If they stole what was meant to be yours... This is bigger than just the prophecy being false, this could cause chaos amongst the Courts. This could be why the Sceptre search led us here—"

"They'll answer for it," I growl, power sparking around me, heat curling through the chamber until the torches flare and the air shimmers like molten gold. "Every single one of them. They stole her from me. Time from me. I will have retribution."

Ellisar's gaze softens just enough to show the sister-in-arms beneath the predator.

"That had better include that bloody Earth bitch. I never liked her. We need to look into them too, Aodh — Varyn is not normally that cunning. There must be a reason for the silence wreath and his breaking of oath." I nod, uncertain how to answer.

"Then I'll find your answers, my prince," she says. "For her. And for you." As she strides from the chamber, I'm left alone with my thoughts — and with the emotions of Lily warring inside my head.

CHAPTER 24

Lily POV

It's been a month since that night. A month since his hands burned against my skin, since his voice — low and deep and reverent — said my name like it meant something. A month since I admitted to myself, finally, that I wanted more. Wanted him. A month of waking in the night with my heart hammering, reaching for a presence that isn't there. A month of realising that while I owe it to Cal to mourn him, I also owe it to Aodhan. That if I want him, want us, I need to be able to give him everything I am. All of me. Not half a heart stitched together with guilt. And to do that, I have to sort out my own mess first.

Every morning for the last month, there's been a bouquet waiting at the door of the café — lilies, pale peonies, wild roses, sometimes wildflowers from the hillsides — all beautiful, all quietly left with a single note: yours always — A. No explanation. Just that quiet, steady presence. His presence.

At first I told myself it was just a gesture. Then I realised it was a message. He understood. I needed space. He was giving it. Willing to wait. The space hasn't been empty, though. It's been full of thoughts. Of grief and guilt and wanting. Of imagining what it would mean to stand in the open with him — not hiding behind loss, not apologising for needing, not feeling like betrayal drips from my fingertips every time I touch him.

But today... today isn't about him.

Today is about my children. About the life I built out of ashes. About proving to myself that I can still stand on my own two feet. That I can hold everything — the past and the possibility — without breaking.

I draw in a breath, fingers brushing the newest bouquet on the counter — lilies, pale and fragrant, their scent curling around me like a whisper — and let it out slowly. The knot in my chest loosens, just a little.

Nyxie pads at my heels, sensing the heaviness in me — the way my chest feels like it's been split wide open.

Six years. Six years since I lost Caleb. Six years since I got the call that told me he was gone — that they found him dead on the scene. Six years since my heart shattered.

Six years since the kids heard their father laugh, tease, or tuck them in at night. I take a breath, steadying myself, and step inside.

The house hums with movement. Daisy is packing the picnic basket with her usual determination. Brow furrowed, lips pressed tight as if focus alone will keep her from feeling too much. Oliver hovers near her shoulder, voice calm but clipped as he checks her list against the items lined up on the counter. His way of keeping busy, of keeping control. Vivienne's already outside, the car engine idling, her usual chatter muted for the day. Emma's in the kitchen, fussing with sandwiches and muttering under her breath about coffee. She never stops moving on this day. Maybe because stopping would mean feeling, and this is the one day even she lets her guard slip.

Dad is there too, leaning casually in the doorway with that familiar, quiet sadness in his eyes. He ruffles the kids' hair as they pass, his gaze sweeping the room like he's taking stock. As though making sure, we're all still here might make the loss a little easier to carry.

But I notice the way his hand lingers on the door frame. The subtle press of his fingers against the wood. He's already been through the house this morning — checked the locks, walked the boundary, whispered the words he still remembers from his grandmother. Wards. Quiet and old. Laid into the bones of this place to keep us safe.

He always reinforces them on this day.

It's not something he talks about — not often. But I see it. I feel it. It's his way of protecting what he has left. Of protecting us. Sal stopped by earlier, her knock soft against the frame. She didn't stay. Just pressed a basket of muffins and quiches into my hands — her warm, work-rough palm squeezing mine, a silent reminder that we're not alone before she turned and walked back down the path without a word. And for a moment, just a moment, I let myself stand there in the doorway, holding the weight of that simple kindness — the reality of what today means pressing in on all sides.

Caleb's grave sits in its usual quiet corner, tucked beneath a stand of gums where the breeze never stops moving and wildflowers creep right up to the stone in spring. It's peaceful here. Just how Cal was.

We spread the picnic blanket — the same one we've used every year, the one with a frayed corner where Daisy once spilled grape juice and tried to blame it on Oliver.

It smells faintly of sun and detergent, and of all the years it's borne witness to our grief.

The kids sit on either side of me, hands brushing mine, needing the anchor of home.

I trace my fingers over his name, etched clean and unyielding in stone:

Caleb James Carvish
Beloved Husband.
Devoted Father.
Always and Forever Loved.

Emma settles across from me, folding her legs beneath her, her bright eyes dimmed.

"Remember when he tried to fix that old car of yours, Viv? The one with the dodgy carburettor? He swore he could sort it out in a day and ended up setting half the shed on fire instead." Vivienne groans, covering her face with her hands, but there's a laugh threaded through it. "Oh my god, yes. Dad still tells that story every Christmas like it's his favourite joke."

Oliver chuckles, sharp and warm, the sound breaking through the heaviness like a shard of light. "He blamed the dog for months. Said Nyxie knocked over the petrol can and the sun caused it. Mum, you nearly strangled him." Daisy, quiet all morning, lets a small smile slip through. "He made the best pancakes, though. No one else can get them fluffy like that. Even when they were burned on the edges, they tasted... perfect."

Her voice wobbles, and I gather her hand into mine. My throat tightens, but I let the sound of their voices wash over me — the laughter, the stories, the memories polished smooth with retelling.

Each one hurts and heals all at once — because loving him didn't end when he did.

We stay like that for hours. Talking. Remembering. Letting the ache stretch out into something softer, something bearable. The kids lean into me as the sun dips low, and I don't hide my tears this time. I let them fall. Grief is just love with nowhere else to land.

When we pull into the driveway, the silence lingers. Vivienne squeezes my hand once, firmly, before heading inside with Emma — the two of them already murmuring about dinner plans and maybe a movie later, their way of cushioning the night. I climb out of the car. My foot hits the gravel. And I freeze.

Aodhan is there, as if he's been waiting in the folds of dusk and shadows. He leans against the gatepost with that careless, impossible ease — one boot hooked on the rail, the gold in his tattoos catching the last of the sun so they blaze like sun-rays themselves. He doesn't look like a man who belongs on a gravel driveway; he looks like someone torn from a dream, a figure carved for the cover of a magazine.

Daisy's breath hitches — a soft, sharp noise — and she shoots me a look that says everything without words. She tucks the picnic basket under her arm and slips inside with the small, efficient silence she's always carried. Oliver lingers at the car, shoulders set like a shield. Nyxie pads alongside him, tail low, eyes glittering with the same unreadable intelligence she always wears. I take a small step forward before Aodhan lifts a hand in a half-gesture, not quite a stop, but close enough. So, I pause looking between them both before staying where I am.

Oliver squares his jaw and walks the short distance between them. He doesn't speak at first; his silence is heavy and patient, like a held breath waiting to break. When he does, his voice is steady but threaded with that edge I know too well. "You like her," he says bluntly.

Aodhan doesn't answer straight away. The look in his eyes — the gold rims and silver flecks sparking like embers — says yes in a dozen languages. When he finally speaks, his tone is calm, measured. "Liking your mum seems far too small a word for what I feel for her. I care for her deeply. Far more than I can put into words. But she's someone I'd very much like to have in my life for the rest of my own."

Oliver's face tightens, an expression that curls like a fist. "You need to understand something." His words come out part warning, part plea. "My dad… he wasn't just Dad. He was Mum's person. They built this." He waves his hands gesturing around the property. "Every beam, every tile — it was their dream. He wanted this to be hers. When he… when he was taken, everything changed." His voice lowers, roughened by memory. "Dad made us as safe as he could. But Mum's been the one holding it all together ever since. She fights to keep the pieces from falling apart."

Hearing him say it like that — clear and fierce — something inside me twists. I think of all the nights running my thumb over my ring, of tucking the kids into bed, staying up late to balance the books so I wouldn't miss a minute with them when daylight came. The scraped knees, the late-night fevers, the school forms. Every heartbeat of survival. "If you're here for her," Oliver says, stepping closer until his shoulder brushes mine, "if you're going to hurt her or take from her—" he swallows hard, then forces the rest out like a dare, "don't. Leave now or I swear, I won't let you." Silence follows.

Aodhan inclines his head slowly — a gesture that feels almost ceremonial. When he speaks, his voice is low and even, each word deliberate. "I would eclipse the world before I hurt her. There's nothing I want to take from her. I want to give her everything I have — my all." There's no flourish to it, no threat aimed to intimidate Oliver — only the bare, barbed honesty of someone who has already measured the cost of his promise.

Oliver studies him for a long, searching moment, as if weighing the weight of that vow against the man who stands before him.

At last, the tension eases from his shoulders; he steps back, though the steel in his stance remains. Trust here will have to be earned. I stand there, rooted, feeling both the small, ordinary relief of the promise and the enormous, complicated weight of it. The words press against my heart until I can almost hear the whisper of hope in their wake. I glance once more at Oliver — at the way he watches me like someone guarding a door — then turn toward the house, letting them finish in their own space.

Behind me, in the softening light, Aodhan stays where he is — a silhouette against the ridge. When I look back, he lifts his head and our eyes meet. There's something in that look I can't quite put my finger on; promise, hunger, protection or danger braided with care.

I turn away, from them both, as Emma calls my name from the front porch.

CHAPTER 25

Aodhan POV

Oliver's voice is calm but firm as he finishes, yet every syllable carries a weight far older than sixteen. Grief. Memory. Love. It presses against my chest like a physical force, like a hand braced there, testing the measure of my heart.

He watches me with his father's eyes. Sharp, too steady for someone so young — assessing me with a quiet scrutiny, as though he can see every vow I've ever made to his mother, every promise I've held back. A quiet challenge. A silent demand: prove yourself.

It leaves me uneasy.

Because if this boy — this young man who carries his father's strength in his shoulders and his mother's fire in his eyes — doesn't accept me, then there will be no Lily. I know that as surely as I know my own name, as surely as the bond humming low and restless in my veins.

I've faced warlords, creatures older than time itself. I've stared down Courts on the brink of war without flinching. Taken a poisoned blade to the back. But this? This boy — her son — tests me in ways I never prepared for.

His steady stare feels like a blade pressed to my throat, meant to warn don't fail her or there will be reckoning.

I need him to see it. To feel it. The truth thrumming in every part of me, that I'd never let her feel alone again. And as I look at him — at the sharp line of his jaw, at the quiet strength carved from grief and loss — I see it. The resilience. The protectiveness. The leader he's becoming for his family.

And beneath it all, the bond between his mother and I stirs — alive, restless — like it knows this moment matters. Like it's waiting for his verdict, praying for his silent blessing. I can feel her even now, inside the house — the echoes of her grief, her exhaustion, the fierce, quiet love she has for these children. Her fear. Her hope. It brushes against my ribs like a phantom heartbeat.

Then, to my surprise, he breaks the silence. "Stay," he says at last, voice clipped but steady. "Have dinner with us. Meet the rest of the family that you would be joining." The words land like a key turned in a lock I didn't dare reach for. For a moment, I don't breathe. The boy's invitation hangs in the air, sharp and heavy, and I feel the bond flare hot in my chest, twisting like wildfire.

Across the yard, Lily catches the flicker in her son's eyes — not just tolerance, but a careful, cautious acceptance. Her shoulders loosen almost imperceptibly; a breath she didn't realise she'd been holding finally escapes. And in the softening of her gaze, in the gratitude written plain across her face, I see it: this is her family.

Her world. If Oliver is willing to let me in — even the smallest fraction — then perhaps there's room for me here after all.

For a second, I can't speak. The words knock the air from my lungs, unexpected and staggering. This boy, this human boy, has just offered me something no court, no council, no prophecy ever has — trust. A bridge. "Oliver..." My voice is rougher than I intend, quieter, strained with the weight of what I feel. "I don't want to intrude. Tonight is about your father. About family. The last thing I would ever do is take away from what this day means to you, to your sister... to your mother."

His jaw tightens, his chin lifting in that quiet defiance that reminds me so much of her. Yet his voice stays even, controlled. "If you're serious about Mum... then you'll understand that this is part of us. Remembering him. Every year. If you want to be here ...then be here. Otherwise, why did you come here tonight knowing what today was?"

The words land like an oath, a challenge and an invitation all at once. They settle deeper than any blade I've carried into battle. Because this isn't just about acceptance. This is about belonging. About being allowed to stand where another man once stood. About carrying the weight of her past alongside the hope of her future. I bow my head slowly, reverently, meaning every word when I finally manage to speak. "Then thank you," I murmur, my voice steady now, threaded with conviction.

"I'd be honoured."

I feel it as soon as I step inside: her element. Not the muffled, heavy stillness of Earth-Court stone halls, where the air presses down and every movement feels contained. Here, the air is alive — high ceilings drawing it upward, sunlight pooling and shifting like liquid gold. It's her world built to breathe; a place that invites movement instead of stifling it. And beneath it all, like a current under the floorboards, her magic hums. Subtle. Steady.

The house is taller than I expected — a cathedral of glass and light, yet somehow still intimate. Black beams stretch overhead, bold against the soft-timber ceiling. Warm wooden tones mingle with muted greens and tan-brown textures, every surface chosen with quiet, deliberate care. Earthy colours anchor the open space; trailing plants spill from shelves and climb toward the sunroof, their leaves catching shafts of light.

It feels like a garden caught mid-breath, a sanctuary disguised as a home.

I feel it as soon as I step inside: her element. Not the muffled, heavy stillness of Earth-Court stone halls, where the air presses down and every movement feels contained. Here, the air is alive — high ceilings drawing it upward, sunlight pooling and shifting like liquid gold. It's her world built to breathe; a place that invites movement instead of stifling it. And beneath it all, like a current under the floorboards, her magic hums.

I've watched this house from the edge of the tree line for months — its lights at dusk, its warmth spilling out like a promise

— always keeping my distance, always guarding without stepping across the threshold. Until now.

The house hums with life —with a steady undercurrent of warmth stitched into every corner. The smell of roasted vegetables drifts from the oven, mingling with the faint sweetness of Emma's perfume and the earthy scent of tea on the stove.

It's foreign and unfamiliar. A belonging I've never known in the Air Court, where affection is rationed and duty presses forward no matter what. Here, love is casual, unspoken, but everywhere.

Oliver clears his throat, and with the kind of crooked grin only a son can get away with, and says, "Everyone — this is the weirdo interested in Mum."

A ripple of laughter cuts the tension. Even Lily rolls her eyes, cheeks-tinged pink, but her lips twitch with a reluctant smile.

Emma is the first to pounce. She whistles low, dramatic, and props herself against the counter like she's front-row at a show. "Well, well. If it isn't the mysterious stranger who likes to hang at the café, or lurk at bars. Nice to see you looking a little less 'stalker' and a little more... committed. Suits you." Her grin is razor-bright, full of mischief.

Vivienne follows, offering me a polite smile that doesn't quite reach her eyes.

"Viv. Lily's older sister." Her tone is pleasant, her posture perfect. But her gaze — sharp, steady — says something else entirely: hurt her, and you'll wish you hadn't.

Then Daisy steps forward, tilting her head. Green eyes — so much like her mother's — lock on me, bright and curious. "I'm Daisy," she says, voice clear. Then, with a smile that's far too knowing for her age, she adds, "Mum's daughter. So... what do you think of her?"

A test. The answer comes before I can stop it.

Quiet. Certain and true.

"She's my sun, my light, my strength."

The words hang in the air, simple and raw. My gaze drifts — helplessly, always to Lily as she fusses with glasses, laughing at something Emma mutters under her breath. And it's the truth, all of it, laid bare for them to see.

Daisy's smile sharpens. She doesn't mock. Just nods once, as if satisfied. As if she's taken my measure and, for now, finds me passable. I exhale, sweat beading above my brow with nerves.

Emma snorts, breaking the moment with a smirk. "And you know me, Emma — best friend. And Secret keeper." I incline my head, lips tugging faintly. "Noted."

Finally, the older man steps forward. Her father, whom bares no resemblance to Lily. His presence is quieter than the others, but no less commanding. His steady gaze weighs me, sharp and unflinching. When he offers his hand, I clasp it firmly, meeting strength with strength. His grip is solid, his silence deliberate. He studies me for a beat, as though looking past the mask, past the prince, to the Fae beneath.

I feel an energy around him. Not Fae, something else and older. It's masked, and masked well. I hesitate to ask, but decide to leave it be, making a note to revisit it later. Then, at last, he nods. "Tom."

When he turns back to Lily, he takes her hand in his, the gesture simple but filled with years of shared grief and endurance. She leans into it instinctively, her shoulders easing. And in that quiet exchange between them, I see it — the love of a father still guarding his daughter, even as he dares to make space for me.

Vivienne clears her throat, her voice even but soft, carrying the weight of ritual. "We all share a memory of Cal before dinner. That's the rule."

Emma doesn't hesitate. "Oh, I've got one." She leans back, eyes glittering with mischief that softens into fondness. "Remember when Cal was in the hospital with Oliver? He swore up and down he was having a girl — had the name Olivia picked out and everything. He'd practised saying it like it was some royal decree." Her grin widens at Oliver. "Then the doctor told him otherwise and I swear he nearly fainted. Full-on pale as a sheet, wobbling at the knees, ready to drop."

Oliver groans, but there's no real heat in it. A reluctant smile tugs at his lips as he mutters, "Yeah, yeah. Hilarious." He shoots Daisy a sharp look — the kind that says "don't you dare laugh"

— which only makes her bite her lip harder.

Vivienne's smile is gentler, touched with nostalgia. "When you first moved here, Cal swore he'd found some kind of rare gem in the soil out by the shed. He came running in, grinning like he'd struck gold, holding this little red shard. Said it was going to pay off the mortgage one day." She shakes her head, laughter threaded with sadness. "Turned out to be coloured glass. Still, he carried it in his pocket for weeks like it was the crown jewels."

That's enough to break Daisy's restraint — her laughter spills out, soft and melodic. "He was so proud of it. Told me it was going to pay for my uni degree one day. I think he even polished it once." Her laughter fades, and when she speaks again, her voice is steadier, almost reverent. "When he took me to my first concert... he learned every single dance move ahead of time. Even the ridiculous ones. He was better at them than I was." She jumps up suddenly, performing one of the moves — exaggerated and silly — and her laugh fills the room.

Oliver snorts, shaking his head, but his grin is real this time. "My first soccer game. I scored, and he dropped his phone cheering. Screen shattered completely. Didn't even notice. Just kept yelling that his kid had scored." Daisy giggles, wiping her eyes. "And it wasn't even a good goal. The ball kind of... rolled in. Barely." Oliver shrugs, mock-serious. "A goal's a goal."

The laughter lingers, warm and bittersweet, until Tom clears his throat. His deep voice carries more than memory — it carries years. "The moment I met Cal he was a bundle of nerves. I swear I thought he was going to drop to the floor when he shook my hand, but he was determined." He looks across the table, eyes soft and shining with quiet grief. "The way he looked at you... I knew right then he was a good man. I could sense it from him, even if we only had him for a short while."

He reaches across, his hand closing over Lily's with that firm, fatherly strength only he can give. "You made each other better. Anyone could see it." Silence folds around the table for a moment. I sit with my head bowed slightly, hands resting still against my knees. I don't dare speak. I don't intrude. Though no words pass, the bond hums inside me, fierce and aching, whispering the truth:

I will honour this man's memory as much as they do. For Lily. For all of them. A man who holds more meaning and memory than most Fae in the millennia they live.

Lily draws a slow breath, her fingers trembling slightly against the edge of the table. "My turn," she says quietly. "My favourite memory." Everyone stills, even the air seeming to soften. "I was seventeen," she begins, her voice threading into the room like a story half-whispered. "He was playing soccer at the oval behind the school. I'd never even noticed him before. He was awkward, a bit of a class clown — trying to tell me about some impossible goal he'd just scored. He spun to demonstrate, did the kick..." Her mouth curves faintly. "...and fell flat on his face right in front of me."

A ripple of soft laughter moves around the table. Lily's smile trembles but stays.

"I couldn't help but laugh," she continues, eyes distant but shining. "Before I even thought about it, I asked if he was okay. And then he jumped up, nose bleeding, laughed and asked if the fall was enough to break the tension between us. He made me laugh so much — that kind of laugh you couldn't help but share. He was my best friend before he was anything else."

Her gaze drops to her hands, knuckles white against the wood. When she speaks again, her voice is glassy but fierce. "It's cruel we didn't get more time. But..." She swallows hard, gathering herself, looking first at Oliver, then at Daisy. "I see him in the kids every day. In Oliver's quiet strength. In Daisy's fire. That makes it easier. Easier for me to..." A small breath. "...to start moving forward. To live again."

The silence that follows is thick and reverent — full of love, full of unspoken understanding. Around the table, heads bow slightly, eyes glisten, but no one speaks because none of them needs to.

Beneath the table, I find her hand. My thumb brushes over her knuckles, and she doesn't pull away. The bond hums between us — quiet but undeniable — a tether thrumming with a silent promise of what's to come.

Dinner flows after that — laughter, teasing, more stories. It's the kind of evening that roots itself deep in your chest, the kind you know you'll carry for centuries. For the first time in my long life, I feel part of something that isn't duty or politics or bloodlines. Something real. Something I didn't know I was missing.

When the house quiets and the laughter fades, I find her standing at the front door. The air is heavy with memory — bittersweet, soft. She turns toward me, her eyes tired but warm, and for a moment the world narrows to just this — her and me. "Stay," she whispers, her voice barely a breath, but the weight of the word settles deep in my bones. "Just... stay with me tonight."

The fire in my chest roars to life, the bond pulling tight, unrelenting. I can feel her emotions mixed with mine. My voice is low, reverent, roughened with the promise of what I can't yet say. "As you wish."

CHAPTER 26

Lily POV

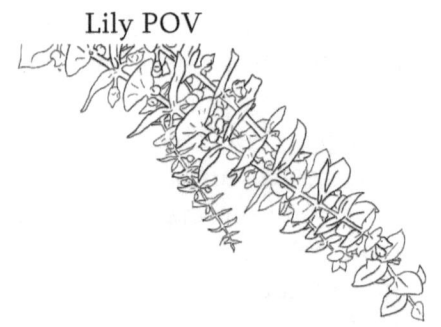

Sleep drags me under, deep and heavy, and when the dream comes it's nothing like the others. Not the café. Not the house. This time, the world blooms around me as twilight — a strange, endless hour where violet bleeds into molten gold, where the sky seems to hover between dusk and dawn. The air hums faintly, alive with a low vibration that thrums in my bones, as though magic has woven itself into the very fabric of this place. The streaks of light blurring with the marring night. The sensation has my body tensed — not quite a safe feeling, but something that calls me home.

My mind feels conflicted and confused.

A narrow dirt path stretches ahead, winding through a field of tall grass that sways as though stirred by a wind I can't feel. Glow-worms blink in the half-light — tiny embers flickering along the path, as if the stars themselves are lighting the trail. I continue forward, unable to turn back the way I came. Flowers unfurl and bloom with each step I take, pollen drifting into the air. A sweet, floral scent following in my wake.

The path narrows in the dark ahead, then splits in two, carved into the ground like fate's hand opened wide: one track leads back toward the familiar mountains — veiled , heavy, committed to memory. The other vanishes into a horizon I can't see, the edges of it shimmering faintly, glowing as though lit from within.

Colours so vivid and alluring. A road that promises something new, an electric current pulling me towards it and a familiar song almost calling me home. And at the fork — waiting as though he's been standing there all along.

Caleb.

He looks exactly the same as the last day I laid eyes on him. Jeans faded and fraying at the knees.

A soft, worn shirt with sleeves rolled to his elbows, exposing those strong forearms I once traced absent-mindedly while we sat under the stars. His hair falls into his eyes — stubborn and untamed — and that crooked grin, the one that used to give me butterflies with nothing more than a glance, curves at his lips.

Although his stance and the way he holds himself are familiar, the air seems to bend around him.

There's something new. A stillness, a gravity I've never seen before. Like the weight of years I didn't get to share with him has settled in his frame. The years lost with his children, all held in calm composure, resigned to his fate.

My chest fractures, breathing laboured— as my throat tightens around his name "Cal..."

The sound is raw, breaking, as though saying it aloud might shatter him back into dust. I take one trembling step forward, then another, unable to stop myself before I'm running at full speed, hurling myself into his arms as though I can crush myself to him and bring him back.

"Hey, love."

He catches me easily, holding me in his arms, feet lifting from the ground.

His voice is everything it always was — steady, warm, grounding. It falls over me like sunlight through leaves, and my knees nearly buckle with the ache of it.

God, how I've missed that voice. How I've missed him. My body tells me he's here — here with me right now — and I shouldn't let go. My mind tells me to hold on, because this could be the last time I see him. And my heart... my heart is torn, breaking at the sight of him — at the faded memories, his voice, all the things I've been terrified of forgetting. And here he is. The ache in my chest becomes unbearable.

My hands shake as tears blur my vision, spilling hot down my cheeks. The sight of him — solid, real, here — is everything I've prayed for in the dark and cursed the stars for denying me. And yet, deep down, I know this can't last. I know this is not life, not truly.

But still, my heart whispers, Please don't let me wake up. Not yet.

Tears blur my vision.

"I miss you. I don't know how to do this without you. I'm scared."

The air shifts — heavy with a familiar sweetness. Jasmine and roses twine together, the scent of our old garden in full bloom, wrapping around me like a memory I could drown in.

Vines I know as well as my own hands curl up around a phantom pergola that hadn't been there a moment ago, blossoms unfurling as if answering to his presence. It smells like home. Like summers that never ended — barefoot evenings spent in the garden, laughter spilling into twilight as he kissed the back of my hand like we were still teenagers fumbling our way through love.

It smells like safety. Like the life we built together, piece by piece, before the world tore it away. Before I got that call. Before I was confirming his body in a morgue. Before I was saying goodbye at a funeral. Before my life changed to a forever without him in it.

He reaches out, folding me into his arms, and the ache in my chest shatters, sending jagged edges through every part of me until I can hardly stand.

His scent — soap, summer rain, cut grass, eucalyptus from hikes — clings to him as if the years never passed, as if I could bury my face in his neck and go home again.

His thumb brushes away my tears, gentle and sure — the same gesture that soothed me through colic nights, heartbreak, and hospital waiting rooms. It's muscle memory for him, and for me. My body leans into it before my mind can catch up.

"You've already been doing it, Lil," he murmurs, his voice like warm honey poured over raw edges. "Every day. Loving the kids. Holding everything together. Breathing even when it tore you apart." He swallows, a flicker of grief tightening his mouth before his tone softens again. "But..." His gaze drifts past me, beyond the phantom pergola to the fork in the road, threaded with something heavier than words — sorrow and pride woven into one. "It's time to stop just surviving."

I follow his gaze. Behind me, the path is lined with blurred silhouettes, each one a memory — nights curled up with his jumper pressed to my face; mornings pretending I wasn't crying in the shower; every time I smiled for the kids when I was breaking inside.

Attending parent–teacher interviews, only to be asked when my husband would arrive. More memories — heartbreak upon heartbreak, pulling back the shattered pieces, trying to fit them together. I watch myself in the flashes of memory, seeing myself for the first time — a hollow, sad woman who looks like she's barely holding on. One who might fly away if given the chance. A fresh wave of tears burns my eyes. My kids — our kids — have had to watch and endure their mum look this way for six years. They deserve more. Better.

"Don't do that, Lil," he sighs, his breath warm against the top of my head. "I can see you blaming yourself."

"You were mourning, just as they were. You cannot blame yourself for your grief. And the kids..."

His voice cracks, tears brimming in his eyes. "They never once saw you the way you see yourself. They see a woman who went to battle for them every single day — a woman who worked full-time, made every concert, every awards night, every soccer game, and a mum who screamed the loudest to make up for the fact I wasn't there."

His arms tighten around me, and I feel the droplets falling on my shoulders, a soft sob echoing from him. "You have been — and are — perfect. You always were meant for more than me. I was just lucky enough to be a small part of your long future."

My throat tightens, heavy with guilt and longing — a physical knot of everything I've carried since the day he died. "I don't know how," I whisper, voice cracking. "I don't know how to start something new, knowing you won't be there. You were always my certainty, and without you…"

"Yes, you do," he says quietly but certain — the same tone he used when teaching me to parallel park, or when I doubted if we could afford the café, or when I wondered if I'd be a good mum. The voice of the man who always believed in me before I did. "I never wanted you to carry me like this."

His thumb strokes my cheek again, and his smile trembles at the edges. The air around us seems to drop in temperature. "I'll always be with you — in the laughter, in the quiet, in every memory that we share, even the sad ones. But you deserve more than this — more than the guilt, the grief, the ache that keeps you frozen in place. You deserve to laugh again. To explore. To love again."

My breath shudders. It's like trying to inhale through water, lungs unable to take in any air — a thought of this is the end. "I don't want to forget you," I choke out, the words torn from somewhere bone-deep, raw as an open wound. My voice breaks on the last syllable, shattering like glass, and I hate myself for how small and pathetic I sound.

Caleb's fingers find my chin, tilting it up with the same gentle insistence that once made me look at him when I was angry, when I was scared, when I wanted to hide. His touch is warm, steady, familiar. His smile is soft — steady in a way that makes my knees weaken — even as his eyes gleam with unshed tears. "You won't," he says, voice low but unshakable.

For a heartbeat, his smile shifts, softens into something so young — from our days in school.

The man before me dissolves into the boy I met at seventeen: grass-stained knees, a second-hand shirt two sizes too big, that ridiculous mop of hair he could never keep out of his eyes. The boy who laughed nervously when he asked me out, voice cracking as if the words were too heavy.

My chest aches with the memory — with the cruel sweetness of it. "You'll never forget me," he whispers gently, the words a balm and a blade all at once. His voice is warm enough to split me open, to unspool every fragile thread I've been holding together. "Remember that ridiculous song I used to sing off-key in the car, just to make you laugh?" His mouth tilts, breaking into the crooked grin that once undid me. "You rolled your eyes every damn time, but you still sang with me. You always sang with me."

A small laugh escapes him — tender, aching — and it cracks down the middle. "That's me, Lil. Still here. Still with you."

His eyes — green, endless, familiar as the seasons — glint with something eternal, something that hurts to look at but I can't turn away from. The smile softens again, melting into something quieter, more fragile. "You won't forget. You couldn't, even if you tried. I'm part of you — carved into your bones, woven into every heartbeat. But it's okay..." His voice falters, trembles just enough for me to hear the cost of the words, then steadies again. "It's okay to let someone else in. To be happy. To *live* — not just for the kids, but for *you*."

His thumb strokes across my cheek, tender, reverent. "But it's time to step forward now. Time to choose where the path goes next." Caleb's hand finds mine, warm and steady, his thumb brushing across my knuckles as though grounding me to this place between worlds.

With his other hand, he cups my cheek, his calloused palm achingly familiar, and for a moment it's as if time folds in on itself — every kiss, every late-night whisper, every ordinary touch layered into this one. His eyes soften, the green of them deepening with a knowing that twists my heart. "I will always love you," he murmurs, voice low but certain, as though he needs me to carry the words with me when he's gone. "You and the kids... you were the best things I ever did. The best choice I ever made. And I will never regret it, Lil. Not one moment. Not one breath."

His thumb drags across my cheekbone, slow, reverent. "No matter what comes, and no matter what you learn later, remember — you were always my choice, and that will never change."

The words send a chill through my spine. My throat closes, but he doesn't let me look away. His gaze holds mine — steady, fierce, filled with a kind of gentle urgency. "There is change coming, Lil," he says, his voice threading with something heavier, older, as if it carries more than just him. "Whether you're ready or not, it's already moving toward you. He will be there for you — I see it, in the way he steadies you even when you don't realise you need it. But you'll need to be careful."

His hand strokes down my cheek again, softer this time, his palm lingering as if to memorise the shape of me. "No matter what happens, don't let your rage consume you. Don't let grief twist into something darker. Be you. You're everything you need to be, Lil. Everything."

The garden stirring as if an unseen wind has brushed through them. The very air holds its breath. The magic in the air, threaded through me, stirs too — a low, electric pulse at the base of my spine, sharp and certain, as though it recognises this moment.

Caleb notices; I see the flicker of awareness pass through his eyes — a weight knowing he won't speak aloud he won't speak aloud. "He's different," he says softly, returning to me, grounding me with the press of his hand still on my cheek. "Not just anyone could make you feel this. Don't run from it. Don't run from him. You were both meant to meet."

Tears spill freely now, hot against his skin where my face presses into his hand. "I... I'm afraid. What if I love him and lose him too? I can't do this again," I whisper, the truth shattering out of me.

"I know." His thumb sweeps gently over the curve of my cheek, his touch both ghost and anchor. His voice lowers to a whisper, breaking but steadying itself again. "But he's already in your soul, isn't he? Like the roots of a tree that's been there all along — just waiting to grow."

The garden begins to dissolve around us — colours bleeding into pale light, petals unravelling into shimmering dust that swirls like fireflies on the wind. The scent of roses fades first, then the jasmine, until only the ghost of summer lingers in the air.

The world is slipping away, but his voice remains — low, steady, clear and precise — the only anchor left as everything else crumbles. He leans down, and when his lips press to my forehead, it's like sunlight breaking through storm clouds. Warm, fleeting, unforgettable. His whisper follows, brushing hot against my skin, words carved so deep they feel etched into my bones.

"Tell him," Caleb murmurs. "Tell him what you feel. Make him love you better than I ever could — or there'll be a reckoning on the other side if you don't. Don't waste this chance, Lil. Don't lock yourself away." His smile curves.

Soft and sure. A smile that once made me fearless, a smile I will spend the rest of my life carrying. "Live, my love. Live well. And love — it's who you are. Don't ever forget it. You are strong. You are resilient. You are... you."

When I glance down, his hand is already sliding from mine — fingers I once clung to like lifelines slipping slowly, irrevocably away. Panic claws at me, a raw, desperate ache that rises in my throat, but I can't hold him. Not this time. I look up at him, and he leans down, brushing his lips against mine — soft, sweet, and salty from my tears. I don't want to break away from him. I know this is the end.

He pulls back slowly, brushing my hair away from my face and tucking it behind my ears. We're standing at the fork now, the paths stretching before us. His road shimmers with golden fields and wildflowers swaying in a wind I cannot feel.

A horizon calling him home. Mine glows faintly, pulsing like a heartbeat in the distance, alive with something unknown but undeniable.

For a breath, we simply look at each other, memorising. His green eyes are endless, shining with love and sorrow and pride all tangled together, and in them I see everything we were, everything we might have been, everything he wants me to be.

"Go," he whispers, the word breaking and steady all at once. "*Live.*"

The last of his warmth fades from my hand, slipping through my fingers like smoke, and I force myself to take a step — forward, trembling, onto the path that beats like a living thing beneath my feet. It hums faintly, alive, as if the very earth is urging me on.

Behind me, Caleb's figure is already dissolving into light, edges breaking apart into a brilliance too sharp for me to hold.

I turn back just once. My throat burns as I lean in, pressing a kiss to his cheek — one last touch, one last memory carved into me. His gaze holds mine with that same crooked love that once made me fearless, and for a moment, I swear my heart stops beating.

"Be brave," he calls, his voice echoing across the twilight as the dream unravels around us. It trembles, then steadies, as if he's pouring every last piece of himself into it.

"Be the strong, unbreakable Lillian I love. I'll be watching over you — always. You, and the kids. My best work. My greatest love." Tears stream down my face, hot and unstoppable, but my feet keep moving. I keep walking. I have to. The path curves away from the estate, twisting through light that bends and sways as if it knows my choice has been made.

Shadows fall behind me, swallowed by the glow. Turning through an overhead hedge with flowers blooming around me and then — slowly, achingly — the world opens. What rises before me is unlike anything I've ever seen. A tall, glass-walled castle hangs suspended in the sky itself, as though it has been plucked from a dream and anchored between stars.

Its walls shimmer with shifting colours, reflecting every hue of dawn and dusk, while mountains cradle it from either side — their slopes draped in iridescent flowers that glow faintly with their own inner light. The blooms sway as though alive, bowing in rhythm with a breeze I can't feel, petals shimmering like liquid jewels.

Dragons soar through the sky — larger than planes and more graceful than anything I have ever seen before.

Below, on the hillside, horses with vines growing across their heads gallop free among deer with an aurora billowing around them.

My mind is stunned, shocked, and in awe of the beauty surrounding me. And then — from somewhere beyond, beyond the castle, beyond even the edges of what my dream can hold — a voice drifts toward me.

Rich. Resonant. Familiar in a way that makes my chest ache, though I cannot yet place it. It wraps around me like a welcome, like a summons — deep and commanding yet threaded with promise.

Welcome home child.

CHAPTER 27

Lily POV

I wake with tears slipping, hot down my cheeks and Aodhan's arms wrapped tight around me. Holding me steady as though he's been here the whole time. A guardian in the dark, protecting me from the storm even in my sleep. His embrace is unyielding yet tender, anchoring me in a way that feels both foreign and inevitable.

"I'm sorry," I whisper into the quiet, my voice raw, frayed around the edges. "I'm so sorry. This... this isn't why I wanted you to stay, or for you to see me like this."

He doesn't answer with words. He doesn't need to. His arms tighten, his chest solid against my back, and the warmth radiates against my skin — just steady pulses of support threading through the jagged edges of my grief until they soften.

"Just take deep breaths, and take all the time you need, I am not going anywhere." The rhythm of his soft rumble above my head is almost hypnotic, a silent vow wrapping around me: I am here. You are safe.

He doesn't ask, doesn't press, doesn't demand answers. He simply holds me. A calming presence. A strength that feels infinite where mine feels unworthy and pathetic.

The dream lingers even as my eyes open, a phantom ache carved deep in my chest — Caleb's voice still echoing at the fork in the road, urging me to live. But with Aodhan's arms around me, steady and warm, something sharper cuts through the ache: I don't want to live inside memories anymore.

Caleb gave me permission. My heart demands I choose to live. And when I lift my hand, fingers trembling as they trace the faint glow of Aodhan's tattoos beneath his shirt, it isn't grief that guides me. It's want. It's hope. It's life. It's him. A Future.

I lose track of time in the quiet rhythm of him — the measured cadence of his breathing, the reassuring strength of his heartbeat thrumming against my spine, the subtle glow of his magic weaving calm through the storm raging inside me. Hours pass like this. The raw ache doesn't vanish, but it softens into something bearable — a dull throb that doesn't consume me.

Finally, I shift in his arms, turning to face him. Dawn spills across the room, gilding everything in soft gold. The light kisses the sharp planes of his jaw, the strong line of his cheekbones, and the faint shimmer of his tattoos. They glow in steady pulses, as if they've aligned themselves with me, echoing the beat of my own heart. And for the first time in six years, the grief doesn't feel like a chain. It feels like a truth I can carry forward — because right here, in this light I am bathed in, I want to. The room looks clearer today, like I have been walking and living in a fogged atmosphere for the light to finally break through and see everything in all its vivid glory.

Without thinking, I lift my hand, tracing the curve of his collarbone with my fingertips, following the glowing marks etched into his skin like a map only I've been allowed to read. The light under my touch pulses faintly, almost as if it's responding to me, and a shiver ripples through him at the contact.

Still, he doesn't move away. This man — this impossibly patient, unflinchingly steady man — has given me space when I asked, silence when I needed it, and a kind of loyalty I didn't know how to name until he walked into my café and shifted my entire world without even trying.

"Lily, careful," he murmurs, voice low and roughened by sleep, carrying that restrained thread of warning that always lights something deep inside me. His breath brushes my lips, warm and uneven. "If you keep touching me like that, I'll forget all my good intentions."

"Maybe..." I whisper, breathless, "...maybe I want you to." His breath stutters — sharp, audible — and his eyes darken as they lock onto mine. Molten gold and silver flakes dancing in the sunlight, sharp and unguarded, his gaze strips me bare, every wall I've built over these years reduced to ash under the weight of him.

"You have no idea," he rasps, voice low and vibrating with restraint, "how much I crave you and your touch, and what I imagine doing to you every time you look at me like that."

My pulse stumbles, heat curling and tugging. Heat coiling tighter with every choice, every moment of patience, every bouquet, every unspoken promise and I can't hold back anymore. "Then show me," I whisper, the words a plea, a challenge, an invitation all at once.

For a heartbeat, the room stills, the morning light holding its breath with us.

Then his mouth finds mine, hot and desperate, yet still careful, always careful, as though I'm something fragile he's afraid to break. "You are perfect and mine now," he groans against my lips, the word torn from his chest — primal, reverent, raw all at once. "Always mine, Lily."

I answer with my hands, sliding them up his chest, down his sides; surrender and invitation tangled together. Every inch of him is heat and power under my palms, but his body trembles faintly with restraint. I answer with my hands, sliding them up his chest, down his sides; surrender and invitation tangled together. Every inch of him is heat and power under my palms, but his body trembles faintly with restraint.

"Stand. And no touching. You need to be patient," I murmur, my voice a whisper in his ear. He obeys without hesitation, eyes locked on mine — unwavering, intense — as if there's no world beyond this moment.

I sink gracefully to my knees before him, I want him to know just how much I want him, an act of claiming him as much as he claims me. The sharp intake of his breath pierces the quiet. His breath stutters, a tremor of control flickering across his features.

"Lily…" My name is a warning, a plea, a surrender all at once — his voice roughened with the weight of everything unspoken, everything we've been circling since the first moment we met.

I rise slightly, my palm sliding up the plane of his abdomen, fingertips grazing the ridges of muscle drawn taut beneath smooth skin. Slowly, deliberately, I push the fabric upward. He simply watches, breathing hard, eyes dark, as if each inch of revealed skin costs him another shred of control.

When my fingers trace the curve of his shoulder, down over the dip of a scar that disappears beneath his waistband, his sharp inhale tells me exactly what my touch does to him.

Then, slowly, I drop lower again, back to my knees before him. His breath falters. A muscle in his jaw ticks.

"Lily," he breathes, my name frayed on his tongue, his chest rising sharply.

"You don't have to, I want you to be the one to unwind and —"

"I want to." My voice is steady, sure, threaded with something fierce and tender all at once. "I want you to feel what you give me. I want you to know."

My hands slide over his hips, my gaze climbing back to his —"Let me, and remember no touching or we go back to bed" I whisper.

For a second, everything freezes. Then he exhales, shuddering, and his hands hover at my shoulders, before pulling back to his sides, I watch his hands clench and unclench, veins tensing. A thrill overcomes me, that he wants me, he wants my touch, just as much as I his.

His breath hitches, ragged and uneven, as I slide my hands up the strong line of his thighs, the fabric of his sweats soft beneath my palms.

His throat works as if he's searching for words and failing. It's all the confirmation I need. I ease his waistband down, breath catching when I free him — thick, heavy, already aching, his need laid bare in a way that makes my pulse stutter.

I pause drinking him in, and murmur to myself "How the hell did you fit" before wrapping my hands around him.

One stroke. Then another. Slow. Teasing. Deliberate.

The groan that rips from him is low, guttural, primal. His head tips back against the door frame with a dull thud

I lean in, pressing a soft kiss to the base of him, then another halfway up his length — tasting, teasing — until his hands twitch at his sides. I can feel the restraint coiled tight in him, every muscle straining with the urge to touch, to guide, but he holds back. Not backing down from the challenge set.

When my lips finally close over him, his sharp inhale and the broken sound that rumbles from his chest go straight through me, heat pooling low and insistent. I take him deeper, my tongue swirling, my hand keeping pace while the other braces against his thigh for balance. "Mo draganín," he groans, voice shredded, reverent and raw.

"Goddess, you're... fuck." He struggles out.

I tighten my grip, stroking in sync with my mouth — slow at first, then faster — savouring the way his breath comes ragged, the guttural sounds tearing loose from his throat. His head tips back again, eyes finding mine through the haze — dark, hungry, questioning, undone.

I only smile around him, leaning forward to swirl my tongue over the sensitive tip, tasting the bead of precum — sharp, addictive, like some forbidden sweetness meant only for me. His answering groan reverberates through the air.

His breath hitches, rough and jagged, his gaze hooded and fixed on me sucking harder this time, my tongue teasing with deliberate, unrelenting precision.

He's so big, thick and hard against my lips, stretching me, filling me, no way to swallow him whole. My hand strokes where my mouth can't reach, every movement calculated, every caress meant to unravel him, how I want to see him come undone from me. And only me.

When I cup his balls, giving a gentle squeeze, a violent shudder rips through him, his restraint cracking like glass under too much weight. His tattoos flare bright, molten fire racing along his skin. "You need to stop you have won, I haven't touched" he groans, voice guttural, frayed, almost broken. "I can't... hold back."

I let him slide out slow just enough to meet his gaze, heat sparking like a live current between us, daring him. "I haven't won yet, remember don't touch," I whisper, before sinking down again, hollowing my cheeks, taking him deep.

His control shatters. His fingers dig into my shoulders, anchoring himself to me, his breaths coming in ragged, uneven bursts. His hips jerk despite himself, the bond thrumming between us, alive, demanding, binding. I drink in every sound — every guttural growl, every sharp gasp — each one hitting me like a mark of worship, like proof of how completely I undo him.

"Lilian—" My name tears out of him, raw and desperate, as his body goes taut, muscles locking tight. Heat floods my mouth as he spills into me, his groan reverberating through the room, through me, through the bond itself until I feel scorched by it.

I swallow him down.

When I finally look up, his gaze crashes into mine — molten, reverent, utterly undone. His chest heaves, every breath rough and unsteady, as if I've stripped him of everything he thought he knew about control.

I don't' get the chance to rise when I am taken in his arms and lifted to meet his eyes, my legs wrap around his waist. He crashes his mouth to mine a kiss so intense I feel lightheaded. His hand cups my face, calloused palm trembling as though he's holding something too precious to risk breaking.

His forehead presses to mine, his breath still uneven. His hands cradle my face like I'm the only thing tethering him to this world.

"That was amazing, but you did not need to do that, I don't want you to ever feel you need to show me you care by getting on your knees," he whispers, raw and reverent, the words not just desire but devotion and promise.

"I see, so your happy to forgo me on my knees moving forward. I will have to note that" I smirk back

"After what you showed me," he says quietly, a slow smile tugging at his mouth, dimples creasing at the corners, "I'll be replaying that moment more times than I care to admit. I don't think anything could top how much I enjoyed the view."

Then his expression shifts — softer. Steadier. "But I don't ever want you to feel like you have to, Lily."

I meet his gaze, heart thudding. "I appreciate that, Aodhan. But I believe in mutual want. If we do this, it's because we both choose it."

He pauses, lifting a hand to tuck a loose strand of hair behind my ear, the touch gentle, reverent. "Okay," he murmurs. "Bath." The sound of running water fills the quiet, soft and steady, grounding me.

Aodhan moves through my ensuite with quiet purpose, his every motion unhurried. He adjusts the temperature, the steam curling around him, and adds oil that blooms into the air. When he turns back to me, his eyes steal my breath. "Come here, Mo draganín," he says, voice quiet.

He simply takes my outstretched hand— and begins to undress me, piece by piece. Each brush of his fingers sending a new wave of heat and hunger in me needing to be fed.

Even when his hands skim over bare skin, steadying me as I step free of the last layer, his gaze never leaves my face. He watches me, calm steady.

The water is warm when I step in, enveloping me in a wave of coconut and vanilla. Aodhan follows, the ripples breaking softly around us as he lowers himself behind me. His long legs bracket mine, and he pulls me gently back against his chest until I'm cocooned there —the bath far too small to hold us both.

"You don't have to talk, I just want you to rest," he murmurs into my hair, his chin brushing the crown of my head. "Just... breathe. Just be."

His hands move slowly, gliding up my arms, across my shoulders, soaping my skin with care. Each stroke exploring a new area of skin, leaving a spark on my skin with each touch.

"Better?" he asks softly, "Yes," I whisper, my voice small. For a while, that's enough.

When I finally tilt my head back, chin tipping so I can look at him, the glow in his tattoos has deepened, faint pulses of golden light moving just under the surface of his skin, syncing with the thrum of my own pulse. His eyes, catch mine.

"You're staring," he says, his mouth curving into the faintest teasing smile, though his gaze burns with something deeper.

"Maybe I like what I see," I whisper.

His smile deepens; "Well I too, like what I see."

He leans in until our foreheads touch, his breath mingling with mine. "I also like what I feel" pausing and dragging his hands across my shoulders, down my side and across my breast, he stills before I feel his lips on my neck and his hand cupping a breast, pinching the nipple and rolling it between his fingers. I arch back a moan caught in my mouth.

"Say it," he breathes, low and rough. "Say you're mine." The plea in his voice breaks something inside me — the last wall I'd been holding.

"Yours," I whisper, trembling but certain.

"I will be yours, Aodhan." His answering smile is dazzling, before the heat reaches his eyes the air feeling heavy around us. He gathers more body wash in his hands and starts rubbing it in slowly. When he reaches my back, his hands slow even more, kneading as he works the lather across my skin, his thumbs pressing into the knots at the base of my spine until I sigh.

Then his palms slide around to the front, over my chest, cupping one breast and then the other, kneading gently as the soap builds into slick foam. The warmth of his hands, the heat of the water— it's all too much. When his thumb flicks over a nipple — already sensitive from his touch earlier — a soft moan escapes me before I can stop it.

His lips brush my ear. "That's it," he murmurs. "I want you to feel this, all of this, only you can make me feel this way. Just you. Just us."

He circles inside my hip before rubbing my bud slowly, then inserting a finger curling and reaching high, my legs give, wanting a release.

Without breaking rhythm, he pushes a second finger inside, slow, deliberate, stretching me further, filling me until the ache sharpens into something hotter, hungrier.

"God..." The word slips from me on a ragged exhale, my head falling back against his shoulder. My body clenches around him, greedy, needy, desperate for everything he's holding back.

"There is no God, here Lily," he whispers, his lips brushing over my temple, his breath sticking against my damp skin. "Take me in. Feel me. Every part of you belongs to me, Lilian and I will taste every part of you starting here." I feel his tongue on my neck followed by his lips, teeth grazing the skin.

I gasp, nails digging into his thighs under the water, clutching at him like he's the only thing keeping me from coming undone completely.

"Do you know what you do to me?" His voice is rough "Every sound, every gasp... you send me mad. And I'll worship you until you believe it — until you know it's only ever been you and will only ever be you."

My hips buck helplessly as pleasure coils tight, white-hot and unrelenting, building and building until it's all I can hold onto. The water laps against the edges of the tub with every roll of my body, every thrust of his fingers, every sharp breath he steals from me.

"I want to hear you Lily," he commands. His pace quickens, relentless now, every motion designed to shatter me.

"Call my name."

My vision blurs, the edges of the world dissolving in heat and water and the electric hum of the bond roaring alive between us.

"Aodhan," I cry out, the word ripped from my chest as my release crashes over me, violent and consuming, wave after wave tearing me apart and piecing me back together in his arms. "That's my good girl," he rasps, his mouth at my ear, his pace gentling as he draws every last tremor from me. "My perfect, powerful mo draganin."

"Aodhan I want all of you, I need you"

He cups my face in his wet palms, eyes blazing molten gold, his forehead pressing to mine. "Are you sure?" he asks, his voice low, rough, almost broken.

"If I take you now, there's no going back. Not for me."

"Yes," I breathe, meeting his gaze, my pulse wild, honesty taking over my lust. "I want you inside me. I want you to fill me. I want you Aodhan."

My palms press to his shoulders as I rise, guiding him, and then — slowly, trembling — I ease down, taking him inch by inch.

A sharp gasp breaks from my throat. He stretches me, fills me, every muscle inside me clenching around the impossible width of him until there's no space left between us, only heat and heartbeat.

"Christ," I whisper, dizzy from the fullness, from the way he seems to reach every place inside me at once. "Why does it feel like your getting bigger"

His jaw flexes, veins standing out along his forearms as he holds me steady, I start to move, slow at first — a tentative roll of my hips, a slide that drags against every nerve ending. The water laps against our skin, warm and silken. Heat coils low in my belly again, deeper, sharper. His eyes never leave me watching every shiver, every sound that escapes my lips.

I ride him harder, bolder now, the bathwater splashing around us. Every shift sends a shockwave of pleasure through me, sparks crawling across my skin. My breasts sway with the motion; he catches one in his palm, the other between his teeth, sucking until my back arches.

A cry tears from my throat, head tipping back, hair clinging to damp skin as the pleasure builds — climbing, winding, spiralling higher with every thrust. He grips my hips tighter, guiding me, his breath a rough growl at my ear. "Let go, Mo draganín," he murmurs, his own control fraying with every word.

The world narrows to heat, to movement, to the way he feels — thick, hard, deep. My body shudders, then breaks open, tumbling over the edge, as release hits, fierce and shattering.

He follows with a groan, hips jerking once, twice, as he spills into me, the pulse of it sending aftershocks through my trembling body. His arms lock around me, holding me through it, keeping me anchored until neither of us can do anything but cling to each other.

When it's over — when the world settles and the only sounds left are our slowing breaths and the soft hum of his magic curling around us — he gathers me close, my cheek pressed to the heated glow of his chest.

His hand slides up my spine, slow and soothing, fingers brushing the nape of my neck. "Mine," he whispers again, softer now, no longer a growl but a vow. "Always mine, my lovely, perfect Lily."

CHAPTER 28

Aodhan POV

I dry her off with slow, steady strokes, water beading and sliding over skin still warm from the bath. She doesn't resist when I lift her; she's exhausted — my Lily. Mine. Her head lolls against my shoulder, damp hair clinging to her neck, and she curls instinctively into my chest, fitting there as though she was made for this place, this moment, for me. I hold her close, chin resting lightly on her hair, and let the quiet stretch around us.

But even with her soft breaths brushing my chest, my mind replays the moments from earlier — each one burned into me. She touched me like I was something holy. Like every inch of me mattered. Her fingertips had traced along my jaw, reverent and unhurried, down the glowing lines carved into my collarbone, lower over my ribs, mapping every mark, every scar I thought no one would ever want to see.

My magic had responded without permission — flaring faintly, golden light pulsing in rhythm with my heart. Above us, the air had stirred — weightless — teasing loose strands of her hair, framing her flushed, beautiful face.

I've never — in four and a half centuries — wanted anything the way I want this woman. Not the throne. And the bond had tightened, that thread weaving tighter and tighter until I could feel her heartbeat thrumming in my chest, perfectly in sync with mine. When we connected — both accepting us — it was like being consumed from the inside out; her name torn from my lips as my magic broke loose, wild and unrestrained.

The air around us had thickened, shimmering ribbons of violet and gold blooming above us like an aurora, casting her bare skin in celestial light. Outside, the lilies by her window had bloomed all at once, their petals opening in reverence, releasing the sharp sweetness of rain and jasmine until it filled the room.

When my strength was spent and the only thing keeping me tethered was her, I'd kissed her. Not as a prince. Not as a Kárith. But as a man stripped bare, hers and hers alone. But even as I hold her, thoughts claw their way through the quiet.

The prophecy. It sits in my chest like a shard of ice. Someone twisted it. Someone with power enough to alter priest-keepers' logs, silence seers, bury every thread of her existence until she was nothing but a void where she should have been a beacon. My gut whispers the Fire Court — but that's too obvious. Too clean. Which makes me suspect hands hidden deeper unseen. Perhaps even someone closer. When, if I find out who thought to curse me into loneliness by erasing her from me... I will raise their name from history, burn every sanctuary they've ever known, and ensure they pay the price. Because she's here. My mate. My equal. My Ríganne.

Still... danger coils in every veiled corner. In the courts. In the whispers that grow louder with each passing day. The Sceptre is no longer a myth to chase; its reality bleeds into every corner of the realms, stirring old loyalties and older betrayals. The Unseelie and Seelie prepare for war and rebellion; Ríganne are being usurped by the power-hungry, Sylvaris plot, and witches remain in hiding in the Verdant Veil. And her magic — raw, untamed, hungry — hums beneath her skin, restless even in sleep, reaching for something she doesn't yet understand.

She's powerful, far more powerful than she realises. And it will only grow stronger. I want to keep her safe. I want to lock the world out, hide her from the scheming hands that would try to claim her for what she is. But hiding her would also mean denying her what's hers. Denying her who she is.

She deserves to see my world — to walk through the shimmering spires of the Air Court, to stand at the edge of the floating cliffs and feel the wind magic hum through her bones like a song.

To taste the endless night skies that belong to her as much as they belong to me. And the Earth Court...

I can already feel the connection she'd have there. Her magic would flourish in those living gardens, where the earth thrums like a heartbeat, where vines and blooms rise wild and unrestrained. She would feel it, hear it — like a second pulse calling her home.

Together, we could unravel the threads of this mystery — dig through the archives, pry open the memories buried and guarded by those who fear what she represents. But I want her to understand, too.

To know what she is.

To claim every piece of herself the way she claimed me tonight.

Tomorrow, I'll start to tell her. No more half-truths. No more waiting.

For now, I hold her closer, the bond thrumming like a steady drumbeat under my skin, golden light weaving faintly where our magic brushes.

"Sleep, Mo draganín," I whisper into her hair, my voice low, reverent.

"What... what does that mean?"

I'd brushed my knuckles along her flushed cheek, letting her see everything I could never say aloud.

"It means... my little dragon," I'd murmured, voice quiet but certain. "Because that's what you are — fierce, untamed... and mine from the very moment I met you in the café, nostrils flaring, defiant."

The sound she'd made — that soft, unsteady laugh "and you still wanted me after that." I stroked her her cheek, "Now. Sleep. I've got you. Always."

The magic hums in quiet agreement, wrapping us in a promise older and stronger than the realms themselves.

Even as she sleeps, the vines along her window tremble,

stretching unconsciously toward her, roots pressing against the floorboards.

The earth answers her, restless — already sensing what she is becoming.

Her power is growing — raw, unshaped — and it will not stay quiet forever.

And as her breathing evens, steady and sure, I let myself drift — into the deepest, calmest sleep I've known in centuries, her quiet presence wrapped around me like the only peace I will ever need.

CHAPTER 29

Unknown POV

The room is quiet.
  Too quiet.
Even the firelight does not dare to crackle.

Its flames burn low, reduced to little more than coals, their glow pulsing faintly like a dying heartbeat. The shadows they cast stretch long and unnatural, warping across the stone as though the chamber itself has been stitched together from fragments of places kept hidden deep within the earth. Rooms and chambers that hold a history of brutal murder and betrayal.

One could hear the howls of those who would have perished in this very room — ghosts holding stories that were never meant to be told.

There are no windows. No sky.

Not even the faintest breath of wind to stir the stagnant air.

The silence presses heavy, oppressive, until it feels as though the walls are listening. Power thrums through the obsidian stone. A low, constant vibration that sets every nerve alight, dark magic rolling across the room in waves that call for blood and the hunt for the weak.

The air tastes of iron and smoke, coppery on the tongue, leaving fear lingering in the back of the mind. And in that silence — in that absence of breath and sky — the unseen begin to stir.

Slow, steady steps echo across the chamber. A pause — eerily silent. The sharp tap of a heel on stone reverberates off the walls. Then, a voice low, silken and lethal — cuts through the dark.

"Explanation. Now."

The command slices through the silence cold and absolute. The voice carries weight enough to bury every other sound; even the air seems to bow to it.

A dozen heads lower in unison. Hooded figures kneel in formation, bodies bent as though the pressure of the room itself grinds them into the floor.

The runes carved into the stone pulse faintly beneath their knees, sickly light crawling through the obsidian, branding it with power.

Each pulse is a reminder that their will, their breath, their very existence, belongs here — bound until death.

"F–finding it is proving... difficult," one ventures. His voice shakes, the words dragged from his throat with effort. Sweat beads at his brow despite the icy chill creeping through the stone. "The traces vanish the moment we close in — as though something... or someone... is masking it."

The silence that follows is worse than a dragon's roar. It is suffocating. The kind of silence that promises retribution. When the voice returns, it is quieter. Softer. Infinitely more dangerous. "Then cast a wider net. Tear through every ridge, every mountain path, every mortal in Crystal Hollow that reeks of him. Leave no stone unturned, no corner unchecked. If you must..." A pause, deliberate, measured. "...burn it all to the ground until it is found."

One of the kneeling figures risks a glance upward — too quick, too small — and immediately regrets it. The wisps of magic respond instantly — dark wind given form. They coil and unfurl in sinuous spirals, moving with the weightless glide of smoke caught in a breath.

Air thickens around them as they slither across the floor, alive, tasting the fear.

One tendril sweeps forward, curling around the trembling messenger's ankle — not touching flesh so much as circling the air around it, a serpent made of wind and night teasing its prey.

He shudders but does not move.

The darkened wind lingers, tightening for a single, breathless heartbeat — a warning carried on a current sharp enough to cut — before it pulls back, dissolving into the dim edges of the chamber like a sigh swallowed by the dark. Disappointed. But patient. For now.

"And the prince? What of his movements?"

"He lingers, my lord," another, replies carefully, each syllable wary, as though the wrong word could summon death. "Near... the woman. Every day, longer than the last. She is—" a sharp breath "—a weakness we could use to our advantage. If the bond strengthens... if his power surges as mates' do—"

The room shifts. A wave of fury ripples outward, shaking the very air. The brazier flame gutters low; the walls groan. Breath catches in a dozen throats.

"Interesting," the voice purrs, venom laced with amusement. "You question how I should act." A pause, dangerous and drawn out. "Predictable. Foolish. He believes his want makes him strong. But it will destroy him. He will be his own undoing." A faint scrape. A whisper of chains. Somewhere far below, a muffled cry echoes through the stone. "Call in my pets."

From the farthest corner, a figure moves. Cloaked in darkness, their very presence seems to drink the firelight. Only their eyes glint beneath the hood — twin shards of steel in a sea of black.

"You." The voice dips, cruel amusement curling through the word. "Stay close. Feed his delusions if you must. Let him believe he can protect her. Let him believe his bond is strength. It will make the fall..." A slow exhale. "...sweeter. I want him broken. I want him to beg for her before I take everything he holds dear. So, like his mother I look forward to the look on his face as I destroy him, his bloodlust will be the perfect sacrifice to unite the pieces."

The cloaked figure hesitates — just long enough to smirk. They bow, mockingly graceful, then fade into the dark. The cavern swallow them whole.

The chamber settles again. Heavy. Expectant.

The air thick with prayers that this failure, at least, will not be theirs. "What of the Courts? Do they stir?"

"Yes, my lord."

Another kneels lower, forehead pressed to the glowing runes, faint light searing his skin. "The Fire Court grows restless. They believe the others hide knowledge of the Sceptre. They search the human realm — contacting witches. The Earth Court watches, silent but wary. Our last spy has not reported in. Their Ríganne dead, their cousin heir apparent — they have sealed their archives."

"The Air Court?"

"Still grieving. Their king remains missing. And the Water—"

"Under my control." The voice cuts him off, quiet and disdainful. "As they always are. It takes only greed to bend them to my will. Let them believe they act of their own accord." A pulse of power rolls outward. The runes flare. The air hums with a sound too low for mortal ears — a predator's growl threaded through the stone itself.

A thud is heard against the door followed by the stench of filth and blood. So strong it overwhelms the senses. A prisoner is dragged forward. Threadbare robes hang from a skeletal frame; the woman's wrists are ringed in iron, raw and blistered from months of chains, blood caked across her frame from beatings.

Her eyes, once luminous, are now clouded with pallor and exhaustion. A seer — once revered. Now broken. All hope of salvation starved.

Behind her, another captive is shoved into the half-light. A witch, young, wild-eyed, blood crusting the carved grooves of protective sigils tattooed into her arms. Her breath comes ragged, defiant even through the fear clinging to her.

The seer wheezes, her voice thin as torn parchment. "The wards... they fray. The magic you wove to blind the bond... it falters. The true prophecy will be told you will not obtain the power you seek following this path."

The chamber stills. And then the temperature drops to a frozen, crushing cold of deep water pressing against lungs. The torches gutter, nearly snuffed, frost feathering across the stone where her blood has dripped.

A silence falls so sharp it could cut flesh.

"Explain." The hiss cuts through the chamber like a blade drawn across bone.

It isn't a question; it's a threat sharpened to flay her remaining flesh.

The witch swallows hard, eyes flicking up once before dropping back to the glowing runes beneath her knees. Her voice trembles, but it holds.

"The bond between them... it grows stronger. There is interference — older, deeper magic. The dark weave you cast is unravelling. Every time they..." she falters, glancing at the seer, "...every time they touch, every time the bond threads deeper, it burns through what remains of the curse. Your magic masked it — but it cannot undo what was forged by the old gods. Not forever, not even with her interference."

The whisps overhead shift, writhing the serpents across the vaulted ceiling. They stretch long and low, pressing inward like a storm coiled and ready to burst.

"Then strengthen it."

The voice snaps like a whip, shattering the stillness.

"I do not care what it costs. Bleed the ley lines. Burn your covens. Drain the bones of the earth. Bind them — at any cost."

The seer lifts her head just enough to meet the darkness. Her hollowed eyes are full of exhaustion, but also something like warning.

"It will not hold. We would need a far greater sacrifice. The bond is growing by the day. The Sceptre... it calls. The shard trembled, as though it heard the claim already — the mortal girl whose power stirs old gods and shatters curses, you should beware what is to befall those who interfere with the goddess's plan—"

A vicious snarl cuts her off. Dark power slams through the chamber like a shockwave, flaring from the runes and snapping their spines backward.

The witch crashes to the stone floor, her wrists sparking where iron meets flesh. Black smoke coils up from the runes and licks at her throat like fingers.

"Then we let them lead us to the shards first," the voice

growls, the edges of patience shredded and bleeding.

"Every last one. Then we take them before she understands what it does. Before he does. When the Sceptre is whole, when its power bends to me, there will be no bond. No prophecy. No Courts. Only one ruler. And by then it will be too late for them. Or I will take her for myself and drain the power from her before the goddess herself."

The witch and the seer exchange a single look — wide, horrified — at what those words mean, at what this thing intends to do. Guards step forward like clockwork, iron boots grinding into stone, dragging the captives back to the dungeons. Their chains rattle like a funeral march. "Ensure they are well rested for my next visit."

The young witch recoils as she's hauled away, revulsion twisting her features as she fixes her captor with a look of pure hatred. The seer does not struggle. She lowers her head instead, as though already mourning what is to come.

A cloaked figure steps closer, moving like a shadow detached from its source.

Pale, elegant fingers emerge from the sleeve and brush the shard with deliberate care. The wood is warm under their touch, humming, hungry.

"Soon," the voice murmurs — quiet but certain, almost tender despite the venom coiled within. "Soon, the world will bow. Soon there will be nothing but obedience and flames. The fools will never see it coming. They will either bend... or perish. There will be no compromise."

The figure licks their lips, slow and deliberate, eyes sweeping the hall — a hall that was once the meeting place of a goddess long gone. Raw power still lingers here, calling for its master to return. A master he will become. A ruler of all rulers.

The shard pulses once — a sharp, violent flare of light — before dimming again, leaving the chamber smothered in silence, like the breath held before a scream.

Far above, where the skies are bright and the towers hum with life, no one feels the storm building in the dark — a war that will make even eternal lives burn to ash.

CHAPTER 30

Lily POV

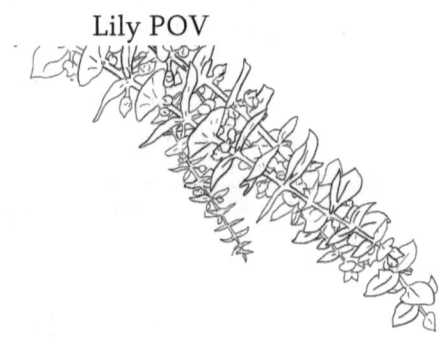

The morning is quiet.
Deceptively so.

I wake curled against him, my cheek pressed to the steady rise and fall of his chest, his heartbeat a calm, grounding rhythm. His skin is warm beneath my cheek, in a way that makes me feel anchored, safe. No grief. No fear. No self-loathing waiting to catch up with me.

Just him. A new start.

His voice breaks the stillness, soft and heavy with sleep, that makes my pulse falter.

"Lily," he murmurs, almost hesitant, like saying my name too loud might break the spell of this moment. His chest vibrates under my cheek, each syllable taut, edged with something he isn't saying. My lashes flutter, heavy with half-dreams, my voice still husky with sleep as I try for lightness, a tease. "Hmm...?"

"I might have to leave soon... to go back home for a while."

The words hang in the quiet, foreign and cold against the warmth of the morning.

Leave. Leaving? He's leaving? Something in me twists at the tone in his voice. My fingers curl against his side before I can stop myself, clutching like my body knows what my voice doesn't dare say aloud.

Because I know there's more to him — there always has been. From the moment he stepped into my café, with that impossible regal stance, always a secret hidden in his gaze and something not quite human. And if he leaves...

If he goes back to wherever it is he's from... What else might that mean for me? For us? My mind races at the thought of opening my heart and not being enough — maybe I didn't show I cared, did I wait too long? My self-esteem plummets.

But then I see it. A flicker. Barely there. The smallest tightening at the corner of his mouth, a faint crease that carves across his golden features and is gone just as quickly. Pain. Guilt. Regret.

He reaches out and cups my face. "Lily, I never want you thinking that again. You are enough. You are perfect, right down to every freckle and callous on your skin. If I could spend every minute kissing every single one I would. Me leaving has nothing to do with how much I care for you. It's to set up protections for you."

"H-how did you know?" It steals the breath from my lungs. The fragile humour I'd been reaching for slips away and is replaced with a sense of dread.

"Aodhan..." His name catches in my throat, thin and trembling. I push up on one elbow, rubbing the heel of my hand against my eyes as though that might banish the dread creeping up my spine. But he's too still. Too silent, unwilling. His jaw tight, his shoulders rigid, as though braced for a blow that could strike at any second.

My stomach knots hard, dread settling deep like a stone. "If you need to go..." My voice is steadier than I expect, though my pulse betrays me, thundering against my ribs, vibrating across my body. "Then say it. But don't sit here and lie to me." The last words slip sharper than I intended, but I don't take them back. I can't. Not when every instinct in me — grief-taught, widow-honed — screams that truth is better than silence.

I hold his gaze — steady, sharp — even though every part of me wants to break, to curl back under the safety of his arms, to smother the crack I've just seen in his calm and pretend it never existed.

Pretend this moment isn't happening. Pretend I don't feel the shift in the air between us, heavy and dangerous, a pivotal point of no return. He looks over my features again and a sigh slips free.

"I can put up with a lot," I force out, my voice unsteady but unyielding. "But trust—" The word fractures in my throat, scraping raw on the way out. "Trust I can't compromise on. I won't. I can't stand lies. Not from you." The words land between us, sharp and unyielding.

For a moment, he doesn't move. Doesn't speak. Then, slowly, deliberately, he shifts. His broad shoulders roll back as he sits upright against the headboard, every line of his body taut with control, like a man preparing to bear something immense. He reaches for my hand and kisses my palm. "I won't lie," he says at last, his voice low but edged with finality. "Not to you. Not ever. Nor will I deceive you — not that I could, being what I am. Just please promise me you won't run out the door screaming."

The words spear through me — being what I am. They coil and twist inside my chest, demanding answers. Answers that feel too big, too impossible, yet too close to ignore.

My throat is dry, my pulse hammering against my ribs, but my voice — somehow — comes steady. Unwavering. "Then tell me," I whisper. A plea for the truth.

His jaw flexes, the muscle twitching as though the truth itself tastes bitter on his tongue. He drags a hand through his hair — restless, almost human in its frustration — before his gaze lifts back to mine. And then the words come, unvarnished, unshielded, each one weighted like a stone dropped into still water.

"I don't know how to say this without you thinking I've lost my mind," he said quietly. "And I know you've had questions — especially since Evans went missing." He paused, as if choosing each word with care. "You know the old stories," he continued. "The ones told as warnings. About forests that don't give people back. Mountains you don't wander after dark. About things that look human, but aren't — that lure you in and leave no trace."

My stomach tightened.

"Dragons," he said. "Storm-bringers. Creatures who could bend lightning and fire with their hands. Fae, creatures that will make you do as they please. Tricksters. You were taught they were myths. Bedtime tales meant to keep children close to home." His gaze held mine, steady and unflinching. "They weren't stories, Lily." The air between us seemed to thin. "I'm not from here," he said. "Not from the human realm. And the things you were warned about... are real."

The words drop like stones, crashing and breaking the silence. His voice is low, deliberate, every word said with a calm as though trying not to scare an injured animal.

"My home is..." He exhales once, steady but raw, eyes never leaving mine. "Another realm. The Air Court. High towers carved of glass and wind. Mountains that float in skies with no horizon. A kingdom where storms bow to their rulers, and the very air itself is alive with magic."

The room tilts. My pulse hammers, loud in my ears. A world beyond this one. Not fantasy. Not myth. A place. Real. He leans closer, his gaze softening. "A world that doesn't just hold magic, Lily. It breathes it. Every stone. Every leaf. Every inhabitant."

The air between us shifts. Heavy. Crackling. Almost electric. As though his confession has pulled something unseen into the room — and it knows me, recognises me, draws me to it. I freeze, my thoughts snagging on every impossible word. My mind scrambles, clawing for solid ground, but the floor tilts beneath me, spinning, pulling everything I thought I knew inside out, questioning everything.

"This has to be a joke or some bizarre dream."

"There's more," he says, softer now, as though the words themselves might break me. His throat tightens, his voice roughened by the weight of what he's about to share with me. "I'm... an Air Fae. Four hundred and fifty years old."

The room contracts around me, my heart battering against my ribs. Fae. Old gods' stories. Wings and tricksters and bargains whispered, cloaked in mystery.

A myth. An impossibility. But the glow under his skin — the tattoos that pulse faintly with golden light even now — the way the very room has always listened to him, the way the air itself stirs when he's present as though feeding from his emotions...

Pieces slam together, fragments of things I've ignored, brushed aside, explained away.

"And—" His voice breaks over the word, quiet but fierce, as though this part is harder than all the rest. The silence sharpens, unbearable.

"And?" The word scrapes out of me, jagged, unsure of how much more I can take.

His hand finds my chin — warm, steady, thumb brushing the curve of my jaw like he's trying to anchor me, to remind me that whatever this is, whatever he is, I'm still here. Safe and he is no threat.

I lock eyes with him, and there— the crack in his armour, the concern and fear bleeding through, the way his mouth tightens at the corners as he hesitates between sentences.

He's scared, his body tense, sensing unease. "And I am a Prince of that same court," he says quietly, every syllable, careful, as though speaking them too loudly might shatter the remaining thread holding us together. "And I have a mate. That mate..." His thumb trembles against my skin. "...is you. The bond has been growing for months, pulling me to you. But I needed to be certain before I said it. Before I risked breaking you by telling you everything. It has been tearing me apart hiding myself from you".

The words slam into me, sharp and disorienting, like a door swinging open onto a world I didn't know existed.

Mate. It doesn't feel real. My chest tightens, my pulse a wild, uneven rhythm, my breath caught between a laugh and a gasp. "A... mate." The word comes out half a laugh. My fingers curl in the sheets, my mind scrambling to focus on anything else.

What the actual hell.

Mate? Magic? Realms? Prince?

My brain stutters, trying to keep up, grasping for sense. Next he'll tell me he has wings and can fly—and at this point, I don't even know if anything else would surprise me.

Then I look at him. Really look at him. The air around him shimmers like morning light breaking across the sunrise. I can see him watching me, my pulse racing under his touch, all this information colliding in my chest. Yet calm washes over me, as though I should have already known magic was real, that mates existed, and my body recognises it before my mind does. The pull. The bond. That invisible thread thrumming between us, tightening, sparking fire in my core.

"Yes," he says softly, quiet certainty in his tone. "It's a bond. A thread that ties us together. It strengthens me, steadies me. And if you let it... it can strengthen you, too. Help you understand your power." Power. My power?

The word coils low in my stomach like a live wire, sharp and electric. I don't even know what it means, but the way he says it makes it sound alive—something waiting inside me to burst free. "You don't look a day over thirty," I whisper, but my voice cracks, fraying in places I can't control. My throat feels tight, words scraping out raw. "Four hundred and fifty..." The number tangles in my mouth, feeling foreign. I laugh, high, almost hysterical—because what else is left? "Fucking Hell, Aodhan..."

I force the words out, my pulse a frantic drumbeat in my ears. "Why are you here? What are you even looking for? Is this about that... that lost item you mentioned?"

His mouth tightens at the corners. "Yes," he admits, the word rough.

A piece of the Sceptre," he said quietly. "One that was meant to be sealed in the human realm." The words landed heavy. "It was stolen thousands of years ago. Without it, the balance between the Courts fractures. Old boundaries weaken. Chaos creeps in where it's been waiting patiently." His jaw tightened, the faint shimmer beneath his skin stirring. "The Courts cannot remain divided forever. They will either fall under a single ruler... or the Sceptre must be destroyed entirely."

He exhaled, slow and measured. "But destruction is unlikely," he continued. "Not with rebellions stirring in the dark. Not with witches still in hiding, watching, waiting for the moment the scales tip. They're already moving — using wyverns to strike at places they think are vulnerable. Outer territories. Border settlements. Crystal Hollow is not as untouched as it once was."

His gaze lifted to mine, steady and grave, searching for some kind of reaction.

"Can you prove it? That what you're saying is true? I want to believe you, Aodhan, I want to say that all the things I've been noticing are related to magic but... this just seems surreal."

He lets go of my hand and instantly I feel hollow. He raises his palm and air rushes through the room, my hair whipping around my face. He looks toward a scrap of paper on the dresser. "Is it important?" I shake my head—then it bursts into flames.

My heart hammers so hard against my ribs it hurts, like it's trying to break free. The room feels suddenly too small, as if every sound is being swallowed by the rush of my pulse. The air itself seems to shift.

"So I'm not hallucinating," I whisper, the words trembling out of me like a confession. "I'm not dreaming. This—" My hand trembles as I gesture toward him, to the impossible glow beneath his skin, to the way the plants on my windowsill sway and hum like they're alive, reaching toward him. "—all of this is real."

Something in his expression softens—sunlight blooms from his palms, golden and fluid, molten and alive, spilling through the quiet room like liquid fire. It dances across the walls, threads through the air, casting an eerie glow across the room like stained glass. It smells faintly of warm rain and ozone, humming against my skin like a living thing.

My breath catches.

My world narrows to the glow in his hands, to the impossible beauty of it, to the realisation that everything I thought was myth has been standing in front of me all along. And then his hands are on my face—warm, steady, firm but impossibly gentle—thumbs brushing the curve of my jaw as though he's trying to anchor me, to keep me from cracking under the weight of what he's revealed. He tilts my chin until my eyes meet his.

"Look at me," he says softly. "Yes," he murmurs again, steady as the earth beneath my feet, steady as the heartbeat I can feel through his fingers. "It's real. Every bit of it. And yes, the danger is real too." His eyes—molten gold, basked in the magic around us—hold mine. "But you are safe with me. Always. Nothing and no one will ever get close enough to hurt you."

The quiet between us thickens, humming with questions and

the rush of my pulse in my ears.

"What does this mean, Aodhan?"

My voice fractures around the words — sharp, uneven. My thoughts spiral, dragging me back to that first meeting on the road: the quiet intensity in his stare, the way something inside me had thrummed even then, long before I had language for it.

"Was I just... a target?" I swallow hard. "Daisy's accident — was that a set-up? Some twisted game to draw you here? Is that why strangers kept appearing, why the attack happened?"

His eyes flash — molten gold edged with pain — and the air between us tightens, charged enough to lift the fine hairs along my arms.

"No. Never."

The word doesn't just answer — it lands, vibrating through the space between us, rough and raw, as if torn straight from his chest.

"Lily," he says, unshakable now, voice iron-steady. "I swear to you — I have never used you. There was no trap. No scheme. Not from me. Not ever."

His voice dips then, low and velvet, the sharp edges softening into something that makes my chest ache. "The first time I saw you, you stopped me in my tracks. You felt like air after drowning—like coming home to warmth. I didn't know it then, not fully. But every moment since, every second I've spent with you..."

His throat works, his mouth tightening at the corners, his eyes flickering with something raw and unguarded—fear, hope. The sound breaks on the edges of his control. "Everything fell into place. Like this was where I was always meant to be. Here with you."

His hands slide from my jaw to the back of my neck, fingers trembling just slightly.

My throat tightens painfully, my pulse thrumming in my ears like a war drum. "This is... a lot," I breathe, my voice unsteady, trembling as my mind scrambles to catch up. Everything I've built, everything I thought I understood, tilts dangerously.

"I know," he murmurs, twirling a strand of my hair around his finger. "But I want you to know me," he says softly, his gaze steady, unwavering. "All of me. The real me. No walls. Not with you." His voice cracks just slightly at the edges.

"This... mate bond," I ask, curiosity peaking. "What does it mean? Really?"

His gaze doesn't waver. "It's a gift from the Goddess," he says at last, quiet but certain, each word falling like a stone in a still lake. "A bond that ties two souls together. It amplifies everything—strength, magic, emotion. It's fated. I was made for you, Lily. To love you. To protect you. To spend every breath proving you'll never have to doubt how much you mean to me."

His voice dips then, darker now, threaded with old pain, his eyes turning inward for a heartbeat. "But it also means that losing you would end me."

"There was a prophecy," he says at last, and the words aren't just spoken—they're dragged out of him, rough and bitter, like an old wound sitting festering. "It was delivered not long after I was born. It spoke of a Fae Sun Prince—one who would unite the Courts, bring balance, end the endless wars. They told me that the one to unite the Sceptre would remain alone. No mate. No love. No family. Just power—and a crown heavy enough to crush whoever bore it. A weapon for the realm."

I swallow hard, my pulse hammering. The image of him as a boy, growing into a man, into a prince, always believing he was cursed to be untouchable, flares in my mind. Centuries alone, carrying that weight. Centuries thinking love was a weapon meant to destroy him. My chest aches like it's been cleaved open. "And you believed it," I say softly, as if speaking it aloud can ease the loneliness etched into his bones.

"For centuries," he says quietly. A flicker of something fractured moves across his face—a trace of pain and memory. His mouth tightens before he forces the words out. "Until you. Until the bond snapped into place, and I realised someone lied. Someone hid you from me. The magic cloaking your existence is weakening now—that's why I found you. Why the bond keeps pulling tighter, no matter how far I tried to stay away."

He lowers his head until his forehead rests against mine, his breath ghosting across my lips. "It will always be you, Lily."

Something fragile inside me shatters to pieces. My hand trembles as it finds his, sliding over his knuckles, grounding me—grounding us both. The golden light beneath his skin pulses faintly against my palm, like a heartbeat answering my own. "So... what now?"

He looks at me, genuinely startled. "*Now?*"

He sucks in a breath. "You... believe me?"

I nod, reaching up to catch his cheek between my fingers, giving it a small, grounding pinch. "Yes. I believe you." A faint smile tugs at my mouth. "You always seemed so regal — distant. Untouchable. But not dishonest."

Something in his expression shifts. The surprise melts into warmth, then into that familiar, dangerous curve of his mouth as he leans into my touch.

"Then let me show you my world," he says softly. "My Court. And the Earth Court, too." His thumb brushes over my knuckles, reverent, almost awed. "If I am to be regal," he adds, a hint of teasing beneath the vow, "then my Rígann should know the realm she stands in."

My breath catches.

"I think you'd feel at home there," he continues, quieter now. "Your magic — your bond to the earth — it hums every time you're near the gardens. Like the land recognises you." His gaze holds mine, steady and certain. "It's waiting, Lily. Waiting to be explored. To be nurtured." He pauses. "Together," he says. "We'll discover what you are. And who you're meant to be."

Fear and wonder twist inside me, thrumming under my skin, making my pulse stumble. "And the danger?" I ask at last.

His jaw tightens. Silver flecks in his eyes spark like lightning against a storm-darkened sky. "It's coming," he says quietly. "You've already felt it. Seen the signs." His voice steadies into something grim and certain. "The scorched leaves. The tremor in your garden wards. The presence at the edge of your land."

His gaze flicks to the window, as if he can still sense it there. "They can't cross," he continues. "Not yet. Something is guarding you — something old. Older than me." His voice lowers, thunder held tight. "But you will not face what's coming alone. Never. I would demand reckoning from the Goddess herself before I let anyone take you from me." The force of it hits like a wave — fierce, unrelenting. Protective. Possessive. My breath stutters before I can stop it.

"Aodhan…" I exhale. "I care for you. More than I think I even realised." I gesture weakly between us, to the invisible thread pulled tight and humming. "I want this. I want you. But it's not just us." My chest tightens. "I have children. A family. And if they're in danger — if this magic touches them—" I shake my head. "I need time. To think. To breathe. This choice doesn't belong to me alone."

Daisy. Oliver. Dad. Viv. Emma.

"I know, Lily." His answer comes without hesitation. No pressure. No frustration. Only quiet certainty. The tension in his face eases, just a fraction — like a man who'd been braced for loss and instead finds a door left open.

I lean in and kiss him — soft, careful, but threaded through with everything we're not saying. "Just… give me time," I murmur against his mouth. "And if I need to run, you tell me. And if I need to fight—" A crooked smile slips free. "You point me at the target."

His hand cups the back of my head, thumb tracing slow, grounding circles. He presses a kiss to my forehead, reverent enough to steal the air from my lungs.

"You have my word," he murmurs. A promise. A vow — old, binding, and unbreakable. I curl into him for one last moment, soaking in the warmth, the steadiness — because when day starts, I'll have too much to process. And he won't be here to anchor me.

CHAPTER 31

Aodhan POV

Two weeks of restraint taste like ash on my tongue. I've honoured her boundaries — to the letter. Morning bouquets left on the back step, blooms chosen with care so she knows I haven't given up. A protection weave anchored beneath her windowsill, its threads humming low against the wards she unknowingly carries. Harrid — the quietest blade I know — stationed in the hedgeline whenever duty drags me away. Unseen. Silent. Lethal if necessary. Always watching. Always protecting. Waiting.

I tell myself this is what she needs.

Space to breathe.

Time to untangle the truth I laid bare at her feet. Time to see the world through new eyes without feeling the weight of mine pressing in. I will wait. But every moment away from her feels like a dragon's talons raking my ribs — a slow, unrelenting burn I cannot quell. The bond thrums low and hungry beneath my skin, restless in a way it never was before. My body calls to her in more ways than lust ever could. Her scent lingers even here, threaded through my sheets and my magic, curling into my lungs until it feels as though I am breathing her instead of air.

At night, when the wards around her house flare — soft, subtle pulses — I sense her dreams. Not their shapes, but their ache. Hope. Confusion. Want. Love. Every flicker of her magic brushes against mine like a heartbeat trying to sync. It drives me half mad, knowing she reaches unconsciously even as she keeps her waking distance, sorting through thoughts she doesn't yet have the language for.

I have endured centuries of discipline. Centuries of withholding — my temper, my hunger, my power — because that is what being a prince demanded.

But her absence makes me feel as though my heart has been torn from my chest and clawed raw. This waiting is its own kind of war. I hold my restraint because she deserves the right to choose. Yet each dawn I rise with the same gnawing truth:

She is no longer just the centre of my want. She is the centre of my world. And the storm building beyond her is drawing closer. Still... I am proud of her. Every day.

I watch in silence when she laughs with Sal in the café, her hair falling loose around her shoulders in soft waves. When she moves through her garden at home, the children trailing at her heels, sunlight catching on the faint glow of magic she does not yet recognise as her own. When she sits on the porch at dusk, knees drawn up, a book balanced on her lap, tucking a stray curl behind her ear as the light fades — unaware that I memorise every movement, every new expression.

I see the change. Her hands no longer clutch at her chest when she thinks no one is watching. She has stopped twisting the ring at her throat with grief sharp enough to bleed. Now, when she stares into the distance, her gaze is quieter. Thoughtful. Not empty, but searching — weighing a future.

A future I pray I am part of. I curl my hand into a fist. Sparks of light bleed from my skin — my magic restless.

Danger does not bend to boundaries. I have already killed one Sylvari — a lean, reeking half-breed that crept too close beneath the cover of rain, stinking of corruption and the acrid burn of dark magic. Whether it came for her because of me, or because of something inside her it could not comprehend, I do not yet know. Its blood steamed black where it struck the soil. The stench clung to my skin long after the body dissolved into ash, burning the grass where it fell.

And it will not be the last.

Before leaving that morning, I stood at the edge of her garden — added another ward and marked my magic to prevent any further Fae from entering in my absence.

Nyxie at my heel, golden eyes reflecting the wards I'd already woven. I give her a scratch; something about this dog seems foreign — most animals flee Fae on instinct, but she held her ground. I scratch behind her ear. She snorts back as though she understands. "No one touches her," I told Harrid, my voice low and edged like the steel on my sword. "No one gets close. Not a whisper of magic, not even a shadow over that fence. If you even think something's off, you tell me. Immediately."

My command was firm, not for refute. His silent nod received. The thread between us pulled in protest, a low, insistent ache beneath my ribs as I stepped back into the veil. Every instinct screamed to stay. To stand guard myself. To kill whatever dared watch her from the dark before it even thought of moving. But I must continue my duties to prevent any other Court noticing my absence.

By the time I reach the training grounds, the need to move — to fight, to burn off the restless ache that's been clawing at me for days — is a roar in my blood. My magic sits too close to the surface, hot and volatile, simmering and needing an outlet before it burns everything around me. The grounds sprawl, a circle carved into the cliffside, its sand marked with deep gouges from decades of sparring. Wind magic sings through the ward stones set into the perimeter, but even the sky feels heavy today, clouds banked low over the floating spires.

I can feel them out there — the Fire Fae. Stalling. Testing. Pushing at the edges of the wards with decrepit fingers, as if they can peel them back, find a crack, slip a spy through before I notice.

I pause, my breathing echoing Lily's pulse even across the distance. Every beat feeds my rage. The ring at the centre waits empty. I step into it without a word, I call on my flames, lightning and fire form as one restless in my hands, a soft flare of gold and silver rippling up their edges. I don't need an opponent.

I need movement. Violence. Destruction. I need blood.

A way to ease the tension before it devours me. I swing my flames — arching wide strikes above my head, letting my muscles feel the stretch, my magic reeling for release. I turn fast, digging a heel in the ground, letting my formed blade fly free and lodge into the stone metres away.

Maricus saunters in slow, drawn-out, leaning against the edge of the arena — all long limbs and lazy poise, shadow like wraiths curling around his boots like billowing smoke. They flicker and shift, restless. His eyes track me with that familiar, infuriating smirk — the one always mere moments from provocation.

"You're distracted," he taunts, voice smooth. "Your magic's off tempo. Even the air is warring. You've been holding back for too long." I don't look up as I adjust my grip, testing the balance of my blade and flames. "Save it," I warn, voice flat, even. "Not in the mood for you."

"Look who's touchy?" His shadows stir, coiling tighter, form like serpents ready to strike. "It's her, isn't it? Lilian. She's on your mind again." His head tilts; the grin widens just enough to show teeth.

"You think the others don't see it? That they don't talk?" My grip tightens; magic flares bright beneath my skin, pulsing like the sun with every beat of my heart. A flicker of sand rises at my feet, caught in the updraft of my temper.

"What talk?" I growl, low and lethal.

Maricus pushes off the wall with lazy grace, circling the edge of the ring. His magic trails behind him, a low-lying haze, ready to smother the arena at a thought.

"You're a fool if you believed no one would notice," he says mildly. "The Sun Prince — the weapon of prophecy — frequenting a mortal. Visiting the same place, day after day." His gaze flicks to me, sharp with amusement. "Did you think the Courts blind?"

I say nothing. The air tightens.

"They whisper," he continues, unhurried. "That you're distracted. That a woman — a mortal — has softened you. Weakened you." A pause, deliberate. "Some say she'll be the realm's undoing. Others think she'll unite the Sceptre." His mouth curves. "Or perhaps the prince has simply found a very effective distraction for his cock."

Heat coils in my chest.

"One that must be worth the risk," he adds softly — almost kindly. The kindness of a blade pressed just shy of skin. "If you've tasted it."

"One day," he murmurs, voice lowering, letting the words sink in, "you'll understand. Humans break, Aodh. They age. They die." His smirk sharpens into something cruel. "And when she does..."

He lets the silence do the damage.

"Don't say I didn't warn you."

My blood hums hot. I raise my blade slowly, the edge catching the morning light like liquid fire, sparks igniting. "Step into the ring, Maricus," I say, my voice a low, lethal thread. "Let's see if you're as quick with your magic and steel as you are with your tongue."

His grin widens — dark, wolfish. Predatory. "Now, now, my young Prince," he, mocks-gentle. "You asked what was being said." He steps forward, crossing the boundary without hesitation. Shadow coils around his hands, tightening, sharpening — claws forming from living darkness. "Come on, Sun Prince," he murmurs, voice rich with wicked promise. "Show me just how badly you're slipping."

His eyes gleam. "Let's see whether the rumours are true."

The restraint I've been clinging to for weeks snaps, clean and brutal. I move before the last word leaves his mouth. My flamed blade sings free of restraint, golden light flaring along its edge as I lunge. Muscles uncoil, honed reflexes older than kingdoms snapping into motion. The sand erupts beneath my boots as I strike.

Maricus is fast — but I've fought wars that lasted decades. I've bled across battlefields where the dark drowned the sun and fire rained down while poison seeped through veins. He meets me head-on, black blade formed from steel and shadow, rising in a razor hiss as wraith-tainted currents coil into snapping serpents.

A black tide racing to eclipse the sun.

The clash detonates—sparks flaring across the ring as heat crashes into wind gone dark and wild. I drive him back instantly. Calling forth the storm.

My body moves before thought can catch it. Muscles coil and uncoil in perfect rhythm; shoulders roll through each swing, lightning itself threads through my tendons. Every strike cracks with purpose, no wasted energy, no second chances. Heat pours off me in waves, sweat stinging my eyes, sliding down my spine, tasting of iron and exhaustion and rage.

Maricus snarls — a low, guttural sound — and the dark air around him reacts. It surges like a living cloak, rippling outward, a black gale trying to choke the sun from the arena. The temperature drops as his magic flares; the air thickens, tasting of old stone and ash.

He ducks under my next blow — a heavy downward cut meant to end this — and my blade slams into the ring hard enough to crack stone. The impact sends a shudder all the way up my arms, rattling bone, and grains of sand spray up like shards of glass, peppering his face.

He spits blood and grit. I inhale fire. My breath tears hot through my chest; every heartbeat is a hammer. Sweat slicks my grip, so I tighten it until my knuckles ache. Light gathers under my skin in a rush — bright, furious, hungry — demanding release.

I shift my weight, blade rising again. The arena hums with the tremor of our magic colliding — heat from me, storm-dark from him — two forces grinding against each other hard enough to shake the air.

He retaliates, gnashing his teeth; a whip of wind-dark magic lashes toward my throat, fast enough to slice the breath from my lungs if it connects. It's a killing strike — clean, efficient, meant to end me. I don't give it that courtesy.

My own magic snaps up, catching its arc mid-flight. The dark air unravels under my grip, dissolving with a sharp hiss. I hurl my blade in the same heartbeat. It whistles past his cheek, missing by a hair's breadth — close enough to shear a lock of hair, close enough to make him flinch.

He stumbles.

A rough sound escapes him — half-sigh, half-grunted shock as he realises how close he came to losing more than balance. He laughs — a sound edged with pain. "There he is," Maricus spits, circling, eyes hungry and dangerous. "The Sun Prince. Losing control. Look at the ring, or were you thinking of her on her knees.."

I bare my teeth. I recall my blades from the stone and lunge, blade singing, aiming not for release but out of rage: kneecap, ribs, wrist. My strikes are brutal, arcs meant to destroy a Kárith's joints. He raises his blade to block and I drive my shoulder through the motion, my weight collapsing his guard.

His boots skid, carving furrows. Sand flies. A jagged spray finds his cheek and the taste of iron hits the ring.

The storm dark veil around him unravels where my heat claws through it; his left arm flashes crimson where a shallow cut bites through skin. He tastes blood and anger, and for the first time in a long while I see his ease crack. He comes at me with everything he has — speed, guile, the blessed contempt of a man who has always thought his wits enough — and I meet him with the kind of force that ends lives.

My blade finds the soft flank beneath his ribs, a hot line that will bruise for a week. He answers with a flurry aimed at my face, and I catch a wrist, twist, wrench; the tendon in his forearm tightens, a sound like a rope snapping in winter.

We trade blood in small, clean measures — a nick on his brow, a rivulet on my hand that stings as the serpents caress it, searching for an opening.

At last, my blade arcs low and true; steel kisses his ankle and the man goes down with a hard, graceless thud. Before he can roll, I'm over him — boot on chest, blade to throat. The heat of my magic coalesces where my fingers grip the hilt.

Blood flecks his lips where a tooth took a careless hit. He swallows and, even with sand in his hair and the world still shuddering from the fight, he grins that damn lopsided, cocky smile.

"This," he says again, softer this time. "...is going to get you killed."

I lean in until the heat of my breath ghosts across his face, my tone low and slow. "No," I say, each syllable deliberate — the calm before a storm. "She is not my weakness. I am hers."

My thumb tightens on the hilt; a ribbon of pain blooms red on his skin where the blade kisses. "And goddess help any Fae, dragon, or Sylvari who thinks to speak of her otherwise."

"If you want a warning for the Courts," I add, voice dropping so low it comes out a rumble, "consider this it. Tell them whatever you must, wrap your story in pretty words. But if a single hand thinks it can touch her — with hunger in its eyes or politics on its tongue — I will answer in a language your kind understands." My words are spoken with the kind of cruelty learned through war and rebellion.

For the first time since childhood sparring, I see the flicker of something that resembles fear — not for himself, but for the shape of the thing I could become.

He exhales a short, brittle laugh, recovering the banter on the surface, but the joke folds around a new, colder truth. "Very poetic," he says, wiping sand from his jaw. "And utterly terrifying. Noted, your majesty — I'll send postcards to those in power."

I withdraw the blade, then offer him a hand. "You might want to watch that left swing of yours. You always leave yourself open. I smirk and hoist him up. He chuckles — a short, startled sound — then lets out a deeper laugh.

He tastes blood and spits sand, his busted lip already healed. I let my magic unfurl and sheath my blade slowly. The fury that drove my arms still thrums beneath my ribs, alive and dangerous, but focused now — sharpened into something I can carry forward with purpose. Maricus falls into step beside me, his hand clapping my shoulder.

"You're quick to rile," he says, voice sliding back toward its teasing cadence. "And you're quicker to finish the fight. Don't die before I get a chance to put you on your arse."

"Like I would give you the chance," I say. We exit together — Kárith, Fíralen, something close to family. The day feels hotter somehow when I step into the sunlight, a clarity settling over me that I hadn't realised I was missing.

CHAPTER 32

Lily POV

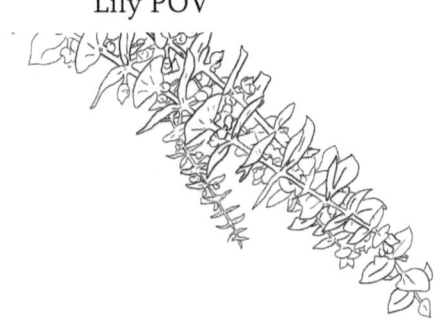

Two weeks. That's how long it's taken me to stop spinning in circles, to stop letting the chaos in my head drown out everything else. Two weeks to breathe.

If there's one thing I promised myself after Caleb, it's that I would never again make choices that cut them out. I won't drag them into the dark, confused, wondering where they fit. Not again will I hide my thoughts from my family.

I sit at the kitchen table, phone in hand, staring at the family group chat. My thumb hovers, hesitates. My chest feels tight.

Then I force myself to type:

Me: *Dinner tonight. No skipping. It's important.*

The reply pings almost immediately.

Oliver: *Got it, Mum.*

Reliable Oliver — always the first to answer. Then Daisy. The typing bubble flickers, disappears, flickers again before her message finally lands.

Daisy: *If this is about your new beau … we get it. We don't need details.*

I can't help it — I roll my eyes, even though no one can see me. Classic Daisy, using sarcasm when she's unsure. I type back, fingers firm this time.

Me: *It's important, Dais.*

Another pause.

The bubble appears. Vanishes. Appears again. Finally —
Daisy: *Got it, Mum.*

I set the phone down, exhaling a shaky breath. It's happening. Tonight the walls come down. I pause, leaning against the counter, phone pressed to my ear as I call Sal. My voice is even as I tell her I won't be at the café today. She doesn't ask why — just tells me to stop nagging.

Even with the windows closed, I feel him — that hum of steady magic brushing against my skin, protective and unrelenting. Aodhan is close. Watching. Somewhere in the hedgerow or maybe near the café, careful not to intrude but present all the same.

Relief washes through me; the bond — if I can call it that — feels calmer knowing he's near enough to reach if I need him.

The house smells of roast chicken, garlic bread, pasta salad — herbs and warmth. Comfort food. The kids come in together — Daisy with her backpack hanging from one shoulder, ready to be tossed at the door; Oliver half-distracted, his mind already on practice.

But when their eyes catch the set table, the extra care in the meal, the spotless house from my nervous cleaning — both of them pause. The air is too thick to ignore.

Oliver's brows knit. His voice is careful. "What's wrong, Mum?" Daisy doesn't speak, but her eyes are sharp, watchful, suspicion tugging at the corners of her mouth. She's old enough now to know life doesn't always go to plan. Then Oli jumps in panicked, "Don't tell me your pregnant!"

I draw in a breath and gesture to the chairs, squeezing the bridge of my nose. "Take a seat." My throat is tight, my stomach knotted, but I keep my gaze steady and my voice even. "I have something to tell you. And it's ... a lot. But I need you both to hear it from me. And I promise — I will never hide things from you. Not now. Not ever. And no Oliver I am not."

Nyxie stirs from her bed in the dining room, lifting her head, ears twitching as though she understands the weight settling over the room. The kids exchange a glance — apprehension in Daisy's eyes, Oliver's jaw tight as he braces — but they sit.

Quiet. Patient. Together. Then they each grab one of my hands, nodding for me to begin. My voice trembles on the first word. "Okay," I whisper, exhaling hard. "So ... let's start from the beginning." And I tell them. Everything.

When I finally stop, the room is quiet. The hum of the old fridge fills the silence, a steady drone that feels suddenly too loud. The kids sit motionless, caught somewhere between disbelief and apprehension.

Daisy blinks at me, wide-eyed. Oliver stares down at his hands, brows drawn tight, thinking harder than he wants me to see. Finally Daisy speaks, her voice quiet but steady. "Are you sure, Mum?"

I let out a shaky laugh, tears pricking at my eyes. "I wish I was making this up, sweetheart. God, I wish I was crazy. It would make this so much easier to explain."

She nods slowly, chewing her bottom lip, then glances at her brother. "I always knew this place was ... different," she says, almost to herself. "Like I could feel it sometimes. The air was heavier. Or lighter. Or just ... alive. Like magic hiding in the hedges or the summer rain." She looks back at me, a half-smile tugging at her lips. "Guess it kinda makes sense now, huh?"

Oliver finally looks up — his green eyes, Caleb's eyes — steady and searching. "Okay, Mum," he says, calm and even. "Well, what do we do moving forward?"

I swallow hard. "That's why I'm telling you. I want to know how you both feel. That matters most to me."

They exchange a look — that silent sibling conversation, a whole debate without words — before Daisy speaks first. "Mum ... despite everything, he cares for you. He was honest with you. We can see it — how much he loves you. And we can see how you look at him, too." She pauses, a mischievous grin flashing. "So if he makes you happy ... then so be it. But — " her grin sharpens into a dare — "if you grow wings, I want the first flight."

I burst out laughing, relief loosening the knot in my chest, as

Oliver shakes his head with an exasperated smile. The tension breaks as Daisy leans back, still grinning. "So what — does this mean we have, like, a new step-dad with secret Fae powers? Can we learn powers or something? Because, Mum, I'd like dibs on invisibility. Or maybe ... dragon fire."

Oliver snorts, stabbing a carrot. "Please. If anyone gets powers, it's me. You'd just burn the house down."

"Shut up! At least I didn't think mum was pregnant." Daisy snaps, flicking a carrot at him. He ducks, smirking, and laughter bubbles up — easy, light — and I let myself breathe it in. Even in the middle of the impossible, my kids are still my kids.

But the question lingers on my tongue. "Have either of you ... noticed anything strange lately?" I ask carefully, lowering my voice as though the shadows might be listening. "Around the house. The café. Anything that feels off?"

They trade another glance. Oliver frowns, tapping the table. "Sometimes, I feel like we're being watched. Like ... when I'm walking home from school. Or even in the yard. I thought it was just me." Daisy shifts, uneasy. "The lights in my room flicker sometimes. And the garden — the vines move when there's no wind. I thought it was just Nyxie being weird, but ... maybe not."

I nod slowly, the truth weighing heavy. "Those are the wards. They give off a vibe, like a hum when something presses too close. And lately ... they've been humming a lot more. Aodhan strengthened them, but if the wrong kind of magic tries to breach ..." I trail off, throat tight. "It means danger isn't far."

For a moment, fear flickers raw across their faces. Then Daisy blows out a breath, forcing a crooked grin. "So ... Pops wasn't so crazy with his salt lines and superstitions after all."

Oliver actually laughs — a sharp, surprised sound. "God, he's going to love this. 'Told you so,' for the rest of our lives." The laughter fades until only Oliver's words hang between us. "Alright then. If this is real — if it's dangerous — then we need to be ready. We need to know what to do. And who ... what we're looking for. This is so weird — I'm talking about unicorns and faeries."

Daisy leans forward, fire sparking in her eyes. "Do you really think unicorns are real too? And you need to teach me how to swing that bat properly, Mum. If I'm going to fight monsters, I'm not going in without the Carvish swing."

The lump in my throat swells — pride and fear twisting together. "Alright," I murmur. "Alright."

Oliver glances toward the door, then back to me, serious now. "Then we need to tell Aunt Viv, Emma, and Pops. Sooner rather than later." And I know he's right.

The calls are harder than I expect. Within an hour, the house is full — Vivienne with her sharp eyes and quiet strength; Emma, a whirlwind of noise and chaos; and Dad, steady as a Huon pine, calm as ever.

I explain it again.

Viv goes pale, blinking rapidly, her usual composure cracked.

Emma is the first to recover, of course — leaning against the kitchen island with a grin forming. "Oh my god, Lil, I knew something was up," she declares, eyes wide and sparkling. "You've been floating lately. Glowing, even. And don't you dare try to deny it." She throws a hand in the air dramatically. "And another thing. I cannot believe I slept with a fairy and he didn't even have the courtesy to show me his ears. No wonder — "

"Emma," Oliver groans, burying his face in his hands. "God. Please. Just. Stop talking."

"Still magical, though," she mutters, utterly unrepentant. It's Dad who steadies the room, his deep voice calm but certain. "Lil," he says, wearing that soft, knowing smile that used to drive me mad as a teenager.

"He's your mate. Your missing piece. This is bigger than you realise."

Something in his tone makes me still. My breath catches as unease coils sharp in my chest.

"Dad ..." I start carefully, eyes narrowing. "How do you know that? I barely understand it myself, and you — " My voice falters, suspicion sharpening. "Did you already know? About the Fae? About magic?"

For a moment his gaze holds mine, unflinching, but behind the calm something flickers — a shadow of hesitation. "I know enough," he says at last, voice measured. "Enough to recognise what this is. Enough to know you're on the right path for now."

The knot in my stomach pulls tighter. "That's not an answer."

"No," he admits quietly. His mouth tightens at the corners, every word chosen with care. "Because it isn't the right time. There are things Viv and you both need to know — but not yet. Soon, when you're ready." Vivienne's head snaps toward him, sharp suspicion flashing in her eyes. "Dad!"

"Not yet," he repeats, voice low but firm, carrying a weight that silences the room. Then, softer — almost tender: "Lil ... your decision's already been made. Cal would be relieved, you know."

I swallow hard. "Why does it feel like you're keeping secrets from me?"

"Because I am," he says simply. No apology — just truth. "But trust me, when you hear it, you'll understand why I waited."

The quiet stretches, heavy. My chest aches with questions I can't untangle. Viv glances my way, the same questions simmering beneath her calm.

I excuse myself, pushing out into the cool night. The air is sharp, grounding, but my thoughts spiral. Dad's words chase me — not the time, not yet, soon — and unease curls deeper.

Tingles run against my skin, soft and electric, like the world itself is calling.

Every hair along my arms rises; my pulse quickens. His emotions ripple through the bond like a storm barely contained — rage at unseen threats, fear of losing me, aching love that burns hotter than fire, and a hunger that refuses to quiet. It crashes through me in waves, raw and undeniable.

"Aodhan," I whisper into the stillness, glancing toward the treeline. "I know you're there. Come out."

The shadows shift, the air shimmering as though the space itself bends to make room for him. Then he steps forward, magic glowing faintly. His eyes lock on mine — unguarded — and the bond pulls taut around my ribs, singing with his want, his fear, his desperate need to hold me and never let go.

"I've missed you," he whispers, voice rough. For a long heartbeat, I just stand there, drinking him in — the man who has upended everything I thought I knew, who carries centuries of pain and still looks at me like I'm the only truth left in his world.

My throat tightens, tears stinging my eyes.

I am ready — ready for him. Ready for his world. And no one will take him from me. "Come on in," I manage, my voice steady, calm.

He crosses the distance in a few long strides, and when his hand brushes mine it's tentative — a question, a plea. I don't hesitate. I lace our fingers together, grounding us both, pouring every ounce of my answer into that touch: yes. yes. yes.

His warmth floods me instantly, steadying my nerves even as I sense how mine steadies his.

He squares his shoulders like he's about to enter battle — jaw tight, posture rigid — and I laugh to myself at how this near-seven-foot Fae warrior looks like he's about to be eaten alive by mere humans. "They'll love you," I say, giving his hand a gentle squeeze — and I mean it.

Whatever comes — questions, laughter, chaos — they'll see what I see. They'll feel it. Him. Us. His answering look nearly undoes me — half relief, half disbelief, threaded with raw, aching hope I can feel vibrating through the bond. What has this man been through in his world...

Inside, the chaos is immediate. Emma is already leaning against the counter, her grin sharp and cutting. "Well, well," she says, eyes glittering with mischief. "Welcome to the family, Mr Fairy. Just... do more than sparkle or blow glitter, okay?"

Laughter bursts out of me, spilling free and uncontrollable until my stomach aches. When I glance up at him through the blur of tears and laughter, I catch the faintest, disbelieving smile tugging at the corner of his mouth, smothered by confusion.

He leans in quietly before looking at Emma.

"Why would I sparkle? Is that something you think we do?"

I bite the inside of my cheek, suppressing another fit of giggles.

Dinner is loud and rambunctious in the way only family can

be — forks clinking, chairs scraping, voices overlapping as Daisy and Oliver bicker over who gets the last piece of garlic bread. Emma fills every pause with running commentary, somehow juggling three stories at once, while Dad sits beside me, calm as a stone, his movements quiet before engaging Aodhan in trivial talk.

Every so often, Aodhan's hand brushes mine beneath the table — a quiet anchor amid the noise.

For tonight, I don't let myself think about prophecies or shadows creeping at the edges of the estate, or the weight of questions yet to be answered. Tonight is just dinner. Just family. Just us.

Daisy, of course, can't help herself. "So," she says, leaning across the table, eyes bright with curiosity, "do you, like... zap people with lightning? Or is it more of a floaty-wind situation? Because if you can fly, Mum has to take back everything she said about bungee jumping being too dangerous."

Oliver groans, nearly choking on his victory slice of bread. "Dais, you can't just—" He waves his fork at Aodhan. "You don't interrogate a guy over the pasta salad. There's a system."

Emma laughs, slapping the table for emphasis. "Oh, please. If I had a fairy prince at my dinner table, I'd be asking far worse questions — and asking when I'd become his princess." She waggles her eyebrows at me, smirk wicked.

Heat rises in my cheeks, and I roll my eyes, lifting a hand to cut through the chatter. "Tomorrow," I say firmly, though laughter threads through my voice. "Tonight, we eat. Tomorrow... we talk."

Daisy huffs but a smile tugs at her mouth. Oliver grins into his plate. Dad only gives me a small nod — approving.

CHAPTER 33

Lily POV

The next morning, sunlight spills soft and golden across the bed, painting the room in a warm glow. I blink awake slowly — the kind of waking where there's no rush, no dread, no weight pressing down on my chest. Just ... peace. A rare, startling ease into the day.

Beside me, Aodhan is still — not guarded, not wearing that quiet edge of control he always carries like armour.

He's serene. At ease in a way I've never seen before. His chest rises and falls in an even rhythm, the faint glint of his magic dim in the morning light — quiet, as though it, too, is at rest. I simply watch him. The curve of his mouth softened in sleep. His hair mussed and falling over his forehead in untidy strands, spilling across the pillows. The faint stubble marking his jaw. Unkempt and yet impossibly perfect, because it's him — because every mark, scar, strand out of place shows the truth of him.

No mask. No walls. Just Aodhan.

Then his eyes flicker open that deep blue, molten gold swirling around the pupil, flecked with silver that shifts like waves beneath the surface, outlined faintly in white like a storm caught in sunlight. They're hazy with sleep, but when they lock on me my breath hitches, my mouth goes dry, my body burning beneath his gaze. His eyes tell me everything I need to know: that this is our beginning — the start of us, of many mornings together.

I want to memorise this moment. To hold it so tightly it never fades — the first morning where guilt isn't clawing at me, where grief isn't gnawing at my soul. The first time I wake feeling not just alive but whole — and it's by my own choosing.

When we finally make it downstairs, my hand laced firmly in his, hoping no one heard what transpired moments ago. The kitchen is alive with noise — coffee brewing, pancakes stacked high on the table, butter melting into golden pools. Oliver is already halfway through his second helping, and Daisy is swatting his hand away from her plate, both of them bickering through mouthfuls. The sound fills the house.

I feel his pulse steady against mine, but the slight stiffness in his shoulders betrays the truth: he's nervous. Nervous of them — of us. Nervous about fitting into this kitchen where we've built our home on burnt toast, chipped mugs, and kids who bicker over the last slice of bacon or the day's pancake.

My heart aches at the vulnerability he's hiding. I rub his hand once before letting go — a silent reassurance. My world. His world. Somehow, we'll find a way to bridge them.

Oliver looks up first, his green eyes glinting with mischief. "So," he says slowly, dragging the word out, "what's your power? What can you actually do?" Daisy leans forward, elbows on the table, already grinning. "Hey! You said no questions while we were eating! But ... Mum's been holding out on us. Spill it."

Aodhan exhales through his nose, the faintest smile tugging at his mouth. "Air," he says simply, voice calm but carrying promise. "I'm an Elemental Fae of the skies. The wind bends to me, the storm answers when I call, and the sun lends me its power. That is my birthright as the ruler of Air."

He lifts a hand, palm up, and the air shifts instantly. The curtains stir. Plates rattle faintly on the table. Daisy's hair lifts off her shoulders like invisible fingers are threading through it, sending it haywire and earning a squeal of laughter. "No way!" she breathes.

His tattoos pulse faintly, golden light bleeding beneath his skin, and when he opens his palm again molten sunlight rolls across his hand — fire and radiance coiled into his touch. "The sun," he says softly. "A blessing from the goddess herself. Heat. Light. Flame. Power enough to burn through the dark if I need to."

Daisy gasps, sitting back. "Okay, that's insanely cool. Like ... superhero-level cool. Do all Fae have tattoos like that?"

"Superhero?" Emma snorts from her perch at the counter, swirling her coffee. "Please. He's like a Fae hair-dryer." Her smirk sharpens. "Alright, Sunshine, what else you got? Don't tell me that's the whole act. And, Lil, I want to know — are those tattoos only on his arms or ... everywhere?"

Aodhan's mouth curves into something sly, almost teasing.

"No, not all Fae have elemental sigils — only those who've been blessed by the goddess. And to answer your question ... they can be anywhere."

Emma sputters into her coffee, cheeks flaming. "I did not need to know! I was joking!" A laugh erupts deep from his chest, startling Daisy, who nearly falls from her chair.

Oliver snickers into his pancake. "So, what else can you do?" he presses, his grin spreading. "I can open portals. Step from one realm into another in the blink of an eye." His gaze flickers to me, then back to them, tone deliberately casual. "Only royalty can do that, those of the purest lines." The table goes still. The words settle over the room.

Oliver leans back, eyebrows raised. "So ... like teleporting?"

"Something like that," Aodhan allows, amusement evident. "But more dangerous — and very, very costly if done wrong."

"And the wings?" Daisy blurts. He chuckles low, leaning back in his chair, muscles no longer taut. "Yes. I can fly." His voice dips darker, smug. "But I won't bring my wings out just for show." His smirk deepens, eyes glittering. "Not yet."

Daisy groans, half-thrilled, half-exasperated. "That is so cool — but so unfair." Oliver folds his arms, though the corners of his mouth twitch. "Super speed, portals, wings, fire, wind and storms. Great. Next, you'll say you heal faster than us too."

Aodhan shrugs, unbothered. "I do. Quicker healing. Stronger reflexes. Better agility and stamina. All of it." His eyes find mine, softening despite the smirk still tugging at his mouth. "But it doesn't make me invincible."

In that moment I feel his emotions crash over me, my cup slipping within my fingers — his fear of losing me, the restless edge of danger thrumming in his chest, the way his need for me burns deeper than pride or power. And beneath it, quieter but unshakable, the simple truth: he wants forever. Safe. Whole. With me. I glance at him and almost hear his voice in my head. *I can't lose her.*

I shake my head, clouded thoughts dissipating as I hear Oliver trying for unimpressed. "Okay. But what about the rest? You said you're a prince. Princes usually have kingdoms, right? So ... what's it like? The Fae place you're from?"

The room stills, the laughter tapering off. All eyes land on Aodhan. He leans forward slightly, forearms resting on his knees, shoulders loose but gaze intent. "There are four main Courts," he begins, spearing a pancake and shifting it around his plate as he talks. "Air, Earth, Fire, and Water — each bound to its element, not just through magic, but in spirit. In history. In temperament." He glances up, checking I'm following. "The Air Court rises high — towers of glass and pale stone carved into mountain peaks, cities balanced where the wind sings and the sun demands perfection above all else." A faint, wry edge slips into his voice at that. "We are shaped by height and light. By discipline."

He nudges the next pancake aside. "The Fire Court burns. Volcanic fortresses and rivers of magma, Kárith forged in heat and fury. They revel in chaos, passion, destruction — and rebirth."

Another shift.

"The Earth Court endures — crystal caverns and living halls grown from stone and root, gardens that breathe, soil that remembers every footstep taken upon it. History lives there. Nothing is ever truly forgotten." His gaze softens slightly.

"And the Water Court flows — sprawling citadels carved into cliffs and hidden beneath the waves. Light bends through everything there. Illusions, memory, tides. Water cleanses... but it also drowns." The words hang in the air, painting a world none of them can quite imagine. Even Emma, usually first to cut tension with a joke, sits quiet, grin gone, fingers stroking her chin as she listens.

"And the people do they all talk in riddles?" Daisy asks softly.

"Fae, mostly," he says — but his tone sharpens with history. "The realm is older than the Courts. Dragons, wyverns, Sylvaris, witches ... many withdrew after the wars and rebellions. Some chose exile. Others hide, waiting. The realms aren't as separate as they once were — old grudges keep us divided, but the prophecy, the Sceptre ..." His jaw hardens. "That's what every Court circles now. Some of those you pass every day — you'd never know they're not human. Glamour hides them well."

Oliver frowns. "Glamour?" Aodhan nods once. "A veil. A way of blending in. When humans encounter us, when they see too much, their minds can't quite tolerate it. Curiosity. Fascination. Obsession. It can be dangerous."

His gaze flickers to Dad then, sharp and questioning — something unspoken. I notice their exchange and file it away to ask about later.

His fork stills mid-air, steady eyes fixed first on Aodhan, then on me. His jaw tightens — I could swear I hear his teeth clench — before he lowers the fork and sets it carefully on his plate. "I know my girl will be safe with you," he says at last, his voice edged, laced with a poisonous calm. "And I can see how much you want this family to accept you. But there's danger you'll need to face sooner rather than later. The wards are being pushed. The Sylvaris and Fae circling too close. This property was meant to be hidden — off the map. So why now? Why has it been found?" His brow furrows, the words turning into something muttered under his breath, more for himself. "*Where did it leak from?*"

Viv and I exchange a look — we know that tone. We heard it plenty in our early childhood, one that still sends a shiver down my spine. Dad was always strict, in a paranoid, overly protective way. But Dad's expression settles into that firm, immovable stance. I feel Aodhan's shock ripple down the bond — his intrigue sharp, assessing. He senses it too: Dad knows more than he's saying.

The words hang, heavy and unsettling, until Dad clears his throat and gestures for Oliver to pass the syrup, as though he hasn't just dropped a stone into still water. For a moment, the table is silent, the weight of his warning sinking in. "I don't know — maybe the bond being strengthened. It's something I've been looking into." The tension fuels curiosity.

Then Emma leans back, smirk flashing. "I still want to see wings. Tell me, Aodhan — bird wings? Butterfly wings? Or are we talking full-on bat wings?"

Aodhan exhales, tension snapping in an instant as everyone returns to their conversations. Emma's eyes sparkle. "Add it to the list for our next girls' trip: cocktails, spa day, and fairy wings."

Laughter bubbles around the table. I glance at Aodhan, and I catch it — that flicker of unease. What he isn't saying. He's preparing for war. And he isn't willing to lose.

Dad offers to take the kids to school. Oliver mutters about being "perfectly capable of driving himself," while Daisy whines about being "chauffeured like a child," but neither puts up a real fight. They know Dad. And they know better than to argue when his tone leaves no room for discussion.

When the front door shuts and the car pulls out of the driveway, the house falls into a quieter rhythm.

Viv and Emma linger, though they make a poor show of pretending it's to help. Viv fusses with stacking plates that are already clean, her sharp eyes cutting toward Aodhan every other breath. Emma, leaning against the counter with her arms crossed, is far less subtle — her grin practically daring him to start talking. I know that look. She wants details. Most of all, she wants to hear more about Maricus.

Aodhan moves across the room with unhurried ease. He lowers himself onto the couch beside me, presence calm but commanding, one arm draped along the back cushions in a loose, protective sprawl.

Nyxie wastes no time claiming him — her great dark head nudging onto his thigh like she's done it all her life. He strokes behind her ears, fingers threading through her fur with a familiarity and quiet acceptance.

When I glance up, I find him watching me. Every breath, every subtle movement. His fingers brush a strand of hair from my face, his stare so intent I reach out instinctively. Just as I lift my hand to touch his ears — the ones I've secretly wanted to explore since he revealed them — a slow, knowing smile curves his mouth, dimples forming.

"If you wanted to touch me, Lily," he murmurs, lips quirking, "you could just say so. Tell me what you want me to strip first."

I roll my eyes and slap his chest lightly, though my pulse stutters, thoughts scattering to far less innocent places. "I wanted to touch your ears, not your ego." His laugh rumbles deep, warm and rich, curling through me like the breeze after a summer storm. "You know they're just like yours. Only a little elongated."

I narrow my eyes, tilting my head. "You wouldn't be avoiding me touching them, would you?" He dips his head, angling closer so I can trace the delicate curve of cartilage, dimples still showing. They're like mine — but not. Finer, sharper, the texture almost silken beneath my fingertips.

My hand drifts lower without thought, brushing over the scars etched across his back — ridged lines that vanish beneath his shirt but can't hide their story.

My breath catches, voice hardening. "And what are these from?"

He hesitates. Just long enough for the air to turn heavy. "Training," he mumbles, detached. "With my father. When I was a child."

The words strike like lightning, outrage sparking hot in my chest. "Your father did this to you?" My hand fists against his chest, fury flaring. "How could—"

He lowers his gaze, resigned. "Fae grow up differently to humans. Our upbringing... training is harsher. Survival is expected, there is no room for weak."

Something fierce rises in me — a fire I don't bother to dampen. I cup his cheek, thumb brushing the corner of his mouth, holding him still. "No one treats you that way now. Not even your father. Not while I'm here." My voice trembles with the kind of hatred I've never known. "I don't stand for bullies. Not in this life. Not ever."

He studies me, as though I've said something bewildering. Then, slowly, a smile softens his mouth — reverent and disarming. "Yes, Mo draganín." My gaze lingers on him. "I can see it. Gods help anyone foolish enough to test you — the ground itself wouldn't survive."

"You're wrong," I mutter, heat creeping into my cheeks. "I wouldn't scorch the earth — I'd destroy a kingdom. Or well a Court..."

A faint laugh escapes him, but his eyes gleam with pride.

"Aodhan, there's a lot we need to learn about each other," I continue quietly. "You've had four hundred and fifty years. I've had thirty-six. We've got a lot of ground to cover. My life's a snippet in comparison."

"We have time, Lily. All the time." He reaches for my hand, eyes steady. "You can ask me anything, anytime. But for now — with the current threats — I need you to know this. My Fíralen or you would call them...soldiers will be at the café, around the property. Watching. Protecting you and the kids."

The way he says it — you and the kids — like it's one promise, one family. My chest swells. "Thank you," I whisper. Then panic slams in. "Oh God — the café! I need to—"

"Handled," Viv cuts in smoothly from the kitchen, voice far too casual. The smirk tugging at her lips gives her away. "I called Sal last night. Thought you might need the morning to ... decompress. She's happy to cover — and she said to remind you that you can take time off, you know."

I blink at her, half-relieved, half-suspicious. But before I can reply, she fixes her gaze on Aodhan, her tone teasing but edged with intent.

"And you — fair warning. Lily may look calm and quiet most of the time, but don't mistake that for softness. There's fire in her, and it becomes all-consuming. When she decides to fight for something — or someone — she doesn't back down. I pity the poor bastard who tests her patience."

Aodhan glances at me, surprise flickering before his expression steadies — silver and gold swirling together like a storm. "I already know," he says simply.

She waves me off, flicking her towel over one shoulder. "Don't thank me, sis. Just don't burn out. And keep the flirting in check — it's too damn early and I would like my food to digest."

Emma leans her elbows on the counter, grin wicked. "Forget the café. Let's talk about these friends. How soon do we meet them? And will they all be as..." she drags her gaze over Aodhan, "...friendly as the last one I met?"

"They'll be here within the hour," he says evenly, voice giving nothing away.

I start to retreat upstairs, but his hand catches mine — warm, steady, unyielding. He draws me back with the barest tug, his breath a whisper against my ear. "Running from me, mo draganín?" The low burr of his voice vibrates through my skin, soft but threaded with something dark and hungry.

I swallow hard. "I can't fall for your tricks right now. I have to meet your friends. What does one even wear to meet the entourage of their mate?"

The word lands between us like a spark in dry grass. He goes utterly still. The faint heat of his fingers tightens, the bond humming like a live wire between us.

"Say it again," he murmurs, voice low and rough enough to shiver through every bone.

"*Mate*," I whisper.

Something primal flashes in his eyes — a predator's hunger and a lover's devotion locked together. His next words are dark velvet dripped in honey. "If you call me that again," he says, tone a dangerous promise, "I'll cancel the meeting and keep you upstairs all day."

I laugh, trying for levity, but the look on his face wipes it from my lips. My palm slides up his chest, passing each button, his breath hitching with every touch until I reach his jaw, thumb brushing the faint stubble there.

"I am yours, Aodh," I whisper.

His eyes close, a long exhale trembling out of him, like the words sink somewhere deep and long-denied. When they open again, the intensity in them hits me like a storm.

"And I am yours, Lillian," he says, quiet and absolute. His arms are suddenly around me, strong and sure, lifting me as though I weigh nothing. The hallway blurs; the half-closed door vanishes; cool tile meets my back.

The rush of water fills my ears, drowning out the rest of the world. For a heartbeat there's only him — his heat, his scent, the bond between us pulling tighter, hungrier.

Steam curls thick and heavy in the air, turning every breath into something molten. My clothes cling wet to my skin, cool tiles shivering against my spine while his touch burns. His shirt sticks to his body, every muscle outlined; I rake my fingers over him, revelling in the shape of strength beneath my hands.

He squeezes my hips before murmuring, voice rough, "As much as I love seeing these..." — his mouth trails lower, my breast caught in his mouth — "...I prefer no interferences."

A flicker runs through me like cold flames dancing across my skin, tickling and igniting at once. Then my clothes vanish, and I'm bare in his arms. Every touch feels like a vow carved into my skin. His mouth traces my throat, slow and deliberate.

"Fuck, Lily," he groans against my neck, voice raw and reverent. "Your scent... your body... you undo me."

"Aodhan," I whisper, arching closer, my nails scraping down the hard lines of his back. His restraint falters, the sound he makes low and guttural. In one smooth movement he hoists me up, my legs locking instinctively around his waist as the firm mass of heat presses against my core.

"Tell me," He rasps, forehead pressed to mine, voice shredded by control. "Tell me what you want."

"I want you," I breathe, the words trembling but certain. "Only you."

That's all it takes. The last of his restraint breaks. He pushes into me slowly, inch by inch, until I gasp — until the ache melts into fullness. His magic flares brighter, lacing the steam like lightning trapped in a cloud.

The rhythm builds — slow at first, then relentless — every movement pulling us tighter, every sound of water and skin and breath drowning out the world beyond the bathroom.

"I am yours" he growls against my mouth, the word rough and raw, possessive. "Forever yours, mo draganín."

The coil of tension inside me snaps, sharp and electric. I shatter with a cry, his name on my lips, clinging to him as he follows — broken sounds torn from his throat, his hands gripping me tight, fingers biting into my flesh.

When it's over, when the only sounds are the soft drip of water and the low hum of his magic settling back into his skin, he stays there — forehead pressed to my shoulder, his breath ragged against my damp skin.

"I've waited a lifetime for you," he murmurs, voice so low it almost disappears into the steam. "And I won't waste another second."

By the time we make it downstairs, my cheeks are still flushed, my legs unsteady, my hips sore, my hair damp and curling against my neck.

Viv glances up from where she's wiping down the counter, one brow arching in silent judgement. The corner of her mouth twitches before she mutters, "Took you long enough…"

Emma doesn't even pretend to be subtle. She leans an elbow on the counter, grin wicked. "Well," she says brightly, "if this is what mornings are going to look like now, I'm going to need a bigger pot of coffee and a cold shower — you about destroyed the upper floor."

Flushing further, my skin turns a new shade of red, while Aodhan holds my hand, ignoring their words, only smirking at me.

My pulse recognises their arrival before my mind catches up. The air shifts — heavy and charged — like the moment before a wave crashes. Five Fae step through the doorway, and my kitchen feels like the centre of something vast and ancient. Power presses against the walls, the pressure in the house crackling.

"This is Lillian," Aodhan says, his voice calm but threaded

with pride that makes my chest ache. "My mate, your Rígann." The word still makes my stomach flip — equal parts fear and wonder.

The first to step forward is tall and elegant, every movement precise. His skin seems to hold the light rather than reflect it, like polished marble, and his eyes are sharp, calculating, missing nothing. Shadows coil faintly at his boots, sliding across the floorboards like smoke before vanishing. When he bows — low, formal — a prickle skates across my skin, like cold ink soaking into parchment.

"Kaelen," he says, his voice smooth, calm as water running over stone. "It is an honour, Rígann Lillian. I look forward to serving you."

"Good morning," I reply quickly, awkwardly, hands twisting in my lap. "Lovely to meet you. And please... just call me Lily." The faintest tilt of his mouth acknowledges the request, though his bow remains just as deep. An aura sways behind him — black and white intertwining.

The next is a woman — shorter, with a halo of vibrant red curls and a face dusted with freckles. Sparks crackle across her knuckles when she folds her arms, the temperature of the room shifting, a subtle rise that beads sweat at the nape of my neck. Her grin is quick, mischievous, her very presence like fire dancing at the edge of a fuse. "Yasar," she says brightly, her voice edged with the confidence of someone who's burned and survived. "At your service, Lady Lily." Her gaze flicks toward Kaelen and she smirks. "Morning." Heat clings to her even as she steps back — a restless fire contained for now, waiting for the right ignition.

The third moves like lightning. Hair the colour of stormlight — shifting shades of electric blue that catches in the morning sun. The faint, sharp tang of ozone prickles my nose, leaving the taste of iron on my tongue. Tattoos coil around her ears in intricate spirals, scars etching her arms — a story not kind, carved into flesh. "Naralle," she says with a wink. Her grin is roguish, all trouble, but her gaze is razor-sharp, scanning the room before she winks again. "You sure are gorgeous — I understand the hype."

"Show her respect and leave your flirting at the door," Aodhan warns lightly. Naralle's wicked grin widens. The fourth hangs back, hesitant. Younger. Boyish. His shifting weight makes the house feel light, nervous energy fizzing through the space like champagne bubbles. He looks barely seventeen, but the quickness in his eyes betrays something sharper. When our gazes meet, he grins — wide, genuine, unguarded — before ducking his head.

"That's Luc," Aodhan supplies, voice softer. "Don't be fooled — he's young but gifted." Luc flashes another grin, like a puppy eager to prove himself, and the fizz of his magic lingers like static on my skin.

The last one steps forward and everything stills. Tall. Wiry. His presence heavier than the rest. Shadows coil thick around his boots, twisting upward like they want to crawl higher, waiting for command. His eyes are dark, void-deep, and they pin me in place.

When he bows, it's deeper than the others, his voice low, regal. "Harrid," he says simply. "A privilege, Lady Lily."

My breath comes shallow and quick, palms slick. And suddenly, I understand — truly — what it means to have this kind of loyalty at Aodhan's back. To stand beside a prince who commands warriors like these.

"Harrid will watch the perimeter," Aodhan says, his tone shifting into command — sharp, absolute. "His gift lets him prowl the shadows unseen. Naralle will be at the café — helping, watching. Yasar and Kaelen will rotate between here and the Air Court. Luc will shadow the kids. He blends best."

I nod slowly, throat dry, absorbing it all. But still — because I can't help myself — I ask, "And Maricus?"

Aodhan's jaw tightens. "Not here. Not unless I call him. He has... other tasks." Everyone mingles — Emma loudest, most intrigued.

When Viv finally gathers her things to leave, she lingers in the doorway. Her gaze moves between me and Aodhan, steady, assessing. "Careful," she warns. "I don't want you hurt again." The door clicks shut behind her.

Aodhan steps closer, his magic wrapping around me like a warm embrace. "You'll be safe." I fold into his arms, coiled tight against his chest. "I trust them with my life," he murmurs.

I meet his gaze. "I trust you."

The house smells of garlic bread and warm spice, the kitchen humming with the clatter of plates. I've cooked enough for an army, and tonight, it feels like one has arrived.

Pasta steams in wide bowls, pizza piled high on platters — a feast to welcome our new guests. The hum of voices is lighter this time, warmer, carrying that rare feeling of ordinary in the middle of impossible.

The Fae sit among us. Luc wedges himself between Oliver and Daisy like a friend known for years, grinning as Daisy tries to explain trends he clearly doesn't understand.

"Is that a spell?" he mutters, bewildered.

Yasar leans back in her chair with the easy sprawl of someone who's already claimed the space, trading sharp banter with Emma about who has the better right hook.

"Careful — I don't punch like a human," Yasar warns with a grin.

Kaelen eats quietly, precise and measured, while Nyxie has claimed his boots as her pillow, rumbling softly like she's known him her whole life.

Naralle flicks sparks across her fingers every time Oliver rolls his eyes — to Daisy's squealing delight.

Harrid stays mostly silent, but the wisps of magic coiling lazily around his chair don't feel menacing; they feel folded into the rhythm of the room, a silent sentinel at the hearth. I curl up beside them, letting myself relax.

"This is surreal," Daisy mutters, spearing a carrot and waving it at Luc. "Two weeks ago, I thought Mum had lost it, new beau, changing her look. Now we've got... what? A warrior, a storm-witch-cross-Fae, a firestarter, and..." — she narrows her eyes at Kaelen — "...whatever you are. Royalty, how exactly are you two related?"

Kaelen's lips twitch — the faintest ghost of a smile. "Something like that. A cousin to the Prince." His gaze flicks to Aodhan, apprehension crossing his face. Daisy beams, triumphant.

Emma snorts into her wine. "Careful, kid. You keep teasing the scary pretty ones and one of them might eat you."

Daisy shrugs, grinning wider. "We never asked that… do they eat humans?"

Luc howls. "Only pretty ones." He winks at Daisy, her cheeks flushing pink.

Oliver, sets his fork down. His green eyes sharpen. "What about the danger?" he asks, voice calm but firm. "You're here for a reason."

The warmth in the room shifts, just slightly. Aodhan meets his gaze across the table, voice steady and certain. "That's why they're here. To keep you safe. To keep your mum safe."

"And if things get worse?" Oliver presses, jaw tight.

Aodhan's answer is simple, heavy as a vow. "Then we'll face it together." The words ring loud in my ears. Not just him. Not just me. Together.

The conversation tilts back to lighter things, stories traded across the table like cards. Emma tries to convince Naralle to take her clubbing "With those tattoos, you'd never pay for a drink again", and Daisy badgers Luc about whether he can glamour himself into looking like someone famous. "No, but I could try," he offers, making her nearly choke on her bread.

Even Viv — who returned halfway through — hides a nervous smile behind her glass at the ridiculousness of it all.

By the time plates are scraped clean and mugs of tea appear in front of us, the house feels full in a way it hasn't since Caleb. And when Aodhan catches my hand under the table, his thumb brushing slow circles against my palm, I realise: my home and my family haven't just survived this change — we're embracing it.

CHAPTER 34

Lily POV

The kids don't even question our new normal. Harrid lingers at the edge of the driveway each morning — tucked into shadow and element alike — his presence so seamless the neighbours have already started joking about my new security system. Daisy rolls her eyes every time, muttering about how extra it looks and how he could be a little less intense about his job.

Oliver, on the other hand... has officially adopted him.

He quizzes Harrid on every movement, spell, and incantation, a newly obsessed enthusiast thrilled to have someone willing to spar. My chest swells at the sight — a quiet sense of ease settling through me with every interaction.

By the time I finish breakfast, Oliver is already out near the edge of the property, backpack half-slung off one shoulder, chattering about footwork and defence like Harrid is some legendary mentor pulled straight from a storybook. Harrid listens in silence, expression unchanged, sharp eyes tracking everything while a writhe of shadows coils at his feet, restless, watching.

Luc is glued to Daisy's side. This morning it's an endless exchange, both of them laughing so hard Nyxie lifts her head from her bed with a grunt of disapproval at her rest being disturbed. Even she seems more relaxed with the Fae presence in the house. As they walk out the door, Daisy's hand brushes Luc's. A faint pink tinge colours her cheeks.

Narelle is already at the café, that electric-blue hair catching the morning sun, her back against the counter like she's claimed it as her throne. Sparks hum around her skin — sharp, alive — but no one notices.

To customers, she's just a sharp-eyed young woman with a quick grin, pouring lattes and trading stories like she's been here forever. Her movements are fast, precise — the kind of efficiency that feels... unnatural. The regulars are enamoured. They're too busy trying to make her laugh, like she's their favourite niece who wandered into town. Sal slides beside me at the register, voice low, gaze flicking toward Narelle with open appreciation. "Normally I'd question you for hiring someone without a single reference," she mutters, lips quirking. "But she's very much my type — in all ways — so... consider me bribed. Has she mentioned if she's single?"

Narelle smirks without looking up, clearly hearing every word. A faint crackle of her magic skitters across the espresso machine. "Oh, I am single, Sal," she says lightly. "And very much ready to mingle."

I bite back a laugh. "Consider it a win, then." But the humour fades when I turn toward the window.

A cluster of figures lingers just beyond the wards — shadows stretched unnaturally thin in the sunlight. At first glance they could be loiterers, but their stillness is wrong. Fae. The air tightens in my lungs as the wards hum low, strained, recognising the presence pressing against their edge of the ward.

Narelle's façade drops. She eases away from the counter, murmurs under her breath, and a shimmering bubble expands around the café. I stare, aghast, at how no one else notices. Narelle just winks before casually sauntering back to the counter. "The Sceptre should be here, in this realm," one voice murmurs, carrying despite its low pitch. "Why else would the prince linger so long?"

Another scoffs, though unease threads through it. "He searches still. Always searching. But the question is — what would he trade if it were found? What would he give?"

A sharper voice hisses, "Silence. Even walls listen." And then — just like that — they're gone.

The group dissolves, clouds breaking into sunlight as if they never existed. The wards hum again, unsettled, vibrating against my skin like a warning. I exhale hard and force my gaze back inside. The café continues as though nothing has happened — machines whirring, mugs clinking, the familiar morning chorus. Normal. Or as close to normal as my life can manage now. But their words loop in my mind.

What would he trade? What would he give?

Mr Fisher shuffles in next, bouncing with his carefree smile. "Morning, Lillian," he says, voice soft but weathered like old timber creaking. His eyes — kind, wrinkled at the corners — crinkle as he takes his usual tea and the slice of brownie he's ordered for years.

"Morning, Mr Fisher," I reply, offering the practiced smile I always do.

But today, he doesn't move to his table. He lingers. Apprehension crosses his face. When he speaks, it's low, threaded with something that makes the room itself feel heavier. Older. Colder. Like time has paused.

"Big things are coming your way, child," he murmurs. "Some of which I can no longer see clearly. Age dulls the edges. But still I see... heat. Gold. Trust, broken."

The smile slips from my face. My hands still against the counter. "Mr Fisher..."

His gaze sharpens. And for the briefest flicker — too quick to grasp — something else peers out through his eyes. Not the kind man I've known for years.

Something ancient. Waiting, lurking. A beast hidden in plain sight. Everything goes frigid. No sound but his voice.

"*Unite them, Lillian,*" he says, voice resonant and impossibly old.

"*Like only you can. A prince bound by false prophecy cannot carry the weight alone. Without you, he falls. With you...*"

He stops. A moment of dread ghosts his expression. "*The Sceptre is dangerous. Bonds, more so. Be careful which one you choose when the storm comes."*

My blood runs cold. Goosebumps ripple along my arms. "What does that even mean?" I whisper.

It drops — darker, colder — layered with power not meant for mortal ears. The words spill out in a foreign tongue I recognise from half-forgotten childhood stories.

"The Sceptre will never fall into the hands of greed or the hands of evil. Only one who bears all elements in balance will wake what sleeps. But to unite... is to risk the end of your mortal life. Sacrifice will be expected, a crown to be returned. If all fails — all realms will fall to ruin."

The words slice through me like ice.

Then he blinks. The veiled mask is gone. Warmth returns to his eyes. His voice familiar again.

"Just an old man rambling," he chuckles, lifting his fork. He eats his brownie as though nothing happened. But I can't shake it. The chill lingers long after he leaves — a wound carved into my chest.

Before I know it, I'm in my room, the sun is dipping low, shades of pink and orange stretching across the sky. My thoughts drift back to the café — to what I overheard, to Fisher's warning. Were they talking about Aodhan? Someone else? Why had Mr Fisher been so cryptic? My hairs rise recalling his tone.

And there he is. My mate — sprawled across my bed.

Nyxie pressed against his side, her massive head rising and falling with the steady rhythm of his breathing, guarding him even in sleep.

For a moment, I just stand in the doorway watching him. He keeps returning to me. Coming home. But the pale colour to his face, the fresh bruises along his ribs...

"You look tired," I murmur, stepping into the room.

His eyes flick open — sharp and bright even through exhaustion. "Training," he admits. "Magic. Weapons. I let my guard down and took a few hits."

I cross the room, frowning. "Aodh—"

"It's nothing," he says quickly, but his voice softens when I sit beside him.

I reach out instinctively, brushing my fingers over the faint bruise along his forearm. His muscles tense, then relax. "You're pushing yourself too hard," I whisper. The bruise looks foreign on him — a reminder that even he can bleed. Even he can break. "You need to stop overexerting yourself. You might be the prince, Aodhan, but you need to take care of your body too. How can you expect to rule a Court if you're not at your best?"

He exhales, slow and controlled, then rolls toward me and rests his head in my lap without a word. My fingers slip into his hair automatically, combing through the silken strands. The tension in his shoulders eases. "I know," he mumbles into my stomach like a child caught stealing snacks before dinner.

"I saw Mr Fisher today," I murmur, thumb tracing the faint glow at his temple. "You've heard me mention him before… he's always been a little strange, but today…"

I swallow. "Today he felt foreign. His words didn't make sense."

Aodhan's eyes open again, gold catching in the fading light. "Different how?"

"Like something was looking out from behind his eyes," I whisper. "Like it wasn't just him speaking."

I hesitate. "He said things about the Sceptre… a false prophecy… about you failing if I wasn't there. And a warning…"

I can't finish the sentence — the part about someone dying.

Aodhan sits up enough to grip my waist and hold me tight. "Thank you for telling me," he murmurs. "I'll look into it. I know you care for him."

"I do." My fingers still against his skin. "But what if something happens to you?"

"You've already done more than you know," he says softly. "When you're near, the noise stops. The rage, the pull, the ache of the bond… it steadies me. You make me a better Fae. Stronger. And more human."

I smooth my fingers along his cheek, protective. "Then rest.

Please. You don't have to fight all the time."

His throat works once. "I want to hear your voice. Talk to me some more." I continue quietly. "What does it look like? The Sceptre."

He's silent for a moment. "No one is certain," he says at last. "Old scriptures speak of a staff forged in all four elements. At its crown, a gem — alive, humming with its own power. They say it held the colours of every element at once, shifting with its wielder."

My breath catches. Before I speak, he hesitates — then slips a hand into his pocket. He withdraws a small shard, faint light pulsing from its facets. "This," he says softly, "is a piece of it. A piece I've kept hidden. A piece I've told no one — not even my father."

He places it into my hand.

The moment it touches my skin, my breath stutters. The shard thrums like a heartbeat — then— Heat. Wind. Stone. Water. And something so blinding my eyes burn. All four elements rush like a storm through my veins.

I gasp and push it back into his hand.

"That power..."

"It's beautiful," Aodhan says, closing his fist around it, the glow dimming. "But in the wrong hands, it would bring ruin."

Silence settles — heavy but gentle — as the quiet hum of his magic lingers between us. I return my fingers to his hair, stroking until the tension bleeds out of him.

"Sleep," I whisper. "I'll be here when you wake." As his breathing deepens, I look down at him — this man, this Fae, my mate — and something in me steadies. My gaze drifts to the crystal on my dresser. Its facets catch the dying sunlight, scattering restless patterns across the wall. It hums faintly in my chest — answering something inside me I don't yet understand.

CHAPTER 35

Aodhan POV

The house a calm shaped entirely by Lily's presence. Her arm is draped across my chest, her breath warm against my throat, the scent of jasmine and rain steeped into the sheets.

I lie still and let it anchor me — a mortal rhythm steadying an immortal heart.

A soft breeze stirs the curtains even though the windows are shut; the room bends toward her without being called, the way everything in me does. My mate. My Lily. Mo draganín. My everything. I press a kiss to her hairline, only easing away when sleep claims her fully. It feels like treason to leave, even for a few hours.

I scrawl a note and set it on her nightstand:

I will be back soon. I'll always find my way to you. —A

Then I step through a cut in the air into the high, cold light of the Air Court. A storm rages along the cliffside, the moon high, my power thriving at the altitude. I'll need to take flight soon and let my wings free. I should've gone for a quick flight before coming straight here, but I couldn't bear to leave her.

I stroll through the halls, every step familiar, each one somehow heavier than the last. Its glass corridors glitter, but beneath the gleam lies power. Guards bow as I pass, though I notice the way their eyes flick toward me — the weight of their silence thick with judgement. Father's men, searching for weakness.

I feel their attempts to corrupt my magic prickle against my skin like a thousand invisible blades.

The Air Lord. My father. A Fae Ruler once celebrated for the way he adored my mother, then feared for the way he turned her death into vengeance. The one who forged me into a weapon — for the Air Court, for prophecy.

A man I once respected. A man I now endure. Paranoid. Hidden from the Court.

The great hall yawns vast and sharp-edged, the throne a spire of glass and light. My father sits upon it, thin and luminous, his hands skeletal on the armrests, the crown of air glimmering faintly above his brow.

He looks frail, his healers claim he is nearing the end— but the golden eyes that spear me are anything but.

No sickness dulls them. No weakness softens them. This frailty is a mask, one yet to be proven. One I must prove to take the Court.

"So," he says, voice icy as frost, "are we any closer to finding the Sceptre?"

"My unit has leads," I reply. "They're being pursued."

His gaze sharpens, contempt flickering.

"The eclipse draws near. The Fire Court arms and pushes boundaries. The Water Court smiles and waits. And you..." His nose wrinkles faintly, like he smells rot. "... reek of distraction."

Lily's name sears against my tongue.

"I am focused."

A sharp exhale — dismissive, cold. "Is that so? Be certain your heart does not cost you your crown. You were not born for love, Prince. You were born a weapon. And weapons are not meant to grow soft or useless. I have no need for a weapon I cannot use."

My jaw grinds, heat flaring in my veins.

"Be certain your crown does not cost us our Court."

For a heartbeat, silence. Then his lips curve into a shadow of a smile. A predator's smile.

"Ah. So, the rumours are true. The prince has found a backbone with his mortal."

Disdain drips from the word mortal, but underneath it — contempt.

"Tell me... what happens when the Court realises their Prince spends his time entertaining himself with fragile flesh? Soft. Breakable and weak."

The words strike like poison. Fury coils tight inside me.

My hands flex, burning, every instinct screaming to unsheathe my blade and silence him where he sits. But if I show him what she means — if I let it slip — he will use it.

Against me.

Against her.

And I do not yet have the Court under my palm.

He leans back, satisfied by my silence.

"Be careful," he says lightly, though the threat thrums sharp as steel. "Hearts burn. Mortals die. And kings don't tolerate disrespect, even from their kin."

"I will remember that." I say, voice low, deadly calm.

Surprise flickers — the faintest crack in the mask — before he dismisses me with a flick of his fingers.

I bow just enough to appease him. No more.

As I turn away, I round the corner and slam my fist into the stone, breath ragged. I must take the throne and the Court soon, or—

My thoughts crash back in, the possibilities if Lily were dragged into my father's war. My fist comes away from the wall, flames licking at my fingers.

The training grounds breathe with morning heat, the hum of steel and wards filling the air. My blade feels heavier today, my mind warring with itself.

Maricus waits in the centre of the ring, his wraiths curling lazily around his boots — mocking, just like him. His smile is already there, sharp and baiting.

"You're late," he drawls. "Did your chat with Daddy Dearest

go well?"

"Same old," I reply, rolling my shoulders, fighting tension.

Maricus' smirk widens. "Stretching, yes. Though not in the way you've been lately." Serpent-shadows slither outward as he circles me, coiling and uncoiling at his heels. "Whispers in Court are loud, Aodh. Our golden prince — bound to a human." His head tilts, mockery sharpened to a blade. "A woman barely halfway through her mortal years while you're... what? Four centuries old? That's not a bond. That's cradle-snatching."

The storm spikes inside me. I keep my face still.

"And let's be honest," he continues smoothly. "She's lived more in her three decades than you have in four hundred. Lovers. Marriage. Children. A life." His smile turns cruel. "Tell me — how does it feel knowing your mortal mate has already loved more deeply, more fully, than you ever dared?"

"Fuck off. Not today."

He laughs, low and pleased. "Politics matter. Perception matters. The Courts whisper that you're soft. And when whispers turn alliances—"

I move before he finishes.

Steel flashes.

The ring detonates in light and shadow.

"Let them," I snarl between blows.

Maricus gives ground, shadows lashing to keep pace.

He doesn't stop smiling. "The Sun Prince undone by a mortal's touch," he taunts. "Tell me — how does it feel playing step-father to children who should have been yours, maybe father would be happy knowing you have two mortal children hmm...?"

Fury slips its leash. Heat cracking stone beneath each strike.

My voice drops, quiet and lethal.

"Fuck off, Maricus. How's your dalliance going with a mortal who sees you as a plaything and nothing more?"

The air thins around him. I step back, taking in the wreckage — scorch marks, fractured stone, the weight of what I almost lost control of.

He laughs, but there's an edge now. "Careful, Sun Prince. You're losing control over mere words... And we both get what we want — it's a clean transaction. Sex. No feelings If I hadn't tasted her myself I would have thought she was Fae, quite the interesting human."

Ellisar appears in the pavilion doorway.

"You left scorch marks," she says evenly. "And Maricus stop baiting him, he is not stable."

"Like that's ever stopped him before."

Her gaze flicks to the ring, then back to me. "You're riding the edge. Overusing portals. If the Courts scent weakness, they'll push harder. Fire. Witches. Rogues." A pause. "Make your moves quieter. And stop thinking with your dick."

I huff a dark laugh. She shifts gears, all business. "What of the wards around Lily's place?"

"No change. Nothing they can penetrate — yet. They probe. They test. I've bolstered them. Harrid and Naralle will run a deeper weave tonight."

Her eyes soften — a rare sibling warmth.

"You can't chain yourself to the house."

"I'm not chaining myself."

She just nods — the silent agreement that she'll take over the rest. "Find the Sceptre, Aodh. And try not to provoke Air Rívaran into killing you or her, not before you take the Court."

I stride toward the west ridge overlooking Lily's land.

The property unfurls in a wave of green. The glass roof throws back sunlight, the garden glowing like it remembers her.

For a moment, I just drink it in — her in the heart of it. Small. Fierce. Stubborn.

Night falls. I remain on the roof line until the stars smear across the sky like a soft cloak.

From here I watch the lanes to the estate, the woods beyond, the old road where curiosity might hide. I watch faces in the dark.

I listen to the night breathe.

And beneath the wide, cold sky, the bond between us hums with steady warmth — a reminder I cannot ignore.

CHAPTER 36

Aodhan POV

It has been weeks now of this strange new rhythm — the closest thing to peace I have ever known. Nights are for the hunt. For following whispers through the mountain passes, for rooting out scouts reckless enough to test the wards, for facing witches who linger too long.

By day, when I am not with Lily, I'm training my mind, my body. I am taking back my Court — rooting out those who would seek to destroy peace from the inside. Discreetly, ensuring my father remains unaware.

I feel it — my power strengthening. Being with Lily feeds it in ways I never expected. She could have been my greatest weakness, yet she has become my fiercest strength. The bond sharpens me, steadies me, makes me more than I was before.

The longer I am with her, the calmer my mind becomes, the sharper my focus. Lily has noticed changes — scents are stronger to her, magic appears as an aura around individuals, and she's reading emotions clearly and accurately.

I see it in her face when she senses the darker side of my work, the firm line of her mouth tightening. She understands. They are trying to hurt her, her family.

But when she discovered the kids had been followed... the

cruelty and rage I witnessed from her still sends a giddy shiver down my spine.

When Luc caught a fae trailing too close to the children, we spent hours interrogating him. Luc's mixed blood makes him sharper, crueller — where most Fae hesitate, Luc does not. He struck without pause, drawing blood and screams with ruthless precision that should unsettle me but doesn't. I kept my distance, my control locked tight, but even my voice could not always drown out the wet sound of bone giving way or the ragged cries he ripped from the prisoner.

Where I pressed with quiet truths and subtle threats, Luc used pain as a language.

Still, nothing. Spells wound through his mind, silencing the truths we needed most. Every time he tried to speak the name of his master, his throat closed, choking the word into silence. Whoever commands them has thought ahead — layers of wards, oaths, geas-bound silence. No secret escaped.

When at last he slumped, magic drained dry, Luc's grin was sharp as a knife.

Mine was frustration. Another wall. Another wasted night. Then Lily was told — and her rage was volcanic. Her threats were gruesome. I relished her cruelty. She was more Fae than human in that moment.

I have seen her fierce, blood on her hands and defiance in her voice. I have seen her laughing with her children, head thrown back, green eyes bright. Yet like this — bare, unguarded, hair messy from sleep — she steals the air from my lungs all over again. She is breathtaking in every form.

I've seen a change not just in Lily, but in her children — and in my Fíralen.

Her children laugh more freely now. The heaviness in their eyes has lightened, grief loosening its grip with each passing day.

Harrid has become Oliver's constant shadow — not only a guardian but a guide. His patience shapes the boy in ways that remind me of old Fíralen, I once trusted with my life. I've seen Oliver's small hands steady against Harrid's massive ones, mimicking a stance, a strike, a lesson in strength tempered by discipline.

Luc trails after Daisy with the stubborn loyalty of a friend. His reckless grin softens into something gentler under her teasing. Where once bitterness lived in his edges, there is now a rough kind of joy. The wildness in him dims only when she smiles.

Naralle has claimed the café as her own. She weaves through customers with sharp wit and sharper eyes, storms sparking faintly at her fingertips when someone dares test her tongue. She banters like she was born for the rhythm, folding herself seamlessly into the heartbeat of Lily's world.

Human and Fae together — united. Something unspoken for a millennia.

I arrive, bare feet whispering across the cool tile, her hair loose down her back in soft, ungoverned waves that sway with every movement. Steam curls from the kettle. The faint scent of coffee and mango mixes with the warmth of the stove, wrapping the small space. She stands at the counter, scrunching her nose in thought as she slices fruit, her mouth tilted in that almost-smile she does when she's lost in her own world.

Light freckles dust beneath her eyes, like a constellation. Her cheeks are flushed from the stove's heat, from the early sunlight streaming through the window.

"I was bringing this up to you," she says, pressing a slice of mango against my lips. Her eyes glint, mischievous and tender at once. "You looked like you needed something sweet."

"Only you," I murmur, my voice rougher than I intend.

I lean down, stealing a kiss that tastes of sun and mango and something dangerously close to peace. I lower myself trapping her with my arms as she leans back against the counter. She squeaks in shock, cheeks flushed.

"I could eat this all day," I whisper, gliding my tongue along her neck, kissing her cheek.

Her breath hitches. And then Maricus's mind-voice slices across the moment — dry and unyielding.

Pants on, princling. Summons. Fire Court. Your father wants you present.

The words clang in my head like cold iron. My jaw tightens. I swallow the curse rising to my tongue and force myself to meet her eyes.

"I have to go," I say softly, brushing my knuckles along her cheek, needing the touch like air. "I'll be back as soon as I can. Harrid will keep a closer watch while I'm gone."

Her flushed face hardens, then her gaze flickers down, catching the faint bruises along my ribs I'd failed to hide. She touches them once — feather-light — but it burns through me all the same, possessiveness flaring hot and bright in my blood at being seen so gently, so fiercely.

"Be careful," she says darkly.

Then sharper still, her voice laced with steel "And if anyone puts more of those on you, no touching when you get back." A huff of laughter escapes me before I can stop it. Heat sparks low in my chest at her ferocity. She would be a formidable Ríganne. My Ríganne. The image lodges somewhere deep, warming a part of me I long thought dead. A Queen, my Ríganne by my side ruling the Court. I bow my head to her threat, despite the teasing curve of my mouth.

"Yes, Mo draganín," I murmur. "I'll make sure they know you are coming."

For a heartbeat, I let myself hold onto that fire — hers. A mortal flame, but no less fierce. Her protectiveness is not politics, nor brittle pride. It is raw, unshakable loyalty, born of love. And it burns brighter than any crown.

I will need that memory in the hours to come.

The Ember City of the Fire Court sprawls in fire and stone — carved into the volcanic mountain itself, alive with rivers of molten light. Towers of black obsidian rise like jagged teeth, glowing veins of magma threading through the cracks, illuminating the streets.

The air is heavy with ash, metallic heat burning in every breath.

The Fire Court thrives in this suffocating brilliance, their Kárith striding across crystal bridges with armour that reflects the inferno's glow.

They look at me as I pass, their gazes sharp and calculating.

To them, I am the Sun Prince — heir of prophecy and war, a blade forged by Air and tempered by every Court's expectation.

"I fucking hate it here." Maricus grumbles — a sentiment I agree with.

"Could this not have been an emissary?" he snaps. "Why me? Which in turn means you?"

I snort. "My apologies, but seeing as you interrupted my meal, I thought penance was due."

He pretends affronted. "You're still holding a grudge from the training grounds! How dare you use your power like this. Such a petty Prince." He waves a hand dramatically. I cuff him lightly in the stomach.

"No — you were right. My mind was elsewhere. I realised after our session something wasn't quite right."

"Interesting," he mutters to himself. I punch his arm.

"Not that I'm promising I won't bait you. I have rather enjoyed it. You do realise in the last few months your emotions have been reckless and haywire — it's something more than the bond—"

"I know, I—"

I stop mid-sentence as we enter the throne room.

The throne room is as merciless as the City outside. Heat ripples in the air, the walls pulsing faintly as though veins of fire run through them.

The Fire Court's relic — a spire of obsidian split with molten veins — glows like a wound at the centre of the dais. It throws long dark shadows, jagged and grasping, across courtiers who lounge in gilded discomfort, all sharp edges and sharper eyes.

The Princess makes her entrance with the subtlety of a flame catching dry tinder. Erif's gown flickers like living fire, every jewelled clasp catching the blaze until she seems almost too bright to look at. Her smile is jagged — beauty carved with cruelty.

"You must forgive our delay," she says, voice silk stretched thin over heat.

"We were occupied reinforcing our wards. Such a shame

about Water's... I hear they falter with every moon. Riddled with cracks a rogue Sylvari could cut through. But the pets are none the wiser, so it hardly matters. Although..."

Her eyes glitter.

"I hear a Fae has been keeping one of his own. In secret."

Her gaze flicks deliberately toward me. Before I can speak, Maricus laughs — low, dark, humourless. "Faulty for Water, perhaps. Yet the bodies left scattered at their borders — those who tried to cross them — burn just as well as any Fire Court execution."

He pauses. "We counted enough to know their ashes tell a different story. So, our little friends, no matter the Realm, should be fine." He grins like a Cheshire cat.

Her smile sharpens, predatory. "How droll. Still — smoke and corpses are hardly proof of strength. They reek more of desperation... or something being hidden."

I let her words linger, then step forward.

"Cousin." The currents stir. "I recall the last time you sought 'entertainment'. You thought to glamour a mortal into dancing for your amusement. Tell me — how would you like to become my entertainment? Dance for me until your feet become bloody stumps and your laughter becomes screams." I smile thinly. A murmur ripples through the chamber. "Stay away from places you do not belong," I finish softly.

Her lips part, outrage flashing before she masks it with brittle poise. But her eyes — dark, flickering with flame — betray the quiver beneath.

Beside me, Maricus throws his head back and laughs — low, delighted, cruel. Shadows coil tighter around him, fanning like smoke.

"Now that," he says, voice carrying, "was worth the trip to this hell pit. Was that diplomacy"

Erif knows now. We walk to the spire. Even from the doorway I feel the change. Where my uncle once walked with easy warmth, the hall is now perfected cruelty. It smells of hate.

The absence of him — the last Rívaran who refused to play for spectacle — has hollowed this place. It is sharper now, less forgiving; the flames here a poor imitation of what was.

The Princess perches near the throne, smirk already set, her gaze sliding over me as if measuring whether I'll make the whole discussion.

Courtiers cluster like moths to a lamp, glittering with expectation.

I reach through the link to Maricus — "two exits only. The one we entered, and the balcony beyond the throne looking over the courtyard. Too exposed if this goes poorly".

He snorts in my head, amusement laced with menace.

"Then I suppose we'll behead the runaway if we need a distraction. Might even improve the place."

The spire at the centre of the room rings, tugging at the magical essence of everyone who draws near.

Torches line the walls in black brackets; their flames crawl, licking the stone.

When the Fire Ríganne rises, the court falls silent — all frivolity gone in an instant, replaced by a frigid chill in the air. She steps down from the throne with the slow, practised grace of a predator casing its hunt.

Where once her voice would have been tempered for my uncle's steadier hand, she speaks now with the sharpness of someone who knows there's no one left to stop her wrath.

"So," she says, velvet burning into iron, "I hear your father bargains for marriage. Peace offered for Air, influence for Fire. A prisoner for a dowry — how convenient."

She rolls the last word over her tongue in a slow drawl, inspecting her fingernails as if they hold more interest than her guests. "Two Courts united beneath my daughter's crown. One less rival in the chase for the Sceptre. A tidy solution for Air…"

The Princess leans forward, her motion practised and cruel. She wants spectacle — chaos. Unseelie to the bone, a living wraith on the realm.

Maricus clears his throat behind me, a pointed reminder. *"Remember you're meant to be calm"*, he murmurs in my mind.

I simply smile and answer:

"No."

The single word lands like a gavel.

The Ríganne's smile thins into something colder. "What do you mean," she hisses, eyes narrowing into twin coals, "that you will not accept my offer? You refuse the Princess's hand?"

"I was not consulted," I say calmly, "nor do I care to please you by marrying her."

Every syllable is iron. *"What happened to staying calm"*, Maricus warns internally.

The Princess's amusement shatters into a sharp, mocking clap. "I hear you promised yourself to a human," she parrots. "To what mercy do you attach your crown, cursed prince?"

The Ríganne's lips curl. "Promised? Intriguing. Then perhaps we should negotiate elsewhere. We had hoped you'd exchange vows for something of greater... utility. A prisoner — the Sylvari captured on our border. He knows something of the Sceptre's trail. One who is missing a hand..."

My hands tighten at my sides. I want that thing dead — he escaped our prisons once, and here he is, how convenient.

"I will not entertain talk of marriage any further," I say. "No alliance is worth the corruption Fire would bring to my Court. Do not think I am unaware of your dalliance with witches." The promise in my voice is slow and inexorable. "Nor," I add, "will I trade a person for mere rumours."

I click my tongue and cross my arms, reining in my rising frustration. A soft, cruel laugh spills from the Ríganne. The Princess joins her — high, sharp, like broken glass. "Then perhaps your courage needs tempering in a cell," the Ríganne purrs. "For your lack of decorum." Her hand lifts in a graceful, contemptuous arc. "We can arrange a night of hospitality for you. You refuse the marriage? Fine. We will teach you manners in our dungeons. Or perhaps your human in our dungeon will change your mind."

Something in me drums low, volcanic.

"Aodhan, remember..." Maricus warns

I step forward until the torches catch the gold beneath my skin.

"You mistake me if you think this chamber intimidates me, Aunt." The title falls like a blade — disrespect sharpened deliberately.

The room feels the sting of it. "This hall is colder now that my uncle is gone. It suits you. But hear this: I will not let you bargain with my life. Not for power. Not for your amusement. And no human will ever enter your cell."

Her smile fractures. "Such insolence," she breathes.

Maricus's mental voice curls like smoke.

"You're reckless, Aodh. Let it be, and you might yet leave with your head, she will not continue to be insulted in front of her court."

My reply is simpler — slower — a promise forged in stone.

"Now, Aunt... you'd do well to remember whose son I am. You continue threatening me, and I may wipe this Court from every map." My magic flares, molten veins tracing heat across my arms. The spire hums in answer, singing with fire. "Tell your underlings who have been breaching the human realm — including your own spawn — that I no longer have the patience or restraint to hold back."

Gasps ripple through the hall — shock, fear, fascination, confusion. The Ríganne's composure cracks for a heartbeat — a tiny, lethal fissure — before smoothing like silk. "Perhaps," she says coldly, "you would do well to remember where you stand, dearest nephew..."

I grunt in response. Courtiers sway like drunkards — intoxicated by tension, drinking in every drop of the looming storm.

"Then we are at an impasse," the Ríganne intones, hands folding in front of her.

Guards shift, armour creaking like stone under strain.

Heat spikes. The torches flare high, serpents of flame coiling and striking before snapping back under control. The air tastes of scorched metal and old ash. Maricus steps forward — polished ease, quiet danger — his tone perfectly pleasant, edged like a velvet-wrapped dagger. "So this is how Fire treats a visiting prince? How very... unfamiliar. Shall we take our leave, Your Highness?"

"You'll leave," the Ríganne replies, voice calm and steady, "when I am satisfied."

She leans back into the throne with a predator's grace.

Flames gutter lower, waiting.

At the edge of my mind, Harrid's presence brushes cold:

Property clear. Lily safe. Luc intercepted a Sylvari trailing Daisy.

Relief hits me so hard my knuckles ache.

I answer quickly, *"Was the Sylvari Fire Court?"*

"Nothing concrete," he replies.

I incline my head the barest fraction — a courtesy, not a bow.

"Then satisfy yourself quickly, Your Majesty. I have somewhere far more important to be."

The Princess tilts her head, lips curving in wicked delight. "I do hope you survive this temper of yours, Sun Prince," she purrs. "I'd hate to be bored."

The Ríganne cuts her a look, unimpressed. "You will entertain me, dearest nephew, and then we will discuss what your options are."

The guards advance a step. Spears and blades hiss as runes heat.

Courtiers lean forward, hungry.

I let a cold smile curve my mouth — clean as high air above the spires.

"Fine," I say softly. The sooner this is done, the better.

CHAPTER 37

Aodhan POV

They ascend at once, hurling blades, magic with all their might. I throw my head back and laugh, a bark laugh so loud it spooks the Fae still dancing, relishing in the chaos. I entertain the first few blows, dodging, moving slightly before the blow strikes. Winking at my Aunt, I roll my shoulders letting my wings unfurl, spreading each tendril then letting them alight. I take flight, the air billowing around the room, sending a wave of air and heat, scattering all the guards sprawled across the room.

Every gust I send remind me of home — of her. If I lose myself here, if they bring me down in this pit of fire and ash, she will be alone. The thought is more dangerous than any blade in this throne room. It sharpens me, steadies me. She is my anchor, even in mock battle.

I look to the Ríganne, laugh again before extending my wings once more, no need for magic, no need to strike. Let the momentum build just enough for gale-force winds to whip around the chamber, sending glasses crashing, guards sprawling.

A flicker of movement from the throne. The Princess straightens, her smirk faltering for the first time. Around her, courtiers shift uneasily, their masks of composure slipping as the temperature in the hall dips sharply despite the flames — a storm rising in a furnace.

Several courtiers glance toward the far-left alcove. A place usually abandoned during audiences. Not tonight. Wisps curl there in uneasy shapes, and I note three Kárith wearing colours not of Fire, but of mixed allegiance.

So... alliances shift already. Cowards. Opportunists. Waiting to see who bleeds first.

The Ríganne doesn't blink. "Enough," she says, the word a whip-crack of command. Fire flares, then stills as though obeying her. "Erif. Out." The Princess bristles, lips parting to protest, but the Ríganne's gaze cuts to her — a single, lethal glance. "I said out. All of you. Leave."

The courtiers hesitate only a moment before obeying. Silk rustles, whispers scrape like embers as they retreat in tight clusters, casting glances over their shoulders. Erif rises last, her heels striking sharp against the stone as she stalks past me, perfume and smoke trailing in her wake. Her eyes promise she'll make me pay for the insult; mine promise she won't like the cost.

The doors slam shut behind them, the hall exhales. We are three now: flame, storm, and night.

The Ríganne sits back against her throne, fingers steepled, her eyes like dark coals. Exhaustion softens her edges.

"You and your theatrics...," she murmurs. "Now we can speak freely."

I let out a humourless breath. "Aunt," I return deliberately, the syllable bouncing between us. "Your hall feels colder than my last visit.

All this fire, yet not an ounce of warmth left. If I had burnt it down, at least it would have been an improvement."

Her brows rise, but amusement glints behind the molten black of her eyes.

"Temper, temper," she says lightly, though her tone is edged. "It hasn't changed at all. Nearly tore the roof off my hall just now."

"I could have," I answer quietly. "Wouldn't have made a difference. The hall's a mess. Nothing but snakes and traitors."

Maricus snorts faintly beside me, though his eyes stay fixed on her — a Water Fae refusing to trust a flame.

"So it's true," she says as she rises, her gown trailing sparks across the stone. For the first time she smiles — an honest grin, almost familial. "The prophecy was no lie. The Air Prince, bound to a mortal… fated to bring ruin and rebirth."

Prophecy. Ruin and rebirth.

The words spear through me. I force stillness.

"What do you know?" My voice is cold, apprehension threading through it.

She tilts her head, eyes gleaming with old fire.

"Enough to know your mortal is not safe. Enough to know every eye is on her — mine included. Watch her carefully, nephew. Or you'll lose more than your throne."

Nephew.

A title she uses only when she means every word.

"Power plays for the Sceptre are growing," she continues, voice low now. "The whispers are louder with every rumour. Old allegiances cracking. Some dream of one ruler holding the Sceptre — uniting or crushing all. Downfall for the kingdoms if they fail to bend. Or something worse. You must be careful moving forward. Especially within your court."

"Then you know why I came," I say. "Release the Sylvari."

Her eyes narrow. "And if I don't?"

Wind coils tighter, bowing banners, rattling sconces, snuffing flames.

"Then I will continue with my theatrics," I say softly.

She sighs, unimpressed.

"Nephew. Four hundred and fifty years, and you still let your power speak before your mind."

The cells sit deep beneath the Fire Court, colder than any mountain cave, damp stone humming with old wards. Shadows cling to corners like cobwebs.

The Sylvari slumps against the wall, wrists shackled, eyes fractured-glass bright.

"You think you can keep her safe," he rasps. "But you can't.

None of you can."

"She's the key," he says, laughing brokenly. "And every realm wants the key." My magic surges, crawling gold up the walls, chains rattling under the strain. "It's not just her," he continues. "The girl burns bright — he can smell her. And the boy... he carries his father's strength. What do you think the other Courts will do with such a weapon? A family... quite intriguing. And you still knows nothing of his families death or the true mastermind."

Wind roars low, slamming him back. "Run home, Prince. Before he finds her. Before her little ones bleed for her power."

"Kill him," I tell Maricus. "Double the Kárith. No one speaks of this."

Far below, where nothing goes unseen a ripple runs through the Fire Court. Erif slips into an alcove, smile fading into something cold.

"Tell our liege," she breathes, "the prophecy holds. The prince burns for her. And the Sylvari sings of children."

The figure's listen. Then vanish.

Erif's smirk returns — harmless, polished — as she steps back into the light.

Midnight settles over the property. Wards hum steady.
And there she is.

Lily lies curled on the couch, wrapped in one of my shirts. Soft. Warm. Peaceful. A book rests forgotten on her lap, lamplight gilding her in gold. She looks like peace. Like home. Like everything I cannot lose. I kneel beside her, letting her presence soften every sharp edge in me. Her lashes flutter open, eyes hazy with sleep.

"You're home," she whispers.

"I will always make it back to you."

She pulls me down into her arms. The storm quiets. The fire fades. No Politics.

Here, I am simply Aodhan.

Here, I am just hers.

CHAPTER 38

Lily POV

I wake to find a note resting on the night stand, written in Aodhan's precise, elegant hand.

Ellisar will be by today.
My first Firalen, my confidant, my oldest friend.
She says she has something important to discuss with us both. —A

I read it twice, then a third time, nerves knotting sharper with each pass. Ellisar. The one he trusts above all others The blade at his side for centuries. A strategist, a soldier, a whisper in war councils. I'd pictured someone carved from ice and steel — older, colder, untouchable. A force to be reckoned with.

She is nothing like I imagined. Tall. Willowy. Lean but muscular. Hair like silver-blonde waves spilling to her waist, catching the morning light as though spun from moon-water. Storm-cloud grey eyes — sharp, assessing — and yet when they find mine, something softens. She is... ethereal.

"Lily," she says warmly, crossing the room without hesitation. She smells faintly of ocean spray and crushed mint as she pulls me into a hug so tight it knocks the breath from me.

"Finally. I've heard so much about you. You're far cuter — and younger — than I expected. He really is not good enough for you," she mutters at the end.

I blink, stunned, hugging her back, suddenly feeling like a child in her presence.

It doesn't feel like meeting a stranger. It feels like meeting an old friend. When she steps away, her gaze sweeps the kitchen with quiet precision. Power hums around her — leashed, disciplined, steady.

"Your mum or dad," she asks lightly, "any chance either of them were Fae?"

The question lands like a rock in a pond. "No," I say quickly. "Not that I know of. My mum died when I was little. Dad's... Dad. Human. Odd but ordinary."

Her brow furrows. "Did your mum look like you?" Her tone stays gentle, but something sharpens in her eyes. "Sometimes traces of bloodlines run quieter than the Courts want you to believe. Prophecy leaves traces... and sometimes those traces can be erased. Other times they're left in plain sight."

My heart stutters. "Erased?"

Before she can answer, the wards ripple. My head snaps toward the door — But Ellisar is already moving.

Aodhan steps through. His shirt is torn, streaked with blood and dirt. His marks pulse beneath his skin, flaring bright. His eyes are dark, dangerous — storm-wrath barely caged. For a heartbeat, I can't breathe.

Then his gaze finds mine. Everything shatters. He crosses the room in long strides, air curling around me like a shield before he even reaches me. "Lily," he breathes, forehead dropping to mine. The tension drains out of him in a single shuddering rush. My fingers grip the torn fabric of his shirt.

"What happened?" My voice trembles.

"I'm fine," he whispers, though he leans on me like he's been holding up the sky. Behind us, Ellisar clears her throat. "Aodh."

Her tone is calm, but her eyes sharpen at the sight of him. He finally turns. Ellisar."

"She's gorgeous," Ellisar says simply. "Exactly as I expected." Then her gaze clicks into action. "But before we continue — what happened? Maricus did not say."

"There was an ambush," he says flatly. "A witch on the run. Then a wyvern. Maricus caught most of it."

Ellisar's face hardens. "Wyverns, openly? That means someone's escalating. The old treaties won't hold if monsters are being unleashed." Her gaze flicks to me, softening.

"Forgive me, Lily. I know this is all new." I flush, but she doesn't pause. "That isn't why I came." The room stills. The mate bond," Ellisar says.

Every nerve in my body tightens. "What about it?" Her magic pulses faintly against my skin, like static. "Someone tried to erase her from you, Aodh. The bond should have pulled you together long before now — but it was muted. Blinded. It wasn't chance. It was deliberate. Ley lines have been destroyed and... Dark magic has been used old, evil." A sigh escapes her lips, "Sacrifices were made."

The words hit like a blow. Aodhan doesn't move. "Who?" he asks, voice iron.

"Your mother." Ellisar keeps her voice low.

"Every trail I followed ended in blood. Whoever orchestrated this killed to keep it hidden. Seers who might have spoken of it are gone. Records erased. I can feel the gaps themselves." Her jaw tightens.

"My mother remembered fragments before they silenced her too. I have my suspicions." A hush falls. My stomach twists.

"Hidden? From who? Why?"

"From everyone," Ellisar says. "But especially him." Aodhan's hand flexes around mine. Ellisar gives a single sharp nod. "I can't confirm the architect. But every path leads back to him — power shifted, prophecies bent, allies silenced. He altered the texts; that much is clear." The room feels smaller, colder. "But the bond," she continues, "that's older magic. Older than I know how to track. There's more than one player involved, and whatever they used... it leaves no normal trace. It's like chasing ghosts in smoke."

Aodhan's knuckles whiten.

Ellisar nods again. "If the mastermind knows you've found her — after all the blood spilled to keep you apart — it will not end well. The Courts are whispering about a new hierarchy. One ruler claiming the Sceptre as their own. The downfall of kingdoms. The prophecy doesn't read the same anymore, Aodh. Someone has been rewriting fate."

Silence follows. Aodhan sends warmth through the bond, steadying me.

Ellisar exhales. "I'll double the patrols. Tighten the guard. If there's a weak link, we'll root it out. And I'll reach out to Perzia. She may know how to unpick what witches have hidden — she's still in hiding from the last revolt in the Verdant Veil."

Aodhan gives a curt nod.

"Do it, she will be hidden in Air for now."

Ellisar's gaze lingers on him — then on me. "He's different with you, Lily. Less weapon, more man. My mother once whispered that a bond like this would shake the realms if it ever appeared. Maybe that's why they tried so hard to erase it."

Then she's gone, her magic folding away like a breath disappearing. The kitchen feels too small. Aodhan stands frozen, jaw locked tight.

"Aodh," I whisper.

His gaze lifts to mine — molten, raw. "She knew," he murmurs. "All this time... she knew."

I squeeze his hand. "Knew what?" His eyes darken with memory.

"When I was a child, Ellisar's mother tutored me, as my mother had already been taken. She taught weapons, lore. Prophecy. My father called her riddles ridiculous. But she was friends with my mother. Once... she pulled me aside after court."

His voice is hoarse. "She told me there would come a time when the wind would fail me, when fire would burn against me, when earth would rise in fury and water would try to drown me. She said the only way I'd survive would be to find the one who carried all of them."

A shiver races down my spine. "All... elements?"

He nods slowly. "I thought she meant allegiances. A diplomat. A ruler." His gaze locks with mine. "But she wasn't speaking of allegiances. She was speaking of you."

My stomach drops. "Me?"

"You felt it when you held the shard," he says quietly. "All four elements answered you. That shouldn't be possible. No one born of this world can wield more than one."

The room tilts.

"And your father...?"

"He dismissed her visions as myth. But when she tried to warn the others — when she tried to record her prophecies — her writings vanished. Then she vanished. No body. No grave. Nothing." His hand tightens around mine. "And now Ellisar confirms the bond was hidden. Deliberately. And my mother possibly being a sacrifice." He swallows hard. "He must have known. He must have feared what she foresaw."

My breath stutters. "If she was right... if I'm what she saw... then this isn't just about the bond, is it? It's about the Sceptre. About everything."

His thumb strokes my hand, gentle despite the storm radiating from him. "It's about war, Lily. And you're at the centre of it — whether we want it or not."

Aodhan goes still — Wind coils around his ankles, sharp and cold as winter breath. His magic flare once, violently, before he clamps his magic down so hard the lights flicker.

He steps back from the counter, chest rising in shallow, uneven breaths. For a heartbeat I think he'll speak — but instead his fist snaps forward, slamming into the edge of the kitchen island. Stone cracks beneath his knuckles with a sharp, brutal sound, like thunder trapped in a small space.

"Aodha—"

He bows his head, shoulders trembling, magic spinning around him in frantic spirals.

"I searched for you," he whispers, voice ragged with something I've never heard from him before — grief. "For years without knowing what I was missing. I felt the absence... like a wound that wouldn't heal." His hand braces against the fractured counter. "And someone stole that from us. He took you from me before I even knew your name. Before I even knew you were a possibility."

The storm inside him lashes outward — then collapses inward when I touch his arm.

He exhales, shaking, forehead dropping to my shoulder. I don't know when I moved, but suddenly I'm sitting on his lap, his forehead pressed to mine. His breathing is ragged, his power a quiet, strained hum. I reach out and hold him, stroking his back slow and calming.

The words echo through me long after they fall silent.

All four elements. One who can wake what sleeps. One who can unite what's broken.

It shouldn't be me. I'm just… Lily. A barista. A mum. Someone who once cried because the dishwasher broke and the kids wouldn't eat their dinner. I'm not a Ríganne, Ruler or a warrior or a chosen anything. But the warning sits like heat under my skin, spreading wider with each breath until I can't tell where fear ends and fury begins. Someone hid the bond. Someone erased me from him. Someone decided I wasn't allowed to exist in his future. And the kids.

My arms wrap around myself before I realise I'm moving. My throat tightens, breath stuttering. What if they come for Oliver? For Daisy?

A cold certainty curls through me, sharp and unyielding. "If this is a prophecy," I whisper, barely audible even to myself, "then they should be afraid. Because if they try to take anything from me… I'll make sure they can't use me."

Aodhan's hand closes over mine, steady and warm, grounding me. "You… Lily, never ever place yourself in harm's way" he says softly.

But deep down, beneath the fear… something else stirs. Something old. Something fierce. Something that feels like the earth itself shifting under my skin, like the wind gathering at my back. Maybe Ellisar's mother was right. Maybe what's waking inside me isn't something to fear…

But something the realms should.

CHAPTER 39

Lily POV

The mornings feel different now. The season has slipped into our pre-summer storms — cooler, sharper. The edges of the air carry that crisp bite that comes after relentless rain and wild winds. Even the light has shifted: longer later dawns, slower dusks everything stretched thin and restless. I can feel it in my bones, the wheel turning, time pulling us forward whether we're ready or not.

It's been eight months since Daisy's accident. Eight months since the veil between the life I thought I knew and the truth of what lay beyond tore open — and nothing has been the same since.

Now, impossibly, she's graduating. Nearly eighteen, her whole life stretching out in front of her like a blank page waiting for her story to begin.

Oliver is only a year behind, restless in ways that ache to watch. Both of them caught on the edge between childhood and the vast unknown, and I can already feel them slipping into it, step by step.

They sit at the kitchen table together, breakfast half-eaten, the scene so ordinary it almost hurts. Daisy scrolls her phone, her cap and gown folded neatly in the corner like a warning —

as if touching it too soon might make it real. Oliver drums his fingers against the wood, gaze distant, already chasing horizons I can't see.

"Feels weird, doesn't it?" Daisy says suddenly, not looking up. Her voice is casual, but poking for interest. "Like... everything's ending and starting at the same time."

Oliver smirks, though it doesn't reach his eyes. "You're just happy you'll never have to sit through Mr Dalton's English lectures again."

She snorts, grin quick and bright, but softer words linger beneath it.

"That too. But it's more than that. Now..." Her voice falters, the admission heavier than she meant to let slip. Oliver bumps her elbow, a crooked grin pulling through the distance in his eyes. "You'll be fine. You're tougher than half the Fae, Harrid tells me about. You're basically invincible now."

From the doorway, Harrid raises one dark brow, dark shadows coiling lazily at his feet like cats in waiting. "Invincible is... generous," he says dryly. "Stubborn, maybe."

Daisy groans, rolling her eyes, but her smile lingers — softened by something quieter. Trust. Safety. A bond I hadn't expected to form so easily. Oliver leans back, fingers still drumming. His gaze flicks toward Harrid, sharper now — not just curiosity, but hunger. "You ever think about showing me more of the realm?" he asks. "The real thing. Not just stories or training drills."

The question hangs heavy, a challenge wrapped in longing, like he's already halfway decided. Harrid's expression doesn't shift, but something flickers in his eyes. The magic coiling at his feet stir, restless. "Perhaps," he says at last. "When the time is right."

The answer snuffs out the lightness in the room. It doesn't satisfy Oliver. I see it in the way his jaw tenses — but he lets it go. For now.

The café hums around us, warm and alive, espresso and

baked bread wrapping every conversation. Sal has extra staff on, moving like clockwork behind the counter. The clatter of mugs, the hiss of the machine, the low murmur of customers — it all runs without me now, a rhythm I built but no longer have to hold.

Mr Fisher walks in with his gentle smile and takes his regular seat, mumbling about the goats getting in and destroying his crops. I chuckle, noting to talk to Oli and Harrid about popping over to help.

Vivienne leans against the counter like she belongs there — sleeves rolled, hair catching the light in a dark ripple. She has always carried herself with control, everything about her precise and well ordered. Her eyes scan my face, sharper than any knife.

"You're thinking about taking time off," she says. Not a question. I sigh, wiping my hands on an already-clean cloth. "Maybe after graduation. Sal can manage here, and Dad can watch the house." I hesitate. "I was thinking..." My voice dips. "Of seeing the realm. With the kids. Maybe."

Vivienne's brow furrows. Her voice softens — but it stays firm. "Lil..."

"I know." I lift a hand before she can start. "I know it's dangerous. I know it's all-consuming. But we've been living with danger for months. At some point, we have to start living with possibility too."

Her expression softens — barely. "I like him, Lil. Really. But mate bond or not, you need to know who you're with. Don't let magic blind you to the man or Fae."

I meet her gaze, steady. "You know me. I would never be with someone who endangered my kids. Yes, we're still getting to know each other, but I see him. I see what he carries. And... it is hard to describe. It is like I have always known him... But I'll be careful."

Vivienne nods slowly, though doubt lingers behind her eyes. "Good. Because the last time I ignored red flags, it nearly killed me. You and Cal pulled me out. I won't watch you walk into the same fire."

I squeeze her hand. "I won't." Her lips twitch — her version of a smile. "Then I'll stop mother-henning. For now..."

That night, the house is quiet. The kind of quiet that feels like the world holding its breath. I dig through an old box of trinkets at the back of my wardrobe, the cardboard soft with age. Graduation deserves something special.

My fingers find it easily: the emerald pendant Cal gave me years ago, wrapped in delicate silver claws shaped like curling vines. Strong. Wild. Beautiful. Daisy to her core.

Tears prick as I hold it up to the lamplight, the green scattering it like living fire.

Memory rises — Cal's warm hands fastening it at my throat, his teasing voice, the affection in his eyes.

It feels right to pass it on now. A legacy. A reminder. Something from her father as she steps out of childhood and into whatever comes next.

I wrap it carefully in tissue, already planning to find earrings to match.

The lights flicker.

Cold. Sharp. Dark. Shadows stretch long and thin across the floorboards.

"Thoughtful gift," a voice drawls, amused.

I whirl, heart leaping into my throat. Maricus steps from the corner as if he's always been there, smirk sharp as a blade.

"God," I snap. "Do you practise being creepy, or does it just come naturally?"

"A bit of both," he says lightly, though his gaze lingers on the pendant with a flicker of interest. "You've changed, Lily. Not the same fragile mortal I first saw. Almost... alive. Dangerous now."

I narrow my eyes. "Is that a compliment?"

"Take it how you like." His shrug is lazy. His eyes are not. "But you should know — Aodhan is more powerful than he lets on. More dangerous, too."

My heart stutters — but my voice stays steady. "And what are you really saying, Maricus?"

His grin falters for a heartbeat — grief or jealousy flickering beneath the mask.

Gone as quickly as it came. But I saw it. "You hide behind that smirk," I say softly. "But it's not the truth. You're hiding something. I don't know if it's to help... or to destroy us."

The mask slips. His jaw tightens, his magic so like Harrids coiling like snakes.

Then the smirk returns, sharper and crueller. "Careful, Lily," he murmurs. "Reading Fae is a dangerous game." I step closer, refusing to back down. "I know he trusts you. I want to trust you too. But if you're playing both sides — I will find out. And I won't forgive you."

Something in his expression ticks. "I think she'll love the gift," he says. "One thing I will say — mothers here in this realm are very different to the Fae. She is lucky to have you." I open my mouth to ask about his family — but with a mocking bow, he melts back into the dark crevess in the corner, leaving the air colder and the pendant heavier in my palm.

Later, Aodhan finds me in the living room, his presence filling the space before he even speaks. The tension in his shoulders, the storm he always carries — eases the moment his eyes meet mine. Before I can stand, Daisy pokes her head out of the hallway, grin wicked, eyes bright.

"Hey, Aodhan," she calls, dragging out his name. "Graduation's coming up, it is a mortal thing. Will you be Mum's plus one? Please?"

He glances at me, surprise flickering, then warmth replacing it. "Plus one?"

"Yeah — her date."

"Are we not passed dating already?" His confusion is painfully sincere.

Daisy giggles. "Will you come and be her guest?"

"I will go," he says simply, "if she will allow me." My heart stumbles, heat climbing my cheeks. The bond hums steady, sure, and I manage a soft, certain—"Always."

Daisy beams, triumphant. "Good. Because I also want to borrow Luc for the after party. He can glam up as my cousin or something. I need a wingman."

From deeper in the hall, Oliver groans. "Gods, Daisy. You're shameless."

"Practical," she fires back. "There's a difference."

Aodhan chuckles, low and warm, the sound loosening something deep inside me. His hand brushes mine as he leans against the doorway.

Though his words are directed at Daisy, his gaze lingers on me with quiet pride. "I think we can arrange that."

Daisy squeals, Oliver mutters about Luc regretting every future party, and for the first time all day, the house feels light again.

When Aodhan's fingers lace with mine, steady and sure, I realise: This warmth, this mess, this life — is what we're really fighting for, it doesn't matter the race or realm.

CHAPTER 40

Lily POV

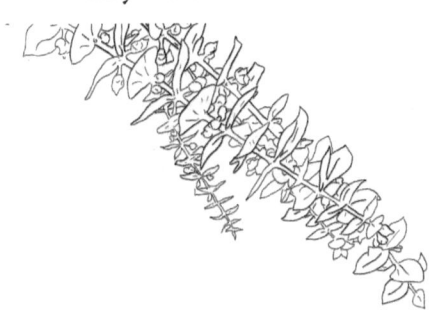

Daisy's graduation — a rhythm that feels both ordinary and monumental all at once. Steam curls from the bathroom, carrying the sharp tang of hairspray and perfume.

Daisy darts between rooms in half-finished makeup, her gown draped over one arm as though it might be lost if she doesn't hold it firmly in her grasp.

Oliver, pretending he isn't fussing, keeps tugging at the knot of his tie in the hallway mirror.

Dad is already on his second pot of coffee, the rich scent filling every corner of the kitchen, grounding us all in something familiar.

I try to pin back a stray lock of Daisy's hair, but she swats my hands away with a grin. "Mum, stop. I've got it."

"Wait." My voice softens as I reach for the small box on the counter. Her eyes widen when I press it into her palm. She opens it slowly, reverently, and the emerald pendant gleams in the morning light.

My heart twists, but not with grief not this time. With awe. With love. My baby — my firstborn — the best parts of us both live in her. Cal would be so proud of the young woman she's becoming. "It feels right that it's yours now," I whisper. "Your graduation. Your future. You'll carry him with you."

Her voice wavers, eyes shining as she clasps the chain around her neck. "Mum..." One word, heavy with every ache and every tether of love that binds us to the man we lost.

Before the tears can spill, I pull out a second gift — new earrings I found in Rivertide, silver with drops of emerald cut to catch the light. They glitter green-gold as I clip them into her ears, catching the tears she tries fiercely to blink away.

Then Luc steps forward, fidgeting like a soldier stripped of his armour. His ears burn red as he slips a bracelet onto Daisy's wrist — a slender band etched with his crest, the faint shimmer of protective runes barely visible.

"So you don't forget your guard up there — with all those other humans," he mutters.

Daisy laughs through the tears and grabs his hand, but she doesn't let go. Not right away. Her cheeks glow pink.

And then Aodhan moves forward. In his hand rests a delicate hairpiece wrought of silver, set with emerald and topaz that shimmer like caught sunlight. His fingers are careful, reverent, as he tucks it into Daisy's hair himself.

"Something fitting for an Air Princess," he says softly, smiling as he squeezes her hand. "I'm deeply honoured you've accepted me... and allowed me to attend."

"Well, of course — we're family now." Daisy beams, cheeks flushed, radiant with youth and the weight of legacy she doesn't yet know she carries. For a heartbeat, she looks every inch her father's daughter — fire and earth twined in green-gold light.

And then it's time.

Daisy's cap is crooked. She pretends not to notice, chin tipped high, lips shaped in that don't-you-dare grin she uses to dare the world to try her. Oliver fixes it anyway, quick and careful, and she lets him — because today she's a storm wrapped around a soft centre, and he's the only one allowed there.

The ceremony is both endless and too quick — a blur of names, applause rising and falling like waves, cameras flashing, gowns too big, shoes too tight, boys grinning as they celebrate the end of school, and girls crying as they promise to stay friends.

The gym smells of flowers and nervous sweat, parents clapping too hard, teachers blinking back pride behind stern expressions. I clap until my palms sting, my throat raw from cheering — because this is Daisy. My girl. Radiant. Full of life. With her future just beginning.

Aodhan stands at the back of the hall, every woman stealing glances at him — he sticks out like a sore thumb, far too tall and far too alluring. Harrid ghosts the aisles unseen. Kaelen keeps to the bleachers, scanning every exit with the precision of a soldier who never stops calculating. Yasar leans against the far doors, posture loose but gaze sharp as a blade — a warrior in plain sight. Naralle texts me a photo of latte art shaped like lilies: All good here, boss.

When Daisy's name rings out, the world shifts. She glows. She looks to the audience, smiles and waves with a nervous hand. Oliver whistles loud enough to shock those around us, sending her into giggles. But then her gaze finds mine — and pride crashes through me so fiercely my chest swells with pride.

The photos are chaos — arms flung over shoulders, faces pressed close, the camera never quite catching the fullness of the moment. Daisy smells of flowers and hairspray and youth; her pendant is cool against my chest when I hug her tight.

"Go on," I whisper, pressing her hands into Luc's. "Go celebrate. Have fun. Look after my baby girl, Luc."

"Muuum..." she groans loudly.

Luc nods, solemn. "I will. You have my word my Lady." And then they're gone — Daisy, Luc, and a whirlwind of friends spilling into cars, their laughter trailing behind them like streamers. I hear one of her friends ask loudly, "When did your mum get with that hottie? And does he have any friends?"

Oliver walks away disgusted before muttering to Aodhan, "High-school girls are terrifying. I'm not introducing any of my mates."

Aodhan claps a hand on his back. "All women can be scary. I wouldn't introduce mine either — they wouldn't be impressed with their high pitch or the amount of talking…" Oliver laughs — camaraderie settling between them.

We head into Rivertide. Dinner feels like a reward — the kind of night that threads itself into memory.

The seafood is fresh, the food rich with garlic and herbs, the scent wafting around the table.

Warm lights, clinking glasses, fresh bread still steaming from the kitchen. Fish platters big enough to drown in. Too many drinks passed hand to hand.

Oliver tells stories that make Dad laugh so hard he hides behind his napkin, shoulders shaking with quiet joy. Emma and Viv slip into their wild-aunt roles, stealing food from each other's plates, bickering like teenagers until the waiter hides a smile. Their joy is infectious, spilling over the table, making the entire night glow.

Aodhan sits beside me, quiet but steady, ever-present. His hand rests on the table near mine, fingers brushing just enough to remind me he's there. He leans in when Oliver talks about next year, asks questions that make my son sit on edge, hopeful for an invitation to the Fae realm.

Pride lights his eyes.

He teases Dad gently, pulling a rare grin from him — the kind that softens years of hard work raising girls and grandkids, revealing the once-youthful man who loved to laugh and drink and cook.

Dessert arrives — rich chocolate cake, bowls of gelato, tiramisu that Emma swears she'll "just taste" before eating half of it without spilling a crumb. The restaurant's lighting dims, candles melting low in their holders. Everyone feels light and carefree.

I look around the table. Aodhan sits opposite, deceptively calm, his attention fixed on my cheesecake with open hunger. I try to sneak a spoonful for him, leaning across the table with a grin—

And the world shatters. The first sign is the pressure.

The air thickens beneath the table, heavy and wrong, as though gravity itself sharply inhales. Dark wisps unfurl from the shadows at our feet — thin at first, like smoke, then solidifying into oily tendrils of living void.

"Under the table!" Aodhan roars.

Chaos detonates in the same breath.

Yasaar appears launching herself onto the tabletop in a blur of motion, overturning plates and sending glassware shattering. Aodhan moves faster than thought — he dives for Oliver and me, dragging us both down as the room is swallowed whole by a darkness so absolute I cannot even see my own hands. Only Aodhan glows.

Light burns beneath his skin in fierce, sun-gold flares. The markings along his arms ignite, throwing angular shadows across his face as he wraps himself around us. A pocket of breathable air snaps closed around the three of us, shielding us from the suffocating, crushing dark beyond.

My body breaks into a cold sweat. My heart hammers so violently it feels like it might tear free of my ribs. Fear seeps into every pore.

"Dad!" I scream into the void. "Viv! Emma!"

Laughter answers me. Not laughter that belongs to a human. A wet, echoing cackle ripples through the darkness, too deep, too hollow, as if it crawls up from an endless pit rather than a throat. Then the voice follows — hoarse, ancient, steeped in rot and malice.

"Well, well, well... little prince. Shall we play a game?"

Aodhan goes rigid around us. His body vibrates with restrained violence, his jaw clenched so hard I can hear his teeth grind. He does not respond.

"Come now," the voice taunts. "You and your precious underlings must decide which path you wish to follow. Will you choose the truth... or the human child who carries the royal line?"

At the final words, Aodhan's grip tightens with a violence I feel through bone and muscle. His fingers dig into my shoulder, not enough to hurt — but enough that I know how close he is to losing control.

The room fractures.

Cracks ripple through the air as if reality itself is splitting like faulty glass. Lightning erupts across the ceiling, forked white-gold bolts streaking over tables and walls. Screams tear through the restaurant.

Chairs overturn. Glass rains down in glittering storms. Oliver begins to shake violently against me.

Aodhan leans down to him, voice low and urgent, steady despite the carnage beyond our shield. "Oliver. I have you. Nothing will harm you. Not you — and not your mum. But I need you to listen now."

Oliver's breath stutters. His eyes shine with fear. "What... what if something happens to you too? I can't lose someone else."

Aodhan cups the back of his head gently. "You won't. I promise you — I will come back. But I need you to stay right here. Hold this pendant and do not let go. Do not let your mum leave this space. Ever. This is important." His gaze is fierce. "Do you understand?"

Oliver swallows, then nods.

A quiet sniffle escapes me. "You'd better come back unharmed, Aodhan. I mean it."

He presses a kiss to the crown of my head, lingering for a heartbeat too long — then he's gone. "Kaelen. Yasaar." His voice turns lethal. "You both know what I expect of you. And what the consequences will be if any one of them is hurt."

A small, terrified squeak sounds from Yasaar — her fear not of what hunts us in the dark, but of her Prince's wrath should she fail.

A chair scrapes across the floor. Fabric whispers through the darkness as something stands and steps forward.

"So," Aodhan's voice growls from somewhere beyond the shield, "what game is it you want to play? Because I am not in a forgiving mood after you threatened my family."

Cold laughter answers him.

"We know your weakness. There will be no more negotiations. Too many of our kind are dying at the hands of your filthy Fae. We want what belongs to the old blood. And you will not have the royal line. You, Fae-killer, do not deserve her — nor the power she carries. She belongs to our Leige."

The floor vanishes beneath my feet. A chasm of pure shadow yawns open, swallowing the light. Black tendrils snake up from the void and coil around my ankles, my calves, burning cold against my skin. I scream. The shadows surge for Oliver.

He shrieks as they wrap around his torso and arms, writhing like living chains as he fights uselessly against them. I lunge for him, clutching his hands as terror rips me raw.

Aodhan snaps his head in our direction — and charges.

He is struck mid-step by an invisible wall of force. The impact is explosive. A deafening crack echoes as he is hurled across the room and slams into the far wall with bone-shuddering force.

Panic consumes me. I pull Oliver against my chest, clinging to him as the shadows tighten their grip. My lungs burn. My throat is raw with screaming. The world collapses into terror and darkness and the violent thunder of my heart. Then—

Rage answers.

Wind detonates outward from Aodhan in a catastrophic burst. The storm he unleashes is alive — cyclonic gusts whip through the restaurant, ripping tablecloths free, sending debris hurtling like shrapnel. Thunder booms so violently the floor shudders.

Golden eyes blaze through the dark.

Lightning slams again and again, faster now, brighter, the light tearing the shadows apart in shredded ribbons. The tendrils around us recoil, shrivelling under the assault.

In the brief flashes of illumination, I glimpse bodies strewn across the restaurant — some unmistakably Fae, others twisted into something more animal than man. Clawed hands. Coiling tails. Too many joints. Too many teeth.

In a sudden, terrible stillness, Aodhan's voice carries cleanly through the dark.

"You want my Lily." A pause. My carefree Aodhan gone. Before me stands a killer. Soft. Deadly. Lethal. His voice echoing through the dark.

"Now it is my turn to play."

What follows is not a battle. It is a slaughter. Aodhan's eyes the only thing visible - a storm flashing with each strike.

Thunder fractures the air. Wind coils through the restaurant, tearing shadows from corners with surgical precision. Lightning answers Aodhan's fury in controlled, lethal arcs, flashing exactly where he wills it, illuminating his path like a spotlight on an executioner. He commands with motion.

One of the creatures lunges blindly through the dark, claws slashing where he stood moments before.

Aodhan is already behind it. His hand closes around the base of its skull.

There is a sharp, yank and twist. The body drops instantly — neck severed cleanly; spine reduced to wet fragments. He does not slow. He does not look back.

Aodhan moves without hesitation. "Yasaar —control the fallout. No breaches near the other mortals."

"Yes, Sire," she answers, voice tight but unwavering.

Lightning strikes again, revealing three shapes slithering together near the fallen wine rack — taloned, hunched, eyes burning ember-red. One opens its mouth far too wide, shrieking as it charges.

Aodhan meets it head-on. He drives his forearm straight through its chest. The creature convulses violently, its scream choking off as golden light floods its ribcage from the inside out.

Aodhan wrenches his arm free, tossing the corpse aside like broken furniture.

The second beast strikes from above. It never lands. Aodhan catches it mid-leap in a cyclone of wind and slams it into the ceiling with bone-crushing force. The impact shatters stone and sinew alike. Its body drops in pieces.

A bolt of lightning lashes from his palm, spearing it through the spine and pinning it screaming to the far wall. He approaches slowly, deliberately — boots crunching over broken glass, his wings of light flaring wide behind him in a silent, terrible display of dominance.

"You shouldn't have come," he says quietly. With two fingers, he snaps its neck.

The body slides lifelessly to the floor. Across the room, a larger shadow shifts — one of the true enforcers, massive and plated in armour engulfed in a smoke, its claws dripping with venomous dark. It roars and charges, uprooting a table as it comes.

The air starts to feel humid, moisture sticking to skin and clothes.

Wind screams inward in a spiralling vortex of flame and sparks, compressing around the charging creature. Its momentum falters — then shatters. The pressure crushes inward with titanic force, collapsing its armour, its bones, its very breath.

It explodes in a sound like thunder breaking stone. Black ichor rains down. Droplets falling, each one leaving an every sound on the surface it hits.

The room stills into pitch black darkness. Golden fire surges through Aodhan's palm and into the creature's torso. It ignites from within. The second assailant does not even have time to scream before Aodhan's wing carves through its body like a blade.

The room reverberates with dying sounds. Not one of them touches the shield. Through it all, his awareness never leaves myself and Oliver.

Every strike he makes is angled away. Every blast of power redirects outward. The storm bends its arc around our pocket of safety as if the world itself refuses to endanger us.

Another enemy bursts from the darkness — this one fast, serpent-like, its body composed of writhing shadow and exposed bone. It coils toward the shield. Aodhan reacts instantly. A spear of compressed wind slams the creature sideways mid-lunge.

Yasaar appears out of the darkness like living flame, her blade glowing molten white as she drives it through the creature's head.

It disintegrates without a sound just a fine dust falling where it stood. Aodhan turns, scanning the battlefield with lethal calm.

His eyes catch the final cluster of intruders attempting to pull back toward the central witch. The pressure drops so sharply several remaining enemies collapse gasping to the floor, their lungs failing as the air evacuates around them.

Aodhan steps through them like a king through kneeling subjects.

Another tries to crawl.

His heel comes down on its spine. Movement erupts in the

darkness — fast, brutal, precise. I hear the snap of bone, the wet rip of flesh, the pop of dislocated joints. Feral snarls echo through the restaurant as Aodhan moves with inhuman speed, his presence marked only by lightning and the sound of things dying.

A scream tears loose beside us.

Then a wet choking gurgle. Another creature lunges too close— its shadowed form half-revealed in a flash of lightning — and Aodhan appears behind it in a blur of gold. He wrenches its spine free with a savage twist. The body collapses like a dropped puppet.

This is the work of someone who has commanded war long before tonight.

Blood slicks the floor. Shadow-ash drifts like falling snow. The restaurant, once warm and glowing with candlelight, is now a shattered battlefield lit only by lightning and gold fire.

I press Oliver's face into my chest, shielding his eyes, my own stomach heaving at the sounds alone. Then, abruptly, the violence ceases. Silence crashes down. Aodhan glances back toward Oliver and I.

"You," Aodhan says quietly as he grips the remaining Fae by the throat and hauls them upright. "I have plans for you. But not where my family can see."

Pain streaks through my leg. I look down to see the last wraith crawling up my body, coiling around my thighs and ribs with icy malice.

Oliver screams as its shadowed limbs graze his back. The pendant in Oliver's hand erupts in blinding light. Pure sunlight floods the space, white-gold and searing.

The wraith shrieks as it disintegrates in a storm of black embers. Oliver collapses against me, sobbing in pain as burns etch across his back in faint, glowing sigils before fading.

Aodhan whirls back to the captive.

"Witches have nothing to do with the Sceptre," he snarls, voice vibrating with restrained violence. "Nor can you wield it. So why are you here, what do you want with Lily?"

The witch laughs — a wet, guttural sound that rattles in their chest. Blood strings from their teeth when they speak.

"You murderer..." they rasp. "You have no right to the power she carries. And we will make you pay for it. This is not the only family you will lose."

Their head tilts, eyes gleaming with something serpentine and cruel. "I saw an old friend here tonight." A pause — deliberate. Needling. "One who betrayed his kind... and tucked himself neatly beneath the Fae's wing."

Aodhan's expression does not flicker, but something immense shifts in the air around him. The storm pauses. Listening. "Don't worry," the witch whispers, lips curling. "His time will come. His secrets won't stay buried forever. The lives taken will seek vengeance." He murmurs a foreign tongue.

The laugh that follows is jagged and triumphant — cut short as blood suddenly gushes from their mouth, spilling hot across their chin and dripping in thick red spatters onto the floorboards.

They choke once... then lift their head. Their gaze slides past Aodhan — and lands on me. The shift is subtle, but it freezes the world.

When he speaks, his voice is so cold it steals the breath from my lungs.

"You have more than one child, do you not?" A slow, wheezing inhale. "One... safe, tucked in his mother's embrace..."

His eyes gleam, dark and knowing. "...and another standing on the edge of adulthood."

His smile widens, cracked and bloody.

"I wonder how she will fare... when the ones who lurk in the dark decide she is next."

The air collapses in on itself.

Before Aodhan can react, the witch bites down on something hidden in their mouth.

Their eyes glaze instantly. Blood floods their pupils. Their body convulses violently before collapsing boneless to the floor, dead.

Aodhan stares at the body in shock.

Then he swears softly. And in a voice that freezes my blood, he murmurs, "We need to go. Now. I can't reach Luc."

CHAPTER 41

Lily POV

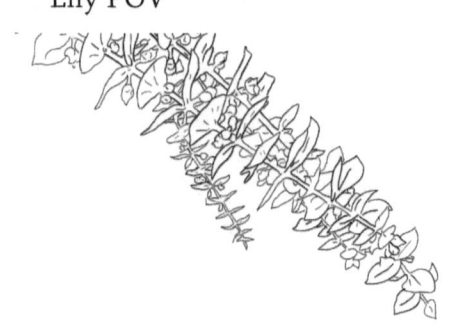

Aodhan tears open a portal and we slam through it, stumbling out at the hedgerow bordering the property. The headlights sweep across the driveway, sending a few wallabies scattering into the scrub. Twilight has drowned the hills in a deep purple cloak, the road behind us nothing but a ribbon carved through lavender dusk.

And there — our house. Glowing like a lone lantern between the gums.

And yet—something is wrong.

The air is too still. A silence that isn't silence, but a held breath. No bark. No paws thundering across the boards. Nyxie always greets us first. Always.

"Stay here," Aodhan says, gentle but unarguable. He's already striding away. Harrid melts into the dark, becoming nothing.

"Lily—" Dad begins, but I'm already moving, heart hammering, Daisy's absence a stone in my palm. The air tastes of smoke. Iron. Copper.

Mr Fisher. He lies sprawled across the boards, his jacket blooming dark. For a heartbeat my mind tries to conjure excuses — resting, napping — until the cough rips the illusion apart. Wet. Rattling. Final.

"Mr Fisher!"

My knees slam into the wood. My hands catch his — cold, calloused, still faintly stained with soil from his endless garden.

His touch jolts memory awake. Cal and I, fresh from the Rivertide, unloading the old ute. Mr Fisher striding over, sleeves rolled, insisting on carrying the heaviest box because I "looked like I had enough to carry already." His booming laugh when Cal argued and lost. Oliver at ten, wobbling on a too-big motorbike. Mr Fisher steadying the back, patient as stone, jogging alongside until Oliver found his balance. "That's it, lad," he'd said, pride warming his eyes. Daisy at seven, knees scraped from falling off her scooter. Mr Fisher crouched low, wrapping a bandage with the same care he gave his roses. "Battle scars," he told her, eyes twinkling. "Means you're fierce."

Then — memories I don't recall.

Mr Fisher with Dad, arguing before Dad storms off. Mr Fisher leaning down to me, holding both my tiny hands. An incantation. A bright halo of light spilling across my vision. His voice: *I will always be watching, Lily. Magic will find you again when you're ready.*

His eyes find mine now — clear, deep, ancient.

"Lillian," he rasps. "Good... you're here."

Aodhan kneels opposite, magic haloing his palm. It flickers, falters. His jaw locks.

"Old magic was used. This was deliberate."

Mr Fisher's laugh is a broken sigh. "Don't trouble yourself, Sun Prince."

He coughs, gaze sharpening on me. "There will be heat of gold and earth. Trust will splinter... and still you must gather it. You are the calm. The key. The final piece."

"Stop," I whisper, tears spilling hot. "Save your strength. We'll get help."

His grip tightens — deceptively strong, life surging through him. And in that heartbeat, the mask of years lifts. Power spills from him in waves — older than Courts, older than crowns. Not a harmless neighbour. Never. A guardian. Mine. Perhaps my mother's once just like the old stories and songs I remember.

Aodhan's voice is steel. "Why did you hide yourself?"

Mr Fisher's lips twitch. "Because playing in gods' games was never mine."

He looks at me again, eyes soft. "The children are safe, little Lily. I have seen to it. But with all that's awakening... and with the millennia I've lived... Ailith's time is upon us once more. You must break the cycle. You must remain strong."

The wind chimes ring one clear note.

The lilies in the garden bloom all at once, frantic and bright — as though the earth itself mourns.

"Who did this?" Aodhan asks, deadly quiet. Mr Fisher's gaze shifts to the treeline. His breath rattles, shallow, final. "Foe," he whispers. "But not the one you expect. Now it's your turn Aodhan of Phoenix Fire, you must protect her." He squeezes my hand once — firm, certain. A benediction.

"Live well, child. And know you are loved... I will see your parents soon. They will watch over you. Proud of your resilience. Your kindness..."

His hand slackens. Warmth drains. The light in his eyes folds inward and chest stills.

The porch holds the silence of a world cracked open. My tears fall unchecked, dripping onto the boards where his blood has already soaked deep.

And the grief isn't just for tonight, but for every day to come — no neighbour waiting with tomatoes at the fence, no quiet whistle through the gums, no firm hand steadying my children, no knowing smile on moving day.

No tea and brownies at the store opening. For the first time in months, I feel small. Untethered. And the only sound left is the wind moving through the lilies, carrying the scent of loss like a dirge.

Silence. A silence so deep it swallows sound, thick enough to choke. Even the cicadas stop.

Then the world crashes back. Harrid erupts from the dark crevices of shadow. Yasar crackles with blue sparks. Kaelen sends rings of compressed air sweeping the fields. Naralle's voice buzzes through the comm on my phone: *Café locked. Staff safe.*

I wipe my face hard. My voice doesn't shake.

"Nyxie is missing. Where is Daisy?"

Aodhan responds, "Luc isn't responding."

Harrid drops to one knee, palm pressed to the ground, shadows bleeding like ink pulling memories from what once was seen.

"There was a fight. Quick. Contained." His darkness crawls across the boards, mapping the unseen. "Scorch marks. Burned resin. Blood. Wolf hair in the hedges. Talon marks. Dark magic — and something older waking. Something I've never felt."

Yasar crouches, fingers brushing the blackened gravel. "Fire Court," she says, sparks snapping from her knuckles. Kaelen frowns, the air around him shuddering like a living veil. "The trail splits."

I sprint to the porch. Daisy's satchel lies torn open by the front door, her phone cracked in two. Distorted. Twisted. Blood smears the wall at knee height, dragged toward the door. And there, in the debris, a single green earring glints — its twin still in Daisy's ear only hours before.

No Nyxie.

No Luc.

No Daisy.

Only the stink of smoke. Smog clinging to the house. Someone has been in my home. Someone has taken my daughter. Someone has killed my friend. I fall knees crashing to the ground.

My heart races. Faster. Wilder. Like a stampede. I hear Aodhan calling to me, but his voice sounds muted, as if underwater. The world dulls, muffles — until I hear nothing at all.

My heartbeat stops its frantic stutter.

And the earth answers.

The ground beneath the porch groans, then shudders. Vines explode upward, tearing through the boards like spears, stone cracking beneath my knees. The house itself seems to inhale. The air howls — wild, furious — a storm spiralling up from the estate, cracking the concrete slab beneath us. Leaves rip from branches in a cyclone. Shutters slam. Glass rattles in its frames like chattering teeth. Power, power burning so strong. I feel it in every bone. Every muscle. It needs to be freed.

"Inside!" Aodhan roars, voice like a thunderclap. Harrid sweeps Viv, Dad, and Oliver into the house, shadows coiled around them wrapping - out of reach. Yasar drags the last warding lines across the door as Kaelen braces the walls against the gale.

But I can't stop. Rage floods me — earth rising, air tearing, a wild scream of magic I didn't know I carried. Vines twist higher, fusing into a living dome, green fire racing along their veins. Roots spear deep, splitting gravel and tile, drinking my fury.

Above, the storm flashes with white-gold arcs, lightning braided with wind and leaf, as though the estate itself has woken to destroy whatever dared to take from me.

My hair whips across my face. My palms glow like embers. The power isn't just mine — it's everything I breathe. It wants to burn. Break. Devour. Destory.

"Lily!"

Aodhan's voice cuts through the roar, but it barely reaches me. The storm continues. Vines thicken, ripping through the hearth, forming tighter domes; some lash across the courtyard toward the jasmine hedgerow, striking at anything that does not belong.

And then—

Wings. They erupt around me in a blaze of molten fire and light. Vast. Terrible. Feathers edged in living flame; each beat throwing sparks into the maelstrom. Phoenix-fire wings, born of a line older than any Court — unfurled in full fury at last. Suppressed magic, unleashed.

Aodhan moves through the hurricane like a god of storms, his arms iron around me, his wings an unyielding wall that forces the elements to bow. The vines writhe but falter beneath his heat; the dome trembles, then shudders still. His tattoos blaze brighter, threads of gold running from his skin into mine like molten sutures, trying to stitch me back together.

"Mo draganín," he pleads against my hair, voice breaking under the weight of it. "Come back to me. You'll tear yourself apart."

The bond pulses once — hot, desperate. Alive like a heartbeat beneath a collapsing sky.

For a moment, the dome flickers with our magic: green vines streaked with gold fire, roots glowing as though the earth itself seeks a new dawn.

And then the world tips.

Darkness rushes in, swallowing storm, earth, fire, and sky alike.

The last thing I feel is his arms his wings — holding me together as everything goes black and my name on his lips.

CHAPTER 42

Aodhan POV

"LILY!" my lungs tear her name free.

Her magic is spiralling. Eating her from the inside.

Ellisar. My voice rips through the bond, raw and unrestrained. Send the witch. Now. She's dying.

Her response is immediate. *Coming.*

I huddle Lily against my chest, her body trembling as power pours out of her in violent, uncontrolled waves. Rage. Grief. Fear. It consumes her, scorching through the bond like wildfire. "I can't lose you," I whisper, forehead pressed to hers. "I can't."

The bond frays. Weakens. I feel it slipping, threads snapping one by one, her life bleeding away through my fingers.

Panic claws up my spine. The door slams open.

"Fool," the witch mutters, striding into the room like a gathering storm. "Put her down. On the floor."

I tighten my hold, unable to release her.

She clicks her tongue. "Fine," she snaps, stalking closer. Her sharp gaze sweeps Lily's body, the burns of magic etched into her skin. Vials clink as she pulls bowls and bottles from thin air, murmuring an incantation under her breath.

"What magic was used?" she asks sharply. I open my mouth, but she cuts me off, eyes snapping to my wrist.

"No, Prince. What did you have placed on yourself?" Her voice goes cold. "It's killing you both. Like a poison."

My gaze drops. The silencer.

"I thought we'd cancelled it," I rasp. "After—"

She exhales hard, fury flashing across her features. Grabbing my wrist, she doesn't hesitate — the blade slices bone-deep. I grunt as blood spills, the pain blinding.

She pours a vial over the wound.

Fire.

My skin burns, peels, screams as the magic eats through flesh and rune alike.

"You will be weak," she says grimly. "But this will destroy the remnants and pull her back from the brink." Her gaze lifts, pinning me in place — eerie, knowing.

"There will be no hiding the mate bond after this."

"I don't care," I snarl. "Remove it. Save her. I will take whatever remains if it means she returns to me."

The witch laughs — sharp and unhinged — muttering words too old to follow. Then—

Magic slams into the room like a pressure wave. Wind howls. The wards scream. The world fractures. I drop to one knee as power detonates through my veins — wild, reckless — furious with purpose. Gasping, I cling to Lily, refusing to let go. She shudders. Then — a breath.

Raspy. Fragile. Real. Alive.

Her heart stutters beneath my palm, then catches, fluttering back into rhythm.

The witch staggers, shielding herself as the bond flares incandescent gold, blazing between us with violent clarity. "It is done," she whispers. Her eyes lift to mine, sharp and unyielding. "You would burn for her," she says softly.

"Now you must ask yourself what else must burn for her return," she pauses, looking at Lily with a gentle fondness. "This child she needs to be taught to control and wield the power. She has been neglected by that fool for too long."

I haven't left her side. Not once.

My hand has been locked with hers for three days, fingers cramped, wings curved around the bed like a shield whenever exhaustion finally claimed me. I've only half-slept — the restless kind where every twitch of her breath, every flicker of magic spilling from her skin, jolts me awake as though my body no longer trusts the world to hold her.

When her fingers twitch against mine, I'm upright in a single breath.

Her lashes flutter, lips parting on a sharp inhale, and then she blinks up at me — dazed, pale, but alive.

"You stayed," she whispers, voice ragged, eyes glassy with disbelief.

Relief crashes through me so hard my knees nearly buckle. I lean down, pressing my forehead to hers, shutting my eyes before she sees the wetness burning in them.

"Always," I murmur. "Gods, Lily... you terrified me. I thought I was going to lose you — not to an enemy, but to your own power."

Her fingers curl weakly around mine, grounding me, defying the panic I've drowned in for days.

"But you didn't," she breathes.

"No."

My voice breaks on the word, jagged edges tearing free. "But if I had..." I draw a harsh breath, the confession clawing its way out. "Lily, I—" It sticks — then breaks loose, raw and unpolished. "I love you. Not the bond. Not the prophecy. You. A life without you isn't worth living."

Her breath catches. Her gaze softens. And in that moment, everything I've fought to bury unravels — the fear, the anger, the helplessness. Love is my tether, my guiding force, the only thing that's kept me from tearing the realms apart with my bare hands.

"Daisy—" she starts, voice trembling.

I press her hand to my chest, over the frantic pulse there.

"We will get her back," I vow. "Harrid is still on the trail. Kaelen has called the army to readiness. Ellisar is on her way. You will not face this alone."

Her eyes burn with tears, but her chin lifts, stubborn even through the weakness.

"Then help me up. I can't lie here while she's out there."

"You need rest," I insist, though pride and terror battle in my chest at her defiance.

"I need my daughter," she fires back. Even fragile, her will blazes hotter than any crown's flame.

"What about Mr Fisher? I need to tell Sal." I squeeze her hand gently.

"It appears that when he passed, so did any memory of him. No one in Crystal Hollow recalls him. No one knows who he was. Even your friend Emma couldn't remember."

I feel her reaction hit me — the pang of guilt, her heart breaking, the overwhelming sense that he could be forgotten like that.

"I need to bury him," she whispers. "He needs a place where he's remembered."

"I'll plant a spot at the back for you," I promise, voice low. "But there is no body, Lily. He is gone."

Silent tears stream down her face. I lean in, pull her into my embrace, and let her emotions hit me like a freight train Her tears hit my skin like embers. Each one burns, branding me with another reason to tear apart whoever dared make her cry.

By dusk, her lounge has been turned into a war room.

It hums with tension and a dark, coiled undercurrent. Maps ripple across the table, golden threads marking where Harrid's shadows have tracked Daisy's scent through the veils.

Every line feels like a blade across my skin. Ellisar steps through the portal, silver hair gleaming like a drawn blade, her storm-coloured eyes sharp with purpose. She wastes no time with greetings. "They covered their tracks well. Fire magic, yes — but layered, cloaked. Too precise for ordinary Court soldiers. Someone higher is moving the pieces."

At her side emerges a new figure — broad-shouldered, quiet, with eyes the pale amber of a predator in moonlight. His presence thrums with raw, shifting power.

"This is Cael," Ellisar says. "Wolf-Sylvari. His nose is keener than any Fae's. If the trail has any heat left, he'll find it." The Sylvari inclines his head once. His gaze flicks to me, then to Lily — lingering there with something like recognition.

A deep bow follows. "I will find her for you, my Ríganne," he murmurs — before straightening, eyes sharp. "I'll track her," he says simply. Certain.

Nyxie has not returned. The absence gnaws at me — a missing rhythm in the hunt — but Cael's steady presence and Ellisar's sharp eyes are ready for the chase.

I glance at Lily. She's pale, still weak in body, but upright, standing beside me with her hand braced on the table. Determined. Defiant. Her presence radiates a strength that makes hardened Kárith pause.

"Don't sideline me," she warns quietly, cutting through the silence. "She's my daughter. I will be part of this and I will find my daughter."

Even Ellisar arches a brow, but there's no mockery — only respect.

CHAPTER 43

The throne room smelled of cold iron and old promises. Light fractured through the high windows in thin, hostile slashes; the polished obsidian drank it up and returned.

My liege's voice cut through the hush like a shard. "Why is the girl not yet secured in the Fire Court?" An easy question with punishment to follow.

My reply was a practised thing, smooth as oil and twice as slippery.

"My unit is preparing the transfer, my Liege I purr in response. The prisoner is contained. We move on the morrow."

He studied me with those gold, calculating eyes — the ones that made alliances and executions feel interchangeable.

"Contained is not hidden. The eclipse draws near. If the Sceptre finds its hand, all is undone."

I bowed. Automatic. Polite. Inside, my gut knotted. His paranoia was acidic. He meant to choke the world into obedience and call it order. I would never tell him I thought the crown had already rotted.

When his back turned, when the courtiers' whispers softened into the hum of the hall, I let the mask crack just long enough to breathe. The part of me he rarely saw — the part that could read loyalties in the tilt of a boot, scent betrayal in a single syllable — flared hot.

One day soon, I promised myself, the parasite on that throne would choke.

For now, I played my part.

"You." His voice again — soft, dangerous. "Yes?" I kept my tone even.

"You've been... distracted." Not unkind. That was the danger of it — the memory of the boy I once had been, bright and reckless, dangled like bait. "You must remember what you are, you may be an illegitimate son, but you will abide by doing. The Court needs you whole. I will not have both sons trying to take my throne from me nor the realm."

"The Court will have me," I answered. "I will not fail it."

Not lie just distorted truths.

I'd failed it long ago. When I stopped believing crowns could hold anything but rot. When I noticed merchants arriving with more coin than sense. When witches died with too much knowledge and were mourned too little.

When council broke, I walked the corridors. Tapestries whispered. Boots thudded like distant thunder. The palace had eyes everywhere; I made my steps deliberate, the way you walk past a sleeping beast.

Once out of sight, my courtesy turned convincingly into weariness. No one questioned a tired courtier. No one checked the man who performed loyalty at noon and conspired in the dark.

I slipped into an arched recess between the kitchens and western ramp. The corridor smelled of stew and hearth smoke — a comfort marble could never match.

Here, I could exhale.

My fingers went to the inside of my forearm. The signet band worn openly showed the world one truth — lineage, power, House.

But beneath the sleeve lay the second mark: a sigil burned into my skin by another ruler, older than treaties, older than the lie I breathed every day.

I pressed my thumb to it. It hummed — faint and eager.

A mechanism clicked. From my cloak I drew a coin the size of a saucer, surface dull and pitted. On its face: the charred symbol of the Fire Court. Under it, an overlay — a secondary engraving no one would notice unless they knew to look. I thumbed the coin once. Its core glowed with ember-light, and the metal sang.

I stilled — but it was only Harrid in the archway. He nodded once, melted back into the dark still trusting not yet aware of the deeds I have done the broken oaths to those we serve.

I pressed the coin to my palm and whispered the message — a sliver of command and intent, sliding into the metal like steam.

The girl will be redirected. Delay. Cause chaos and confusion. He must not know. Chaser must be found I need his assistance moving a child once more.

An answering whisper bloomed in the coin, heat curling across my skin:

It will be done.

I swallowed the thrill. Some men wore loyalty. I had learned to wear masks.

I returned to the Court viewing hall. My father, the Air Rívaran immersed himself in proclamations. He glanced up, paternal pride grazing his features. I returned my polished obedience.

"Maricus, see that the Fire delegation is welcomed, especially the Princess, make sure she is accommodated by any means," he ordered smirk curling in the corners of his mouth.

"Of course."

The mask settled like armour, my gut curling in disgust at what the Princess will be wanting and who that person will be. The coin in my sleeve cooled — an ember waiting to stoke the next blaze. If anyone asked where my loyalties lay, I would give them the only truth that mattered:

I am not for crowns. I am for the game. And in this game, the better the masks you wear, the longer you survive. And I must see this game out to the end.

Tonight, the players shifted. Tonight, someone would lose far more than spoils.

Tonight, the real pieces moved.

The prison lay buried beneath stone and deep enough even

the wind forgot the path. Damp air clung to the skin, thick with copper and old runes. Light seeped through cracks reluctantly from the moonlight outside, warping the space into iron bars and illusion.

My boots struck slow echoes as I walked the corridor, magic wrapped tight to my spine. Controlled. Camouflaged. The only way to survive my father's rule.

The guards bowed and stepped aside. I didn't spare them a glance. Inside the cell, tension sat like a living thing. Daisy Carvish lay curled on the stone slab — pale, breathing, unbroken. But the mark on her arm halted me.

Black ink, coiled and thorned, running shoulder to wrist and intricate design that is born of magic. It hadn't been there when we brought her in. It had bloomed the second old Fisher died.

Guardian. Relic. Myth. Torchan.

The moment his tether snapped, this brand had erupted across her skin — prophecy recognising blood.

A regrettable loss. Now no fae magic would touch her. Not mine. Not the Kárith'. Not even the Rívaran's scrying. She was wrapped in something older, hungrier. A safety she will need now she is a piece in the game.

In the corner, Luc crouched, half-shifted. Amber claws dug into stone. His eyes glowed with animal hatred — cold, patient, lethal.

I tilted my head, amused. "Still snarling, half-breed? Careful. You'll blunt your claws before you touch me."

His growl shook the chains above.

"You think you can protect her," I murmured, crouching. "But you're a mistake. A half breed of Fae and sylvari. When the Courts tire of you, they won't bother burning your bones." After-all I had seen it again and again.

Sparks scraped where his claws gouged stone. I turned to Daisy. She shifted in sleep, lashes trembling. The mark on her arm pulsed once — a key sliding into a lock.

There, the hesitation. The small flicker of something almost human. I hadn't wanted this. Not her. Not like this. But Lily's power only bloomed under pressure. Under loss. Under heat.

I know that I won't be forgiven. Daisy was a lever. A necessary cruelty. But she will survive it. Luc, though...A weapon made of chaos. Useful. Temporary. I'd slit his throat if I had to.

I straightened. "Wake her," I told the Kárith. "Our Liege wants her moved. Soon."

Luc snarled; the stone under his claws cracked. Daisy stirred. Her eyes opened — fear, confusion, fire, she looked so much like her mother. I almost faltered. Almost I smiled instead — thin, sharp.

"Welcome to the Fae realm, little mortal," I murmured. "Enjoy it while you can." Her hand brushed the mark. Luc moved closer. His glare promised my death. I paused at the door. Small. Mortal. But Lily's. I will not let them break her.

Now with Torchan gone I must do what I can to guide her down the path, to be what I need her to become. The door shut behind me, and the mask sealed over my face. They'd move her soon. And then?

The real game would begin.

CHAPTER 44

Lily POV

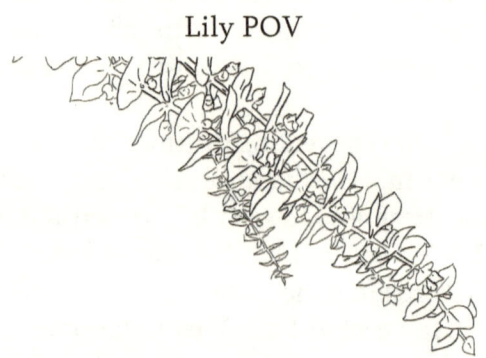

The house feels different now.
The repairs are finished, thanks to some Fae magic, but it's more than that.

I feel it — all of it. The shift of the earth beneath the foundations, the way the gums outside hum softly, vines pressing against the walls as if listening.

Even the air feels thick and alive, threaded with unseen currents. Since the night my power broke free, I can't stop feeling it — the call of everything. The estate sings, and I am its tuning fork.

And Aodhan... I feel him too.

Every beat of his pulse, the weight of his stare even before I lift my eyes.

His guilt coils around me like smoke, heavy and relentless. His rage simmers under his skin, sharp as molten steel — always there, waiting for release. Through the bond, it bleeds into me, and though it should terrify me, it roots me.

Because I know it means he will never stop fighting for us. For Daisy.

My family gathers in the kitchen — the same kitchen where we've spilled wine and laughed over dinners, whispered secrets, patched scraped knees, held birthdays and quiet grief — now heavy with maps and charms and weapons spread across the table.

The smell of coffee lingers, the only remnant of normalcy.

I press my palm to Oliver's cheek, memorising the hard line of his jaw, the way his father's eyes stare back at me from his face. He's trying so hard not to frown, trying not to look like the boy who still sneaks biscuits at midnight when he's watched a horror film.

"You're staying here," I tell him firmly, before he can argue. "With Pops. With Harrid." He opens his mouth — then hesitates. His gaze drops to his arm, to the inside of his forearm, where a faint shimmer has risen like breath beneath the skin. A tattoo, not of this world, spiralling in gold and black, geometric lines that hum faintly with a power I don't understand.

"Since the night Fisher died," he admits quietly. "It just... appeared. There's more on my back." My throat tightens. "Why didn't you tell me sooner?"

"Because I don't even know what it means," he mutters, shoulders tense.

Then softer: "And because I knew you'd look at me like that." I touch the mark, and the hum of it pushes into my bones — deep and strange. It feels like something old. Something watching. Not a curse, but not a blessing either — a whisper of destiny, coiled tight. The plants beyond the window lean toward us, as though they feel the shift too.

"We'll keep him safe," he says, voice low, meant for me alone. "Harrid, Narelle, Kaelen and Yasar will remain here. They'll guard Oliver and train him if this power grows. No one will breach this property ever again."

Harrid inclines his head, his magic curling lazily around his feet, already slipping into the corners of the house as his watch begins hiding in the shadows watching and lying in wait. Naralle tosses her braid over her shoulder and slides her phone onto the counter.

"I'll stay at the café. Someone has to keep Sal from panicking. And the wards are stronger there now. Anyone tries sniffing around, they'll get a shock they won't forget."

For a heartbeat, the heaviness cracks. Sal's voicemail from earlier plays in my mind — her indignant snort when Naralle started "helping" customers in only the way a Fae could. Then Dad speaks. His voice is rougher than usual, older.

"Lily."

I turn to him, and for a heartbeat he looks like he did when I was small — broad-shouldered, strong, a man who could fix anything with steady hands and a steady smile.

But now his eyes are, heavy with something unspoken. He has yet to tell me what he knows of Fisher, of magic, of all the things he's kept from me. Why Fisher mentioned seeing my parents...

"There are things I need to tell you," he says quietly. "About your mother. About the past, about the one who attacked us the night Daisy was taken. But not now. Not while Daisy's out there.

When she's back—" His voice cracks. He swallows hard. "When she's back, we'll talk I will owe you all an explanation and apology." I force the words out. "Did you know Fisher?"

"Yes, love. I did. And for a long time too. His loss..." Dad shakes his head. "It's a loss the realm will feel."

The realm.

Realm. My stomach knots. "Dad... are you human?"

He freezes. He takes a step toward me, resolve flashing across his face — then it vanishes, shuttered tight. "We'll talk later," he says, voice low. "I'm not going anywhere. I'll call in favours — old ones." His eyes lift, distant and wary, as if listening for something only he can hear. "Something's brewing, Lil," he murmurs. "And it's bigger than all of us." The words drop like stones inside me.

Emma exhales loudly, dragging the boiling tension back into motion.

"Well, if we're doing this, we're doing it properly. I've packed — snacks, knives, and my best pair of boots. Don't look at me like that, Lil. If we're going into Fae territory, someone's got to keep you entertained."

Viv crosses her arms, chin tilted high. "And someone's got to keep Emma alive, which means I'm coming too. You're not walking into this storm without us, Lily. We've been through too much for me to sit here and wait." I close my eyes, overwhelmed

— then laugh, soft and broken but real. "You two…"

Viv steps closer, pressing her forehead to mine like she used to when we were little, whispering secrets in the dark. "Be careful, sis. Mate bond or not, I need to know he's the man you think he is. But I'll be there. For you. For Daisy."

Aodhan's hand slides to my lower back, steady and warm. His golden eyes catch the lamplight, flashing with something raw — promise, fury, love. Through the bond, I feel every piece of it.

And just like that, the kitchen — this home, this fortress of memories — shifts from a place of waiting into a war room. Not just a family anymore. An army. "If Nyxie were here," I say quietly, more to myself, "I'd feel… steadier. She knows when I'm collapsing." She knows when to sit on my lap and refuse to move." My hand drifts to a nearby chair, instinctive. "Or Oliver. He'd feel less alone with her."

Emma snorts, but it's the comforting kind. "Then he'd stop pretending he's not scared. Dogs fix people. Or wolves. Or whatever Nyxie is. Giant lap dog — perfect for biting suspicious ankles." My throat tightens.

"I'm touched," I whisper. "That you'd both come. That you'd fight with me." The vines along the walls stir as if answering. Leaves tremble, leaning toward the lamplight, and somewhere in the garden a sapling shudders awake. Power thrums under my skin — no longer frantic but coiled and waiting.

Aodhan's fingers close over mine, iron and warmth intertwined. "We move at first light," he says, quiet and unarguable.

Emma lifts her chin, grin wicked and brave. "And if anyone gets in the way, well — let them see what a five-foot-six human who does cross-fit can do."

A short laugh bursts ragged but growing. The fear is still there, sharp and humming.

But something else is taking shape now — something harder. Stronger. Resolve. The hunt has begun. The house braces, wards whispering. It comes softly at first — a tremor beneath my ribs, a breath that burns instead of soothes.

It is not anger. Not fury. Not the wild grief that once hollowed me out. This is different. Older. Truer. A pulse that rises from somewhere deep beneath my skin, where the earth remembers my name even when I do not.

The world shifts in a single heartbeat — not breaking this time, but opening, as if every moment of fear, every wound, every loss has carved out a place for this fire to bloom. My magic wakes like something long-caged, stretching, unfurling, tasting the air.

And the ache inside me — the one I thought was all I had left — is replaced by something sharper. Fiercer. Something that demands to be answered. I will not crumble.

I will not run. I will rise.

Because the world has taken enough from me. Because my daughter's absence is a wound that will never close. Because love has roots no blade can sever. Because the power stirring in my veins is no longer a whisper — but a promise.

And when I breathe, the air itself seems to tremble.

This is not grief. This is awakening.

And gods help the ones who thought I would break for I will be their reckoning.

BONUS CHAPTER

The night Lily was meant to die, the sky bled fire. It should have been an ordinary night — a baby in her cradle, a mother's lullaby still clinging to the rafters like a memory too gentle for this world. A warm breeze drifted through the cracked window, carrying the scent of eucalyptus and milk and newborn skin.

But the wraiths slipped across the wards anyway. They came with blades in their hands. The guardian moved first. To the town, he was Mister Fisher — the man who smelled faintly of engine oil, who whistled when he gardened, who waved to children and fixed leaky taps without ever asking for payment. A quiet man. An old man. A man who belonged to no one and was therefore trusted by everyone.

But long before he grew into that mask, he had borne another name.

Torchan.

To most Fae, Torchan was a myth — a legend spoken about in the same breath as the fallen goddess and lost wars. A Kárith forged in Ailith's court, sworn by blood and fire to guard her line until his last breath. He had stood beside her through uprisings and betrayals, through the night she lost her king and the day she lost herself. He had held her tears, held her secrets, held her hope. And decades later, in a small human town where no one remembered the old world, he held her heir.

Even now — even after years of burying his power, years of pretending to be mortal — he felt the shift the moment the wards broke.

He felt the wind recoil. He felt the fire stutter. He felt the enemy approaching the cradle he'd sworn to protect.

Torchan didn't think. He moved.

The Shadows lunged, and he answered with magic older than

storm, older than crowns. The cottage shook with the force of it. Light split through the floorboards as if the earth itself screamed in warning. Glass shattered in the windows. Ash rained from the rafters.

And still — the shadows came.

One blade grazed his ribs. Another shattered against his warded palm. A third found purchase between his shoulder blades, sinking deep.

He staggered. Too many years spent hiding.

Too much of his strength locked away for Ailith's line. Too much of his magic bled into the binding that kept her hidden.

But even weakened, Torchan stood as he always had: Between cradle and blade. Between prophecy and ruin. Between death and Ailith's last hope.

The child — Lillian — slept through the chaos at first, tiny fists curled beneath her chin, unaware that the world was already trying to take her.

Her mother, the Hidden Ruler of Earth did not sleep. She pressed herself between attacker and child, hands shaking but eyes fierce. "Torchan, she must live," she cried, voice cracking under terror and love. "Promise me — I cannot lose her too. Please. She must live, even if the world forgets what she is. You must uphold the oath to Ailith no matter what happens to me old friend." And Torchan — who had failed Ríganne's and kings and entire realms — looked at the infant with Ailith's eyes and made the vow that would cost him the rest of his life.

He spoke in the old language, the one mortals could never hear without breaking. Power surged from his chest, weaving silently around the child, cloaking her heritage, burying every thread of her lineage so deeply that even the mate-bond meant to find her could not.

Better hidden than dead. Better the prophecy delayed than the child destroyed before she could choose her fate. But all magic has a cost. When he locked her power away, he locked himself with it — guardian and ward, one tethered to the other until her destiny woke.

It was agony. It was sacrifice. It was love. As the last attackers fled — burned, broken, their shadows torn — Torchan collapsed to his knees. His breath came shallow, his blood black with spent magic, but he gathered the crying child in his arms. He cradled her close to his chest, kissed her brow, and whispered his oath into her soft hair.

"Live well, child. Live long enough to choose your path." And then he walked into a new life. For decades he kept that promise. He became Mr Fisher — a harmless man with dirt under his nails and laugh lines around his eyes.

He taught Cal how to fix broken pipes. He watched Lily fall in love. He held Oliver steady as he learned to ride. He sat on Lily's porch on quiet mornings, just to make sure she hadn't shattered under the weight of a grief he knew would one day shape a queen.

He watched her grow. He watched her break. He watched her heal. And through it all, he kept her secret, even from herself. He wore his mask so well that even Lily believed he was mortal. But he had always been Torchan.

Guardian of the Lost Line. Oath-bearer of Ailith's blood. The last soldier of a dying prophecy written by the Goddess herself. And when his light finally dimmed on Lily's porch — when the tether broke free in a flare of grief and flame — the magic he'd kept locked for decades rushed out in a final burst.

It marked Daisy first. Black vines spiralling across her skin like a brand of destiny igniting. A warning. A summons. A beginning. The prophecy stirred. The bond awoke. Those who had been waiting in hiding clawed forward, ready to begin the chase.

And somewhere, in a realm where eyes watched from the dark and power tasted like hunger, a smile curved. Gods game had begun again.

Acknowledgements

Firstly, thank you to my daughter — for being dragged from location to location, patiently letting me take photo after photo in the same dress and braid for weeks on end while we searched for the perfect cover location. Your patience, enthusiasm, and ability to make the entire process fun made this book possible. We built some core memories in 2025, and it became a whole learning experience as I pieced it all together with you.

To my husband — who has listened to my excited ramblings, endured my rants about characters, and watched me spiral, bang my head against the desk, and obsess over words while learning far more about subjects I didn't realise, I knew nearly enough about. Thank you for your constant support, patience, and belief in me.

To my besties and hype girls — my very own Viv and Emma — Stace and B. You have edited, ranted, read, reviewed, critiqued, and blushed along with me every step of the way. I couldn't have done this without you and your support.

And finally, to the Sceptre Circle — thank you for your patience, your feedback, and the love you showed this story so early on. Without you, the readers, there would be no Of Earth and Gold.

Yany and Lisa – Thank you for being the first to jump in and give a new indie author a read and shout out. Your belief helped this indie author, and your kind words of encouragement meant the world when self-doubt was high.

About the Author

Shona Barton is an Australian author of romantic fantasy, writing stories rooted in magic, resilience, and second chances at love.

Inspired by the misty ranges and quiet towns of Queensland, Shona blends elemental fae lore with emotionally grounded characters, exploring grief, healing, family, and the strength it takes to begin again. Her work is known for slow-burn romance, immersive worldbuilding, and heroines who find their power not in perfection, but in perseverance.

When she isn't writing, Shona can usually be found with a coffee in hand, juggling family life, sketching character art, or daydreaming about fae courts, hidden realms, and the magic that lives just beneath the surface of the ordinary world.

Of Earth and Gold is her debut novel and the first book in the Elemental Fae series.

https://sites.google.com/view/s-barton-author/home
https://www.facebook.com/shonabartonauthor
https://www.goodreads.com/author/show/shonabarton
https://www.threads.net/@shonabartonauthor
https://www.tiktok.com/@shonabartonauthor
https://www.instagram.com/shonabartonauthor
https://linktr.ee/ShonaBartonAuthor

www.ingramcontent.com/pod-product-compliance
Lightning Source LLC
LaVergne TN
LVHW041617060526
838200LV00040B/1323